FORTUNE

I scrambled to my feet, blocking the next blow almost by accident on Phoebe's edge. But burned-out thermite is brittle as dead wood, and the blade snapped in two as the slimy thing flew past to hit me square upside the head. I caught the blow on my helmet instead of my face this time, but the hit was still enough to make me see double. Cursing, I shook my head to clear it as I dropped Phoebe and went for my last gun.

Sasha jumped into my hand as I flung up my arm, firing shot after shot into the tentacles I couldn't see but knew were there. I saw the bullets hit and stick as they would in a thick shield, but no shield was this strong. They were buried deep in the creature's invisible flesh, but the thing didn't even seem to feel pain now. It rose with a screeching roar that brought tears to my eyes, and I fell backward, emptying my clip as the tentacle plunged toward my head, ready to snap my neck through my armor. I could almost see it now, a faint shimmer against the gray clouds above me as it fell. And then, just before I died, I felt the most peculiar feeling I've ever experienced.

It was like someone stuck a hand inside me, grabbed hold of my spine, and jerked me away. I saw the ground crater as the tentacle crashed down, but I was no longer beneath it. Instead, I was flying backward, the hand on my spine dragging me through the air toward the clearing's edge. I could see the trees flying up around me, and I braced for another impact, but I never felt it. Just before I was sure I'd hit, something brushed across my mind, and I could have sworn I heard a soft voice whisper.

Sleep.

By Rachel Bach

Paradox
Fortune's Pawn
Honour's Knight
Heaven's Queen

By Rachel Aaron

The Legend of Eli Monpress
The Spirit Thief
The Spirit Rebellion
The Spirit Eater
The Spirit War
Spirit's End

The Legend of Eli Monpress (omnibus edition)

The Revenge of Eli Monpress (omnibus edition)

FORTUNE'S PAWN

RACHEL BACH

www.orbitbooks.net

ORBIT

First published in the United States in 2013 by Orbit
First published in Great Britain in 2014 by Orbit
Reprinted 2014 (three times)

A CIP catalogue record for this book
is available from the British Library.

ISBN 978-0-356-50235-9

Printed and bound by CPI Group (UK) Ltd, Croydon, CR0 4YY

Papers used by Orbit are from well-managed forests
and other responsible sources.

MIX
Paper from
responsible sources
FSC® C104740
www.fsc.org

Orbit
An imprint of
Little, Brown Book Group
100 Victoria Embankment
London EC4Y 0DY

An Hachette UK Company
www.hachette.co.uk

www.orbitbooks.net

For Travis, who means more to me than words.

CHAPTER

1

"You're quitting the Blackbirds?" The shock in Anthony's voice was at odds with the finger he was languidly sliding over my naked back. "*Why?* You just made squad leader last year."

"That's why," I said, swatting his finger away as I pulled on my shirt. "Nowhere left to go. Squad leader's the last promotion before they stick you in a desk job."

I stood up, grabbing my pants from the chair. Still naked, Anthony rolled over to watch me dress with growing displeasure. "I don't get you, Devi," he grumbled. "The Blackbirds are the top private armored company on Paradox. It takes most mercs ten years in a lesser outfit before they can even apply. The fact they let you in straight out of the army should be the miracle of your career. Why the hell are you leaving?"

"Some of us have ambition, Anthony," I said, sitting back down to put on my shoes. "I had five good years with the Blackbirds, made a lot of money, got my name out there. But you don't get noticed if you sit around on your laurels, do you?"

"If you got any more noticed, I think they'd have you arrested," Anthony said. "They were talking about that stunt you pulled on Tizas in the office just yesterday. The duke of Maraday's apparently thinking of offering you a fat contract with his Home Guard."

I rolled my eyes and combed my fingers through my hair,

wrestling the dark brown mess into a ponytail as best I could. My hair never could take mornings. "I am *not* joining the Home Guard. I don't care how good the money is. Can you imagine me sitting around on some noble's pleasure yacht playing bouncer for his cocktail parties? No thanks."

"Home Guard *is* dull," Anthony agreed, his boyish face suddenly serious. "But it's safe." He reached out, catching my hand as it dropped from my hair. "I worry about you, Devi. You've done eight full fire tours in five years. I know you want to make a name for yourself, but that kind of work will kill you, and I'm not talking about taking a bullet. If you got a job with the Home Guard, you could take it easier. Hell, if the Maraday thing actually came through, the duke never leaves the capital. You could live here, with me. I'd even let you redecorate, and we could be together every night."

I didn't like the way this conversation was going, but I knew better than to let that show on my face. Instead, I smiled and gently pried his fingers off mine. "It's a sweet offer, Anthony, but I'm not looking to settle down. Here or anywhere else."

Anthony heaved a huge sigh and collapsed on the bed. He lay there facedown for a moment, then rolled onto the floor and started pulling on his boxers. "Can't blame me for trying."

When he was dressed, we took the plush elevator down to the building café. I didn't regret turning down his offer, but I had to admit Anthony had a nice setup. His apartment was in one of the new sky towers that dominated Kingston's shoreline. Through the enormous windows, the royal capital lay spread out as far as I could see. Enormous skyscrapers rose like silver and glass trees from the dense underbrush of the older, smaller buildings. The sky was hazy with the usual smog and the clouds of commuter aircraft darting between the official sky lanes. The café was on one of the sky tower's middle floors, but we were still high enough to see the starport and the towering shadow of the Castle behind it from our booth.

I might just be sentimental, but seeing the Castle's shielded battlements and the shadows of the building-sized batteries of plasma guns behind it always filled me with pride. It wasn't the tallest building in the city anymore, but the Castle was still the largest, dwarfing even the deep-space trawlers that were waiting their turn to dock in the starport below. It was a good, strong fortress, feared by all on planet and off, and a worthy guard for the Sainted Kings of Paradox.

As always, I bowed my head before my king's sacred fortress. Anthony followed suit a second later. He'd never been as much of a believer in the power of the king as I was, but then, he hadn't taken as many bullets as I had.

Once we'd paid our respects, Anthony called the waiter over. He ordered large and well, and the spread of food that arrived at our table was a mini-heaven all in itself. Thanking my king again, I fell to with a mercenary's efficiency. Anthony watched me eat with amusement, drinking something red out of a tall, frosted glass that looked like a cocktail. I really hoped it wasn't. Even I didn't drink this early in the morning.

"So," he said, spinning his now nearly empty glass between his fingers. "Why are you really here, Devi?"

"Last night wasn't enough?" I said, popping a tiny coffee cake into my mouth.

"Last night was marvelous," Anthony admitted. "But since we've established you aren't exactly pining for my company, I thought we might as well get to the point before you crush my ego again."

He was still smarting from the rejection, so I let the comment slide. I'd known Anthony a long time; we'd been in the army together before he got his captaincy and his cushy desk job with the Home Guard. We had good chemistry, and he was always the first person I called when I came home. We'd been friends with benefits for nearly seven years now, and I'd thought we had a good understanding. Obviously, things had changed. Still, this was Anthony. An apology would only make him feel worse, so I honored his request and got to the point. "I need you to tell me the qualifiers to become a Devastator."

I had his full attention now.

"Are you out of your goddamn mind?" he cried. "*That's* why you quit your job?" He flopped back against the booth's deep cushions. "Devi, you can't be serious. The Devastators are the king's own armored unit. They're *above* the best."

"Why do you think I want to be one?" I said. "I'm sick of wasting my time on the edge of civilized space crashing pirate camps for corporate money. Devastators serve the Sacred King directly. They get the best armor, the best guns, they go on the most dangerous and important missions. They have power you can't buy; even the nobility listens to them. I was the best in the Blackbirds—"

"This isn't like the Blackbirds," Anthony snapped. "I can't even tell you the qualifiers, because there are none. You can't apply to become a Devastator. They ask *you*, not the other way around, and they don't ask anyone who hasn't spent a minimum of twenty years in active field service."

"Twenty *years*?" I cried. "That's ridiculous!"

"They want experience—," Anthony started.

"What do you think I spent the last nine years getting?" My shouting was attracting weird looks from the other diners, but I didn't care. "I got twelve commendations in four years when I was in the army. You know, you were there. *And* I've gotten five promotions in five years in the Blackbirds. I'm not exactly fresh meat."

"Devi, you're not even thirty." Anthony's voice was calm and reasonable, the sort of voice you'd use with a child who was throwing a tantrum. It made me want to punch him. "You've already proven that you're exactly the sort of suicidally brave, workaholic lifetime soldier the Devastators look for. They'll come calling, I'd bet money on it, but not yet. Not until you've got at least ten more years on your record."

"In ten more years, I'll be dead." I said it plainly because it was a goddamn fact. The average life span of an armored mercenary was just shy of twenty-five. I was two years past that. After thirty, survival rates fell to almost nothing. Shooting for cash was a game for the young. You either got a desk job, applied to the Home Guard, or went back to your parents in a body bag. A desk wouldn't impress the Devastators any more than it impressed me, but I couldn't do crash jobs and pirate clearing forever.

"I'm good enough to serve the king right now," I said, lowering my voice. "I've seen Devastators in their thirties, so I know they make exceptions to the experience requirement. I want to know what and how, and I'm not letting you out of here until you tell me." And just in case he didn't believe me, I kicked out my leg and slammed my boot onto the booth beside him, blocking him in.

Anthony glanced at my foot with a deep sigh. "You're impossible. You know that, right?"

I didn't answer, just leaned back, crossed my arms, and waited for him to cave.

It didn't take long. Less than a minute later, Anthony shook his head and pulled out his ledger. "It just so happens you picked a good time to have your crazy idea," he said, tapping the screen with his thumb. "Here."

I took the ledger he offered, squinting to read the glowing screen in the bright sunlight. It took me a few moments to recognize the short paragraph for what it was, a job listing from the general employment boards. A tiny one, too, barely three sentences long, but what I saw was enough to make me think Anthony was seriously trying to jerk me around.

"This is for a security position on a trade freighter."

"Not just any trade freighter," Anthony said, smiling for the first time since we'd gotten out of bed. "That's Brian Caldswell's ship."

"I don't care whose ship it is," I said. "I am *not* doing guard work." Guard work was just above deep-space mine clearing for crap armor jobs. No Blackbird would be caught dead on a freighter, even an ex-Blackbird like me.

"I wouldn't have shown it to you if it wasn't something you'd be interested in," Anthony said. "Have a little faith, darling."

When I finally relaxed my scowl, Anthony went on. "Caldswell's a bit of a legend in trading circles. They say his ship is cursed. He gets into more trouble on one route than an entire fleet could find in ten years, and he goes through security teams like tissue paper. That's where you come in." He leaned closer. "Don't spread this around, but the Royal Army considers one year with Caldswell to be worth five anywhere else. If you can survive a full tour on that ship, I'm pretty sure even the Devastators would sit up and take notice."

I glanced down at the ad again. It looked perfectly normal, the sort of short-notice grunt job that kept army dropouts in beer money, nothing like the deadly golden ticket Anthony was painting it to be. "You're not putting me on, are you?"

"I wish I was," Anthony said. "Maybe you missed the part about how quickly Caldswell uses up his people? I like you as you are, all in one piece."

It was mean to laugh at his concern, but I couldn't help it. "And maybe you've forgotten who you're talking to."

"I haven't forgotten," Anthony said, his voice deadly serious. "I've seen you fight, remember? That's not something you forget. But this is the fast and dangerous route, Devi. I know you're ambitious enough for any five normal mercs, but there's nothing wrong with a life of being safe, prosperous, and happy."

"I am happy," I said, pulling out a pen and writing the dock number from the ad on the back of my hand. "And the faster I get to be a Devastator, the happier I'll be." I handed his ledger back. "You'll tell them, right?" The Devastators did whatever the king told them to, but they were technically part of the Home Guard. Anthony worked for them sometimes, which was why we were having this conversation.

"If Caldswell takes you, yes," he said. "Don't know if they'll listen, they mostly don't, but I'll be sure to tell everyone what a reckless glory hog you are."

I grinned and dropped the leg that had been fencing him in. "You're a prince as always, Anthony," I said, sliding out of the booth. "Thanks for the breakfast, and the job tip."

"I'll put them on your tab," he said. "You can settle up next time you're in town."

I kissed him on the cheek one last time and walked away. The last thing I heard before I squeezed into the crowded elevator was Anthony calling the waiter for another drink. I worried about that as the elevator whipped me down, but twenty seconds and seventy floors later, I had more immediate concerns.

The crowd on the street level was brutal, and I had to throw my weight around to break through the rush to the cab stand, something I enjoyed more than I should have. I'm five six on a good day, and between that, my bird bones, poofy brown hair, and the fact my face looks closer to thirteen than thirty, normal people tend to underestimate me. It used to piss me off to no end, but that was before I cultivated an appreciation for watching the patronizing look fall off a businessman's face when the little girl he was trying to push aside elbows him in the stomach hard enough to knock his wind out.

After a few minutes of unnecessary roughness, I'd made my way to the front of the taxi line and flagged down a ground cab.

Air would have been quicker, but I wasn't in enough of a hurry to justify the cost. Fortunately, my cabbie was a stereotypical Kingston driver, utterly insane. Despite it being rush hour on a workday morning, we made it to the starport in less than twenty minutes.

He offered to take me into the departures plaza, but one look at the traffic and I told him to drop me on the street. I tipped him well for not getting us both killed and ran up the pedestrian ramp, ducking through the enormous mirrored doors with the rest of the morning crowd before taking a sharp left toward the lockers where I'd bunked my gear when Anthony had picked me up late last night.

I found my locker and opened it with a thumbscan, pulling out my duffel. My handset was on top, right where I'd left it. I flipped it open, working fast. I trusted Anthony, but only an idiot applies for a job without doing her research first. A quick search for Brian Caldswell turned up surprisingly little, but Anthony hadn't been kidding about the prestige of serving on his ship. After five minutes of searching, I'd found no fewer than seven of his former security grunts who were now enjoying fantastic positions, including one who'd gone on to be a Devastator.

But my digging also showed that Anthony hadn't been exaggerating how dangerous Caldswell's ship was, either. The number of crew deaths and disappearances he had on file with the Trans-Galactic Trade Union was staggering for any vessel, but it was especially bad when you considered that Caldswell captained a ten-man freighter on a fairly safe route through the major systems. From his numbers, you'd have thought he was helming a battleship on a bloody front. All of this should have made me think twice, but I'd made my career by beating impossible odds. As soon as I'd verified Anthony's tip to my satisfaction, I got to work hauling my armor case out of the locker.

In addition to my fast elbow, I'm a lot stronger than most people think, a product of spending all day in armor with my resistance turned way up. Some mercs let their suit do all the work. Why bother with flesh-and-blood muscles if you're in powered armor all the time? But I don't like being weak in any way if I can help it, and real muscles come in handy when the most precious thing in your life folds up into a hundred sixty–pound case and all you can get is a top locker.

Bracing my knees, I heaved my armor case down and set it on its wheels. When it was balanced, I slung my duffel over my shoulder and started walking toward the dock number I'd written on my hand.

Considering its black reputation, I expected Caldswell's ship to look sinister, but the freighter sitting at dock C23503 was disappointingly shabby. Its belly sat directly on the ground, while its hull rose in an old-fashioned, ungraceful beige block six stories into the air. The whole ship was spotty with patches, but thanks to a fresh paint job I couldn't tell if the repairs were from cannon fire or just the usual wear and tear you saw on older vessels.

Old or not, though, Caldswell's ship was still an impressive hundred and fifty feet long from nose to thrusters, with the vast majority of that in its cargo hold. The ship's nose was boxy as the rest of it, a squat thrust of metal with its windows covered by steel shutters coated in high-burn plastic against the heat of entering the atmosphere. The tail of the ship was all engine, a pair of long-haulers and a hyperdrive coil that looked pretty new.

That gave me hope. Hyperdrive coils weren't cheap. If this Caldswell could afford a new model, he could certainly afford a top line Paradoxian armored mercenary with an exceptional record.

Like all the noncommuter ships, Caldswell's was docked in the overflow landing. But, despite being in a good spot relatively close to the main port, no other ships were docked around him. That didn't surprise me. Spacers were a superstitious bunch. Docks would have to be pretty scarce for a captain to risk leaving his ship where Caldswell's curse could reach it.

I believed the Sacred King could do miracles just like any good Paradoxian, but I didn't believe in curses. Neither did a lot of people, apparently, or maybe most mercs just didn't bother to do their research, because as I rounded the nose of the ship, I saw that the ramp in was packed with people hauling armor cases not so different from my own.

Never one to let a little competition scare me off, I walked right up and got in line. There were fifteen people ahead of me, but the crowd was dwarfed by the enormous and strangely empty cargo bay. Other than a few dusty crates lashed down in the back, the only thing inside was a suit of armor.

Unlike my armor, which could be broken down to fit in a case, this was a serious heavy combat suit, Count class, the kind the army used to rip up Terran tanks. Even powered down, it was seven feet tall and obviously someone's baby, judging from how nicely the bright yellow paint job sparkled. I scowled. Armor like that belonged to a serious professional who'd spent a lot of time in the armored corps. Clearly, someone had already gotten a job today. The ad hadn't said how many openings were available, but the ship wasn't that big. It couldn't take more than two security guards to cover it all, and if one of those spots was already taken, then this wasn't the sure thing I'd been counting on.

I eyed the line with new rancor. None of them looked like serious competition, but then, standing around in the tight pants and flowy shirt I'd worn to meet Anthony with my hair tangled in a postsex ponytail, I probably didn't either. Nothing for it but to wait and see. I used the time to fix my appearance, brushing and braiding my hair as discreetly as I could. The line moved quickly, and by the time I was decent, I was next.

There was a stair leading up from the cargo bay to the rest of the ship where the interviews were being held. People had been going up and coming down again with only a few minutes between the whole time I'd been waiting. Some looked dejected, but most looked relieved, and I bet they were the ones who hadn't actually wanted a job on a ship that had a reputation for being a flying coffin, no matter how scarce armor work had gotten now that the king had wrapped up all our wars.

The man ahead of me was certainly one of these. He was almost grinning as he walked back down the steps and stabbed his thumb over his shoulder, letting me know it was my turn. Grabbing my bag and lifting my armor case so it wouldn't bang, I started up the stairs to tempt my fate.

The interviews were being held in what looked like a combination lounge and ship's mess. There was a tiny galley kitchen with a bar, a table for meals, and a small sitting area, all empty. My interviewer sat at a folding table with a small desk fan pointed at his face. He was older, maybe early fifties, and wearing an old-fashioned white button-up shirt and brown flight vest. His short, red-brown hair was frosted with silver, but his stocky body was still fit and solid when he stood to shake my hand and wave me to the chair.

"Name?"

I flinched. He was speaking Universal. I spoke it, of course. Everyone did. It was the standard language of civilized space. But the Blackbirds were solid Paradoxian, and we spoke our own King's Tongue exclusively in everything we did. I'd been all over the universe, but because I'd always been with my unit, I hadn't spoken Universal other than to ask where the bathroom was for almost three years.

Looking back, I don't know why I was surprised. Traders, even Paradoxians, always spoke Universal. It was, after all, the language of trade. But the man at the desk didn't look Paradoxian, he looked Terran, and that could be a problem. After so long not speaking Universal, my accent was pretty thick, which put most Terrans off. Usually, I wouldn't care. Paradoxians don't like Terrans any more than they like us. We might both be from Old Earth, but a century of border wars carries a lot more weight than a shared ancestry from some dead rock a thousand years ago. Still, if the Terran was the one with the job, then that was all water under the bridge so far as I was concerned. I'd just have to trust that he was willing to overlook a few dropped consonants in return for a stellar record.

The man glared at me, still waiting for his answer, and I snapped into business mode. "Deviana Morris," I said, pronouncing each syllable as crisply as I could. "I go by Devi."

I set my handset on the table and tapped the button for the projected screen. It flickered to life, throwing my record, commendations, and references into the air right in front of his face. The man flicked through my history with a finger, his expression neutral, though I saw his lip quirk when he got to my last tour with the Blackbirds. A glorious time, even for a glory hog like me.

"That's quite an impressive record, Miss Morris," he said at last. He spoke the words grudgingly, like he didn't like being impressed. "It's my understanding that most Paradoxian mercenaries spend their careers trying to get into the Blackbirds. Why did you leave?"

"I'd reached the top of the active duty promotions, sir."

The man smiled. "Your ambitions don't run to desk jobs, I take it?"

I smiled back. "No sir."

"Fair enough," the man said, glancing at my armor case. "What equipment are you bringing?"

My smile turned into a full-on grin. This was my favorite part of any interview. I reached down and turned my case so he could see the insignia on the front. "Custom Verdemont master craft knight's armor."

My opinion of the man rose significantly when his eyes widened in an appropriate expression of shock. "And this is your suit?" he said. "Not leased from the Blackbirds?"

"No sir," I said proudly. "I own all my own gear." It had taken me two years' wages plus some pretty extreme hazard pay to buy my armor, and it was worth every cent. "I also have my own guns and ammunition as well, and an automated repair case for my suit."

"We'll supply your ammo," the man said, leaning back in his rickety folding chair. "This is a security position. Your job will be to work with your fellow security officer to protect this ship, its crew, and its cargo at all times. We usually run a wide circuit spanning Paradoxian space, the Terran Republic, and the Aeon Sevalis, but that can change without notice. The contract is for one galactic standard year with fifteen hundred Republic Script paid monthly. Shifts are twelve hours during flight with overtime for planetary landings and time off when we're in hyperspace, plus one day paid shore leave per month. So long as you are an employee of this ship, we'll provide food, lodging, and ammunition, as I said earlier, plus a stipend for maintenance and repair of your equipment."

I considered this for a moment. It was a pretty standard contract, but the pay, while high for ship guards, was pretty low compared to what I'd earned in the Blackbirds. I might not be doing this for the money, but a merc had to protect her worth. "Is there hazard pay?"

"Thousand RS for every incident," the man said.

I bit back a smug smile. That was where the money was hiding. Considering this ship's reputation for trouble, that hazard bonus might well end up making me more than I'd earned as a squad leader.

"Sounds good to me, sir," I said, reaching for my armor case. This next bit would be pure fun. I loved showing off my armor. "What would you like me to do for my demonstration? I can do any accuracy challenge you can think of, maneuvers, a strength test, whatever you want."

"I don't think we'll need any of that," the man said, turning off my handset and handing it back. "You've got the job."

I blinked. "That's it?" I blurted before I could stop myself.

The man shrugged. "Unless another decorated ex-Blackbird with her own suit of custom, high-end armor is waiting in my cargo bay, then yes. That's it." He held out his hand. "I'm Brian Caldswell, welcome to the *Glorious Fool*."

I took his hand, head spinning. That was the fastest interview I'd ever had. "Fool?"

"The *Glorious Fool*," Caldswell repeated, smiling like this was an old joke. "My ship."

Weird name for a ship, but I didn't give it much thought. I was too busy absorbing the fact that the short, stocky man in front of me was the cursed captain, Brian Caldswell. The man who went through security like tissue paper, and I was now in his hands.

"Thank you, sir," I said before I found some way to ruin things.

The captain nodded. "We'll get you a bunk when we're ready to go. In the meanwhile, you can store your stuff behind the bar. No one will touch it."

No one but me could touch my armor without getting ten thousand volts, but I kept my mouth shut about that and stowed my bags as directed. Honestly, I was still reeling. My brain couldn't quite get around the idea that after years of fighting like a dog for every step up the ladder, I'd gotten what could well be the make or break job of my career with an interview that had taken less than five minutes.

While I was putting my things up, the captain walked over to the cargo bay door and shoved his head out. "Position's filled!" he yelled, and then he shut the door.

I thought that was a bit harsh, but the captain seemed to have forgotten the other applicants entirely the moment he turned away. "I have to go take care of some business," he said, walking past me toward the hall on the opposite side of the lounge. "Basil will get you settled. He's my second, and you'll obey him as you would me."

"Yes sir," I said, following him. "Who else do I follow?"

"Mabel, our engineer." The captain wasn't looking at me, but I caught his smile and gave myself a mental pat on the back. I'd impressed him. "But she won't be here until later. For now, just worry about making Basil happy. You'll find him on the bridge, straight ahead."

He nodded down the hall toward a closed door at the opposite end. I noted it and then turned to face my new captain head-on. "Yes sir," I said, bowing formally from the waist as was proper now that he was my superior. "It will be an honor to serve you, sir."

The captain shook his head. "This is a Terran ship, Morris. We don't do any of that bowing and scraping here. Just do your job, obey orders, don't backtalk too much, and we'll all be happy."

"Yes sir," I said, without the bow this time. Not bowing to a superior went against my training, but it was his ship. If he didn't want me bowing, I was happy not to. Bowing to a Terran felt a little blasphemous.

The captain nodded and walked down the hall away from me, toward the engines. I watched him until he started down the spiral stairs to the lower levels and then turned toward the bridge as ordered. The hall ran down the ship like a backbone with the bridge as its head. Surprisingly, though the hall was reasonably clean, it was almost as patched as the ship's hull.

The outside damage I could understand; pirates liked to take potshots, but the hall's gray metal walls were peppered with blaster burns, bullet holes, even a few blast shadows from what I could only imagine were grenades. I've walked down worse, but not many, and only in war zones. Whatever had happened here had been serious, and I made a mental note to ask how the last security team had ended their tour.

The bridge door slid open the second I stepped up. I marched inside and stopped at parade rest just as I had back in my army days, glancing around for this Basil I was supposed to be taking orders from. What I saw confused me greatly.

The bridge itself was a perfectly normal three-layer setup and far less scarred than the hall had been, though there was still a bullet hole in the ceiling. At the top where I stood was the monitor deck and systems desk, both empty. Down a step was the captain's chair, its leather seat and consoles worn nearly black from years of use. But at the bottom of the bridge, the seat at the ship's nose where the pilot usually sat was gone. In its place was what looked like a nest of bright-colored fabric, and sitting in this nest was a very large bird wearing a headset.

I'd seen aeons before, but never in person, and certainly never this close. The ones I'd seen had been brightly colored, pink and blue and green and every other neon hue you'd expect from a giant alien bird. This one was brown as a common sparrow. Sitting in its nest, it looked like an overgrown fluffy stork with short chocolate and cream feathers layered over white down. Its neck was long as my arm, and the head at the top was crested with a ridge of rust-red feathers that bobbed back and forth as the aeon studied the projected star map in front of it. Its wings, which looked large enough to be useful, were folded at its sides, each one tipped with four tiny, clawlike fingers at the joint, but the bird wasn't using them. Instead, it was tapping the ship's flight handle impatiently with its long feet, the yellow talons clicking so fast on the padded grip I could barely follow them.

Despite being the most populous race in the galaxy, beating out even humans for sheer numbers, the aeons stuck to their Sevalis and their own kind. I'd heard they disliked the other races with a passion bordering on violent xenophobia, which was a waste, because they were supposed to be the best navigators in the universe. Once I got over my initial shock at seeing a large alien bird sitting in a literal pilot's nest, that fact that Caldswell actually had an aeon to fly this hunk of junk ship was what astonished me the most.

The bird hadn't noticed me yet, and I took a moment trying to decide if it was safer to call the thing sir or ma'am. Neither seemed good. I didn't even know if aeons had the usual genders, actually. But since this was a Terran ship with no appreciation for proper hierarchy, I decided to risk dropping the honorific, just this once.

"Excuse me," I said. "Are you Basil?"

The aeon's head whipped around, and I found myself being glared at by a pair of yellow eyes as large as my fists with round, black pupils set in a flat face above a long, curving yellow beak that practically dripped with disapproval. "Oh goody," it said. "A Paradoxian."

The bird's voice was more like a whistle than words, but I didn't like the tone of it one bit. "That's what you get when you advertise for a security team on Paradox," I said, fighting the urge to cross my arms and glare.

The aeon arched a feathered eye ridge and then, in a flurry of flapping, launched itself into the air. It cleared the captain's chair in one leap and landed right in front of me. Standing, the bird's head was a foot higher than mine. Its yellow eyes gleamed as it set down, no doubt waiting for me to scramble out of the way. But I'd faced down much scarier things than overgrown chickens with bad attitudes, and I held my ground.

The bird looked disappointed. "My name is"—it gave a shrill whistle that faded into a chirp. "But your soft human palate couldn't possibly manage that, so you may call me Basil. I'm the *Glorious Fool*'s navigator and Captain Caldswell's second in command. You will address me as sir at all times."

"Yes sir," I said, hiding a smile. An officer with literal feathers to ruffle. This was going to be rich. "The captain said you would show me around."

The bird heaved an exaggerated sigh and pushed past me. "Come along, monkey. And don't touch anything."

We spent the next hour going over a ship that should have taken ten minutes to walk through. The *Fool* had the fairly standard spacer setup of cargo bay, engine room, lounge, two levels of crew cabins, and a surprisingly nice infirmary (or not so surprising with as much action as this ship supposedly saw). The most interesting thing I noticed was that the damage I'd seen in the main hallway continued through most of the ship.

Hearing about trouble was one thing, but going by battle scars I'd say the *Fool* saw more action than my former crash team's ship, which we routinely dropped on pirate camps. Everywhere I looked, things had been damaged and patched over. Even the out-of-the-way bulkheads were burned or scraped in some fashion, and more than a few still had bullets lodged in them. The floor was rubber coated for traction, but the coating was melted in several places from what looked like plasma blasts. We didn't run into any other crew members, but that didn't matter. In between boring me to tears with details of the ship's mechanics, Basil took every opportunity to talk about them.

"As our engineer, Mabel is responsible for everything mechanical," he said as we walked up the tiny spiral stair from the engine room. "You'll obey her as you obey the captain or myself. Nova is our systems analyst. She helps me run the bridge. The two of you will be bunking together until I can talk some sense into the captain."

His head swiveled to glare at me. "Honestly, if we weren't short on room, I'd never have let it happen. A nice girl like Nova shouldn't be exposed to Paradoxians. Sometimes I don't think you people even understand words that don't have to do with armor, fighting, and king worship."

"We also talk about shooting, sir," I said dryly. "And bird hunting."

"Good thing for us then that you and that other idiot are the only of your barbaric kind here," Basil snapped, feathers standing on end. "Though two is more than enough." He pressed his wing-tip to his head. "Moving on, and do try to remember this because I'm not telling you again, cleaning duty follows a standard rotation. The cook takes care of the lounge, but all other responsibilities are shared between the crew. You'll be expected to contribute at least five hours a week or face a pay dock. In addition, our records require that you file daily reports…"

I tried not to let my eyes glaze over as I tuned him out. Normally, I am the perfect picture of the professional merc. I try not to swear because swearing is for grunts, not officers. I maintain decorum, I follow orders, I never drink on duty, and I do my job with a flair and efficiency designed to land me glowing reports. But after half an hour of listening to Basil squawk, my professional front was starting to crumble.

Even without the bird's talk about cleaning rotations, the tour had been unappealing. The blast marks were exciting, true, but the rest of my duties sounded dull as, well, guard duty. I had a patrol path I was supposed to maintain during flight, hourly check-ins, report writing, inventory control, all the routine, mind-numbing idiocy that had led me to avoid guard jobs like the plague my whole career. Much as I'd grown to dislike crashing pirate camps over the last five years, the idea of hopping out of a drop ship on some remote moon and landing on a pirate's head was starting to sound like heaven at the moment. When the bird turned us into the lounge and launched into a lecture on fire regulations *again*, I rolled my eyes to the ceiling and prayed to my king that all those dead security teams had actually died in combat and not from boredom.

Basil's safety lecture was interrupted by the sound of someone coming up the cargo bay stairs. I looked over, hoping to see the captain or maybe my fellow security team member, anyone who could save me from the bird. But it wasn't the captain or a merc, it was a girl. I placed her at about fourteen, maybe a little older. She was dark skinned with a cap of straight dark hair cut just above her shoulders and almond eyes that were almost too focused as they moved from me to Basil.

If it hadn't been a horrible breach of decorum, I would have rolled my eyes again. I hate kids when I'm working. If Caldswell tried to make me babysit on top of report writing, I was going to tell him he could shove this job, fantastic recommendation or no. I was already working out all the excuses I could use to get out of any potential kid duty when I caught sight of the man behind the girl and everything else became superfluous.

Now this, this was more like it. The man was gorgeous. He was tall and pale, but beautifully so, with shoulder-blade-length black hair tied at his neck. His eyes were a lovely bright blue under dark eyebrows, and his mouth looked quick to smile. He was wearing a black suit, not the ones they wore in Kingston with the wide lapels, but the old-fashioned Terran kind with the high collar that I'd always considered dashing. Even hidden behind the girl, I could see enough of his posture to know that he had some military training. Combine that with his long-fingered hands and broad, sloping shoulders and I was suddenly feeling much, much better about this job.

"Ah," Basil said, his snarky tone fading just a hair. "This is Ren, the captain's daughter."

It took me a few seconds to realize Basil was talking to me. I looked away from the man with some difficulty and studied the girl instead. She must have taken after her mother, I decided, because no matter how much I looked, I could see nothing of the stocky Captain Caldswell in the girl's dark, delicate features. The disconnect made me curious, but I stomped down the urge to question. Nosy mercs were dead mercs. Instead, I nodded to the girl politely: "Miss Caldswell."

Ren didn't even look at me. She just walked past Basil and me like we weren't there and sat down on the couch behind us.

If her antisocial behavior bothered him, Basil didn't let it show. A second later, I let it go as well, because Basil was now introducing the man. "This is our cook."

The tall man's face broke into a smile that only made him more handsome as he held out his hand. "Rupert Charkov," he said, his voice curling around the letters with a soft accent I couldn't place.

"Devi Morris," I replied, doing my best not to let my own, far less attractive accent leak through as I took his hand.

When you live around mercs, you get used to bone-crushing handshakes. It's a dominance thing, a power game, and like all games, I play to win. But Rupert took me by surprise, closing his hand around mine gentle as a caress. His soft grip forced me to dial back my own at the last second, which had the funny effect of sending my fingers sliding under his in a way that felt shockingly intimate between two people who'd just met.

Rupert must have felt it too, because the sudden, knowing look he gave me made his eyes sparkle. "I look forward to working with you, Devi."

"Same," I said. I could certainly stand hearing him say my name in that lovely accent a few more times.

Terrans accuse Paradoxians of being overly forward and completely unable to comprehend subtlety. I think that's an exaggeration, but I have to admit I watched Rupert blatantly as he walked behind the kitchen counter and began moving supplies from the bag he'd been carrying into the fridge. I can't help it, I'm not a subtle girl. When I see something I like, I go for it, and I liked what I saw very much. Even unloading groceries, Rupert moved gracefully, and as Basil led me back toward the bridge, all my earlier misgivings seemed less damning. Yes, I decided, Rupert would definitely make this job more bearable. All I needed now was for my fellow security merc to be minimally competent and this guard business might not be half bad.

Feeling more confident than I had since Caldswell told me I'd gotten the job, I strode after Basil, nodding where appropriate as he started explaining the dreadful burden of navigation, which my unevolved brain couldn't possibly comprehend.

CHAPTER
2

Basil's tour ended at the tiny cabin that would be my home for the next year, but despite his warning that I'd have a bunkmate, the room was empty. Either this Nova girl was one of those who kept everything they owned with them at all times (I've known several over the years; fighting for hire makes people paranoid), or Basil had actually convinced the captain to separate us and just didn't know it yet. Either way, the empty room suited me just fine, and I settled down to the serious business of unpacking my equipment.

Unlocking my armor case always felt like opening a birthday present. I've been obsessed with powered armor for as long as I can remember. There's just something magical about the idea of a lovely machine that slides over your body and makes you super-human.

It also helped that I'd always been good at it. We Paradoxians don't mess around with our armor. Our schools have armor teams starting at age ten, and I'd been at the top of every one since I could compete. My mother used to say it was good I liked armor since I'd never be able to get a real job with my grades. I won't repeat what I said back to her, because now that Basil was gone, I was official on duty, and I try not to swear when I'm on a job.

Whatever my mother's opinion on the matter, my armor obsession had gotten me a place in the Royal Armored Corps my very first year of mandatory military service, and when all the other kids had gone home after their required two years, I'd gotten a promotion. Two years after that, I'd landed a spot in the most prestigious armored mercenary unit on Paradox. Not bad for a girl whose mother said she'd never be anything but an arena groupie.

The Blackbirds had been on the far edge of Terran Republic space when my contract had run out, and between all the flights and the Republic's idiotic armor regulations, I hadn't worn my suit in almost a week. As was always the case after a dry spell, putting it on again was a rush. I pulled the pieces out one by one, examining each segment to see if it had been damaged during all the lugging around. It hadn't, of course. Even the cheapest Paradoxian armor isn't like that plastic Terran junk. It wouldn't get damaged in transport even if you shipped it in a bag of ball bearings. Still, my armor was my baby and my beloved all in one. I checked everything.

When I was finally satisfied, I stripped down to my underwear and dug my underarmor suit out of my duffel. The underarmor wasn't strictly necessary. My armor has a self-cleaning cycle, but sweating in something I paid so much for was unthinkable, so I zipped myself into my skintight underarmor suit and started putting on the Lady Gray.

The Lady Gray was a suit of Verdemont Knight-class armor made just for me. Verdemont Armory is one of the oldest armor companies on Paradox, which is saying something considering our age-old obsession with the stuff, and they only make custom suits. Nobility or common born, Verdemont is the best you can buy, and I'd dumped two years' wages to make sure I was buying the best. My equipment is my life; I only buy quality.

The Lady Gray was broken up into a series of interlocking pieces that fit over my body like a shell. Each segment overlapped and locked into those around it, connecting via a close-gap system, no wires for me. The disassembled armor looked stunning in the case, but it was when I put her on that the Lady's true beauty showed. My suit was the color of morning mist, a light, silvery gray chased through with a spiraling pattern that was only visible in direct light. It was a speed suit, built for strength and flexibility, but the money I'd spent really showed in the suit's size.

Usually, size is a good indicator of the strength potential for a suit of powered armor, but not always. Fully armored, the Lady added only six inches to my height and a mere hundred and fifty pounds to my weight. Her plates clung to me like a second skin, looking more like a slimmed down armor costume than a full working suit. Her engine case was on my back and so small you'd miss it if you didn't know what to look for.

Even I'd been a little skeptical when the Master Armorsmith first showed me her power ratings, but my worries had died the first time I'd put the Lady on. Over the two and a half years we'd been together, my suit had jumped me hundreds of feet onto escaping thruster ships and punched armored combat marines through bulkheads without pushing into the red. She might look like a light racing suit, but my Lady was ruthless to those who underestimated her, or me, and I've never regretted a cent of the fortune I'd paid for her.

Putting on my suit and feeling its comfortable weight lock around me again was its own kind of wonderful, but the real treat came when I slipped on my helmet. The Lady Gray was well-enough made to follow my movements with or without her head, but in order to really use Paradoxian armor, you have to activate the neural net. As I put on the Lady's sleek helmet, the neural sensors slid through my hair like a comb to lock onto my scalp. The moment the helmet locked in place, my world shifted.

It was like waking up from a dream. My vision sharpened as my cameras took over for my eyes, and suddenly I could see everything around me in a 360 degree circle. Infrared readings hovered over my normal vision like ghosts for a few seconds before fading into the background as my brain adjusted to the new information the Lady's neural net was feeding me.

As my senses adjusted, my suit became an extension of my own body. I could feel the floor under my armored knees and the slick surface of my suit beneath the articulated joints of my gloves like I was touching it with my own fingers. All my systems flickered on the edge of my thoughts: ammo, power, maps, chat systems—even my music—were all ready and waiting to flick into my field of vision the second I thought of them.

Feeling infinitely more myself now that I was back in my suit, I moved to my weapons. I hadn't quite managed to get my guns up to the Lady Gray's level yet, but my girls were no slouches. As always, the first to go on was Sasha, my anti-armor pistol. She was a variant of the Paradoxian standard sidearm I'd used in the army, but with some major modifications that jacked up her power and a custom sight that linked into my armor's camera control system whenever I touched her. I locked her into the custom holster on my hip and then reached for Mia's case.

If Sasha was my bread and butter, Mia was my statement piece. She was a plasma shotgun the Blackbird quartermaster had sold to me after I pulled her off a tank and refused to give her back. I'd already modded her charge to shoot seven shots instead of six, and I was saving up to get her a sight that hooked into my suit's targeting system like Sasha's did, but I wasn't in too much of a hurry about it. Plasma shotguns aren't exactly hard to hit with.

My thermite blade was already in place, folded into a nook in my armor beneath my left arm, so once Mia was fixed on my back, I was ready to go. I locked my armor case, stowed my duffel and gun cases, as well as the tiny army-issue concealable hand pistol I kept for those rare occasions when I was out of my armor, under the lower bunk. When everything was in place, I stepped out into the hall, ready for business.

As I left my room, I noticed for the first time that the *Glorious Fool*, though a Terran ship, was retrofitted to Paradoxian armor standards, with ten-foot ceilings and reinforced floor panels. This raised my opinion of my new captain yet again. The Lady might be smaller than most suits, but I was still six feet and almost four hundred pounds once suit, guns, and ammo were counted in. I can and have performed just fine in tight quarters, but I appreciated the extra room. Low ceilings made me claustrophobic.

Being back in my suit put me in full-on merc mode, so when my density sensor told me there was another person in armor standing in the lounge, I put my hand on my gun and went to investigate. I was confident that I could defend a ship this size by myself against pretty much anything. All I needed was for my fellow security officer to not be terrible enough to drag me down and everything would be fine. Caldswell seemed to know what he was doing, so I wasn't too worried until I stepped into the lounge.

You spend enough years as a soldier for hire and you find that most mercs tend to fall into three categories. There are the career professionals like me who are in this business because they're excellent at what they do and love to do it; there are the grunts who put on the armor and do what they're told because it doesn't take too much thought and the pay is good; and then there are the skullheads, the macho idiots who do it for the power trip. I should have known what I was in for the moment I'd seen the canary yellow Count's suit parked in the cargo bay. Count's armor is the biggest suit a peasant can own outside of the arenas. They're huge, seven feet tall and nearly four feet at the shoulders, and impractical for anything other than wading through infantry and ripping up vehicles, which is exactly why skullheads love them.

This Count's suit was a piece of cheap Maraday assembly-line garbage, but it was polished to a sheen. Caldswell was standing beside it, neck craned back as he talked to the man with the shaved head who was leering with a superior sneer from the armor's open cockpit. But if his looks and armor hadn't been enough to clue me in that this man was a jerk, the first words out of his mouth removed all doubt.

"Morris," Caldswell said as I walked in. "This is Jayston Cotter, the other half of your security team. Cotter, this is Devi Morris."

The man's face broke into an enormous grin as soon as the captain said my name. "I've heard of you," he said, eying me up and down even though he couldn't possibly see anything of interest through my armor. When I didn't answer at once, he switched to King's Tongue. "You're the Blackbirds' crazy slut."

I gritted my teeth. Of all the crap that got thrown my way, "slut" was the putdown I hated the most. Sure I had a lot of flings, but all mercs did. It was stupid not to live your life to the fullest when you could die tomorrow, and I sure as shit wasn't about to take hell for that from some macho skullhead idiot.

But I knew better than to show my anger, so I kept my face neutral as I flipped up my visor to give Cotter a slow once-over. "That's funny," I drawled, switching to King's Tongue as well. "I haven't heard of you. You'd think an asshole as big as yourself would be famous by now. Guess you need to work on your insults."

Cotter stepped forward, his enormous boot landing so hard I felt the rumble through my shocks. I grabbed my pistol, ready to shoot this moron's stabilizer right out of his cheap suit and send him tumbling over like a turtle, but Caldswell got between us first.

"Children," he said, his voice low and deadly. "That's enough."

We both stepped back, Cotter giving me a lewd wink in the process. I smiled cold as I could and made a note to deal with him quickly before he got any ideas. If we were going to be working together, I'd have to make sure he understood the boundaries in a real and bloody way.

Now that his security team had been introduced, Caldswell took us down to the empty cargo bay and showed us where we could strap in for launch. The second the captain was gone, the heckling began. It wasn't even original, just more of the same old armored whore catcalls I'd heard since I was a teenager. Now, I knew how to follow orders. I also knew doing this before we'd even left Paradox was a bad idea, but nine years as a fighter had given me some instincts that had nothing to do with fighting.

Mercs are a lot like animals in some ways. Dominance is very important. Dicks like Cotter were everywhere in the merc world. They got their power by bullying anyone they thought was weaker, pushing at whatever vulnerability they could find. If they locked on to you, the only way to get them off again was to push back so hard they learned to keep their mouths shut. That or kill them, but I didn't want to make a mess quite so soon into my new job. So, with shove not being an option, I had to make do with push, and the moment the captain called two minutes to launch, I dropped my safety harness and motioned for Cotter to come to the center of the cargo bay.

"What?" he said, grinning as he clomped over, his giant suit clanging on the scuffed metal floor. "If you want a tumble, sweetheart, you'll have to wait until we get—"

I was in the air before he finished. The Lady Gray couldn't fly, but she could jump so high and fast it didn't matter. I shot up until I was eye level with the cargo bay lights and then dropped, flipping in midair to land hard with both feet on Cotter's broad shoulders. I'd angled to land right on the weight balancer that kept his tank of a suit upright, and my impact sent him tilting with a strangled gasp.

It only knocked him for a moment, but a moment was all I needed. I reached down and popped the hidden safety that's always in the same place on assembly-line suits, yanking up his face shield with one hand while my other dove to grab his now-bared throat. It was a move that would never have worked on small armor like mine, but then people who wore reasonably sized suits rarely needed this sort of discipline.

The moment I touched him, Cotter froze. Snapping his neck would be nothing to my armor-powered hand, and he knew it. Very slowly, taking my time, I reached up and plucked the neural net off his shaved head. As was the default in cheap suits like this, his armor went into idle as soon as I broke the connection, trapping him inside.

Now that he couldn't throw me off, I shifted my weight and crouched down, lowering my head until I was an inch from his nose. I stopped there a second, letting him take a good, hard look at the reflection of his terrified face in my silver-tinted visor while my fingers slowly tightened on his throat until I was pressing on the last millimeter of space he needed to keep breathing.

The launch timer ticking just out of sight on my left told me we were running short on time, but I didn't pick up my pace. Dominance is an animal game. You've got to give the animal part of your enemy time to understand they've been defeated, otherwise you'll end up fighting the same fight a dozen times before they get it.

When I was certain I'd scared him enough, I whispered into my suit's speakers, nudging the levels slightly to make sure my voice had just the right metallic edge that made people hear your words in their nightmares.

"Now that I have your undivided attention," I said slowly, "here's what we're going to do. We're going to start this relationship over. This time, you're going to be a gentleman, or I'm going to make sure you end up a casualty of Caldswell's infamous bad luck."

For a second, it looked like he was going to try and fight. I tightened my grip, cutting off his last fraction of air. "Do you know how to be a gentleman, Cotter?"

Eyes bulging, Cotter nodded.

"Show me," I said, relaxing my hand just enough to let him take a gasp. "What does a gentleman say?"

"I'm sorry," he choked.

I tilted my head. "I'm sorry... what?"

Cotter was starting to turn a little blue. "I'm sorry, Miss Morris."

I smiled and released my hand. He collapsed at once, slumping into his idled armor. I let him pant a bit before I slapped the neural net back on his head and hopped down. "You'd better get strapped in," I said, walking back to the wall and sliding my arms through the harness as the ship began to rumble. "Launch in thirty seconds."

This was the point where a normal jerk would have told me I'd pay for this insult or something else equally stupid, but Cotter, for all his skullhead flaws, was a merc like me. We both understood that this had been a fight for control, and I'd won. Of course, that didn't mean he had to like it.

"You're a crazy bitch," he said, stomping back to his harness.

"Crazy bitch I'm fine with," I answered. "But hit on me again and I'll hit you through the bulkhead."

He didn't say anything else, just locked himself down as the thrusters kicked in, pushing us off the planet with a deafening roar.

I fully expected to have to make my point at least two more times before it stuck, but Cotter didn't bother me again. He was still a complete ass, bossing people around and bragging endlessly about the time his team saved some minor baron's life to anyone who would listen, but he never said anything else untoward about me in my hearing. He wasn't quite as good about not leering when I was out of armor, but he kept his comments to himself, so I let it slide.

Given Caldswell's reputation, I was braced for attack the moment we left Paradoxian orbit, but none came. I quickly fell into the rhythm of ship life. Cotter and I had split shifts; I had the night cycle and early morning while he took the ship's day. With a nine-man crew on such a small vessel, I'd expected to be up to my elbows in crewmates, but I didn't actually see anyone except for the handful of people I'd met my first day. When I managed to catch Basil outside the bridge long enough to ask where everyone was, he gave me a huge lecture about minding my own business and then told me they were waiting for us at the Fishermarch.

"You left your crew on the Fishermarch?" I said, horrified. "Why would they want to stay on that waterball when they could have come to Paradox?"

"It's called a vacation," Basil snapped. "Captain Caldswell is very thoughtful when it comes to his people, and he wanted them to have a little time off. The captain kept back only those who were absolutely necessary for the trip to Kingston."

His puffed-out chest told me what the bird thought about himself being included in the "absolutely necessary" category.

A skeleton crew and no cargo meant nothing much to guard when I was on duty and no one to talk to when I was off. As a result, I ended up spending most of my downtime in the lounge with Rupert. Not that I minded. In fact, sitting at the bar watching him chop vegetables with the quiet intensity of a heart surgeon was one of the few times I didn't worry I'd made the wrong choice taking this job.

Caldswell kept a liquor cabinet in the lounge where he sold drinks to the crew at cost. Rupert tended it in addition to his cooking duties, and he'd been very kind about sneaking me free drinks, a habit that made me like him even more. I had one in my hand now, a Terran whiskey with a deep, smoky burn that made me feel lovely even though I was fresh off twelve hours of standing around.

I was still standing, actually. I hadn't taken off my armor yet, and I didn't trust the bar stools to hold the Lady's weight. Instead, I leaned on the counter that separated the tiny kitchen from the rest of the lounge with my chin on my discarded helmet, holding my glass delicately between my armored hands as I watched Rupert's knife turn a pile of fat turnips into neat little sticks.

"I saw what you did the other day," he said, never looking up from his chopping.

"Hmm?" This was my fourth whiskey, and I was already more drunk than I'd intended to get. I still trusted myself to shoot straight, but translation was getting difficult, especially when he kept speaking in that delightful accent of his. The fact that he'd taken his jacket off and was working in his shirtsleeves with the cuffs rolled up didn't help either. The man's arms went on forever.

I was surprised to see a small black tattoo across the inside of his left wrist, a thin, delicately lined pattern about two inches long. He didn't seem like the tattoo type. I smiled, wondering if he had any more.

"Your fight with Cotter," Rupert said as he scraped the white turnip sticks into a bowl. "You were fantastic. That flip was what, forty feet?"

"Wait, you saw that?" I said, snapping out of my daze. "How?"

"We have cameras in the cargo bay," he answered, his words rich with hidden laughter as he pulled a bunch of leafy greens onto the cutting board. "I'm glad, otherwise I'd have missed the show."

"Crap." The curse slipped out before I could stop it, another sign I should stop with the whiskey. Of *course* they'd have cameras in the cargo bay. The real question was what kind of idiot was I for forgetting them. Disciplining Cotter should have been the captain's job, not mine. That little stunt could have cost me my position.

"Well," I said at last, putting my glass down with a *clink*. "I guess if Caldswell hasn't fired me yet, he's not going to."

"He wasn't happy," Rupert said. "But you didn't do any serious damage, and Cotter was out of line. The captain prefers to let people settle their own disputes so long as it doesn't hurt the ship."

"Good to know," I said.

He smiled at me, his face lighting up. I smiled back automatically, suddenly giddy. He really was good-looking, and he seemed to have an easygoing sense of humor. Add in the free drinks and I was sold. But before I could turn the conversation back to something more pleasant, his eyes slid over my shoulder.

I turned. Ren was sitting on the couch in the corner, just like she'd been every time I'd seen her. The captain's daughter was leaned over a small table, playing with a battered game set that used stylized pieces on a checkered board. Chess, it was called, one of those ancient Terran games from Old Earth. I'd thought it was a game for two people, but Ren was moving the pieces like she didn't need any opponent but herself, so maybe I was wrong.

"Does she ever talk?" I asked, lowering my voice as I turned back to Rupert.

"Sometimes," he said. "Not often. She's had a hard life."

His voice changed as he said that, and for a second, I caught a look in his eyes that was completely at odds with the happy, flirtatious Rupert I knew. "I watch her as a favor to the captain," he continued, his easygoing expression snapping back to normal as he resumed chopping. "He worries about her."

"And it's not hard to watch something that doesn't move."

Rupert just smiled at that and slid the drink I'd set aside back toward me. "Don't waste other people's gifts," he said with a wink.

I gave him my best slow smile as I raised the whiskey to my lips and finished it in one long drink. By the time I set the empty glass down, Rupert was looking better than ever, but he was still on duty when it was time for me to go to sleep, so nothing came of it. As I fell into bed, I drunkenly promised myself I'd be taking him there with me before the crew came back.

Despite my best efforts, I didn't manage to get Rupert so far as the hall over the next two days, much less my bed. It wasn't for lack of trying, either. I don't normally bother to dress up for men, but the day after he'd slid me a drink with that knowing wink, I'd worn my favorite low-cut shirt in the hopes of spurring things along.

But while the shirt earned me a long, appreciative look and a slow smile, Rupert behaved the same as ever, talking politely with me while I ate but never really taking his attention off the soup he was simmering. I'd finished my food quickly and was about to start trying to move things closer to the direction I wanted them to go—namely the two of us toward my bed—but Cotter had come in then, and as much as I wanted Rupert, I wasn't about to do anything in front of the skullhead.

I'm not one to give up, though, and the next day I tried my black dress, a scandalously short little thing that showed off my legs and had yet to fail me. I wasn't disappointed. Rupert grinned openly when I came in. "What's the occasion?"

"Laundry day," I lied, sliding onto what was becoming my usual stool as I looked for somewhere to put my elbows. There wasn't much room. Rupert was busy shucking a basket of grenade-sized seeds, and their soft shells were all over the counter.

His mouth quirked as he watched me try to clear a space. "You're free to help, if you'd like."

I made a show of considering his offer. "Drink with me and maybe I will."

This was my new plan. I was hoping a few drinks would loosen up his wall of politeness, and helping with kitchen work on my off

Rachel Bach

hours seemed like a small sacrifice compared to the potential pay-off. Rupert shrugged, and five minutes later we were both seated at the large dining table in the middle of the lounge with two bowls, the basket of seeds, and a bottle of whiskey between us.

"So," I said, cracking the first nut on the table with a solid whack. "Where did you learn to cook?" I was betting the army, but I wanted to see if I could get his military record without turning this into an interrogation.

"Here and there," Rupert said, filling my glass to just below the rim before pouring a much smaller measure into his own. "Seemed useful. My mother always said that no woman wanted a man who couldn't feed himself."

"How's that working out for you?" I asked, picking up the drink he'd been so kind as to pour me.

"Well enough," Rupert said with a sly smile. "After all, if I didn't know how to cook, we wouldn't be sitting like this, would we?"

I took a sip to hide my smug smirk. Now this was more like it. But even while I was congratulating myself on an excellent start, things were already going downhill. See, I have this bad habit of drinking whatever is in front of me, and Rupert was remarkably quick at refilling a glass. As a result, an hour later my hands were aching from splitting seeds and most of the bottle of whiskey was in my stomach.

I can drink with the best of them, but even I have my limits, and I was now very drunk. Way more drunk than I wanted to be in front of a stranger, even one as attractive as Rupert, and certainly too drunk to hold my tongue like a good merc should. So when the conversation drifted to how I was enjoying life on the *Fool*, I answered a little too honestly.

"I'm bored stiff," I slurred, peeling half a brown husk before giving up and throwing the seed in the bowl. "This curse nonsense is crap. We haven't had so much as a potshot since leaving Kingston."

Rupert reached over and snatched my half-peeled seed before the flaky shell could shed all over his pile of carefully hulled white nutmeats. "We're still deep in Paradoxian space," he said, his voice indulgent as he finished shucking the seed with three neat cracks. "Surely you have more faith in your king than to expect bands of pirates the moment we leave orbit?"

"My life to the Sainted King, holy be his name," I grumbled dutifully. "But I signed up for some action. I thought Caldswell was supposed to be this magnet for trouble. I came here to expand my reputation, but all I've done so far is walk in goddamned circles." I waved my hands in drunken ovals. "If I don't shoot something soon, I'm going to pop."

"I don't think I've ever heard of anyone dying from *not* getting attacked by pirates," Rupert said with a laugh as he tossed the now naked seed into the bowl with the rest.

Drunk as I was, his laugh went right through me, and I suddenly decided I was done talking about work. I hadn't come here to actually help him cook, after all. "You know," I said, leaning forward so my low-cut dress could do the job I'd worn it to do. "It wouldn't be so bad if I had something to take my mind off it."

If Rupert had missed my meaning before, there was no way he could fail to catch it now. Even I would have been a bit shocked by how forward that move was had I been sober enough to care. But I wasn't sober, I was drunk and frustrated. Not to be cocky, but I'm not used to men giving me the runaround. I don't do up my face like a noble lady, but I know I'm attractive. Given Rupert's earlier looks, I was pretty sure he didn't disagree, but while I'd practically spray painted a welcome sign across my chest, he still hadn't taken the bait. It was enough to push my patience, already strained thin by a week of dull guard duty, to the breaking point. I'd put more effort into attracting Rupert over the last few days than I'd wasted on anyone in a long time. A sensible girl would have cut her losses by this point, but I've always been pigheaded. Plus, after all this trouble, getting Rupert into my bed was now a matter of pride.

Pride, lust, and whiskey are a potent combination. I stood up, pushing back my chair with a scrape. Rupert put down the seed he'd been working on but otherwise didn't move as I walked around the table and settled my hands on his shoulders. As I leaned down to press a kiss against his cheek, he turned and caught my face in his hands.

"Devi," he said quietly. "You are very drunk."

"So?" I said. He'd gotten me this way, after all. And given how beautifully blue his eyes looked when we were this close, my level of drunk seemed like a minor concern.

Rupert sighed and stood, bringing me up with him. "Come on, pretty girl," he said. "Let's get you to bed."

I grinned wide.

"Not like that," he chided gently, clamping his hands on my shoulders and steering me toward the door.

I heaved an enormous sigh, but my disappointment was soon replaced by the surprising difficulty of standing upright. As the room started to tilt, I realized with a start that I was even drunker than I'd thought. Suddenly, going to bed sounded like a very good idea. Rupert slid his arm under mine and helped me to my bunk. I was so gone, I didn't realize he'd left the room until he came back with a glass of water.

"Drink," he said, wrapping my hands around the cold glass.

"What's my motivation?" I asked, but the words slurred so badly I was honestly surprised when he answered.

"Not feeling like death tomorrow."

That sounded like a good reason. I drank the whole glass while Rupert pulled the sheet over me. When he took my empty cup, I said, "Wait."

He stopped and looked down at me.

"Thanks for being a gentleman and all," I said, snuggling into my pillow. "But really, it would have been okay."

He reached down, gently pulling my hair out of my ponytail and spreading it out over the pillow. He stroked it once, almost like he was petting it, and then he stood up, tossing my hair band on the dresser. "We'll try this over again tomorrow when you're sober enough to know what you're saying," he said, walking to the door. He stopped when he reached it, and the smile he gave me made my whole body feel warm. "Good night, Devi."

I wanted to ask him to stay and keep smiling at me, but I never got the chance. As soon as the lights went out, I was asleep.

I woke up to a throbbing head and the sour feeling that comes when you've made a fool of yourself. It took me a full ten minutes to haul myself out of bed, strip off the dress I was still wearing from the night before, and pull on my armor. That left no time for breakfast before my shift, but I didn't even want to think about food, and I certainly wasn't ready to face Rupert just yet.

But while I managed to avoid the cook and the reminder of the idiot I'd made of myself that he represented, my day only got worse as my shift wore on. For a supposedly cursed, insanely dangerous ship, the *Fool* was letting me down. Today marked a solid week that I'd been Caldswell's security officer, and *nothing* had happened. So far, this job had been exactly the sort of mind-numbingly dull guard work I'd avoided all my life, and I was starting to get seriously depressed. If Anthony had been wrong about this job, I'd end up wasting a year of my life for nothing.

By the time Cotter showed up to relieve me, I was so low I could barely choke down dinner. A long, hot shower helped tremendously, though, and by the time I got back to my berth, I was feeling a little more human. I'd just sat down on the edge of my bunk in my towel to work the tangles out of my wet hair when the ship's alarm began to blare.

On a normal day back in the Blackbirds, it would have taken me twenty-six seconds to put on my armor. Now, after seven days of waiting to hear that sound, I did it in nineteen. I barely took the time to throw on my underwear before diving into my suit. The Lady Gray must have been as ready for action as I was, because we were running down the hall before I'd actually figured out where I was going.

As it turned out, the alarm was for the bridge, and Cotter got there first. As well he should have, being as he was on duty. His hulking armor blocked the bridge door, but his suit was large enough that I was able to duck between his legs. I came up fast, pistol in hand, only to nearly drop it when I saw what the alarm was about.

Caldswell was on his feet in front of the captain's chair. Behind him, Basil was cowering in his pilot's nest, his feathers tight against his bony body. And standing beside the captain, with the barrel of a large pearl-handled energy pistol pressed directly under Caldswell's chin, was Rupert.

CHAPTER
3

I almost didn't recognize him. He looked the same as always—
same black suit, same dark hair, same handsome face—but the
expression on it seemed to belong to a different man. Rupert smiled
when he saw me come up, but not the warm smile he'd given me
yesterday. This expression was cold and calm as a frozen lake, and
his hand was rock steady as he pushed the pistol's muzzle deeper
into the soft spot below Caldswell's jaw. I started to say something,
but the captain caught my eyes through my visor and shook his
head as far as Rupert's grip allowed.

"Now that we're all here," Rupert said slowly, that lovely accent
as cold as the rest of him. "This is how things stand. If anyone
speaks without my permission, I will shoot the captain. If anyone
moves, I will shoot the captain. If you do not lower your guns, I will
shoot the captain. Understood?"

He was looking right at me as he spoke, and though it made
me sick to do it, I nodded. When my gun was pointed at the floor,
Rupert continued.

"We are going to change course toward the Hereford colony," he
said. "When we get there, I will give you further instructions."

"Ignore that order," Caldswell said. "This ship stays on—"

He cut off with a strangled sound as Rupert stabbed the big

pistol deeper into his throat, barrel pointed up. "Change course, Basil," Rupert said calmly. "Or I will blow his brains out."

Basil gave a frightened squawk, and I tightened my grip on my lowered gun. This was a bad, bad situation. I'd thought Rupert had a military posture when I'd first met him, but his steady finger on the trigger told me for certain that he'd used a pistol to kill at close range before, and he meant to use it this time. This wasn't the Rupert who'd slipped me free drinks and refused to take advantage of a drunken girl. Maybe that Rupert never even existed. Maybe he was just a mask for this Rupert, who was almost certainly going to shoot Caldswell in the next minute if the ship didn't start turning.

He'd set himself up well for it, too. On the small bridge, there was no room to get behind him, and while my suit could move faster than he could, with his gun pressed into Caldswell's neck like that, all Rupert had to do was pull the trigger. He was standing in the classic hostage position with the captain in front of him as a shield. If I shot to wound, body, leg, or arm, I would almost certainly hit Caldswell, too. But he'd left one area open. For all that Caldswell's wide, stocky body made for good cover, Rupert was taller than the captain by a good six inches, and that was where I took my chance.

With bitter regret at the waste of such a nice face, I snapped up my pistol and squeezed off a shot. It happened so fast my targeting program didn't have time to line up the sights, but I've never needed a computer to shoot straight. Sasha struck true, her armor-piercing bullet hitting Rupert right in the middle of his forehead.

I caught one last glimpse of his face before it hit. He was shocked, which was normal in people realizing they were about to die, but the fear and anger that were usually mixed in were missing. Instead, Rupert looked almost...impressed. That was all I saw before he was flung across the bridge by the force of a shot from a pistol meant to take out armored targets, crashing into the railing beside Basil's pilot's nest.

I was moving before he landed.

"Get the captain!" I shouted to Cotter as I surged forward. I saw through my rear cam that he obeyed, grabbing Caldswell and dragging him back. Technically, he didn't have to take orders from me, but after our dustup in the cargo bay he wasn't going to argue.

I wouldn't have listened if he had. I was killing mad. Try it again tomorrow, he'd said. Bull*shit*. Rupert had planned this from the start, and I'd eaten it up. I'd let him lead me around by the nose like a goddamn idiot, and someone was going to pay.

The first thing I noticed when I reached Rupert's body was there was no blood, which made no sense. A shot like that should have splattered his skull, but while he wasn't moving, his head was still in one piece. I reached out to grab him for a better look, but my fingers ran into something that felt like stiff jelly an inch above his shoulder. I guessed what it was the second I felt it, but my display quickly flashed the truth across my vision. Rupert was covered in a personal shield.

Snatching my hand out of the shield's invisible barrier, I grabbed Sasha and pointed her barrel at the hollow of Rupert's jaw, just as he'd done to Caldswell. I couldn't push my gun through the shield without damaging her, but the plasma had already deflected one of my bullets. There was no personal shield in the universe that could take two shots from an anti-armor pistol, especially if the second was point-blank.

As I paused to let my computer calculate exactly how hard Sasha would need to fire to punch through the shield without risking the bullet going through the floor and possibly out the hull, it briefly occurred to me that I should probably stop here. If I killed Rupert, Caldswell couldn't question him, and we'd never know why he'd betrayed us. But my instincts were pounding louder than my common sense or curiosity right then. That, and I don't like being made a fool of.

"Stand down!"

Caldswell's voice tore through my bloodlust like a gunshot, and I glanced through my rear cam to see the captain shoving his way out of Cotter's hold.

"Stand down, you damn bloodthirsty Paradoxians!" he yelled again as he succeeded in ripping his way free, something he really shouldn't have been able to do given how strong Cotter's armor was. "He's out, threat's over, so you stand down right now or so help me I will shove you both into space!"

Caldswell was furious, and Cotter stepped back instinctively. I wasn't so smart. Keeping my gun pressed against Rupert's shield, I spoke without turning. "You mind telling me what the hell is going on, sir?"

"Ease up the gun, Morris," Caldswell said, holding out his hands. "You did it. You passed the test."

If I'd been seeing red before, I was almost blind with it now.

"*What?*" I screamed, whirling around.

Caldswell's fury vanished in the face of my own, fading to something insultingly close to open amusement. "It was a test," he said again. "Response time, ability to act decisively under pressure, who would take the leadership role. It's a dangerous business out here. If I'm going to trust you with my ship, I had to see how good you are."

"A test?" Cotter said, his voice as bewildered as I felt. "You mean, you and the cook?"

"Charkov's a friend of mine," Caldswell said, stomping down the bridge steps. "I asked him to help, and he agreed to play his part. I gave us both a shield in the hopes that you would shoot and I could keep you around." He looked down at Rupert. "Of course, I didn't expect you to use an anti-armor pistol on an unarmored target, or armor-piercing rounds, or to shoot him in the head. Most mercs have normal guns and take the body shot." He sighed. "Should have known better with you crazy Paradoxians."

44

I stared at him. "You've done this *before*?"

"First thing I do with any new team," Caldswell said, kneeling beside Rupert's prone body. "You can drop the gun now, Morris."

I obeyed, letting my arm fall to my side as Caldswell deactivated Rupert's shield.

"How bad is he?" I asked cautiously, fighting to contain my anger until I figured out who most deserved it.

"Just knocked out," Caldswell said, his voice strained with effort as he heaved Rupert up. "He'll be mad at me when he wakes up, though. This wasn't part of the plan." He glanced at me. "Little help?"

Holstering my pistol, I grabbed Rupert from Caldswell. The Lady can carry up to six hundred pounds, but even so, Rupert was heavier than I'd anticipated, and I had to pause a moment to let my stabilizer adjust. When I was steady, I slung Rupert's body over my shoulder and followed Caldswell to the infirmary.

"Thank you," the captain said as I laid Rupert down on one of the long beds. "Good shooting up there, Morris."

"Thank you, sir." I bit the words out. Much as I despised Caldswell at the moment for putting me through this farce, he was still my employer, and I had ambitions to fulfill. That meant I needed to get out of here fast before my temper got the better of me, so I was more than a little upset when Caldswell spoke again, forcing me to stop and listen.

"I'm not going to apologize for doing this," the captain said. "In my line of work, I have to be sure I can trust the people below me. But I'm glad you passed. Cotter's everything I expect from a Paradoxian—rude, violent, and simple. Men like that have their uses, but you're different. You seem like you could make a damn fine officer someday. Maybe even a Devastator."

I froze, but Caldswell just smiled. "Oh yes, I know why you're here," he said. "I saw the ambition in your eyes the moment you walked into the interview. After that, a few questions around the Royal Office cleared up the rest."

He reached into one of the cabinets, pulling out a plastic-wrapped trauma dampener for Rupert's head. "I'm watching you, Deviana Morris, and I meant it when I said you did well. I know you're probably not feeling very kindly toward me at the moment, but that shouldn't stop a good soldier from doing her duty, especially since I'm the one who can get you what you want." He glanced over his shoulder. "My recommendation carries weight even on Paradox. Do me proud, and I'll make sure you get your ambition. We understand each other?"

"Yes, Captain," I said slowly. "Thank you, sir."

He nodded. "Dismissed."

I bowed out of habit and walked into the hall. Back by the bridge, I could hear Basil's whistling voice as he lectured Cotter both for not shooting first and for letting me jump on Rupert to shoot him again. Cotter screamed back that he didn't see the damn bird doing anything, to which Basil replied he was *acting*, a refined art Cotter wouldn't understand. The argument was still going when I entered my room and shut the door, cutting off their voices. I sloughed off my armor with less care than usual, fitting the pieces into their slots with shaking hands.

I still hadn't decided who my fury was for—Caldswell for testing me, Rupert for tricking me, or myself for getting so spectacularly taken in. I tried to lighten my mood by remembering that I'd passed the test. Passed it well enough that Caldswell had dangled the bone of a recommendation to the Devastators in front of me. But the fact that he'd found out so easily exactly what he needed to lure me along made me angrier still, and I fell into bed with a smothered scream.

I punched my pillow a few times for good measure and turned

over, throwing myself into sleep. Maybe when I woke up, things would be less insane. Somehow, I seriously doubted it.

I was still pretty mad when I got up six hours later. I was also starving. I'd eaten like a bird yesterday, and I was feeling it. This wasn't helping my mood at all, so I threw on my sweats, shoved my hair in a messy bun, and set off to raid the kitchen.

I didn't even want to look at Rupert or Caldswell yet, but the captain would be on the bridge, and I'd had enough head injuries to know that Rupert would be out of commission for at least another few hours. My plan was to get some food, get suited up, and do my damn job, but when I saw that the door to the infirmary was open, I couldn't help sneaking a peek. Considering how he'd looked when I'd gone to sleep, I expected to find him still flat on his back, so you can imagine my surprise when I looked in to see Rupert sitting on the bed putting on his shoes like he was about to get up.

"What are you doing?" I cried, running over in horror. "I'm pretty sure you should be lying down." That's what doctors were always yelling at me to do whenever I got knocked out.

"I'm fine," Rupert said, waving me away with a small smile. "Didn't expect to see you here, though."

I stiffened, suddenly remembering I was angry at him. Not as angry as I was at Caldswell, but still. "Don't get any ideas," I said, folding my arms over my chest. "I was just making sure I hadn't killed you."

Rupert's smile widened slightly. "Not yet."

"I'm not going to apologize," I announced, just to be sure he knew. "The moment you pointed a gun at the captain, shooting you became my job."

"No apology necessary," Rupert said. "Risk of the business." He returned his attention to his shoe, knotting the laces deftly into a perfect bow. "In case no one else mentions it, that was a good shot. I didn't even see it coming."

"Of course you didn't," I scoffed. "Do you know how fast my suit can move?" I blew out an annoyed breath before I remembered my manners. "But thank you for the compliment," I added grudgingly.

He chuckled and reached up to rub his forehead with a sheepish look. "I do wish you'd picked somewhere other than the head, though."

I shrugged. "Hey, if you give me the shot, I'm going to take it. Next time tell Caldswell to find someone shorter than himself to play his villain."

"I'll be sure to pass it on," Rupert said, sliding off the table. "I was going to the kitchen to start dinner, care to join me?"

I stared at him for a moment before I remembered that I'd been coming off my shift when the alarm went off, and since my shift ended in the morning, it was now dinnertime. Even without the time confusion, though, his invitation took me by surprise. I wouldn't expect a man I'd shot in the head to invite me to spend time with him, not that any of them had ever lived to ask. And then there was the part where he had a lot of nerve acting like we were still friendly after the stunt he'd pulled. But Rupert was looking at me with that same warm smile I'd noticed the first time I'd seen him, and I found myself walking down the hall beside him before I could think of a good reason to say no.

I took the chance to sneak glances at him. I don't know what I was expecting to see. He looked exactly as he always did: tall, handsome, his dark hair tied behind his head in a sweep that emphasized the sharp line of his jaw. Even knowing it had all been a trick, I couldn't reconcile this Rupert with the cold killer I'd shot six hours ago, and the disconnect was starting to get to me. Finally, just before we reached the door to the lounge, I snagged his sleeve.

"Listen," I said as we stopped. "If we're going to be stuck on this ship together for a while, I need to know—was all that stuff before an act?"

I expected him to look at me with those clear blue eyes and ask what was I talking about, but Rupert didn't. Instead, he leaned on the door, his dark brows furrowed as he considered my question. "Some of it," he said at last. "The captain thought the test would be more effective if you liked the man you'd be shooting."

"He wanted to see if I'd shoot a friend?" I'd thought as much, but hearing it confirmed brought my rage roaring back. I crushed it ruthlessly. If I was going to be mad at anyone, I'd save it for myself. No point in yelling at Rupert for following orders when I was the one who'd let herself get suckered in. No point in mentioning that we both knew how ready I'd been to take it past friends if he'd let me either. "That's why you did it?"

"That's why I sought you out," Rupert said. His voice was casual, but there was a hesitation between his words that told me he was picking them very carefully. "But it wasn't all an act. You're an entertaining person, Devi." He glanced at me, and his smile came back. "You will have to start buying your own drinks, though."

Despite everything that had happened, I laughed. "If it can't be helped," I said. "But I think you owe me at least one more freebie for putting up with all this."

"I might be able to swing that," Rupert said, eying me suspiciously. "You want it now?"

I'd woken up not half an hour ago, but it was technically evening, and I needed something after dealing with this crap, so I nodded and motioned for him to get a move on. Rupert shook his head and went into the kitchen, unlocking the bar and pulling out my usual. "I've never seen a woman drink like you," he said, pouring two fingers of whiskey over ice and sliding it down the counter. "I'm surprised you have a liver left."

"Nice part about being a merc," I said as I caught the glass. "Surviving long enough to have liver problems is considered a major achievement." I tipped my glass at him. "King's health."

He watched disapprovingly as I took a long sip. "Now that I'm no longer under orders to get you drunk, I'm going to start cutting you off."

I set the glass down, savoring the whiskey burn. "You can try," I said. "But fair warning, being drunk doesn't slow down my head shots."

He sighed at me and started getting things out for dinner.

I sipped my drink and took the chance to study him, and not with an eye toward getting him into bed, either. I was well over that. I liked my lovers simple, and Rupert was clearly not simple. Anyone who could switch his personality like that was not one to be trusted. So instead of admiring his skilled hands or graceful shoulders, I started looking for other things, signs of his military training, scars, anything that could give me a hint of the truth, but I found nothing. Just Rupert, lovely as ever, his face a smiling mask as he worked.

I sighed in frustration and finished the last of my drink. But as I tipped my glass back, my eyes drifted to the spot on his forehead where my bullet had hit. The skin there was as pale and unblemished as the rest of his face. There wasn't a bump, not even a bruise, and the more I thought about it, the more that bugged me.

Shield or not, I'd shot him from under ten feet with an anti-armor pistol. The shield may have kept the bullet from smashing his skull, but the force had still been enough to send him flying across the bridge, where he'd hit his head a second time against the railing, maybe even a third time when he'd landed on the floor. All of that trauma should have left some kind of mark, but there was nothing. Rupert was standing over the cutting board looking alert and calm as though he'd just gotten up from a pleasant night's sleep, his eyes locked on the knife's tip as it slid with delicate finesse between the flesh of a large fish and its tiny bones.

"What?"

I jumped, but Rupert's eyes never left the fish. "You're staring," he said. "What is it?"

"Nothing." I set my empty glass on the counter and stood up. "I'm going to get suited up. Thanks for the drink."

"See you later," he said.

I waved, but I didn't look back as I walked down the hall to my room.

I was still brooding about Rupert's miraculous lack of injury while I put on my suit. Fortunately, when I came back to grab dinner before my shift, the captain made an announcement that took my mind off it. We'd reached the Fishermarch, the last of the Paradoxian colonies, and now that the security team had passed their test, it was time to pick up the rest of the crew of the *Glorious Fool*.

Like any good Paradoxian girl, I'd never been to the Marches. Slum settlements on the edge of known space? Sure. Pirate camps hiding in the xith'cal hunting grounds? Dozens of times. But if I was in Paradoxian space, I saw absolutely no reason not to be on Paradox itself with the king and the nobles and everyone else who mattered. The Marches were the borderlands, the buffer zone planets used to slow down anyone trying to get to Paradox, the only planet that actually mattered. They were where old people went to retire and immigrants lived while applying for Paradoxian citizenship, definitely not my first choice for a vacation destination. But as our ship set down at a spaceport that seemed to be nothing more than a white speck floating on an endless blue sea, even I had to admit the Fishermarch was kind of pretty. For a colony.

The planet was larger than Paradox itself, but where Paradox had mountains and forests and cities that stretched to the horizon, the Fishermarch was nothing but sea. Endless, virtually bottomless blue sea teeming with life, both the small, tasty kind and the large, dangerous kind. What "land" there was was all man-made, mostly enormous floating platforms like the starport and the cabana city that surrounded it, serving as a base for the thousands of boats that raced under the glaring white sun. Shimmering shields protected the spaceport from the worst of the blasting wind, but they did nothing to keep out the light, and my visor went almost black trying to adjust for the glare as the captain and I walked out onto the landing pad.

I'd gone with the captain as a matter of course, not because I thought there'd be a threat. The king kept his lands well, and the Fishermarch was as safe as any territory in Paradox. But as my visor adjusted to the light, I was suddenly very glad I'd decided to come out with him, for there, standing at the edge of the landing pad like he was waiting for us, was a xith'cal.

There are four space-faring races in the known galaxy: humans, aeons, lelgis, and xith'cal. Any of these could be dangerous under the right circumstances, but xith'cal were *always* dangerous. The second I saw it, I snapped into action.

I stepped in front of the captain, my suit blocking all of him and my arm holding him in place to make sure it stayed that way. My other arm came up, gun in hand, to point at the xith'cal. The alien didn't look terribly concerned at having an anti-armor pistol aimed at its face. Instead, it tapped its long black claws against something flat and silver in its palm and then held it up for me to see.

The light was so bright that it took me a few moments to recognize that the thing in the alien's claws was a handset. The screen was blacked against the sunlight, and the white text across it stood out strong.

Must we go through this every time?

"Stand down, Morris." Caldswell sounded like he was trying very hard not to laugh. "He's with us."

I stared at the captain's face in my rear cam, but he didn't seem to be joking. Caldswell tapped my arm, and I let him go, but I kept my pistol up as the captain walked over to the xith'cal.

"Hyrek," he said, grinning as he held out his hand. "How are you?"

The xith'cal ignored the captain's extended palm, clicking its claws rapidly against the handset instead before holding it up again.

I'm terrible. But then, you knew I would be terrible when you chose to leave me in this miserable, bright place, so I can only assume your question is a bad attempt at humor.

Caldswell actually had the guts to laugh at that. If a xith'cal had told *me* he was feeling terrible, I would have shot him before he decided to do something about it. But then, I would have shot him before he'd had a chance to tell me anything, so it was a moot point.

Shooting xith'cal was a natural reaction. After all, they ate humans. They ate pretty much anything they could kill, actually, but they liked the sentient races best. Most of my pirate hunting had been ferreting out xith'cal slavers who raided the smaller colonies to get fresh breeding stock for the "herds" they kept on their tribe ships. Combine that with a violent temper, complete disregard for any laws other than their own, and a scaly, naturally armored body that was three feet taller than any human and three times as dense, and you had something that any sensible person would shoot on sight.

"Morris!" Caldswell yelled, glancing at me. "Put that cannon away and get over here."

Though it went against every instinct I had, I obeyed. Shoving Sasha in her holster, I walked over to stand beside the captain. This particular xith'cal must not have been one of their warriors. He was a good bit smaller than the ones I'd seen, and his scaly head was smooth, lacking the enormous ridges warriors grew.

That was something at least, but even if he was short for a xith'cal, he still towered over me even in my suit. Nearly eight feet tall, his body was covered in long, thin, overlapping scales, almost like feathers, but they were sharp enough to cut through ballistic steel, something I'd found out the hard way. Most xith'cal I'd seen were black or dark brown, but this one was green, a soft, mottled forest green that reminded me of winter trees. His eyes were like any other xith'cal's though—long, honey yellow, slitted, and deep set below a heavy bone ridge that made him look like a scowling snake. His snout was long like a lizard's, stronger than a steel vise, and full of sharp yellow teeth that were starting to make me seriously regret not shooting when I had the chance.

"Hyrek," Caldswell said, completely ignoring my wariness. "This is Devi Morris, our new security officer. Devi, this is Hyrek, our doctor."

Forgetting protocol for a moment, I reached over and grabbed Caldswell's arm, pulling him back out of the xith'cal's earshot.

"Are you kidding me?" I hissed over my suit speaker. "*Doctor?* Xith'cal *eat* people. Having him for a doctor is like having a butcher for a vet!"

A sound like someone was running a metal plate through a shredder made me jump, and I glanced in my rear cam to see that the xith'cal was laughing. He tapped his claws against the handset again and held it up for me to see.

Actually, the text read, *I was a butcher before I joined Caldswell, which is where I gained my excellent understanding of the anatomy of the lesser races. Also, xith'cal hearing far surpasses human. Just thought you should know.*

I ground my teeth, though whether it was from anger or fear, I wasn't quite sure. Finally, in a last-ditch effort to recover some of my dignity, I put my hands on my hips with my fingers resting comfortably on the butt of my pistol. "And I suppose you're body cleanup as well, then?"

Sadly no, the xith'cal typed. *Our dear captain is still rather squeamish about some things and we are forced to waste good meat. If it makes you feel better, though, Basil is the first on my list if we're ever stranded in deep space and forced to eat one another. Aeons are most delicious.*

From anyone else, I would have called that a joke, but xith'cal didn't make jokes. Beside me, Caldswell had given up trying to keep a straight face and was now smirking openly. I liked being the butt of a joke about as much as I liked standing next to a xith'cal and not shooting it, but for good or ill, it looked like Hyrek was a permanent fixture.

"I guess I'll just have to make sure I don't end up in your infirmary," I grumbled. The way he was looking at me, I wouldn't be surprised if I woke up with one less arm and Devi on the menu.

You can hardly avoid it if you're going to be a guard on this ship, Hyrek typed. He smiled wide at me, showing all his teeth, and then turned back to Caldswell. *The others are on their way. They did not share my enthusiasm for a swift departure. Now that you're here, I'm going inside. Would you mind coming with me to ensure the other half of your new pair of gun-happy meatshields doesn't try and blow my head off?* He turned the handset toward me. *No offense to present company.*

I didn't like the meatshield comment any better than I liked being laughed at, but the lizard had a point. Cotter would have the same reaction I'd had if he found the xith'cal in the ship without the captain. Caldswell clearly understood this as well, because he told me to wait on the ramp while he escorted the doctor.

I stood in the shade where he'd pointed, taking my helmet off so I could feel the sea air. I was still trying to work my brain around the idea of living in close quarters with a xith'cal when I spotted another figure walking across the landing pad toward the ship.

Fortunately, this one appeared to be entirely human. She was a tall, lithe, middle-aged woman in a bright pink sundress with a towel draped over her head against the sun. She had a small crate under one arm, while the other was guiding an enormous pile of boxes stacked on a very battered hover platform floating along behind her.

"You must be the new security," she called when she was close enough for her voice to carry. "Congratulations on passing the test! I hope you didn't beat Brian too badly."

It took me several seconds to remember that Brian was the captain's first name. "Not at all, actually," I said. "It was Rupert who got shot."

The woman stopped in front of me with a broad smile. "Poor boy," she said. "Where'd you get him?"

I pointed at the center of my forehead, and the woman winced. "Well," she said. "That's what he gets, going along with Brian's schemes. I'm just glad you're still around. We're five days behind schedule already. If we had to wait around while Brian found another team, I'd be forced to call this route off altogether." She stuck out her hand. "Mabel Cobb, engineer and cargo."

I shook her hand, careful not to squeeze too hard with my armor. "Devi Morris."

"Paradoxian." Mabel sounded impressed. "Good. Last time Caldswell went to Paradox he got a pair of Terrans. Horrible waste. Why hire on Paradox if you're not going to get actual Paradoxian armored mercs?"

I decided right then that I liked Mabel very much. "Can I help you with your luggage?" I said, nodding toward the crate under her arm.

"No, no," Mabel said. "Pickers stays with me."

She held the small crate up, and I peered in to see an enormously fat cat curled up in a miserable ball.

"Poor old lady." Mabel sighed. "She hates leaving the ship, but Brian doesn't tolerate her if I'm not around."

"Cute," I said, reaching a finger in. Mabel caught it before I'd gotten close.

"Wouldn't try it," she said. "We named her Pickers for a reason." She curled her fingers into claws and made a scratching motion.

There was no way a cat, no matter how mean, could scratch my armor, but I didn't push the issue.

"You can get the cargo, though," Mabel said, tucking the cat crate back under her arm.

"Cargo?" I said in mock astonishment. "I was beginning to think the *Glorious Fool* didn't ship anything but trouble." We shared a laugh at that, and then I asked, "What are we hauling?"

"From the Fishermarch?" Mabel wrinkled her nose. "What else? Fish. Tons of it, pickled and fresh frozen."

I wrinkled my nose as well. Shipping fish seemed so...unglamorous. But work was work.

"So," I said, grabbing a two-hundred-pound cargo crate with one arm. "How long have you been in this outfit?"

"Forever," Mabel said, stepping aside so I could grab the next box as well. "Caldswell's my brother-in-law. This ship's sort of a family business. My son worked on the *Fool* as well until I sent him to school last year."

The idea of Caldswell having anything so normal as a sister-in-law and a nephew struck me as absurd, but like a good merc I kept my mouth closed, unloading the crates as Mabel directed. Surprisingly, Cotter came out to help when a truck arrived with another three platforms of goods. He introduced himself to Mabel briefly but said nothing else while she was around. Soon as we were inside, he opened a private channel to my com.

"Did you know about the xith'cal?" he whispered in King's Tongue.

"Met him right before you did," I answered.

We shared a look. Whatever our differences, killing xith'cal was something all mercs could bond over. Letting one onto your ship felt like letting a rabid animal sleep in your bed.

"We'll just have to live with it," I said. "It's not like we can do anything anyway."

"This damn ship just gets weirder and weirder," Cotter said, tossing his box on top of the pile. "First that bullshit on the bridge, and now a lizard for a doctor." He shook his head. "I thought the stories were made up, but I'm starting to believe Caldswell really is as crazy as they say."

"Too late to run now," I said, handing him the next box. "We already passed the test."

Cotter snorted, and then his voice took on a note of grudging respect. "I hate to say it, but that was a stone cold shot. Glad to see you're not all bravado."

I didn't have to ask what shot he meant. "We do what we gotta do," I said. "It's weird having a man I shot in the head cook for me, though."

"At least he's a good cook," Cotter said, eying the mountains and mountains of fish crates. "God and king, I hope we're not eating all these."

"Me too," I said, turning to get the next crate.

By the time we were done loading all the crates, the enormous cargo bay was almost full. So was the ship. With the crew back, the *Glorious Fool* was finally the packed box I'd worried it would be, but it wasn't actually as bad as I'd imagined.

I'd always thought of spacers as constantly being in each other's noses with every square inch given over to cargo, but the *Fool* felt more like a house than a trade ship. The lounge actually meant we had a good bit more room than I normally had on merc ships, and, except for meals, everyone seemed to stick to their own areas.

Mabel stayed mostly in the engine room or the maintenance shafts fixing the seemingly endless problems that kept cropping up on the *Fool*. Our xith'cal butcher doctor stayed in his room or the infirmary, and Basil never seemed to leave the bridge.

Pickers went wherever she pleased, which mostly seemed to be under my feet. Fortunately, I have cameras looking down at all times, so I didn't have to add a fat cat to my death toll. She got tired of me eventually and went to sleep on the lounge couch next to Ren, who didn't seem to notice.

My shift ended just as we were clearing orbit. I switched off with Cotter and went to my room to get out of my armor and into a much needed shower. I was so caught up in the thrall of cleanliness and sleep, I didn't see the changes in my room until I was three steps in.

The once bare walls of my tiny bunk were now festooned with pictures of stars and nebulae. Long transparent cloths covered with gold moons hung from the ceiling like seaweed, and the tiny port window had been framed with silver ropes like a shrine. The previously empty top bunk was now made up with a pink and gold bedspread and piled high with colorful pillows. Several strings of bells jangled as my helmet brushed them, filling the room with silver music.

"Hello Deviana," said a girlish voice. "You have a lovely aura. I think we're going to be friends."

It took me a moment to find the voice's source with all the decorative confusion, even though the girl was standing right in front of me. The first thing I noticed was how pale she was. She was almost translucent under the ship lights, small and thin with short-cut white-blond hair that curled around her ears. Her eyes were wide and dreamy but so light they looked colorless. Her lips were faded too, little more than a pink blush around her mouth, and my first thought was that she had some kind of iron deficiency.

"Novascape Starchild," she said, taking my armored hand and holding it between her palms in a motion that looked both ritualistic and utterly ridiculous.

I had no idea what "novascape starchild" meant. I mean, I knew the words, but they didn't make any sense, and the fact that the girl was still holding my hand was throwing off my translation attempts. Finally, I gave up.

"I'm sorry," I said, pulling my hand away as gently as I could. "I don't understand what that means. I'm a little rusty at Universal."

"No worries," the girl said, smiling beatifically. "All languages are but crude translations of the music of the cosmos. We are all of us struggling to speak to true meaning."

That time I was sure I'd translated correctly, but I still had no idea what she meant. My confusion must have been plain, because the girl started to laugh. Softly at first, and then harder and harder as I grew more and more confused.

"Novascape Starchild is my name," she gasped at last, flopping down on my bed. "You can call me Nova, though."

That, at least, I understood. Nova was the girl Basil had mentioned, the one he was afraid I'd corrupt. Now that I'd actually met Nova, I wasn't surprised Basil had treated me like some kind of barely domesticated dog. If this dreamy girl was the bird's idea of a good human, I probably seemed like a violent ogre. "I hope you don't mind I took the bottom bunk."

"Not at all," Nova said. "There is no top or bottom in space. We are all exactly where we are meant to be."

I had no idea what to say to that, so I just nodded. After several seconds of silence, I made one last stab at bringing the conversation back to something I could understand. "What do you do on the ship?"

"Sensors," Nova said immediately. "And I talk to all the traffic controllers Basil's too angry to deal with. I also manage ship power, though my true reward is the chance to travel through the heavens. Getting this job was a dream come true. Most of us never leave the station."

Unless you wanted to become a Devastator, I couldn't think of a single reason getting a job on this ship could be considered a dream. "What station?"

"The Unity of the Cosmos," she said. "We are those who have abandoned the terrestrial to live in harmony with the stars and search for the larger oneness that connects all things. My father's the abbot, he got me this job."

I'd heard of the Unity of the Cosmos. Bunch of crazies who'd sworn off planets and lived on deep-space stations seeking enlightenment. Of course, it would probably be best not to mention the crazies part to Nova.

"Well," I said. "It's nice to finally meet you."

Nova beamed at me. I smiled back and knelt beside my armor case. I was relieved to see it hadn't been touched. It would have been an awkward conversation if I'd had to explain to Caldswell that my security system had accidentally fried his weird space girl.

"My case has an electrical shock security system," I warned her, opening the lid as I popped the pressure release on my suit. "It won't go off unless you try to open it, but it's probably best if you don't touch it at all. Also, I keep a backup pistol under my bed as well as my other gun cases. They're unlocked for easy access, so it's probably best if you don't touch those either."

"I would never compromise your personal sphere," Nova said. "It is my pleasure to share space with you in harmony."

"Mine too," I said, stripping off my suit and putting each piece in its place. "Any idea where we're going next, since you're on the bridge?"

Nova tilted her head thoughtfully. "Mycant," she said. "We're jumping late tonight."

I grinned wide. Unlike Paradox, which kept its colonies to reasonable numbers, the Terran Republic claimed planets like it was afraid they were going to run out, even ones that were clearly way more trouble than they were worth. Mycant was one of these, a far-flung outpost on the edge of the swath of space the xith'cal fleets claimed as their hunting grounds. Not shooting the xith'cal today had left an itch in my hand, one I'd get to scratch if Caldswell's bad luck combined with a trip into xith'cal space turned out the way I hoped. After a week of boring shifts, the infuriating test on the bridge, and the mess I didn't even want to remember with Rupert, I was more than ready for some good, honest shooting.

"What are you smiling about?" Nova asked behind me.

"Nothing," I said, grinning wider as I lovingly stowed Sasha in her case. "Nothing at all."

CHAPTER
4

We didn't get to jump that night.

When Nova left for work, I tried to get some sleep. I was tired, but all the new floaty things in our room kept triggering my finely honed paranoia reflex, jerking me awake every time I started to drift off. After two hours I gave up and decided to do some work. I was sitting on the floor in my pajamas checking my armor's fluid levels when the alarm began to blare.

By the time Caldswell's voice buzzed through my helmet to tell me what the alarm was for, I was suited up and out the door.

"Xith'cal." He said it so calmly it would have been funny if I'd been in a mood to appreciate irony. "Two ships. Big ones, probably slavers."

Cotter's voice came next. "Can't be," he said. "We're four hours from the Fishermarch. No xith'cal would dare come this far into Paradoxian space."

As if to prove him wrong, the *Fool*'s main cannon fired with a rumble I felt through my stabilizers. Outside, other cannons fired faintly in response, and Cotter began to swear.

"Shut up," I said, getting down to business as I cleared the com channel. "Are they going to try a breach?"

"Xith'cal?" Caldswell snorted. "Always. They'll probably go for the cargo bay." There was another hail of fire, and then Caldswell added, "Definitely the cargo bay."

He'd barely gotten the words out when something hit the ship so hard the metal groaned. The *Fool* rolled sideways under my feet, and the gravity flickered a moment before slamming me into the wall.

"Boarding pod's hit us," Caldswell said unnecessarily.

"We'll get it," I said, trusting my suit to adjust as the *Fool* righted itself. "Can you keep the others away, or should we plan for another pod?"

The floor rattled as the cannon fired again.

"Shouldn't have to worry about that." It was Mabel's voice in my ear this time. She sounded as calm as her brother-in-law, and I began to wonder how many xith'cal slaver boardings it took before you started treating them as routine. "I've got the second gun up now, that should keep them from sending anything else out. Basil's getting us out of range, but you'll need to clear out the ones that are already here."

I gave the mental trigger that brought up my active ship map. It flickered across my eyes, and I saw that Cotter was in the cargo bay already. That made me smile. Whatever else might be wrong with him, Cotter's instincts were right on the mark.

"Cotter," I barked, sprinting down the hall toward the lounge. "Stay right there. I'm on my way."

"Don't give me orders," he snapped. And then, a second later, "Hurry, though. They're starting to cut through."

"Mabel," I said. "Close the blast doors to the engine room." The engine room was the only other way into the cargo bay besides the lounge. I didn't want anyone killed by stray fire.

"Already done," she said cheerfully. "Good luck!" And the com went quiet.

I was glad of it. My adrenaline was running high now, and the Lady was responding, throwing all my systems into combat mode. I embraced it wholeheartedly, letting the intense focus of the coming fight burn away the frustration I'd been wrestling with over the last week of mind-numbing patrols. By the time I grabbed the doorway to the lounge and spun myself inside, I was as clear and calm as I'd ever been.

As I entered the lounge, I slammed my fist down on the emergency blast door release. The hunk of steel fell with a squeal behind me, locking off the bridge and the rest of the ship from the lounge and cargo bay. The three-inch-thick door wouldn't hold back a really determined xith'cal with time on his side, but it would stop runners and stray blasts. Of course, I didn't intend to let so much as a blood splatter get past me tonight. I was ready to fight; no more tests, no more waiting. This was what I was on this ship to do, and I meant to show Caldswell exactly what kind of merc he'd hired.

I was turning to run for the cargo bay when I caught a flash of movement out of my side camera. The xith'cal hadn't even broken through yet, but I dove all the same, rolling through the tiny galley opening into the kitchen and coming up with my pistol ready, only to see Rupert sitting on his heels in the corner like he was taking a break.

And just like that, my momentum stumbled.

I swore loudly in King's Tongue before I could stop myself. Rupert's eyebrows rose, and I snatched my gun back, switching to Universal. "Why didn't you say something before I locked up?"

"I tried to," he said, his voice impressively calm for someone I'd just trapped on the wrong side of a blast door. "You were too fast."

I swore again. This was a complication I did not need, though thank goodness Ren wasn't there. The cook was bad enough, but there'd have been hell to pay if I'd trapped the captain's daughter.

I stood up and leaned over the counter, trying to look down the stairs to the cargo bay. I couldn't see the breach from this angle, but I could hear the pounding of the xith'cal shipbreaker getting higher pitched with every blow. The hull was going to give way any second, no time to tell Caldswell to override the blast door and let Rupert out. It looked like we were going to have to do things the hard way.

"Do you have your gun?" The big cannon he'd had against Caldswell's head would have been handy right about now.

Rupert shook his head. "That was just for show."

Remembering how sure his finger had been on the trigger, I sincerely doubted that, but this was no time to push the point. I dropped back into a crouch and grabbed Rupert's hand.

"This is Sasha," I said, unlocking my pistol and pressing her smooth, heavy handle into his palm. "She's made to be used with a suit, so she kicks like a mule. She'll break your arm if you let her, so be sure to keep your elbow slack." I put my hand on his elbow and pressed until he let it go limp. "Just like that, let the kick roll through you. Even Sasha can't take an angry xith'cal down with a body shot, though. You have to hit them here."

I made a pistol out of my free hand and poked the barrel finger at the dip between Rupert's eyes, ignoring how uncomfortably close I was to where I'd shot him. "Right below the bone of their eye ridge. Don't be afraid to take your time lining up the shot. You have to kill a xith'cal with one hit, because he won't give you two. Got it?"

His eyes met mine through my visor. "I understand," he said, gripping my gun. "Be careful, Devi."

I smiled at the absurdity of the unarmored cook earnestly telling the armored merc to be careful. "Just stay out of sight," I said.

I knew he could handle a pistol, but I checked his grip one last time, just in case. I wasn't going to give him a chance to fire, of course. Even though I'd told him to loosen his arm, I'd neglected to mention that still wouldn't be enough to keep Sasha's kick from doing serious damage. But telling him that shooting would really, really hurt would likely make him too hesitant to land the kind of shot he'd need if it came to that, so I saw no reason to give him the whole truth. Whole truths usually just made things worse, anyway. I avoided them whenever I could.

Satisfied that Rupert wouldn't drop my darling, I stood up and hopped the counter, slinging Mia off my back as I went. I felt naked without Sasha, but she really would do him more good than she'd do me in a fight like this, even with the kick. Anti-armor pistols were meant for blasting through ballistic plates and into the people beneath, but xith'cal had no soft insides. Those damn lizards were built like cement pillars.

The shipbreaker's pounding was vibrating through the whole ship now, but it was the squeal of ripping metal that I'd been waiting for. The hull breached with a scream, and then the *Glorious Fool* rocked as the boarding pod punched itself deep into our side, sealing out the newly opened vacuum with an audible pop. They were in.

The first thing I saw as I flew through the door to the cargo bay was Cotter. He was in his armor, standing before the breach with an enormous gyro ax in his hands. I hadn't seen an ax in his equipment, but I wasn't surprised he had one. Skullheads loved their big two-handers, and with nearly a thousand pounds of armor behind it, even I had to admit an ax was a pretty effective weapon. Especially at times like these.

Now that the hull was breached, the xith'cal cutters quickly ripped fifteen feet across what had been our cargo doors and the blast plating around it. Then, with a roar that made my speakers squeal, the sundered hull fell, and they poured out. The xith'cal came like a black tide, enormous crested warriors that made our butcher-turned-doctor look like a house pet. They charged forward under a cover of blaster fire from their ship, their razor sharp scales clattering like an ancient cavalry charge as they pounded toward Cotter.

Cotter answered with a roar of his own and leaped into the fray, his ax biting deep into the front line. This was the sort of fight his huge armor was made for, and it showed. With the full weight of his suit behind him, Cotter's ax went through the xith'cal like a hatchet through soft meat. The blaster shots bounced off his shield, making him look like a firework as the red bolts arced and faded. With another shout even louder than his first, Cotter swung his ax again, and the xith'cal charge broke in front of him like water hitting a rock.

It was a damn beautiful sight. Cotter's voice was roaring over my com with the battle cry of the king. I wanted to scream in answer, but I held myself back. My position was too sweet to waste on bravado.

While the xith'cal focused on Cotter, I jumped down the cargo bay stairs to the first landing, starting Mia's charge as I did. My plasma shotgun whistled to life, going from a deep tone to the almost inaudibly high ready note in less than two seconds. The moment my feet hit the deck, I lowered Mia's short barrel and pulled the trigger. A white-hot slug shot out, hitting a xith'cal on the back line. The plasma exploded when it hit, flinging my target into the xith'cal beside him and taking both down in a rain of burning, sticky fire.

Cotter must have seen the flash, because his ax turned midstrike to come down on the wounded pair, finishing both in a single blow. But I was already on the next target. I switched Mia to my left hand and reached over my shoulder with my right, grabbing a grenade from my string. I armed and threw it in the same motion, lobbing the small explosive over the xith'cal line and into the boarding ship itself. The soft clink of the grenade's landing was lost in the sound of battle, but the blast that followed drowned out everything else.

I was using low-power ordnance since even I wasn't crazy enough to pack real explosives on a spaceship, but they were enough for what I was trying to do. The grenade exploded in a blue-white flash. The blast lit up the boarding ship's dark interior and blew the second line of xith'cal, the ones who'd been firing all those blaster shots, into Cotter's reach.

My grenade caught a lot more than I'd expected it to, and I started to wonder just how many xith'cal we were dealing with. The moment the question crossed my mind, the Lady picked it up and counted, displaying the result on my screen.

"Nineteen!" I shouted over the com. "Fifteen active, four down! Cotter stay front, I'll get the rear!"

I might as well have saved my breath for all Cotter seemed to hear. He was swinging his ax like he was the star of his own gladiator match, scattering the xith'cal as they scrambled to get out of his way. It was a stupid thing to do. If they got behind him, this could get very ugly.

The xith'cal were screeching to one another, a cacophony of calls that sounded more like compacting metal than voices. Then one screech rose over the others, and order began to emerge from the chaos. The xith'cal divided themselves. Ten began trying to circle Cotter, the obvious threat; the other five went for me.

Even after fighting them for so many years, I'm constantly surprised by how fast xith'cal can move. I always expect something that large to be slow, but the first two seemed to fly up the stairs at me, and even the Lady Gray wasn't fast enough to dodge the clawed hand that grabbed my leg.

Quick as a thought, I swung Mia down, blasting the lizard in the head with a plasma slug. The grip loosened, and I spun, firing my next shot into the stomach of the xith'cal coming in on my left just as its claws hit my neck.

Had my armor been anything less than what it was, that would have been the end right there. But the Lady Gray was everything I'd paid for, and my head stayed on. The blow to my neck did take me down, though, but the xith'cal was in no position to follow through, not with Mia's shot burning a hole through its stomach. It screamed a last, rattling death call as I kicked it off and let my suit roll me to my feet, scanning for my next target.

I had my pick. Cotter was almost completely surrounded. A lizard jumped up on the cargo above his head as I watched, and I fired before I could think, catching it in the torso. The xith'cal fell with a scream, nearly dropping on Cotter's shoulders, but he was too busy trying to keep back the others to care.

They were too spread out now for him to get a good blow, so he was just swinging his ax wide, trying to keep them back with sweeping strikes. But even swinging wild, Count's armor is slow, and a gyro ax is even slower. The xith'cal were dodging easily, watching for their chance to jump.

I didn't let them have it. Shifting Mia to a wide spread, I leveled her barrel and fired low. White fire exploded out in an arc, catching the four xith'cal that had been coming in on Cotter's left in the legs. The spread out blast wasn't enough to kill them, but it hurt like hell and sent them scrambling. It also drained the last of Mia's charge.

Of the five xith'cal who'd come for me, three were left. They'd kept a respectful distance while Mia was singing, but now that her whistle was dead, they started to advance again. I kept my eyes on them as I returned my now useless shotgun to her holster on my back and flung out my arm. At the command, the clamps under my left arm popped, and my thermite blade swung out in a beautiful arc.

I grabbed the long handle as it flew by, and the second my hands clamped down, I thought the activation word. The name had barely formed on my tongue before the blade's dull edge flashed blinding white as the thermite lit up. With a cry to rival Cotter's, I swept the thermite blade over my head and into the neck of the closest xith'cal.

The burning edge sliced clean, cutting scales, flesh, and bone with the same ease. The xith'cal crumpled as the blade slid free, but I didn't stop to watch it fall. Once you fired them, thermite blades were the most powerful cutting edge in the galaxy, but only for eighty seconds. After that, they burned out, turning black and brittle. Hell of a time limit, but then, if you used them right, eighty seconds was enough.

Swinging my blade back around, I lunged forward, trusting my armor to balance me as I slammed the thermite's sun-bright tip into the shoulder of the next xith'cal who'd rushed up the steps. It screamed when the hit landed but still managed to get a shot at my chest. My shield, which had kicked on automatically after the xith'cal had hit my neck, absorbed the worst of it, but the xith'cal had shot me with a heavy slug, not a blaster, and the force was still enough to knock me back.

My suit knew what to do better than I did. While I was still reeling, the Lady carried the blow to its end, slicing the xith'cal clean through the shoulder. I snapped back into control just in time to yank my blade free as the xith'cal fell with a screech.

Four of the five that had come at me were now down, but I'd lost the fifth in the chaos. I glanced through my cameras just in time to see the xith'cal jump before it slammed into my back. The last of my shield shattered under the blow, and I staggered forward. The Lady Gray can lift twice her weight, but she's as susceptible to physics as anything else, and the xith'cal was bigger than I was. It had hit me running from above, and the momentum was more than enough to carry us both over the railing.

We fell in a tangle on top of Mabel's endless crates of fish. I landed in the worst position possible, facedown on the bottom. The xith'cal squealed and tried to bite me across the back, its claws scrambling over my sides as it looked for a gap in my armor. Its enormous weight pinned me down as it tried to pry my armor apart to get at my flesh, but the Lady Gray was too well made for that. The xith'cal's claws found no purchase, and its teeth slid harmlessly over the smooth shell of the Lady's linked plates.

While it was busy trying to find a weakness in my suit, I switched all my power to my arms. With one mighty push, I shoved us both into the air. I landed on my feet, while the xith'cal landed in a crouch just behind me. Using my rear cam, I swung my blade around and stabbed backward, striking the lizard clean through the chest before it could move.

I held the blade steady until the xith'cal stopped struggling and then looked around. Cotter was below me, standing with his back to the wall of cargo crates. His ax was gone, and he was shooting at the remaining three lizards with a shotgun that, while not plasma like mine, was still big enough to be a pain even for xith'cal. His suit was a little worse for wear, and there was a long claw scratch across his faceplate, but he was most definitely still kicking.

He pumped four shots into the xith'cal on his chest before it let go, and then he turned to shoot the one that had jumped up on the cargo above him, only to find I'd gotten there first. My thermite was burning fast and hot now, and I sliced the xith'cal above Cotter clean down the middle without feeling a bit of drag on the blade. The moment it fell, I opened my cameras wide and looked around, letting the Lady count the bodies for me.

"Sixteen," I panted. There should be nineteen bodies total. "Where are the—"

My question was answered by gunshots, three of them, echoing from upstairs.

The final shot had barely sounded before I leaped off the cargo and hit the stairs running, my nearly spent thermite blade hissing in my hand. I exploded into the lounge and skidded to a stop, blade raised, only to see three dead xith'cal lying on the floor with Rupert standing over them, Sasha in his hand.

For a moment I just stood there, panting and speechless, and then Cotter's voice crackled in my ear. "That all of them?"

"Yeah," I answered, looking at Rupert. "That's the lot."

Caldswell said something over the com that sounded like "Good job," but I didn't hear it. All my attention was focused on Rupert as he stepped over the dead aliens and handed me my pistol as calmly as he would hand me a drink. I took it silently, but as my glove made contact with Sasha's grip, her ammo counter popped up at the bottom left of my vision. Of her thirty-shot clip, she had twenty-seven left.

Three bullets, three dead xith'cal.

My eyes went back to Rupert. In my armor, when I'm ready and if the lizards are charging me in a line, I can take three xith'cal with three shots from Sasha. Out of my armor, even relaxed and knowing what to expect, her recoil would have ruined my arm after the first one. Rupert had never shot my pistol before, and he certainly wasn't in armor, yet there he was, standing in the middle of the lounge with two apparently unbroken arms and three dead xith'cal. My brain was spinning so fast trying to make sense of this that I didn't understand Rupert the first time he spoke.

"What?" I said, raising my visor so I could see him without my display cluttering his face.

He smiled like I'd made a joke. "I said, 'Does the blade have a name, too?'"

He pointed at the now-dead thermite blade in my hand, its edge spent and black. I stared at it a moment, then looked back at Rupert. "Phoebe," I said quietly. "Her name is Phoebe."

Rupert nodded like naming all your weapons was perfectly normal, and then he reached over and pressed the com by the kitchen counter. When Caldswell answered, he calmly asked the captain to raise the blast door. I watched him a moment more, and then I turned and walked back to the cargo bay stairs without a word.

Cotter was crowing over the com, his big voice grating in my ear with the usual macho bullshit, and I fought the urge to turn my connection off. I wanted nothing more than to go somewhere quiet where I could sit down and sort out all the questions that were rapidly filling my head, but Mabel was talking too now. So was Caldswell. Orders were coming in one after the other, and I forced myself to pay attention. The fight might be over, but it was still time to work, so I put a grudging lid on my worries and pulled myself together, stomping across the cargo bay to help Cotter start cleaning up.

The movies they make back home about the nonstop action of merc life never show how much time you spend on cleanup. It took us almost three hours to drag the dead xith'cal back to their ship and get all the blood off the floor. I don't mind mopping, but I do mind having to do it alone because my partner's too busy bragging to do his share.

"That's why you wear the big armor," Cotter announced to anyone who would listen, which at the moment was myself and Mabel. "This baby can put three thousand pounds of pressure behind an ax swing. That's enough to slice a suit of king's armor in half."

"Only if the person in the armor is dumb enough to let you," I said, slamming my mop into the bucket of very bloody water by the stairs. "Only three kinds of people wear king-class armor: the king, royal knights, and Devastators, and none of them would be that dumb."

"What are you talking about?" Cotter scoffed. "Gerald Reddeath is the undisputed master of ax work, and he's taken two Devastators."

"Gerald Reddeath is a hack," I snapped. "He doesn't even fight in the actual gladiatorial games. He's in the demonstration league, which is *scripted*." I made my voice as disgusted as I could. "His whole career is a publicity stunt, and he didn't take two Devastators, he took two guys in Devastator armor. There's a difference between actual Devastators and idiots dressed up to look like Devastators. *I* could beat Reddeath."

Cotter gave me a nasty look. "Don't insult the Red Death, Morris. He was the Kingston Count-class champion before he went into the demonstrations. He'd wipe the floor with you."

"I'd like to see him try," I scoffed. "Gladiator battles have as much to do with real combat as being carnival king has to do with actually being king." I slapped my mop down on the sticky patch by my feet. "In a real fight, all that matters is killing the other guy before he kills you. If you waste time standing around swinging your ax, you're going to get shot."

"Says the little girl who fights in a dancing suit," Cotter sneered. "You gonna get a pony next? Maybe some pink ribbons to —"

He cut off when my mop hit him dead in the face shield.

"Ass," I muttered, walking over to where Mabel was working on getting the crashed xith'cal boarding pod detached from our ship.

"Please tell me you need some help," I said, crouching down beside her. "If I have to listen to Cotter say one more thing, his ax is going to be in his head and your security team's going to be down to one."

"In a sec," Mabel said, examining the seam where the xith'cal's pod had fused into the *Fool*'s hull. "They slagged us good. There's two anchors outside as well."

"Can you fix it?" I asked.

"Oh sure," Mabel said, grinning at me. "We've had worse."

I paled at the thought and left her to her work, turning to grab the last of the dead xith'cal only to see a live one had beaten me to it. Hyrek crouched over the fallen warrior, his claws hooked delicately under the larger alien's head as he examined the back of the creature's neck.

Suddenly, I felt like I was going to be sick. "Oh, god," I groaned. "If you're going to eat that, can you please do it somewhere I can't see?"

Hyrek fished his handset out of his pocket, typing on it rapidly. *Really, Devi, these warriors were killed by two humans. I'd never eat such unworthy meat.*

I made a face. "What are you doing, then?" I asked. "Making sure the 'unworthy meat' wasn't someone you knew?"

Hyrek didn't answer me until he'd checked the necks of each of the three remaining xith'cal. It was almost funny to see him standing over the warriors. The dead xith'cal ranged from nine and a half to nearly eleven feet. At seven foot eight, Hyrek looked comically small beside them, like a child playing doctor over its parents. But there was nothing childlike in the matter-of-fact way he straightened up and wiped the blood off his claws with a tissue before he touched his handset again.

In a manner, he typed. *The captain asked me to check their tribe marks. These warriors were Reaper's flesh.*

"Reaper?" I said. "As in Reaper's Fleet?"

There were three known xith'cal tribes whose hunting grounds touched colonized space, and of them, Reaper's Fleet was the nastiest. Nastiest, but also supposedly the farthest away. "Wait," I said. "What are Reaper's lizards doing way out here?"

A good question, Hyrek typed back. *His hunting grounds range wide, but this is a bit far. My guess is they were out here for some other reason and decided to take a risk when they spotted us.* He looked at me with a proud smile. *Caldswell is one of Reaper's blood-sworn prey. As such, his flesh attacks our ship on sight, no matter the circumstances.*

I whistled. "No wonder Caldswell gets in so much trouble."

The real wonder was that Caldswell was still alive after pissing off Reaper that much.

Our captain is a resourceful man, Hyrek typed. *He manages.*

I would have asked more, but Mabel was calling for me to help get something off the wall. I went over and lugged down a battered industrial shield generator under her direction, placing it on the floor in front of the hole the xith'cal had punched in the metal hull surrounding what had been our cargo bay doors. Mabel hooked it into the ship's power and fiddled with it for a few minutes before straightening up with a smile.

"That should do it," she said, dusting off her hands. "Soon as we clear the blockage, we can seal the hole." She grinned at me. "Ready to push?"

"Cotter!" I yelled. "Time to earn your keep."

Cotter muttered something about bossy women, but he didn't dare say anything more as he stomped over. Mabel, meanwhile, grabbed Pickers, who'd been watching from the stairs, and walked back to her engine room. Hyrek followed as well, his clawed feet clicking on the wet and still bloody floor. Once they were inside, Mabel closed the blast door.

"Lounge is already sealed," she said over my com. "Hit the red button on the generator when you're ready to deploy the patch."

"Got it," I answered, turning to Cotter. "On three."

He rolled his eyes behind his face shield but waited for the count. When I got to three, we both pushed as hard as we could on the edges where the xith'cal pod had fused to the *Fool*'s hull. The make-shift seam popped after barely ten seconds, and my suit flashed a warning as the cargo bay's atmosphere started hissing out into space.

The anchors hooked into the outer hull were more difficult to remove. Cotter and I had to actually climb through the blasted remains of the hull and out onto the ship's exterior to pry them off by hand. Only when the final hook snapped did the landing pod and the dead xith'cal we'd tied down inside it break off and float away into the blackness.

We were working weightless by the time we climbed back into the cargo bay. For reasons I'd never bothered learning, it's harder to generate gravity in a vacuum, and with a giant hole in its side, the cargo bay had lost both its pressure and its pull. Fortunately, my Lady is certified for spacewalks, and I was able to fly around no problem on my small thrusters. Cotter's suit, on the other hand, had no thrusters at all. He spun like a piece of space garbage, kicking his legs while I laughed at him.

I left him hanging for a few minutes before I pulled him inside and hit the button on the shield generator. It shook for nearly a minute after I turned it on, and then a blob of rainbow-colored plasma shot out, filling the hole in the ship's side that had been our cargo bay doors plus a good five feet of hull. The plasma hardened instantly, forming a bulbous seal that locked out both the vacuum and the radiation. When the breach was fully sealed, the vents started pumping in air to pressurize the cargo bay again, and I gently set myself and Cotter back on the floor before the reemerging gravity could yank us there.

"Thanks," he grumbled.

I nodded, but my attention wasn't really on Cotter anymore. I was staring at the seal. It had hardened to an off-white color with a rainbow sheen across its surface, almost like oil on water. However, though it was more opaque now than when it had started, it was still semitransparent, and that gave me the jeebies. Seeing space through a window is one thing, seeing it through a temporary patch so brittle I could probably put my foot through it without my suit's help was something else altogether.

I brought up the engine room com. "Mabel, are you sure this thing will hold until we get back to the Fishermarch?"

"Oh sure," she said, her voice distracted. "But there's no reason to go all the way back to the Fishermarch. We're headed to Mycant anyway, so we'll just get the repairs done there."

My heart jumped so fast my suit almost switched back into battle mode. "You mean we're going to do a hyperspace jump with a *patch*?"

"Course," Mabel said. "Do it all the time."

"All the time?" I cried. "How often do you get giant holes in your hull?"

I could almost hear Mabel's shrug. "Pretty often. Whose ship do you think you're on?"

She had a point. "We're all going to die," I muttered, eying the patch one more time before stomping up the stairs toward the lounge. "Finish mopping up, Cotter."

"*What?*" he roared. "Why do I have to clean?"

"Because I cleaned while you were standing around giving speeches," I answered, hitting the pressure lock on the lounge door. "Do it right or Mabel will just make you do it again."

I cut off our com link before he could start complaining and shut the door behind me.

We'd cleaned up the bodies here first, so the lounge looked the same as always. Ren was back on her couch, playing with her chessboard like nothing had happened. I saw her and dismissed her in the same moment, looking instead for the man I'd been trying my best not to think about.

For once, Rupert wasn't in the kitchen. He was sitting at the battered dining table in the middle of the lounge where we'd shelled the seeds, reading something on a ledger. When I got closer, I saw it was a Paradoxian cookbook.

"I thought I'd make something for the glorious heroes," he said, flicking off the projected display.

I stopped in front of him. "You mean that wasn't a test, too?"

"Anything can be a test if you want to make it one," Rupert said, his voice calm as he looked up at me. "Caldswell didn't pay the xith'cal to put a hole in his hull so he could test his security team, if that's what you're implying."

I wasn't, though the thought had crossed my mind. "I was just wondering," I said. "You're normally a pretty smart guy. Why didn't you run when the alarm went off? Why did you duck behind the counter?"

Rupert shrugged. "Panicked a little, I suppose. As I said, you got here pretty fast. I never had a chance."

He was lying. First, Rupert didn't panic. Even when I'd shot him in the head, he'd never been anything but calm, cool, and collected. Second, even if I hadn't known anything about him before this moment, I still wouldn't have believed his story. No one with enough training, experience, and guts to one-shot kill three xith'cal in a row would let himself get caught anywhere he didn't want to be.

But I didn't call him on his lie. Instead, I smiled, told him I was going to wash up, and walked out. He watched me the whole way.

Back in my room, I shoved the Lady into her case and hit the self-cleaner. Once my suit was taken care of, I went down the hall to the showers.

Alone at last, standing in the tiny stall as the recycled spray ran through my hair, I finally gave in to the flood of questions I'd been holding back during the whole cleanup. Why had Rupert stayed? Was it because he'd wanted to or because Caldswell had asked him to stay as backup in case Cotter and I failed? And if so, what kind of fighter was he, walking without fear into a xith'cal raid when he had no armor and wouldn't have had a gun if I hadn't given him mine? And most important of all, how had he killed three xith'cal with *my* Sasha and not broken his arms? Did it have to do with his ability to get shot in the head and thrown across the bridge without so much as a bruise?

By the time I turned off the water, I didn't have any answers, but I'd made up my mind that I was going to get some. Nosy mercs might be dead mercs, but there was a point where not knowing was more dangerous than snooping, and we'd passed that when Rupert had fired his first shot. This job was my ticket to the Devastators, and that was too important to risk being ignorant.

Feeling infinitely better now that I'd made a decision, I padded down the empty hall to my room. Technically my shift had started while we were cleaning, but with all the time Cotter had wasted bragging, I figured I could grab two hours or so before I'd need to go back out. Enough time to catch up on a little rest. Can't go sticking your nose where it doesn't belong on zero sleep, after all.

I set the alarm on my handset and flopped into my bunk. This time I didn't even see Nova's hangings. I was out the moment my head touched the pillow.

CHAPTER
5

Of course, now that I'd decided to uncover the truth about Rupert, I didn't actually know where to begin. I'm a merc, not an investigator. "Shoot first, question later" is practically tattooed on my forehead.

If I were still in the Blackbirds or the army I'd just report my suspicions up the chain of command and let them deal with it, but Rupert was Caldswell's man, so I couldn't very well go to the captain for answers. With my normal route cut off, I was floundering to come up with a suitably clever plan that would uncover what I needed to know without risking the most important job of my career. I still hadn't thought of anything by the time we reached the hyperspace gate the next morning, and by that point I was entirely sucked into preparations for the jump.

A hyperspace jump is always a grand affair. Everything has to be locked down, because even with the best equipment, the transition can be rough, especially on a smaller ship. It made sense. We were, after all, leaving our own dimension and slipping into the strange space between realities. I didn't understand much more than that, but neither did anyone who wasn't a hyperspace engineer. All I knew was that it involved a lot of math, and while any ship with a hyperdrive coil could jump into hyperspace with or without a gate, the gate was the only safe way.

Free jumps were horribly dangerous, though not because hyper-space itself was dangerous. Hyperspace was actually the safest place you could be, because when a ship went into hyperspace it cre-ated its own miniature dimension where it was the only thing that existed. That was why Cotter and I were off duty during jumps: no need for security when there was nothing to attack you. No, what made jumping dangerous was time, or, more specifically, the dif-ference between time in hyperspace and time in the real universe.

It had been the discovery of the hyperspace coil that had gotten humans off Old Earth. Back then, it wasn't uncommon for ships to vanish for years, sometimes centuries, though their onboard clocks said they'd only been in hyperspace for a day or two. It was called time dilation, and it was a huge problem. So far as science knew, time only moved forward, but how much and how fast got fuzzy once you left the boundaries of our dimension.

Getting into hyperspace was simple—all you needed was enough energy of the right kind to jump out of reality, sort of like a fish jumping out of a creek, but the math of landing again at the right place and time was something else entirely. There were millions of variables involved with leaving hyperspace, and an error on any of them could mean coming out decades later than you'd planned to. For centuries this meant only the craziest ships used hyperdrives and everyone else stuck to what they could reach through near light speed travel.

The gates changed everything. They weren't even gates, really. "Gate" implies something you go through, but a hyperspace gate is nothing but a space-station-sized supercomputer capable of quickly and accurately doing the computations needed for safe jumps. A gate's math guaranteed you'd come out of hyperspace exactly where and, more importantly, *when* you wanted. Jumps across the universe were routine these days. I'd done hundreds of them in my career, but I still prayed to the Sainted King every time to bring me through safely. After all the service I'd given him, I figured it was the least he could do.

We were using the Portcullis, the newest and largest of Paradox's three hyperspace gates, and we were not alone. The wait to jump was nearly two hours, and I spent the whole time with Caldswell yelling in my ear as I tied things down like a damn deckhand.

"You *do* remember that I was hired to be security, sir?" I snapped as I helped Mabel finish securing the engine room. "You know, the reason you and your entire crew aren't languishing in some xith'cal slave pen right now?"

"Your heroism never leaves my mind," the captain drawled. "But we all pull our weight around here, Morris, and soldiers don't complain."

I closed my mouth and slammed the last of Mabel's enormously heavy tools into the wall case. Fortunately, the engine room was the last of it, and when Caldswell called for everyone to prepare to jump, I stomped upstairs to the lounge windows to watch the show.

Outside I could see dozens of ships, mostly Paradoxian cruisers, floating around the fat, lumpy sphere of the Portcullis gate station as they waited their turn to jump. One by one, the ships lit up and vanished, winking out like dying stars as the gate guided them on their way across the universe. The flashes grew closer and closer until, at last, it was our turn. I felt the thrum through my boots as the hyperspace coil began to spin up. Outside, the hull of the *Fool* was lit with glorious white light as the coil glowed brighter and brighter.

As always, the actual jump took me by surprise. On the other ships it had looked like a firecracker popping and fading, but when you were standing on top of it, the jump flash was like a splash of cold water in the face. The light filled the ship, creating the tiny dimension where we would wait out the journey. I could almost feel myself being pulled out of space and time as it passed over me, and

I had to fight not to throw up. No matter how many jumps I made, I never got used to that feeling. Human bodies just aren't meant to change dimensions. Thankfully, it lasted only a second, and then the ship bucked hard, like a boat hitting a wave.

My suit handled the bump without much fuss. The bottles in the locked bar clattered, but otherwise it was a pretty smooth transition. The shaking stopped after that first lurch, along with all sense of movement. Outside, the black expanse of space disappeared, replaced by the grayish purple wall of our tiny pocket dimension. We were in.

"Jump complete," Basil's whistling voice said over the ship com. "Seven hours until Mycant, and before any of you say anything about the bump, that was the shoddy Paradoxian gate's fault, not mine." I caught the sound of Nova's laughter before the com clicked off.

Because there was nothing that could bother us and nothing to do but wait, hyperspace was time off. I shed my armor and went looking for Rupert with the vague idea of asking him some subtle questions. He was nowhere to be found, though, and I wasn't so out of options that I was ready to go banging on his door just yet.

While I'd been gone, Cotter had commandeered the lounge and was using the vidscreen to watch some god-awful armor exhibition game, the kind with impractically large weapons and tank-sized suits piloted by men with egos to match. I guess all that talk about Reddeath had put him in the mood, and since I wasn't about to have *that* argument again, I went to my room to put in Phoebe's new blade. When I opened my door, though, I found Nova sitting on the floor with her eyes closed and some music that sounded like a duet between a flute and a malfunctioning com system coming from the speaker in front of her.

"Am I interrupting anything?"

"Yes," Nova said. "But I don't mind. Meditating to feel the flow of the universe is a bit of a waste when you're not actually in the universe anymore."

I laughed. "No oneness in hyperspace?"

"None except that which we hold in us always," Nova said, opening her eyes. "What can I do for you, Deviana?"

I was about to tell her to just keep doing as she liked since I was going to work on my weapons, but then another thought occurred to me. "Actually," I said, sinking onto my bunk. "Maybe you can answer some questions for me."

"Questions are the first step toward knowledge," Nova said in a way that made me think she was quoting someone.

Taking that as a yes, I set in. "How long have you been on this ship?"

"Almost two years," Nova said proudly. "The captain says I'm the longest serving sensors operator he's ever had."

That didn't sound like something to be proud of, but I kept my opinion to myself. "Has Rupert been here that long?"

"Oh no," Nova said. "Mr. Charkov came on about six months ago. Before that, we ate precooked rations." She wrinkled her nose. "The food is much better now."

I bet. "And do you know anything about what he did before joining Caldswell?"

Nova thought a moment. "I don't think so. He told me once that he taught himself to cook, though."

"Has he ever fought on the ship?" I said, pressing a little harder. "Like in a pirate raid or something?"

"Not that I remember," Nova said, shaking her head. "I don't think he does anything but cook and help look after the captain's daughter." Her face fell. "I feel so bad for her, her aura is so dim."

"Ren?" I didn't believe in auras, but Rupert had mentioned she'd had a tough life.

"Yes," Nova said. "She used to talk only to the captain, but now she talks to Rupert, too." As suddenly as her face had fallen, Nova was smiling again. "I'm glad he's here."

"Me too," I said thoughtfully.

"I'm happy you're here, too," Nova said, her dreamy voice growing serious. "Thank you for saving us. I'm sorry I didn't get to tell you earlier."

I sat back in surprise. I couldn't remember anyone ever thanking me for doing my job before. "Thank you for saying so," I said at last. "I thought you would be mad at me, actually."

Nova's wispy eyebrows shot up. "Why would I be angry?"

Because all the spacey religious types I'd encountered before had been nut job protesters who thought you shouldn't shoot other people, even xith'cal. "You just seem to be a peaceful sort of person," I said instead.

"Life and death are equal parts of the universal harmony," she said with a shrug. "Though I am always where I am supposed to be, I don't exactly want to end up in a xith'cal feed pen."

I grinned. That was the most normal thing I'd ever heard her say.

"We have six and a half hours before we have to return to our duties," Nova said, getting up off the floor. "What would you like to do?"

I'd meant to keep working on Rupert's mystery, but Nova looked so happy about having someone to hang out with, and it wasn't like I knew what my next step was anyway. "Let's see," I said, leaning over to dig into my duffel. "Want to play cards?"

Nova's eyes went wide. "I'd love to," she said. "How do you do it? I've never played cards before."

That was music to my ears. I love corrupting innocents. "It's not hard. Here." I pulled out my deck and, after a quick shuffle, dealt her five off the top. "We'll start with poker."

Nova caught on quick. She couldn't bluff to save her life, but she counted cards like a pro right from the first hand, no doubt a result of all those years of math you have to master in order to qualify for systems work. I taught her the five basic poker variations and all the common cheats. By the time we got to the royal rules, she was a little cross-eyed.

"You know a lot about this," she said after winning our second game. I'd had to cheat a little to be sure she would, but letting people win their first few hands is vital to hooking them in.

"Survival mechanism," I said. "When you're stuck on an asteroid on minimal power for weeks while your superiors decide where they want you, you learn to like cards or you go insane."

"I've never been on an asteroid," she said as I did a fold shuffle.

I shrugged. "It's a rock floating in space, you're not missing much."

"Actually," she said, her pale eyes counting the cards as I dealt them. "I'd never stepped onto a planet before I joined Caldswell's crew."

"How did you manage that?" I asked, picking up my hand.

"Father didn't allow it," she answered, picking up her own. "The Unity of the Cosmos believes gravity clouds clarity. We don't have it on our stations."

I stared at her. "You grew up in zero gravity?" At least that explained why she was so small boned.

"Not quite zero," she admitted. "But close enough. And they changed it all the time so we'd never start thinking in terms of down or falling. There is no down or up in the cosmos, only us and the infinite space."

"Sounds like an interesting place to grow up," I said. Actually, it sounded horrible.

"It was necessary to achieve our attunement to the latent energies," Nova said seriously, as though this explained everything. "Here, watch."

She closed her eyes and started to hum. After thirty seconds, I was getting a little worried, but then the humming stopped, and Nova's eyes snapped open with a dazed expression.

"Wow," she breathed. "That was much harder in hyperspace."

I knew I wasn't going to like the answer, but I asked anyway. "What was?"

She gave me a funny look and pointed down with the hand that, last I'd seen, had been holding her cards. I followed the gesture, and then my cards went flying as I jumped back. Nova's poker hand was floating in a perfect fan of cards six inches off our cabin floor.

"What the hell is that?" I asked, a little sharper than I should have.

"The latent energies of the cosmos," she answered, smiling as she tilted her head. In front of her, the cards began to spin slowly in the same direction. "The flow of power at the heart of all life. It can also be called plasmex."

I'd heard of plasmex. I'd also heard of gremlins, black magic, and space monsters. Of course, only one of those was making a hand of cards spin in front of me. I stared in wonder for a few more seconds, and then something occurred to me. "Wait," I said. "So you *actually* see auras?"

"Of course I do," Nova said, her dreamy face collapsing into an expression that almost managed to look insulted. "You didn't think I would just make something up, did you?"

"No," I said quickly. "Of course not."

I got down on my knees and reached out to touch the cards. They stopped spinning when I put my finger against them but started again when I let them go. Now that I'd had some time to absorb the idea, plasmex didn't actually seem so odd. After all, I'd been in Kingston when the king's execution of the traitorous baron of Salsley had lit up the whole sky with white fire. Stuff like that was to be expected from a living saint, but after witnessing his magic first-hand, it wasn't such a stretch for me to believe Nova could channel the energies of the cosmos. "Can all Unity of the Cosmos members do this?"

"Most of us can use plasmex," Nova said. "But only a few can actually do anything useful." She sat up straighter, and a hint of pride crept into her voice. "My brother and I are the best on the station other than my father himself. That was why I got to come on Captain Caldswell's ship. That, and he and my father are old friends, of course."

I wondered what kind of father would let his daughter anywhere near this ship, but then Nova's dad probably had the same weird ideas about the privilege of being on the *Glorious Fool* as she did. Still... I reached out and picked one of the cards out of her floating hand. It felt normal, and it fell to the floor like any other card when I dropped it.

"I can move much bigger things when I'm not in hyperspace," Nova said. "Bigger things even than my brother Copernicus."

I rolled my eyes covertly. Copernicus and Novascape Starchild. Of course. What was their father's name? Galaxior?

"But he can read people's minds to tell if they're lying," Nova continued. "So I guess that's better."

"No way," I said. "I'd take throwing stuff with my mind over a lie detector any day."

That made Nova laugh so hard the floating cards fell over. She was still giggling when her handset chimed. As she pulled it out, I noticed the handset's silver surface was spangled with yellow moons, just like her hangings. "Basil says everyone else is in the lounge," she said, reading the flashing message. "Want to join them?"

"Sure," I said, standing. "I'm going to see if I can't trick Cotter into playing us for serious money. You count the cards, I'll bluff, and we'll get enough out of him to keep us both in drinks for the next month."

"But I don't drink," Nova said as I ushered her into the hall.

"That's okay," I assured her. "I'll drink yours for you."

Basil hadn't been exaggerating. The entire crew had indeed drifted into the lounge while Nova and I had been playing cards. Cotter was still watching armor matches and commentating on the action to anyone unfortunate enough to get pulled in, which at the moment were a suspiciously amused Hyrek and an incensed Basil. Basil and Cotter were the only ones actually watching the screen, though. For all that Hyrek was sitting directly below the action, his eyes were on his ledger.

The doctor read a lot, actually. I knew, because when I'd asked him jokingly what he did locked up in his room all the time, he'd made me read the entire mile-long list of his current books, complete with his scathing comments. It had been one of the more bizarre experiences of my life. Who would have thought a xith'cal could be such a book snob? Before Hyrek, I hadn't even known they could read.

On the other side of the room, Mabel and Caldswell were standing by Ren's couch, talking over her head while she played chess like there wasn't a party going on around her. As the cook, Rupert was the only one whose job didn't stop when we went into hyperspace. He was at the bar taking orders, but though I'd be bitter if I had to work while everyone else was partying, Rupert only smiled and asked what we'd like.

Nova got some kind of fruit salad, I got a grilled cheese sandwich and a bottle of dark beer I hadn't known we had until Rupert offered it. Food in hand, we walked over to the windows. Thankfully, in order to win some argument with Basil that I hadn't been following, Cotter had switched from exhibition matches to last year's royal gladiatorial arena finals. Real fights, in other words. I was about to ask Cotter what round we were on when someone bumped my arm.

I looked to see Mabel standing right beside me. "Congratulations on a good pirate clearing, Morris," she said, tapping her beer against mine. "Cheers."

"Cheers," I replied. "Is the patch holding?"

"Of course," Mabel said with a grin. "Don't worry so much. Except for the bump on the way in, hyperspace is much easier on the hull than regular space. Nothing to run into."

"Other than the dust we came in with," Nova put in between nibbles on the red melon at the end of her fork. "That's one of the variables in the hyperspace calculation."

This launched Mabel and Nova into a discussion about whether gates took exact dust measurements from the hyperspace coil during the power-up or if it was an estimated equation. I got lost immediately, but while I couldn't follow the conversation, I realized that this was a perfect opportunity to do some recon. So while Nova and Mabel went back and forth with more acronyms than words, I settled back against the window to drink my beer and watch Rupert.

I don't know what I expected to see. Some sign that he wasn't what he appeared, I guess. There were implants you could get that would let you shake off a massive blow to the head and shoot a gun like Sasha barehanded without harm—bone lacing, synthetic muscles, trauma washes, and so on—but those were all incredibly expensive, not the sort of thing a cook would have.

Anyway, implants generally left the people who got them looking obviously changed, or at least scarred, but other than being generally lovely in his ubiquitous black suit and dark blue apron, Rupert's body looked normal to me. If he had implants, they were very, very good. So good that he'd have to belong to a government to have them, and thus wouldn't be working here. Unless Caldswell was a spy, of course. I could have almost believed that if the idea of a spy who did nothing but fly this rust bucket around and get attacked by xith'cal wasn't so absurd.

"Devi?" Mabel's voice was rich with laughter.

"Hmm?" I said, not looking away from Rupert. If he was a spy, that would explain the suit.

"You're staring."

I blinked and then glanced over to find both Mabel and Nova looking at me. *Shit.* Caught red-handed. I was scrambling for some kind of believable excuse for why I'd been staring at Rupert that didn't make me look like an idiot when a remarkably simple idea came to me.

I wanted to figure out what Rupert was, didn't I? Well, what better way was there than to just ask? Everyone knew he'd shot three xith'cal just like they knew Cotter and I had slaughtered the rest, so it wasn't like I was revealing some secret. With that, I switched from defense to attack.

"Just trying to figure out how he shot three xith'cal with my anti-armor pistol without shattering his arms," I said casually, taking a long draw from my beer to show how unshaken up I was at being caught staring. "I mean, I couldn't pull a stunt like that."

"Oh, that's nothing," Mabel said. "I saw his application when Brian hired him. He was in a fringe branch of the Republic military for a while, and they taught him some kind of fighting style that has to do with relaxing the muscles or something. I bet he just relaxed his arms and let the kick go through them."

I frowned. Could there be a martial art that would let you do that? I'd never heard of one, but Terrans had a lot of things Paradoxians had never heard of. Still. "I don't think that would be enough," I said. "My gun kicks pretty hard."

Mabel shrugged. "Why not? He's pretty good at it from what I hear, and martial artists can do all sorts of crazy things. Makes sense to me."

I'd never seen Rupert practice a martial art, but Mabel's suggestion had given me an idea. A really good idea. Because I was no slouch at hand-to-hand combat myself, in armor or out, and one thing I knew for sure was that instincts were hard to suppress in a fight. That made secrets like implants, even good ones, very hard to keep.

"Well," I said, placing my half-empty bottle on the window ledge. "If he's that good at it, why don't I ask him for a match?"

"He looks kind of busy," Mabel said, but I was already walking over to the kitchen where Rupert was collecting plates.

He must have sensed something was up, because his shoulders stiffened when I stopped and leaned on the counter beside him. "So," I said casually. "I hear you're a martial artist?"

"I know a little," he said, turning to me with a cautious smile. "But it's been a long time since I practiced."

"You shot my gun with no problem, so you can't have forgotten everything," I countered, giving him a smile of my own. A nice, predatory one. "How about a friendly match? Give us something to do besides listen to Cotter and Basil fight over the vidscreen."

Rupert's face didn't change, but I could tell from the stiffness in his posture that he wasn't thrilled by my suggestion. His unwillingness didn't necessarily mean that he had something to hide, but it certainly didn't dispel suspicion. Of course, if he wasn't going to volunteer, then I'd just have to push a little harder.

"Captain," I said over my shoulder at Caldswell, who was sitting on the couch beside his daughter. He glanced up at my voice, and I gave him an earnest, innocent look. "Can I borrow your cook for a little sparring practice? I hear he's pretty good, and I need someone besides Cotter to kick around."

The captain looked at Rupert. "You want to get kicked around?"

"Not particularly," Rupert said. "Forget it, Devi. After a crash ship full of xith'cal, I'm no challenge for you."

"Hey!" Cotter yelled. "I killed most of those!"

"How do you know that if you never try me?" I said, ignoring Cotter completely. "Come on, it'll be quick. Best two out of three."

Rupert looked at Caldswell again, but the captain just shrugged. "Up to you."

Rupert closed his eyes and took a deep breath. "Fine," he said, taking off his apron. "But I'm warning you, you'll be disappointed."

I stepped back and motioned for him to lead the way.

Because there was nowhere else large enough, we set up in the cargo bay. Cotter, being Paradoxian and thus always excited about a fight, got into his armor and moved the crates of fish around to make us a nice little ring. Since we were far and away the most exciting thing going on, everyone came down to watch, even the captain, dragging Ren along behind him. Cotter tried to start a betting pool, but it didn't work out because everyone was betting on me. People were far more interested in getting a good seat on the cargo crates surrounding our little pit, anyway. For my part, I was watching Rupert.

If I hadn't known better, I'd have said he was embarrassed by all the attention. He took off his coat slowly and threw it up onto the crates, out of the way. He swung his arms twice and rolled up his sleeves, but otherwise he didn't do any sort of warm-up.

Neither did I. I could have used one since my joints were still stiff from the fight earlier, but I didn't want to give him any clue as to what was coming. If I was going to learn anything useful from this, I'd have to trick him into doing something that would give himself away, and that meant catching him by surprise. Fortunately, Rupert hadn't seen me do any fighting out of armor yet. No armor meant a whole new bag of tricks.

I was dressed for the occasion, at least. I'd kicked off my ship flats, and my bare feet gripped the scratched metal of the cargo bay floor nicely. My pants were soft, lightweight, and loose fitting, great for kicking. Even better, I was wearing my favorite tank top, a thin, tight black sheath that left my arms free and showed off my chest. I might have staged this fight for very legitimate information gathering purposes, but I was still going to be fighting Rupert, and while I'd written off getting him into bed days ago, I wasn't *dead*. If I was going to be rolling around on the floor with Mr. Charkov, then I was going to look hot while I did it.

But if Rupert appreciated my outfit, he didn't show it. "Last warning," he said as we took our positions on opposite sides of the cleared square. "This will only end in disappointment."

I just smiled wide and lunged.

It was bad form for a mock fight. I'd attacked early, no warning, no salute. But this match wasn't actually about fighting, so I burned every bit of the energy I'd built up waiting for him to be ready, closing the distance between us as fast as I could.

Being so tall gave him serious reach on me, but I was used to fighting larger opponents, and I went in low, aiming for his stomach. I was there before he could defend, my fist flying straight for his abdomen. But the moment I touched his shirt, he faded. His body slid away from the blow, matching my speed perfectly and leaving me overbalanced. I stamped my foot and spun to catch myself, coming back around to brace for the counter—only to see Rupert lying on the floor looking up at me with a scowl.

"*Charkov!*" That was Basil, who'd gotten himself worked into a furious fluffy ball of feathers. "You're not going to let the little Paradoxian knock you around like that, are you?"

"I'd be worried if she didn't," Rupert said, pushing himself up with a hand on his stomach like he was in pain. "It's her job. I'm just the cook."

There were a few more catcalls, but I didn't hear them. I was too busy working over what had just happened.

I knew I'd felt Rupert under my fist, shifting his weight away with a skill I hadn't faced before, and I'd fought some scary people. His fall had been perfect, too, a neat collapse that spared every muscle. But he looked so cross as he stretched his supposedly bruised abs that I started to feel guilty. Maybe his dodge wasn't the amazing skill it had felt like? Maybe he really had gone down like a leaf? Maybe I'd let my paranoia get the best of me and I was just kicking around a man who wasn't a fighter and who'd been nothing but nice to me?

Except, of course, when he was only being nice to set me up.

I eyed Rupert as he stepped back into position. His posture spoke of sore muscles and irritation, everything expected of someone who'd been thrown into a fight he didn't want with a stronger opponent. It was a good show, and I would have bought it and ended the match right then had it not been for his eyes. Rupert's eyes were locked on my shifting feet with a fighter's attention. Every now and then, he'd glance up at my face, and though he tried to hide it, I caught the shadow of a smirk.

I stiffened. That's how he wanted to play it, did he? All right, I'd play. The next time his eyes flicked to mine, I smirked back and ran in.

I didn't kick, I didn't punch, I didn't try to strike him at all. Instead, I went for a throw, putting myself well inside his reach in the process. He'd have to choose. Was he going to stand there and let me throw him? Or was he going to take the opening and throw me instead? It was much harder to fake a bad throw than it was to fake a fall, but if he let me throw him without any sort of counter, no one would believe he'd had any sort of training, certainly not enough to absorb the kick of my gun, which would prove that something fishy was going on. Of course, if something fishy *was* going on and I forced him to reveal it in front of the crew, I would probably end up the dead, nosy merc from my motto, but I was in way too far to stop now. Part of being Paradoxian means never knowing when to quit.

The closer I got, the more certain I was that Rupert was going to let me throw him. By the time my fingers touched his shirt, I knew it for sure. But as I shifted my weight to pull him over my shoulder, Rupert's arm appeared from nowhere, and then I was down on my back with no idea how I'd gotten there.

A chorus of cheers rose, and Rupert's hand appeared again, this time to help me up. I grabbed it with a glare, letting him pull me to my feet. The moment my legs were under me, I lurched back without warning, pulling him with all my weight.

For a second it was like pulling on a mountain, and then Rupert collapsed in another of those perfect falls, tumbling neatly before sprawling almost too pathetically on the floor beside me. To the crew it must have looked like I'd just sent him flat on his face, but I caught a flash of a grin as he got his hands under him. He made a tired, hurt sound and then pushed himself over onto his back with such overplayed stiffness that I rolled my eyes.

"That's that, I guess," he said, staring at me with a pathetic look. "You got me two downs out of three."

"That didn't count," I said, rolling to my feet. "One more down."

"Leave him alone, Devi," Caldswell called. "You've embarrassed him enough for one night."

That sounded like Rupert's out, and I fully expected him to take it, but to my surprise Rupert shook his head. "She wants to knock me over one more time," he said, sitting up stiffly. As he got to his feet, he shot me a sly smile. "Who am I to deny a lady?"

Oh, he knew what he was doing. He was baiting me clear and strong. His posture was defeated, but his eyes were all mocking challenge. I've never been able to turn down a challenge, which was how I got into so many fights growing up. My mother always said that idiots never learn, and I guess she was right, because idiotic as it was to let Rupert bait me, I swallowed it hook and sinker.

All at once, I stopped playing. I stopped bouncing around and grew very still. And then, without shifting my weight, without making a sound, without giving a warning of any kind, I launched a roundhouse kick straight to Rupert's side.

I must have been better than he'd thought, because his body didn't slide out from under the blow this time. There was no overbalancing, no feeling of a spoiled shot. I hit him straight, hard, and solid with all my strength. It was the kind of kick I've used to crack ribs on much bigger men, and Rupert just stood and took it.

Kicking Rupert for real felt like kicking a metal post. The shock and pain went all the way up my leg until I was gritting my teeth against it. For a second I was sure I'd broken my ankle, but I didn't hear anything crack. My eyes were locked with Rupert's the whole time, and I saw the moment I connected that I'd actually done it, I'd caught him by surprise. It lasted only a breath, and then Rupert fell, dropping sideways in perfect, controlled collapse.

The room was silent. Everyone seemed to know that kick was different, even those who'd never thrown a hit in their lives, and except for Cotter, who looked smug, and Nova, who couldn't look mean if she tried, they were all giving me the evil eye. Big, bad Devi, picking on the little guy.

Steeling my face so I wouldn't wince, I lowered my throbbing leg and walked over to Rupert. Every step hurt like hell, but I refused to let it show as I knelt down and helped him sit up. "Okay," I announced. "Show's over. You were all right, this was unfair." I looked down. "Sorry, Rupert. Thanks for being such a good sport."

He sighed. "Just don't go beating up any other crew members."

"I won't," I promised, sliding my shoulder under his arm before he could move away. "Go back and have a drink on me," I said to the watching crowd. "I'll take Rupert to the infirmary and patch him up."

Hyrek moved to help anyway, but Caldswell got up first. "Fine," he said. "Let's go drink Miss Morris's combat bonus while she cleans up her mess."

That was all it took to snap everyone back into action. The rest of the crew followed the captain up the stairs to the lounge, including Hyrek, who didn't look happy about it. I supported Rupert with my shoulder while we walked to the engine room door. Pickers gave us the stink eye as we entered, but she couldn't tell any tales, so the moment the door was closed I sank down and clutched my injured leg.

"God and king," I groaned, glaring up at Rupert. "What's your chest made of? Lead?"

He folded his arms. "You brought that on yourself."

He was right, of course. I had no business throwing a kick like that in a friendly fight. But still. "*You* baited me," I snapped.

Rupert arched a dark eyebrow. "Just because someone baits you doesn't mean you have to take it."

I shook my head and focused my attention on my throbbing ankle, rolling up my pants to get a better look. The bruise ran from the top of my foot up to the middle of my shin, and it was already starting to darken. In a few hours it would be an ugly purple. I was just about to try walking on it again when Rupert swooped down and picked me up.

"Oh, I get it," I said, folding my arms and glaring at him as he carried me through the engine room. "Charity to the fallen enemy."

I felt Rupert's sigh through his chest. "You're not my enemy, Devi."

We climbed the spiral stair up from the ship's lower level to the main hall where the infirmary was. The sound of partying got louder as we got higher. No doubt Caldswell was making good on his promise to spend my combat bonus. With so much noise they couldn't possibly hear anything we said, but neither of us spoke again until we were through the infirmary door.

Rupert set me gently on the table and went to get an ice pack from the freezer. I watched him the whole time, noting how the "pain" from his bruised ribs had vanished completely, leaving him free to move gracefully as he always did. When he came back, ice pack in hand, I put my hand on his chest, stopping him midstep.

"What?" he said.

I ignored the question, reaching for his shirt buttons instead. I undid them one by one, starting at the middle of his chest and working my way down. He didn't move a muscle the entire time, but I could feel his breathing picking up under my fingers. Not so long ago, the idea that I was making cool, collected Rupert's breathing jump would have delighted me, but right now I was more concerned with inspecting the spot where my kick had landed.

I pushed his shirt back to reveal a solid wall of pale, unmarred skin and well-defined muscle. Almost hesitantly, I moved my hand to his side, letting my fingers brush over his ribs and down his waist. It might have been my imagination, but I think his breathing stopped when I touched him. I did smile then, but I didn't let myself get distracted. I'd risked a great deal to get here, and I wasn't about to let things slide now.

"I kicked you hard enough to nearly break my foot," I said, drawing my hand away and folding his shirt back into place. "But you don't have so much as a mark." My eyes went up to his. "Why? Who are you?"

Rupert dropped to his knees in front of me and pressed the ice pack against my bruised ankle, holding my foot to keep me still. "I'm a cook," he said quietly. "And if I am other things, they happened long ago. But you have nothing to fear from me, Devi. I promise I will never hurt you."

"I'm not worried you'll hurt me," I said, confused. Even in the middle of our fight, the idea that Rupert might actually hurt me hadn't even crossed my mind.

I was still thinking it over when Rupert leaned closer. His head was bowed so I couldn't see his face, but his hands were gentle as he pressed the ice pack against my skin. Some of his hair had slipped free of its tie during our fight. It hung down in long, black tendrils around his face. A few of them were long enough to brush the skin of my leg. They felt soft as silk, and the urge to wrap one around my finger was overpowering. My hand had actually twitched forward before I realized what was happening, and all at once, I felt very stupid.

What the hell was I doing? My plan had worked, I'd revealed that Rupert was more than human, but though I was the one with the swollen ankle, Rupert was the one who'd gotten hurt. Whatever he was, it was clear he didn't like it. He'd done his best to keep it hidden, and everything had been fine until I'd gotten curious and started ripping things open.

I closed my eyes, feeling stupid and mean. In hindsight, picking that fight had been a pointless risk. Even if I had discovered some huge secret, it wouldn't have changed anything. I wasn't leaving this ship unless Caldswell kicked me off, so what did it matter if his cook was something other than he appeared? Rupert hadn't done anything with it other than keep his head down and try to stay alive. I was the one throwing her weight around and hurting people in the process.

With a shamed sigh, I opened my eyes. Rupert was still on his knees in front of me, his face turned down as he studied my injured leg. The sight filled me with tenderness, and I leaned down slowly until my forehead bumped against the crown of his head. "I'm sorry," I said softly.

Rupert stilled. "For what?"

I shrugged. "Everything. I got nosy and made a mess when I should have known better. I'm not afraid of you, Rupert. I never have been and I never will be. Whatever you are, it's none of my business, and I'm going to keep my nose out of it from now on. I just hope you can forgive me for being such a pushy bitch about things."

"You're not a bitch," Rupert said quietly, stumbling a bit over "bitch" like he didn't like the sound. "And it was my fault, too. I shouldn't have taken you up on the fight."

"I put you on the spot," I said, shaking my head against his. "I can be pretty pigheaded when I get stuck on something."

He laughed at that, dipping down to drop a kiss to my knee. It was the tiniest motion, a bare brush over almost before I could feel it, but I was still reeling from the shock it sent through me when Rupert stood up.

"That you certainly can be," he said, handing me the ice pack. "Hold that down while I get something to tie it with."

I obeyed, holding the ice against my ankle while he found a roll of gauze. Together, we tied the ice pack to my leg, and then he picked me up again despite my protests and carried me to my cabin.

Everyone was still in the lounge, so we were able to slip in unseen. Rupert hit the light with his elbow and dodged Nova's fluttery hangings to set me on my bunk. He propped me up gently, using my spare pillow to elevate my leg. I expected him to leave after getting me settled, but he didn't. Instead, he plopped himself down on the floor beside my bunk.

"What are you doing?" I asked, smacking his shoulder, which was right by my hand.

"Keeping you from getting up," Rupert said, like this should be obvious. "We've got four more hours before we leave hyperspace, and there's probably going to be a party going in the lounge right up until then. As your bartender, I don't trust you not to hobble over and join in, so I'm going to sit here and make sure you stay off that leg."

I fell back into my pillow with a dramatic sigh. "Great," I said. "I'm paying for a party and I don't even get to go."

"It's not so bad," Rupert said, folding his arms behind his head as he stretched his long legs out beside my bed.

I stared at him, dumbfounded. If I'd been in his shoes through all this, I'd be fuming, but Rupert looked content as a cat in a sunbeam, and eventually, I relaxed as well. If I was honest with myself, I had to admit it was nice to just spend time with him again. Between my initial ill-fated attempts to sleep with him and all the crap that had happened after, I'd almost forgotten how much I enjoyed his company.

"I guess you're right," I said, smiling at him. Then I caught sight of my cards, still sitting where I'd left them, and my smile widened with sudden inspiration. "So Rupert"—I reached over him, grabbing my deck off the dresser—"do you know how to play poker?"

His insulted look told me everything I needed to know.

CHAPTER
6

Rupert turned out to be even more of a card shark than I was, mostly because he was such a good bluffer. If we'd been playing for money, I'd have been in trouble, but we weren't, so the only damage I suffered was a bruised ego. It was hard for me to see the cards when he was sitting on the floor, so, after our third game, Rupert joined me on the bed, sitting on the far side with my injured leg stretched over his knees.

It couldn't have been a comfortable position. He was too tall to sit up straight under the bunk, so he had to lean sideways, but he didn't seem to mind. In fact, his posture was more relaxed than I'd ever seen it, and I relaxed as well, letting myself enjoy having Rupert in my bed at last, even if it wasn't the way I'd planned.

We talked about stupid, common stuff, mostly how I'd dominated my duchy's varsity armor league when I'd been in school. He seemed to find the idea of me as a teenage armor jock hilarious. I, however, saw nothing funny about it at all.

"It was serious competition," I snapped, bidding two even though I knew he had to have a better hand than I did. "The suits are stock for league play, no custom anything. The fights are all skill. They recruit gladiators out of the varsity leagues, you know."

"So why aren't you in the arena, then?" Rupert said, matching my bid with a pair of the hair clips we were using for chips. "I can't imagine a recruiter would pass up someone like you."

"Who said they did?" I huffed. "I got plenty of offers, but I didn't want to be a gladiator. They make the girls fight in bikinis, and that's not the sort of glory I was looking for. Even if I could have gotten a real suit, I wouldn't have taken a gladiator contract. I've never wanted to be anything but a Devastator since I saw the royal squad when I was thirteen, and they don't recruit out of the arenas."

"Why?" Rupert asked, glancing at me over his cards.

"Because all gladiators, even the good ones, are more about showing off than fighting," I said authoritatively.

Rupert laughed. "No, no, I meant why do you want to be a Devastator?"

"Because they're the top," I said. "The absolute pinnacle of how far a peasant like me can go. I'd be under the direct command of the Sacred King himself. It doesn't get much better than that."

He arched an eyebrow, and I smiled. "You gotta understand, I grew up in the middle of nowhere. I didn't even know what I wanted to be when I was a kid because I never saw anything except fishing and farming. Then my dad took me to Kingston to watch the parades, and when I saw the Devastators, it was like the whole universe suddenly opened up." I could still remember that day clear as a photograph, the crowded streets, the confetti falling from the sky, and the Devastators in their shining golden armor that screamed power. No matter how many years went by, the memory still made me shiver.

"I found my calling," I continued with a shrug. "Looking back, it was kind of obvious. Armor was always the only thing I really liked to do, and the Devastators are the best armor users in the galaxy. One look was enough. From that moment on, I knew exactly what I wanted from my life."

"You seem pretty determined to make it," Rupert said, rearranging his cards.

"Can't be a Devastator if you're not determined," I said, tossing my losing hand down with a grin. "I'm well on my way, though. All I've got to do now is stay alive."

"You might have chosen the wrong ship for that," Rupert said quietly. His eyes flicked up from his cards as he spoke, and the look in them was so intense that my hands began to shake.

"Whatever," I said at last. "It'll take a bigger monster than Caldswell's *Fool* to eat me."

To my surprise, Rupert's face broke into a wide smile. "I believe it," he said, folding his hand neatly as he started gathering the cards for the next game.

My arm shot out to stop him. "Wait. Aren't you going to collect your winnings?"

He shook his head. "I don't need clips for my hair, and besides"—he gave me a sly look—"you won that hand."

I released him with a groan. He'd bluffed me again. I'd thought for sure I'd lost. Should have bid harder. Rupert's smile grew infuriating at my indignation, and I wrinkled my nose at him. "Are you always like this?"

"Only with you," Rupert said, shuffling the cards in a neat fold.

I flopped back against my pillow with a huff. "So that's me," I said. "But why are you here? Surely there are better places to be a cook." My voice was almost sleepy it was so casual, but I was holding my breath. I'd promised I wouldn't pry into his past, but I was just so curious. I also wanted to know more about his relationship with the cursed captain. Back on the bridge, Caldswell had said they were friends, but Rupert always seemed to treat him like an officer, not a friend, and I'd never seen them spend time together as friends would. Actually, I'd never seen Rupert spend time with anyone except myself and Ren.

But despite the relatively innocent question, Rupert didn't speak. He just lay there, flicking the cards with his long fingers. The silence was so sudden and dour after our happy conversation I was about to tell him to forget about it when he answered.

"I requested to be on this ship," he said, keeping his eyes on his cards. "Caldswell is very respected. It is an honor to serve under him."

"I'm afraid you're going to have to explain that one to me," I said. "All I've seen him do is play mean tricks on his employees and manage to get himself attacked by xith'cal in the king's own space. Not that that isn't a feat, but it's hardly what I'd call respectable."

He still wasn't looking at me, but I saw Rupert's lips quirk in a smile before he hid them behind his cards. "I'm sure he'd be flattered to hear you say so."

"Just don't tell him," I groaned. "I have to get through a year of this, remember?"

"My lips are sealed," Rupert promised.

We were about to start the first round of betting when a soft beep interrupted us. Rupert pulled his handset out of his pocket, glanced at it, then slid off the bed, gently moving out from under my bruised leg.

"Let me guess," I said. "Caldswell?"

"Who else?" Rupert said.

"Speak of the devil," I muttered, sweeping the cards into a pile in front of me. "Have fun babysitting."

"Stay off the leg," he ordered as he dodged Nova's hangings. "I'll be back to check on you before we exit hyperspace."

"Yes, doctor," I said dutifully. "Rupert?"

He stopped at the door.

"Thank you," I said, waving the deck at him. "It was fun. If

I promise to get you ribbons to win instead of clips, can we do it again?"

"You wear the ribbons and I'll play whenever you like," he said, his voice rich with laughter. "See you later, Devi."

I took a deep breath. My name still sounded so lovely when he said it. Rupert vanished into the hall, and I caught the loud chatter of the now very drunk party I'd been funding in the lounge before the door slid shut, cutting off all sound except the hum of the ship.

I stretched contentedly, pressing my legs into the lingering heat Rupert's body had left in the mattress. That had ended much better than I'd thought it would when I'd limped out of the cargo bay. True, my fumbling attempts at investigation had fallen flat, but I had a much firmer grip on where I stood with Rupert.

I still didn't trust him, of course. No one with any sense would trust someone who could fake a fall that well, but I wasn't worried anymore about what had happened during the raid. Whatever Rupert's secret was, it didn't seem like the sort that would come back to bite me unless I poked it, and I was done being nosy for a while. In any case, it was certainly more enjoyable to be Rupert's friend than his enemy. I had enough enemies, and I was ready to take what I could get.

I hadn't meant to fall asleep, but I must have because the alarm for our imminent exit from hyperspace snapped me awake. I blinked and sat up, wincing as the movement jostled my bruised ankle beneath the now-melted ice pack. Pathetically, my first thought was disappointment that Rupert hadn't come back to check on me like he'd promised. Shaking my head at my foolishness, I swung my legs over the edge of my bunk and nearly stepped on a covered tray.

I jerked my feet back and leaned over, eyeing the tray like it was a wild animal. As though on cue, a delicious smell drifted up. My stomach rumbled in reply.

I let it growl, folding my arms as I glared at the tray. I knew it was from Rupert. He was the cook, after all. What I couldn't figure out was how he'd gotten it in here without waking me up.

I've never been a heavy sleeper, and I've only gotten warier about it over the years. Sleeping through the door opening I could maybe see; the doors were about the only quietly operating parts the *Fool* had. But sleeping through someone coming in, putting a tray down right beside me, and leaving again? That was unheard of.

I worried over it for a good minute before I decided I was being stupid. Rupert was a nest of secrets already, was I really so surprised he could sneak into my room? Maybe if he'd been coming to put a knife in my chest I'd have cause to complain, but it was just bad form to be angry at someone for bringing you dinner. With that decided, I leaned down and lifted the tray cover.

The food was all Paradoxian, and most of it was from Ambermarle, my duchy. There were red potato cakes, fried greens, shredded mushrooms, even a little steamed chocolate cake. Best of all was the shot of whiskey on the tray's corner, the chilled glass beaded with condensation. I stared at it in wonder for several seconds, and then I picked up the tray, shook the silverware out of the paper napkin, and fell to.

Everything was delicious. True, the greens were some variety I didn't recognize, the mushrooms were Terran, not Ambermarle longstems, and the potato cake was stuffed with fish stew rather than the traditional creamed chicken, but it was as good as anything I've had back home, and I ate well past the point of being full just for the pleasure of it.

Stuffed and happy, I put my dishes on the tray and stood up. My ankle was still sore and probably would be for another few days, but I could limp along well enough, and once I got into my armor and made some adjustments to compensate for the injury, letting the balancers pick up the extra tension, it didn't hurt at all. Well-made armor is a beautiful, beautiful thing.

When I was dressed and ready for work, I gathered my dishes onto the tray and took it back to the kitchen. The lounge was empty when I got there. I rinsed out my dishes in the sink and loaded them into the washer, no small feat in armor. When I was finished, I pulled up the ship's com grid and looked up Rupert's connection. It wasn't as good as thanking him in person, but I sent a quick message to his handset thanking him for the food and assuring him it had been delicious. The response was immediate.

My pleasure.

Grinning, I closed the message and walked over to the windows, propping myself against the glass to watch as Basil announced our exit from hyperspace.

We left hyperspace smoothly, coming out in orbit above Mycant with only one second's difference between the local space controller's clocks and our own. Mycant was one of those sparsely populated Terran colonies on the edge of civilized space, the ones that were so far out from the Republic's core worlds you wondered why they bothered. It was pretty, though, with lots of strange, spindly forest, stormy, dark gray seas, and a population of about a million spread so thin it was easy to imagine there weren't twenty people together in the whole place. The starport was little more than a dirt field walled off with chain-link fence, a fact that bothered Basil more than anyone else. He was cursing so loudly about getting dirt in the thrusters I couldn't hear Caldswell when he called with our orders.

"I'm going out to meet a potential client," he repeated after sending Basil off to have his meltdown somewhere else. "He has family, so I'm bringing Rupert and Ren with me. The buyer will be here to pick up our current cargo in the morning. I'll be gone for three days, and I want you to stick to the *Fool* like glue the whole time, understand?"

"Do you think something will happen, sir?" I asked.

"No," Caldswell said. "But that never stops it from happening. Just don't budge until we get back. I'll contact Basil if plans change."

"Yes sir," Cotter and I said in unison as the captain cut the connection.

I hadn't noticed that the *Glorious Fool* had two atmospheric skippers stowed in a special berth beneath the cargo bay until Caldswell had Cotter roll one out. They were pretty drab compared to the silver-plated beauties I'd seen nobles flying around Paradox, but they were still much nicer than anything I'd expected him to have.

Caldswell loaded himself, his daughter, and Rupert, who was presumably stuck on Ren duty, into the newer of the two and took off without so much as a look back, zipping through the overcast sky and disappearing behind the tall trees in a handful of seconds. I couldn't decide if he was in a hurry or if the quick, cold departure was just the captain's nature. Both seemed plausible.

Now that we were on planet for a few days, the crew began to scatter. Hyrek, of course, never left his room, but everyone else seemed determined to get outside. Since it was my job to watch them as well as the ship, I had Basil make me a sign-out system and forced them all to log their destination whenever they left the ship. I'd expected Basil to grumble about this, but the bird actually seemed to like me more for having suggested it, and I got the feeling he'd been trying to impose some sort of order on shore leave for years. As it turned out, the only person who did grumble was Cotter, mostly because I'd told him to do it, too.

"I never heard the captain make you head of security," he

growled in King's Tongue when we were sitting on the downed ramp a few hours later, watching the night rain turn the spaceport to mud while we waited for Nova and Mabel to get back from a shopping trip in the tiny clump of buildings that somehow qualified as a planetary capital.

"He didn't," I said, keeping my eyes on the adjustments I was making to Phoebe's new thermite blade. "But someone has to do it, and I'd rather it be me."

"Bet you would," he said. "But I didn't see you in the thick of things when the xith'cal attacked."

"That's because I was killing the ones jumping you from behind," I snapped. I didn't have to lift my head to look at him, but I did. Some things are instinct. "Let's get this straight, Cotter. Only an idiot would doubt your ability to be a deadly fury after that last fight, but I'm not taking orders from you. If you want to try and make me, go right ahead, but we all remember what happened last time you fought me one on one."

"That doesn't count!" Cotter cried. "You got the jump, it wasn't fair."

"I'm not fair," I said. "But if you'll shut up and listen when I tell you things, you'll find I'm the one who's going to get us through this year with our skins intact."

Cotter leaned forward. "Where do you get off being such a bossy bitch?"

I looked him dead in the eyes. "I was born a bossy bitch, so you can either roll with it or get rolled over. Your choice, sunshine, but remember, Caldswell already treats me as lead because I shot first on the bridge, and I haven't led us wrong since. Stick behind me and all you'll need to do is follow orders and be a good merc. Try to pull ahead, and your life's going to get a whole lot more complicated."

Cotter surged to his feet, towering over me, and for a moment

113

I thought we were about to throw down again then and there. But then he swore and turned away, and I knew I'd just won dominance struggle number two. He was mine until the next outburst, which would probably be his last unless I screwed up. Cotter was a dick and a braggart, but he wasn't dumb, and you've got to be pretty stupid to bang your head against the brick wall of Devi Morris more than three times.

"So, *boss*," he sneered, folding his armored arms as best he could over his suit's massive chest. "What should I do now?"

I ignored his snide tone and answered in Universal. "Go inside and make sure Basil isn't cooking birdseed for dinner. I'll keep watch here. We'll switch at lights-out."

He must not have expected such a reasonable order, because he stood speechless for a second before turning on his heel and marching back into the ship without so much as a dirty word. I turned my head back to my thermite blade as he clomped over the remains of the plasma patch and through the hole the xith'cal attack had left in our ship, but I watched him through my rear cam until he disappeared up the lounge stairs. Only then did I reach down and slide Sasha's safety back into place.

The first quake hit just as Caldswell's buyer showed up to unload his fish.

Cotter, Basil, and I were on hand to do the deal. As head of cargo, Mabel should have been there, too, but she'd run off at dawn to go visit some mechanic friend. How there was any mechanic worth knowing on this dirtball, I had no idea, but I wasn't pleased by her sudden disappearance. Especially not when the buyer climbed out of his huge truck and started eyeballing the three of us like this was some kind of joke.

Though Basil was technically in charge with both the captain and Mabel away, I did all the talking, mostly because the buyer couldn't stop gawking at Basil long enough to listen to him. I was taking his payment when the Lady's alarm dinged in my ear a split second before the ground started shaking.

Cotter and I balanced instantly—stabilizers are worth their weight in gold in situations like this—but Basil and the shopkeeper we'd been dealing with both stumbled. I caught Basil by the wing before he fell, and he squawked at me, fluttering out of my reach before landing again with a huff as the shaking faded.

"Are you trying to pull my wing off?" he cried, his head bobbing right in my face.

"Sorry, sir." I shrugged. "Next time I'll let you fall like a—"

The next quake hit before I could finish. It struck like a crash, harder than the first. This time, Basil leaped into my arms, his long feet clenched around my legs so hard he might have broken them had I not been in armor.

"Easy, birdie," I whispered, sending a quick message to Cotter not to laugh.

"What is going on?" Basil squawked, jumping off me the moment the ground was still.

Our fish buyer, who'd clung to his truck through both quakes, sighed and wiped his forehead with a handkerchief. "That was a bad one," he said. "We've been having quakes planet wide for the last week and a half."

"Planet wide for a week and a half?" Basil said, regaining a bit of his composure with a shake of his feathers. "I thought colony grants are only given to stable planets. Do you think we should move the ship?"

"We are stable," the man snapped. "Mycant started out as a mining colony, and we've got geologic surveys of everything, before and after terraforming. This rock's as solid as any of the core worlds. We're just having a spot of activity is all."

I frowned. "Did you ask the local scientific council?" Scientific councils were the only part of Terran colonial structure I knew.

The man glared at me. For all that I wasn't an aeon, I was obviously Paradoxian, which most Terrans considered nearly as bad. "Don't have a government seismologist on a colony this small," he said at last. "Local council didn't see the point in paying for one when nothing's going on."

"Well," Basil said. "I'm sure that's a great comfort to you n-OW!"

I lifted my boot off his long toes before he could add anything else, completely ignoring his murderous look as I moved between him and our buyer. "You and the captain agreed on the price in advance?"

It took him a second to catch up with the change in subject, but once I'd gotten him back on business, we stayed there. He paid up front, transferring a surprisingly small amount of money onto Basil's ledger, and then Cotter and I helped him load the crates of fish into the back of his hauler. The minute it was full, he drove away, his big tires squishing through the mud left by last night's rain.

We didn't get another quake until that afternoon. I was keeping an eye on the repair crew that had come to fix the busted cargo bay, and I was in a foul mood. Mycant was cold and wet, and the dreary weather was starting to get to my suit. Also, the repair crew had been late. It was bad enough that Mabel had vanished who knew where, but she wasn't answering her com either. That meant I was the one left waiting for the repair crew, and then, when they did finally arrive, I had to stand around watching to make sure they didn't put the new door on backward.

Normally, I enjoy being in charge. I like seeing things done right, and the only way to be sure of that is to keep an eye on things yourself. But I knew nothing about ship repairs, and the numbers the foreman was tossing at me kept getting higher and higher.

Basil approved each one without hesitation, though, and I watched in horror as all the money from the fish vanished. By the time the crew left, the broken hull was repaired, the new door was in place, and I had serious doubts about how Caldswell stayed in business. This deal he was off doing had better be a fat one, or else I didn't see how I'd be getting paid this month.

I was still grumbling about money when the entire ship bucked under my feet so hard even my stabilizer couldn't balance me in time. I fell sideways, and the Lady switched to emergency protocols, flipping me back onto my feet in a show of acrobatics I never could have managed on my own. Cotter, who'd been coming down the stairs to get back into his armor after his break, had to grab the railing to keep from going down the rest of the way on his ass.

"What the hell was that?" he shouted, clinging to the stairs for dear life.

"Quake," I said unnecessarily, glancing up at him as the shaking gradually faded. "You okay?"

He straightened up at once, rolling his shoulders. "Course," he said nonchalantly. "Nice flip."

"Thanks," I answered, ignoring the sarcasm in his voice. He hurried down the stairs and jogged across the bay toward his armor, stumbling only a little when a mild aftershock rattled the floor. I let it roll through me, watching the mud outside wobble.

"We need to get off this planet," I muttered.

"Fat chance of that," Cotter said, tapping the front of his suit. It swung open, and he hauled himself inside. "Damn turkey nearly pecked my eyes out when I said something similar. You tried calling Mabel?"

"All day long," I said. "She must have her handset off." And sister-in-law or not, I'd be reporting that to the captain. Vanishing when you're needed is not the way to run a ship.

"Could be the interference." Cotter's voice was coming over the com now as his suit locked in. "Nova said something about that when I was up on the bridge."

I turned to the stairs and jumped, flipping once to land in the door. "Cover for me a sec," I said, jogging into the lounge. "I'll go ask her about it."

"Watch out for bird attacks," Cotter replied, and then his com cut out. I smiled. Nice to know Cotter could be half decent when he forgot to be a jerk.

When I reached the bridge, Nova and Basil were standing around Basil's projected star map. They both jumped when I came in, so I didn't bother with preamble.

"We're having communications problems?"

Basil glared at me, but Nova just nodded. "There's magnetic interference. Basil thinks it's from the quakes."

"Nothing too serious," Basil said, placated now that he was the acknowledged authority. "The main channels are working fine, it's just the smaller sets that are having problems."

I heaved a relieved sigh. "That explains why Mabel's ignoring my calls."

"I certainly hope you weren't implying that the captain's sister-in-law wasn't doing her job?" Basil said, his voice more scornful than I'd thought such a whistling sound could be.

"Not at all." I'd been ready to report her, but really, no one likes having to tell her commanding officer that a family member is shirking. Of course, it would have been great if Mabel could have waited to go visiting until *after* the hull was fixed. "Just worried. Protecting the crew is my job, after all."

Nova beamed at me, and even Basil looked satisfied. I would have been too if the business with Mabel had been my only worry. "So," I said. "What's wrong with the handset signals?"

I should have known better than to ask a technical question in Basil's presence. The bird pulled himself to his full height and launched into a long and detailed lecture on the difference between the bandwidths used for smaller sets versus satellite communication and how magnetic interference interacts with each. I glazed over almost immediately. My patience for technical description drops off once I get away from armor, guns, and other fun things, but I did catch his last sentence: "...my real worry is the clocks."

"What about the clocks?" I asked.

Basil gave me a nasty look. "Didn't you listen to any of that?"

I lifted my visor so he could see my wide grin. "Ignorant monkey, remember? Now, clocks?"

Basil harrumphed. "I *said* that our ship clock keeps losing time. Every time the *Fool*'s computer checks in with Republic traffic control, we're off the standard galactic time by a fraction of a second."

I shrugged. "Fraction of a second doesn't sound like a big deal."

"It's a very big deal," Basil snapped. "If our clock is damaged it could throw all our other systems out of whack." He punched something on the console in front of him, and the large monitor at the front of the bridge flashed up a time display divided down to picoseconds. I froze when I saw it, and an uncomfortable tightening dread began to restrict my chest. See, I keep the time in the corner of my display at all times, and my clock? It didn't match Basil's at all.

I cursed in King's Tongue and pulled off my helmet, examining the inside. I didn't see anything out of the ordinary, so I stuck it back on and brought my clock right to the middle of my vision.

Basil's head bobbed toward me. "Don't tell me you're off, too?"

"By almost ten minutes," I answered. "I don't understand. Everything else is working. Why am I so far off?"

"Probably because your suit doesn't check with outside clocks," Nova said, her dreamy voice tinged with worry. "Are you on a vibration system?"

I shook my head. "Atomic clock, guaranteed accurate to within one second for three centuries." My clock was part of my FWL, or

Final Word Lock, the almost indestructible knot at the base of my spine designed to survive no matter what so that my officers could pull my data later and see how I'd died. Morbid, but useful—and, up until today, completely infallible.

"I don't like this," Basil announced, speaking for everyone. "But business is done and the captain comes back tomorrow. I'll ask him to put in at a real space dock and we'll have a professional electrician take a look at things. Maybe he can find the problem."

I frowned. "I thought you said it was the quakes?"

Basil rolled his enormous yellow eyes. "Quakes don't hurt clocks, idiot. We might be up to our eyefeathers in magnetic interference, but it shouldn't matter to the clocks if we all turned into magnets. I'm more inclined to think this is more of the *Glorious Fool*'s usual bad luck. We'll just have to hold our breath and hope nothing breaks too spectacularly before we can get to a repair bay."

"Basil," Nova said gently. "You're not making Deviana feel more confident."

"It's not my job to be her mother," Basil sniffed, but his voice was much kinder to Nova than the look he gave me. "Just keep your monkey mouth shut and try not to panic your fellow gun-toting barbarian. You would not *believe* how rude he was to me earlier."

I believed it. "I'll keep the rabble in line," I assured him, turning back to the hall. "I'm going to shower and catch a few hours' sleep. Go to Cotter if you need anything shot."

"Like either of you would wait for us to-ask!" Basil shouted after me.

The quakes didn't let up for the rest of the day, though we only had one more as bad as the one that had thrown me in the cargo bay. Also, and maybe this was just my paranoia, but the quakes seemed to be coming faster and lasting longer. That alone would have been enough to put me on edge for the remainder of our stay, but now that I knew it was wrong, my clock was bugging me more than anything. I kept it at the center of my vision, but while it continued to lose time, I couldn't tell if it was losing it faster or slower than before.

Other than this, the night passed uneventfully. No one bothered our ship, not even the guys in the control tower, who were usually the first to stick their noses in. When I walked Basil and Nova into town the next morning for a non-reheated breakfast, the whole place felt like it was holding its breath.

The quake damage wasn't as bad as I'd expected. Mycant had a lot of room, so all the buildings were low, wide, and spaced well apart. Still, people had pulled everything off the walls, and several roofs were cracked. And though I looked for them, I didn't see a single clock.

"I hope the quakes ease up soon," Nova whispered to me when we were walking back to the ship half an hour later. "This place is black with fear."

"Natural phenomena like this can take a while to sort out," I said. "Who knows? Maybe they'll have to abandon the colony."

Nova paled, something I didn't think was possible since she was already the color of bleached flour. "I'm glad we're leaving soon."

"Me too," I said.

We prepped for launch when we got back, and then we sat down on the ramp to wait for the captain. And waited. And waited. Mabel was late, too, and I was starting to get frustrated.

"Where is everyone?" I snapped. "The coms are damn near useless now. You'd think that would be enough to send someone with any sense running home. I know that leaves the captain hanging, but Mabel at least should know enough to get back."

"I'm sure she's just delayed," Nova said, but her face was worried as she watched the trees at the edge of the starport's clearing wave in the wind.

"Mabel can take care of herself," Basil said. "And she has plenty of time since we're stuck here until the captain gets back." But while his words were flippant, his head was bobbing nervously, the little crest of rust-colored feathers on top wobbling like gelatin.

Nova saw it, too, and she reached out to touch his wing reassuringly, but just as her fingers brushed his feathers, another quake began to shake. It was a small one, little more than a quiver, but it was enough for me. I looked at Cotter, catching his eye through my visor as I cut my outside speakers and opened a private com just for him. "One hour," I said in King's Tongue.

Any merc who makes it past their second year develops an almost supernatural instinct for danger. Mine had been screaming at me for two days, and I knew Cotter's was going off as well when he accepted the order with no back talk. He just nodded and pulled out his pistol, checking each chamber with deliberate slowness. I followed suit, checking each of my weapons with my delayed but still functional clock square in the center of my vision as I watched the hour tick down.

Ten minutes before our deadline, Cotter and I stood up in unison.

"I'm going to get the captain," I announced. "Cotter, get everyone inside and secure the ship. We're launching the second I get back."

"Now wait just one moment!" Basil screeched, his growing fear forgotten in his rage at having his command usurped. "Caldswell left me in charge, and—"

"He did," I said, cutting him off midsentence. "But your job is to obey the captain. Our job is to ensure the safety of ship, crew, and cargo. Right now, our job takes precedence. If the captain has a problem with that, he can take it out on me."

Basil's eyes went wider than I'd thought possible, but I was already jogging down the ramp. "Get 'em loaded, Cotter."

I heard Cotter making shooing sounds as he swept Basil and Nova into the cargo bay. Basil must have realized he was outgunned, because he went inside with only minimal protest. I saw the bird shooting me nasty looks through my rear cam, but not nearly as nasty as I'd expected. He wanted off this planet, too, I realized, and below his anger at having his authority overturned, he was happy I was doing something to get us out. At least, I hoped he was. Otherwise, this stunt was probably going to be my last on this ship. But every instinct I had was screaming at me to get us off Mycant as soon as possible, and my instincts had never led me wrong before, so I left Cotter herding the others up to the bridge and went around to the hold under the cargo bay where the atmospheric skippers were stored.

Caldswell had taken the better of the two, but the one he'd left flew just fine. I unlocked it from the berth and rolled it out. Skippers are flat, light aircraft meant for getting across a planet comfortably and quickly. They're civilian craft, but they weren't that different from the Paradoxian landers I'd been taught to fly in the army, so I hopped in and hit the ignition without much worry.

The faded plastic seat wheezed under my suit's weight, but the skipper flared to life after only a few shudders. The moment it came online, I punched at the control pad, flipping through options until I got to one marked SECURITY. I hit it, and my face lit up in a grin. No trader captain would ever keep a skipper without putting in some kind of location program to prevent theft and joyrides, and, for once, Caldswell was no exception. The skipper's security tab showed a map with two marked dots: my skipper and the ship. A hundred miles away, a third dot glimmered in the middle of a large, blank spot on the map, our missing skipper, its signal clear and strong despite the interference.

I plugged in the coordinates and hit the thrusters hard, jumping the skipper into the air. The ship, starport, and small town beyond shrank beneath me as I set off in a straight line toward the missing skipper and, I hoped, my missing captain. Far below, the trees wobbled as another quake shook the planet.

CHAPTER

7

Atmospheric skippers are built for speed, and it took me barely half an hour to clear the hundred-plus miles to the spot where my map said Caldswell's skipper was. Mycant was sparsely populated, so I didn't expect to see much when I got there. A little town maybe, or a commercial farm. What I got was endless forest stretching as far as I could see in all directions. I spotted Caldswell's skipper sitting abandoned in a clearing not much larger than the *Fool*'s footprint. I set my skipper down beside it and jumped out, turning every sensor I had to full sweep.

The Lady's sensors filled my perception. Suddenly, I could see the whole clearing through all twelve of my separate filters, the information overlapping and merging until the flood of input was almost overwhelming. I might as well not have bothered. The clearing was blank on every frequency, just a hollowed-out stretch of scrubby grass and bushes. I didn't see so much as a rat, much less a person, but I didn't find any corpses either, so that was something.

I toned down my scan and looked around at the tree line as I tried to imagine what kind of business took Caldswell to a desolate place like this. The only captains I knew who did their dealings this far from civilization were smugglers. Caldswell being a smuggler would explain a lot, actually. I didn't usually care for smuggling, but if Caldswell was shipping something other than fish, the chances of my getting paid went up tremendously. Assuming, of course, someone hadn't left him out in the woods to die.

Such dour thinking was hardly helpful, so I pushed the worst-case scenarios out of my mind and walked back to the skippers to decide my next move. On the way, I tried to raise the ship to let them know what I'd discovered, but my com was now completely dead. I was giving it a mental poke to see if I could at least get text out when my cameras began to go fuzzy.

I stopped midstep, six feet away from my skipper. Static lines were dropping through my vision on all sides, popping in my ears as they passed. I glanced at my suit monitor to see what the malfunction was, but everything looked perfectly normal.

I reset all my cameras anyway, but the lines didn't go away. I kept trying, changing every setting I could think of, but my screen refused to clear up. I bit my lip in frustration. Nothing bothered me more than a problem with my suit. The com I'd expected, but my cameras were my eyes. My clock going wonky was bad enough, but—

I froze, eyes locked on the time display I'd kept large and forward ever since I'd realized something was wrong. It was still there, the numbers glowing like phosphorus despite the static lines running over my vision, but they weren't ticking over. My clock was no longer slowing, it had stopped altogether.

And that was when something enormous hit me from behind.

It felt like I'd been slapped with Mabel's plasma patch. The thing that hit me was soft and slightly yielding but so heavy I couldn't do anything except grunt as it threw me forward. I would have fallen on my face, but while her cameras might be on the fritz, there was nothing wrong with the Lady's emergency mode. My suit flipped me just like it had in the cargo bay, and I landed on my feet, boots skidding through the vegetation as I whirled around with Sasha in my hand.

I'd fired twice before I realized there was nothing behind me. My shots hit a tree on the clearing's edge, shredding the soft trunk to streamers. I pulled my gun back and swirled my cameras, but I saw nothing. The clearing was empty as ever and, except for the lingering echo of Sasha's shots, utterly silent. There was no wind, no bird cries, nothing but the soft whisper of my suit's motor and the crush of my boots as they dug into the grass.

The next blow hit me low and from the left.

I grunted and stumbled forward. As soon as I realized what had happened, I left my balance to my suit, trusting it to catch me as I focused all my attention on my side cameras, trying to catch some hint of what was attacking me. But I saw nothing. The air was completely empty. No matter what filter I tried, all I saw was the empty clearing, even as the thing lifted me up and hurled me at the trees.

Again, it was like getting picked up by something soft, and squishy, but enormously strong. In the second before it tossed me, I could actually feel the shape of it as it wrapped around my middle, two feet thick and articulated like a snake. It flung me so hard my teeth knocked, but not before I'd painted a target on the air where I'd just been. I fired without looking, and Sasha jerked in my hand, her barrel homing in on the spot I'd marked before firing a burst right into its center.

A screech stabbed through my mind as I crashed back-first into the forest, and my suit went dark. My cameras, my internal monitors, even my vitals all flickered out as I fell hard, hitting the ground without stabilizers for the first time in years. The crash knocked the wind out of me, but I barely felt it. All I could feel was the scream.

It wasn't even a sound. It was a feeling, an intense surge of pain, surprise, and fear that vibrated through my brain and gave me an instant splitting headache. For a moment I lay there in my dark suit, unable to move. I don't think I could have moved even if the Lady had been working. I was too busy gritting my teeth against that horrible sound that wasn't a sound. Slowly, the screech began to fade, and as it did, my suit came back online.

The ground filled my vision as my cameras flickered back to life. I was lying on my stomach, trapped beneath the half-broken trunk of the tree I'd crashed into. I pushed off the ground with enough force to break the rest of it, surging to my feet.

I'd landed ten yards out of the clearing, and though I still couldn't see anything, I could hear something moving. The underbrush rustled at the edge of the tree line closest to my position, and I felt the screech again, lower this time. Predatory. My screens went snowy as the sound increased, and I decided I'd had enough.

I reached up and thrust my visor open. My naked eyes saw even less than my cameras, but at least they stayed on when the thing roared. Thanks to my neural net, I could still see my suit's vital info off to the side, but my targeting system was useless.

I sighed and glanced down at my pistol. I'm a good shot, but running and gunning without my targeting system was suicidal. If I was going to be fighting with my own eyes, I needed a lower bar, so I shoved Sasha in her holster and grabbed Mia off my back. The plasma shotgun whined to life as I dialed up her charge, running sideways through the trees as I did.

The clearing still looked empty, but I could see something floating in the air just above where I'd hit the trees. I tried to zoom in out of habit before I remembered I was using my eyes and not my cameras. I squinted instead, then grinned as I realized that the something I was staring at was actually three bullets in a tight, familiar spread, floating in midair like they were lodged in something I couldn't see.

After that, the next step was easy. Dropping Mia to one hand, I reached over my shoulder and grabbed a grenade from my stash. Grenade in one hand and Mia in the other, I ran through the forest quiet as a silver ghost until I was directly across the clearing from where I'd seen the floating bullets. The thing must still have been poking at the trees where I'd landed, because I could see the tall trunks bending like something was pushing them aside.

It wasn't much of a target, but it was good enough. I crouched down, trusting my suit to shift the power even though I couldn't see the readings with my visor up. I couldn't see the ready light either, but the Lady and I knew each other well enough that signals were unnecessary. A second after I crouched, I shot into the air.

The Lady Gray launched up like a rocket, and suddenly I was flying high over the clearing. The thing must have heard me jump, because the trees stopped rustling. I could almost feel it looking up, but it was too late. Punching the grenade's manual trigger with my thumb, I wrenched back and threw it hard as I could at the ground where the trees had been bent back.

The grenade exploded with a deafening bang, and the thing screamed again, sending all my readings to static. This scream wasn't as loud as the first, though, and I knew the grenade hadn't hit, at least not directly. But it didn't matter. The explosion had done its work.

Down below, the clearing was filled with blown-up dirt and a haze of hot smoke that would cling to an enemy like paint and give me a solid target on my thermographics. Of course, without my cameras, I didn't have my thermographics at the moment, but what my eyes saw was almost as good. The smoke and dirt fell in a mist, settling on the invisible shape of something I'd never seen before.

It looked a little like a shrimp, only it was the size of a bus. A haze of tentacles rose from the underside of its body, the long, thick bludgeons that had slapped me around earlier. The thing seemed temporarily stunned by my grenade blast, but then the roar increased and the tentacles flew up into the air, casting off their fine coat of dust as they lunged for me.

I didn't give it the chance. I swung Mia down as I began to fall and fired three blasts as fast as I could pull the trigger. The first struck the thickest part of the thing's body, the next hit its tail, and the third struck its front, where, if it had been a shrimp, its head should have been. I had no idea if this thing even had a head, but since most of the alien critters I'd seen did, I took the chance.

If it had screamed earlier, that was nothing compared to what the thing did when Mia's plasma hit. The wail hit me so hard I nearly blacked out. My suit sputtered around me, and for a moment I was terrified it would go dark before I hit, and instead of landing and rolling, I'd splat on the ground. But the Lady held together, and we landed perfectly, rolling sideways as the thing's tentacles crashed down after me.

I fired another plasma shot as soon as I was up, aiming over my shoulder by pure habit even though I couldn't see a thing behind me with my cameras off. But with Mia, I didn't have to be a good shot. Her blast hit the tangle of tentacles racing for me, and I turned just in time to see the brilliant white plasma fire spider up the long, snakelike tendrils before they jerked away with a scream that made me go cross-eyed.

Using the fire as a guide, I launched three more shots at the thickest part of the tendril I'd spotted before it vanished. The first shot missed, but the next two hit, and I heard something clump to the ground as the creature's wailing ramped up again. Apparently, I'd shot off a tentacle.

But there was no time to celebrate. With my seventh shot, Mia's power was drained. I dropped her gently on the ground and threw out my arm to let Phoebe unfold into my hands.

It took three tries to get the automatic latches to pop. The creature's screaming was scrambling my systems, and my own thoughts weren't much better. The scream might have been more mental than sound, but it stabbed through my ears like a field knife, and

I had to focus hard to send commands that the Lady Gray could understand.

Eventually, it worked, and Phoebe swung down. The moment she hit my hands, her thermite edge flared bright as the sun. The light blinded me without my cameras to adjust the glare, but it also helped me focus. I gripped the blade's long handle and, one by one, turned off all my systems except for the most basic movement controls. The pain in my head dropped with each system I switched off, and by the time I was running on minimals, I felt almost normal.

The thing's shape was starting to fade as it threw off the dirt from the blast. But I knew it now, and I could still see well enough for my next strike. With a furious scream, I leaped into the air, kicking off the tentacle that launched up to grab me to launch myself onto the thing's back.

I landed with a thud and immediately started to slide. The creature was slick as half-set jelly. I scrambled for purchase, my boots digging into the soft, squishy flesh. For a few frantic moments I thought I was going to slide off entirely, but then my feet caught, and I brought my blade down.

Phoebe's burning edge cut through the thing like an acetylene torch through a spiderweb. I still couldn't see anything except the blade in front of me, but I could feel the creature's flesh curling away as I cut down and down and down until I couldn't reach any farther. The monster was screaming and thrashing now, and the bucking cost me my footing. But even as I slid down its side, I kept my blade lodged, opening what had to be an enormous gash as I fell.

I gasped in shock as the thing's blood began spraying over me. At least, I thought it was blood. I couldn't see the stuff at all. It, like everything else with this creature, was invisible. I could feel it, though, slimy and shockingly cold as it hit my bare face through my open visor.

By the time I hit the ground, I was drenched. The slime was so slick I couldn't stand. Every time I tried to get my feet under me, they slipped away again. Fortunately, the creature wasn't attacking me anymore. It thrashed madly, rolling away with a terrified squealing that turned my thoughts to mush and sent my suit dark twice. The second time I came back online, I jumped away, rolling through the stubby grass in an attempt to get the burning-cold invisible slime off me.

Phoebe's handle was dry where my gloves had been, but her blade was covered in it. The creature's blood smoked yellow white as the plasma burned, and the smell was toxic. Even so, I held the blade firm, not daring to let go for fear the creature's slippery blood would get under my gloves and I wouldn't be able to keep my grip.

Across the clearing, the creature was still thrashing. It had thrown off all the thermal smoke and dirt by this point, but now that I knew what I was looking for, I could see its shape where it crushed the weeds. Its screams had faded to whimpers, and my suit was back online and humming around me. Sensing this was as good a chance as I was likely to get, I gripped my blade tight and rushed forward.

The thing's blood must have been everywhere, because the clearing was slick as an ice rink, but the Lady Gray was pounding now, my boots slamming into the ground so hard and fast they never got the chance to slip. I hit the creature with all my momentum, driving my smoking blade into its flesh again and again. I had no idea what part I was hitting, but it didn't matter. Lost in battle lust as I was, I could have carved it to shavings. I swung and swung, screaming as I went until Phoebe's blade burned out at last and the creature lay still.

I stood panting for several seconds, and then I reeled back and kicked the invisible body as hard as I could. *"Ha!"* I screamed in King's Tongue. *"How do you like that, you overgrown slug?"*

I kicked it a few more times for good measure and then fell back to catch my breath. I was about to pull off my helmet to try to get the freezing slime off my face when I heard something rustle in the undergrowth.

I shot to my feet, brandishing my now useless and brittle thermite blade, but I saw nothing. I was about to dismiss the sound as nerves when a tentacle hit me in the face.

It didn't hit me nearly as hard as before, but the blow was still enough to knock me on my back. Worse still, with my visor open, I actually felt its slimy skin touch me, but the horrible, freezing cold feel of its invisible flesh was quickly replaced by the too familiar pain of getting socked in the eye.

The soft, squishy tentacle hurt a lot less than a bony fist, but as luck would have it, a piece of my grenade shrapnel had gotten lodged in the tentacle's tip. The blow slammed the metal shard against my face, missing my eye by a fraction of an inch to slice sideways along my cheekbone. My blood, burning hot after the freezing cold of the creature's, started pouring down my face and into my suit. But despite that and the pain of what was sure to be one hell of a shiner, my eye still worked, and I kept going without missing a beat.

I scrambled to my feet, blocking the next blow almost by accident on Phoebe's edge. But burned-out thermite is brittle as dead wood, and the blade snapped in two as the slimy thing flew past to hit me square upside the head. I caught the blow on my helmet instead of my face this time, but the hit was still enough to make me see double. Cursing, I shook my head to clear it as I dropped Phoebe and went for my last gun.

Sasha jumped into my hand as I flung up my arm, firing shot after shot into the tentacles I couldn't see but knew were there. I saw the bullets hit and stick as they would in a thick shield, but no shield was this strong. They were buried deep in the creature's invisible flesh, but the thing didn't even seem to feel pain now. It rose with a screeching roar that brought tears to my eyes, and I fell backward, emptying my clip as the tentacle plunged toward my head, ready to snap my neck through my armor. I could almost see it now, a faint shimmer against the gray clouds above me as it fell. And then, just before I died, I felt the most peculiar feeling I've ever experienced.

It was like someone stuck a hand inside me, grabbed hold of my spine, and jerked me away. I saw the ground crater as the tentacle crashed down, but I was no longer beneath it. Instead, I was flying backward, the hand on my spine dragging me through the air toward the clearing's edge. I could see the trees flying up around me, and I braced for another impact, but I never felt it. Just before I was sure I'd hit, something brushed across my mind, and I could have sworn I heard a soft voice whisper.

Sleep.

As the word formed, the world went black, and my mind folded over into a deep, peaceful sleep.

I woke up to Caldswell screaming in my face.

"What the hell were you thinking?" he shouted, smacking my helmet. "What part of 'stay with the ship' can't your Paradoxian brain handle?"

I blinked at him in surprise, and then everything came back in a rush. I shot to my feet, nearly knocking him over in the process, and staggered in a circle, hand going for Sasha, only to find my holster empty.

"Gun," I whispered. "Where's my gun?"

Caldswell gave me a funny look, and I realized I was still speaking King's Tongue.

"Where's my gun?" I said again, in Universal this time. "We

have to go. There was a…" I didn't even know how to describe what I'd fought. "A monster," I said at last.

Caldswell was still staring at me like my words made no sense, which they probably didn't, but I didn't care. All I knew was that this place was dangerous and I had to get us out. By this time my head was clear enough that I noticed Ren and Rupert standing a few feet away beside the skippers, mine and Caldswell's. Rupert was watching me like a hawk, his face drawn with worry. Ren was staring off into the distance, her short, dark hair twitching in the cool wind.

I turned back to the clearing, flicking my eyes over the blown-out ground and torn-up trees for any sign of movement. I saw nothing, of course, but that didn't mean anything.

"Get in the skippers and get in the air," I said, stumbling forward. "I have to find my guns."

"Devi." Rupert's voice was so gentle, I had to look back. He caught my eye and pointed at his feet, where my weapons were lying in a pile.

I didn't realize until I saw them how scared I'd been that I'd lost my girls for good. It took every ounce of dignity I had not to run forward and hug them to my chest. Instead, I marched over, picking up my guns and Phoebe's broken blade. I tucked each one in place, breaking off the last of the spent thermite before I folded Phoebe in thirds and stowed her away.

As I was packing my guns, I realized with a start that I was clean. I stopped, running my hands over my armor. It felt like it always did. The cold, invisible slime was gone. My face was clean as well. My eye was puffy and painful, but the blood, both mine and the creature's, had been wiped away. The Lady was still running on only the most basic systems, but none of my displays were flickering anymore, and my clock was ticking over like normal. I reached up hesitantly and flicked down my visor. My cameras came on smoothly, opening my vision so I could see the growing concern on Caldswell's face behind me.

I ignored him, running through my systems instead. I flipped everything on, off, and on again. When I was satisfied my suit was working, I pulled up my camera footage from the last thirty minutes. Or, rather, I tried to. When I reached for the records, all I got was static.

"What happened?" I asked, turning around.

"We were coming back from the meeting when we heard a plasma shotgun," Caldswell said. "You're the only person crazy enough to use one, so we ran over and found you lying here. You just woke up."

"And you didn't see anything?" I said before realizing how stupid that question was. "I mean, there wasn't anything here?"

Caldswell shrugged. "It was quiet as it is now." He squinted at me. "Have you been drinking, Morris?"

"*No!*" I shouted. "No sir," I amended at his hard look. "I am completely sober and I'll take any test you like to prove it. When you were late showing up, I told Cotter to lock down the ship while I went to find you. I know I was disobeying orders, but this planet is unstable and we couldn't get you on the com. Under the circumstances, I deemed that you, your ship, and your crew were in real and immediate danger, so I tracked your skipper here. When I arrived, I was attacked by an invisible creature approximately fifteen feet long with tentacles strong enough to throw me like a ball. I sliced it to pieces defending myself, but it wouldn't die. It attacked me again right before I blacked out."

While I was talking, Caldswell's expression changed from angry and confused to blatantly skeptical. "Tentacles, eh?" he said when I'd finished. "And how did you see all this if it was invisible?"

"I blasted it with dirt using a grenade," I said, working hard to keep my temper in check. "I can only guess it died while I was out. Its body should be around here somewhere, but it might be rotting quickly. The blood it got on me is already gone."

Caldswell stared at me a moment longer. "And you really think you fought an invisible monster?"

"I fought something, sir," I said hotly. "I don't go around in the woods wasting grenades, ammo, and a thermite blade just for kicks. And I sure as hell didn't punch myself in the *face*."

Caldswell's glare sharpened. "Easy, Morris."

I forced myself to relax. "Sorry, sir," I said with what I thought was some pretty impressive calm. "But I fought something."

"I believe you," Caldswell said. "Your guns were hot when we gathered them, I just don't know what from, and I'm not going to waste time finding out. We'll deal with your insubordination later. Right now, we're getting back to the ship." He glanced up. "Charkov?"

Rupert straightened. "Sir?"

Caldswell nodded at me. "I think Miss Morris is a little punch-drunk. Why don't you drive her back and I'll take Ren in my skipper."

"Yes, Captain," Rupert said. Caldswell turned away, touching Ren's shoulder as he led her to the skippers. Meanwhile, Rupert walked over to me and gently took my arm. "You ready to go, Devi?"

I yanked my arm out of his grasp and walked past him without a word, jumping into the skipper and slamming the door behind me. He got into the pilot's side a moment later, and the clearing was filled with the roar of thrusters as the two skippers hopped into the air.

Whatever was wrong with the coms must have been clearing up, because Rupert called Basil no problem. I couldn't make out Basil's side of the conversation, but I could hear the relief in his reply when Rupert told him we were coming back. Rupert turned off the com after that, and we flew in silence for several minutes.

I spent the time sorting through the Lady's backup, trying in vain to find any footage at all from my fight. But just like my first try, I got nothing but static. Whatever the creature had done to my cameras must have fried my records, too. After the third try I tore off my helmet with a growl, slamming it onto the bench seat between Rupert and me. He glanced over, but I looked away, tearing my sweat-damp hair out of its ponytail and letting it hang around me as I leaned forward and gently banged my head down on the dash.

"Devi," Rupert began.

"Don't," I snapped, tilting my head so I could glare at him. "I fought something in that clearing, Rupert. Something that threw me around like a rag doll. Something I couldn't see even when it was bleeding all over me and couldn't kill no matter how much I sliced it. Mycant was terraformed. Terraformed planets don't even have large animals unless someone brings them in, and I've never even heard of anything like that giant invisible whatever-it-was."

Rupert sighed. "I don't think—"

"I fought it," I said again, my voice shaking. "I'm not making this up!"

"I know you're not." He reached over, gently brushing my hair out of my face. "I believe you, Devi."

Foolish as it was, I leaned into his touch. I hadn't realized how scared I'd been that no one would take me seriously until Rupert said he did.

"And I'm sure the captain believes you, too," he said, dropping his hand quickly. "He's just angry because you disobeyed orders."

"Part of being a soldier is knowing what orders to disobey," I said. "I did what I thought I had to do to keep you all safe. And if Caldswell wants to punish me for that, he can go ahead." I just hoped he didn't kick me off the ship.

As though he'd read my mind, Rupert shook his head. "He'll punish you, but he won't fire you." His eyes were on the sky in front of us, but his sudden smile was just for me. "You're the best merc he's had in a long time. You'd have to do something really terrible before he'd let you go now."

"Don't tell me that," I warned, sitting up. "I might push just to see how much he'll put up with."

"I believe you would," he said, smiling wide.

I grinned back, or I tried to. Smiling hurt like a bitch, actually, and moving my cheeks caused the cut under my eye to start bleeding again. I reached up to wipe the blood away with my glove, but Rupert's hand stopped me.

"Wait," he said, catching my wrist. When my hand stopped, he released me and reached under the dash to pull out a battered first aid kit. He flipped the latch expertly with one hand and grabbed a gauze square from the pile, handing it to me.

"Thank you," I said, taking the gauze from him and pressing it against the cut. The contact stung like hell, and I hissed involuntarily.

Rupert gave me a worried look.

"Don't look like that," I said, wincing as I patted the cut dry. "It's my own fault for raising my visor in a fight. Don't know what else I could have done, though. That thing did something that messed my suit all to hell and scrambled my cameras. I don't even have my recordings."

"That's too bad," Rupert said. "I bet it was something to see."

"It was," I assured him. "Big slug didn't have a chance. Maybe next time my camera will actually work and then I can play the whole thing for you in the lounge like Cotter with one of his gladiator matches. Of course, it might not look so impressive since all you'd see would be me flipping around shooting and slicing up thin air."

Rupert chuckled. "I think that would still be pretty impressive," he said, laying his arm across the back of the seat. His hand ended up just a few inches from my head, his fingers barely brushing the tips of my hair. "But then, impressive seems to be what you do, Devi."

The compliment filled me with pride, but it was the way he said my name that made me squirm. He was smiling as he flew, and the expression lit up his face. It was always surprising to see Rupert smile for real. He was nice to the crew, but he didn't really smile for them. Not like he did for me, anyway. The sudden rush of warmth I felt at that realization was way more than I could handle at the moment, so I turned to the window to stare down at the much less attractive but far safer scenery as we flew over Mycant's wooded hills back to the ship.

CHAPTER
8

Caldswell and Ren's newer skipper beat us by a good ten minutes, and I was relieved to see Mabel was back as well. The ride hadn't improved Caldswell's temper, though. He handed Ren off to Rupert and then stood around glaring at me while I stowed both skippers back in their berths. When I was finished, he casually informed me that, as punishment for disobeying orders, I had the choice of a month's docked pay or forty hours extra cleaning duty.

I had gun upgrades to finish, so I chose the cleaning. That suited Caldswell just fine, and we marched into the ship. He didn't mention the clearing again. Neither did I, but I didn't forget it for a second, either.

We were cleared for liftoff soon as Mabel okayed the repairs. She checked them first thing, which was the least she could do considering how she'd abandoned us. I was all prepared to be mad at her over that for a good while, com trouble or no, but to my surprise she sought me out before we were even off the ground, coming into the cargo bay while Cotter and I were lashing down for liftoff.

"Thanks a bundle for stepping up, Morris," she said with a sincere smile. "I never would have left if I'd thought the contractor would have problems with something as simple as a hull patch and door replacement, or if I'd realized the coms weren't working. I didn't even notice my handset was out until I tried to call Brian to tell him I'd be late."

"Must have been some visit," I said, though less sarcastically than I'd intended.

Mabel just grinned. "You know how it is when two tinkerers get together. Max and I spent the whole time in his warehouse trying to get his old Republic Wasp Fighter working. We didn't even notice the quakes until one knocked a wrench on my head."

I had to laugh at that image, and Mabel laughed with me. "Really, though, thanks a ton," she said. "I told Rupert to put your next bottle of whiskey on me."

That brightened me up considerably. "Thanks!"

Mabel grinned at me and jogged off toward the engine room, scooping up Pickers as she went. I watched her go with the distinct feeling that I'd just been bribed, but I didn't waste time worrying about that. If Mabel and I were straight, then that was good enough for me. I had bigger targets to shoot.

Once we were safely back in space, Cotter and I divided our shifts to match the new day schedule. Cotter's came up first, so I left him to his work and went to my cabin. I had only four hours before I went on duty, but though I was exhausted from days of anxiety and the fight with the monster in the clearing, sleep was the last thing on my mind. I stripped out of my suit but kept my helmet and chest piece on. Then, sitting on my bunk, I pulled up my footage from the clearing, both the recordings from my cameras and the backup from my Final Word Lock, and started going over them frame by frame.

It was a short, frustrating process. My cameras were fine right up until a few moments after I'd set the skipper down in the clearing, and then everything went to static. After that, the next clear image I had was Caldswell leaning over me.

That was it. Between those two points I had nothing but a wall of fuzzy white noise. I went through it all again, hoping to at least cal-culate how long I'd been out, but with my clock stopped, the video's time stamp was worthless. In the end, I did it manually, playing the whole thing in my helmet while I timed the static against my handset's clock.

What I found made no sense at all. There was less than ten minutes of recorded static between where my cameras cut out and Caldswell's waking me up. That was barely long enough to account for the fight, much less however much time I'd spent knocked out. I put down my handset and skipped the video back to the beginning.

As I watched myself hop out of the skipper yet again, my heart began to pound. Now that I thought about it, that part made no sense either. All my assumptions up to this point stemmed from the idea that the creature's screams had scrambled my recording. Considering how many times the thing had blacked out my suit, it just seemed obvious that was what it had to be. Now, though, I was starting to doubt. After all, if the scream was responsible for destroying my recordings, then my cameras should have gone out *after* I shot the creature, not when I'd landed.

Maybe just being near the thing was enough to fry my feed? But I had the footage of my landing just fine. If proximity to the crea-ture was what caused the problem, then it seemed to me that my video should have faded out as I'd gotten closer, not just cut off like it did. And none of this explained why I only had ten measly min-utes of ruined footage to cover what was probably closer to an hour of lost time.

I paused my video feed, staring at the frozen wall of static. I didn't like where this was going. The more I thought about it, the more I felt that it wasn't the creature who'd messed up my footage, at least not entirely. And now that I'd opened that can of worms, there were the other mysteries to consider.

Taking a deep breath, I shut my eyes against the static and

thought back to how the fight had ended. Or, rather, I tried to. I remembered getting punched just fine, and I remembered empty-ing Sasha's clip as the tentacle came down to crunch me. After that, though, things got fuzzy.

I knew something else had happened, something...strange, but I couldn't make my brain pull it up. It was like the memory was floating just on the edge of my consciousness, but every time I reached out, it flitted away. It seemed to want to be forgotten. Grit-ting my teeth, I tried harder, forcing myself to go over every detail I could recall.

It wasn't much. I vaguely remembered being pulled away, though how and by what I had no idea. And though I'd woken up by the skippers, I was almost certain I'd been in the forest when I'd blacked out. I couldn't put my finger on how I knew that, though, and just thinking about it was giving me a pounding headache.

I rubbed my temples and moved on to other worries. The crea-ture had been huge, but I hadn't found so much as a stray tentacle when I'd quickly searched the clearing. Unless the invisible thing melted like snow when it died, that meant someone had disposed of its body. Someone had certainly cleaned mine. If I believed that, then was it such a stretch to believe that perhaps my dim memories were correct, and someone had pulled me to safety in the woods? Perhaps the same someone who had cleaned the slime and blood off my armor. And to clean me, this mysterious savior would have had to remove my helmet, which meant they would have access to my computer, and my footage...

My heart began to pound. My suit hadn't been locked, so it wouldn't have been too hard to get my helmet off, but erasing my footage was another thing altogether. A little hacking would have taken care of my main cameras, but my Final Word Lock footage was sacred.

All Paradoxian suits come with an FWL by Royal Law. The

lock and all the information inside it was protected by several levels of the king's own security. I could look at my FWL all I liked, but I couldn't erase or change anything it recorded. No one could except crown-appointed judges, high-ranking generals, and members of the royal family. The idea that some random stranger on Mycant could somehow tamper with my FWL was absurd. Almost as absurd as being rescued from an invisible, unkillable monster whose roar blacked out my suit.

I opened my eyes again with a deep breath. I *really* didn't like where this was going. As the pile of things that didn't add up got larger and larger, I realized that the question now wasn't *if* something had happened while I was out, but *what*, and how badly did I want the truth?

Pretty badly, came the answer. Messing with me was one thing, but messing with my suit was something else altogether. If I'd been hacked, bugged, or compromised in some way by persons or creatures unknown, I could be putting the whole crew in danger. I had to know, which meant it was time to break a few rules.

Pulling off my helmet, I stood up and hit the cabin's door lock, arming it to the highest privacy setting so even Nova would have to knock. I was pretty sure there were no cameras in our room, but I turned all the lights to black, just in case. It made getting around hard, but bruised shins were a small price to pay to keep someone from seeing what I was about to do.

I made it to my armor case with minimal stumbling and put away my helmet by touch. Once I was sure it was locked and deactivated, all cameras off, I took off the Lady's chest piece. If I hadn't been so familiar with every inch of my suit, this next bit would have been tricky. I sat on the floor and placed the back half of the Lady's chest piece in my lap. Finding her spine with my fingers, I ran my hand down to the small plate that covered the small of my back, just above the knot of the FWL. Curling my pinky finger under the plate's lip, I squeezed into the gap and felt around until something stabbed my finger.

Even expecting it, the pain still made me jump. I snatched my finger back and sucked at the tiny bead of blood welling on its surface while I waited for the biolock to verify my DNA. I didn't have to wait long. A second later, the small plate popped open with a click, and a black silicone chip no bigger than my thumbnail slid out.

Gentle as a surgeon, I pinched the chip between my fingers and pulled it free. I couldn't see it in the dark, but I knew it was glossy as black water. It certainly felt slick against my skin, slick and ice-cold, but then, the Mercenary's Bargain was an icy sort of deal.

The point of the FWL was to record your final moments so your officers could see how you died, but that wasn't always how it worked. Sometimes, soldiers died in a way that made their officers look bad, especially in a mercenary company like the Blackbirds whose operations weren't always on the sunny side of interstellar law. When that happened, FWL footage tended to get "accidentally" erased. That was fine if you were dead, but if you were unlucky enough to actually survive the kind of incident that required the loss of your FWL, then you needed some serious leverage to keep yourself from getting erased as well. That was where the Mercenary's Bargain came in.

It went like this: the Mercenary's Bargain was an aftermarket armor modification that recorded the video track that fed into a suit's FWL onto a second backup completely separate from the suit's main computer. Even if the FWL was physically removed, the Bargain would stay in place, preserving the truth of what had actually happened just in case you needed it. This way, even if your FWL footage was destroyed, you always had your own copy.

The Bargain was a merc's final line of defense against anyone who wanted to screw us over, and, obviously, it was about as illegal as you could get. Footage recorded by the FWL was considered sacred under Paradoxian law, as good as the king's own witness. By creating a second Final Word, the Bargain undermined the FWL's absolute authority, and the king did not tolerate anything that undermined his authority. Admitting you had a Bargain going, even as a private mercenary, was as good as putting your neck in the noose, though I'd always thought I'd count it as worth my life. After all, if things got bad enough that I'd actually have to use my secret footage, I was probably dead anyway, and I saw no point in not taking the bastards down with me.

Fortunately, things weren't that bad yet, but thanks to my mercenary's paranoia I had a resource no one expected. If the static on my records really was from the monster, then the footage recorded by my Bargain would be just as snowy and short as my FWL's. But if my mysterious rescuer *had* somehow erased my FWL, the Bargain would show the truth, which was exactly why I'd risked the king's wrath to install it in the first place.

I took out my handset and flipped it open, using the glowing screen as a flashlight as I made my way back to the bed while balancing the Bargain delicately on the palm of my free hand. I sat down on my mattress and scooted into the corner until my back was against two walls. Only then did I flip my handset over and open the side, sliding the tiny black chip into the handset's feed port.

The screen went black as soon as the chip was in, and then a password request popped up. I keyed in the sequence, speaking a completely different code out loud at the same time. My handset screen flickered as the Bargain chip's double security unlocked, and I hunched over, curling myself into a ball around the screen to watch the truth come out.

In the years I've had it, I'd never actually had to use my Bargain other than my annual check to make sure it still worked. Its interface was minimal, and it took me a bit of fiddling to find the footage I was looking for, especially since I had to use my fingers instead of just scanning through clips with my mind via my neural net. Fortunately, Mycant hadn't happened too long ago, and I found the spot quickly, starting the footage at the point where I landed the skipper, fifteen seconds before my FWL's feed cut off.

The Bargain's video quality wasn't quite as good as my FWL. There was no sound either, a sacrifice to the size of the chip, but I could clearly see my main camera and my primary display just as they'd been at the time. Silently, the footage rolled on as I watched myself hop out of the skipper and take the step that, every other time, had ended in static. But there was no static now, and I barely dared to breathe as the Devi in the footage moved out to start scouting the clearing.

After that, everything happened just as I remembered. The feed cut out in several places from all the times my suit had blacked out, but the footage never went to static as it had on my FWL. I saw everything, lines and all, right up to the bitter end when I'd sat defeated, waiting for the tentacle to come down. And then, just like in my fuzzy memories, the camera spun wildly as my body was flung backward.

By this point I was hunched over so far that my nose was nearly touching my handset's screen. The trees raced by as my body flew into the forest, and I held my breath, waiting for the crash. But it never came.

Quickly as I'd been thrown, my body stopped. Up in the right corner of the screen, I saw my vital signs go from jagged panic to calm sleep like someone had switched me off. For one long second, I hung there like a puppet, floating impossibly in midair with my camera running while my body slept soundly inside my suit. It was so unbelievable, I was about to go back and watch that part again when the screen spun like I was doing a pirouette, and two figures whirled my camera's vision.

Considering everything that had happened today, I'd thought I was past the point of being surprised, but what I saw on the tiny screen of my handset stopped me cold. Ren was standing between the spindly trees. Her dark eyes were spacey and unfocused as ever, but her arm was thrust out in front of her with her hand balled into a fist like she was holding something very tightly. Weird as it was to see Ren, though, she was nothing compared to the thing that stood behind her.

"Thing" was the only word for it. The creature behind Ren was a good two feet taller than she was and covered head to toe in black. I couldn't see what the covering was exactly through the white lines that were still falling over the camera like streamers, but I could tell it was glossy and segmented, almost like scales.

The tall body had a humanoid shape with a long torso, arms, legs, and a head all in human proportion. After that, though, the similarities stopped. It had no hair or flesh, nothing but the scales. Its head was ridged along the temples, the scales rising in sharp, aggressive lines. It had ridges on its elbows, knees, and shoulders as well, all of which looked functional as fighting spikes. Its hands and feet had long black claws sharper than a xith'cal's, and its face was a flat mask with two glittering black eyes, a protrusion in the vague shape of a nose, and no mouth at all.

The alien reached up to lay its clawed hand on Ren's shoulder, and even though I'd seen the girl not an hour ago, I sucked in my breath. But the claws didn't slice into her as it seemed they should, only squeezed her softly. This must have been a signal, because Ren uncurled her fist immediately. The moment her palm was open, the camera swirled wildly as my unconscious body fell face-first on the ground at her feet.

Dirt was all I saw for about five minutes. The white lines that had been falling over my cameras constantly since just before the creature had first punched me disappeared around minute three, and then the world came back as someone rolled me over. The flat wall of Mycant's cloudy sky filled my screen, edged with treetops, and then the trees began to move as someone started to drag my body backward.

If I'd had my actual six-camera feed, I could have easily seen who or what was dragging me, as well as where they were dragging me to, but the FWL, and thus the Bargain, only recorded my forward camera, so I could do nothing but sit and watch the trees slide by until, at last, they vanished, leaving only open sky.

The clearing, I realized. This was where the alien had dragged me back to the clearing. We kept going for several more feet, and then the movement stopped as it let me go. My head must have fallen to the side when it released me, because suddenly the camera was looking sideways out over the scrubby grass of the clearing. I was beside the skippers, right where I'd woken up. Across the field, I saw Ren again. She was standing in the crater of my grenade blast where I'd fought the invisible creature, and someone was kneeling down beside her.

The video quality was so bad I almost thought it was the black alien from before, but when the figure straightened up, I saw it was Caldswell. The captain turned and yelled something over his shoulder. There was no sound, but I didn't need any now. I knew who I'd see next.

A second later, a familiar pair of dress shoes stepped into the shot, and then Rupert knelt down in front of me. His face was detached and cold as he reached down and turned my helmet slightly so that I was looking directly at him. He yelled something back to the captain, but his eyes never left me.

With Rupert in the way, I couldn't see what the captain was doing, but I could see Ren clearly. She was looking up at her father like she was listening. After about a minute, she turned and held out her hand with her fingers up and palm flat, almost like she was pressing it against something I couldn't see.

The creature. I realized the truth with a shock as cold as the monster's icy blood. Ren was *touching* the invisible creature's body.

I was still coming to terms with that when a flash of light whited out the screen. It was so sudden I jumped, nearly slamming my head into Nova's bunk. When the white didn't go away at once, I started to worry that the Bargain's feed was ruined, but eventually the glare faded, and I saw Caldswell turning Ren away. I wanted to see more, but at that point something wiped over my camera.

It happened a few more times before I realized what was going on. Rupert was wiping down my helmet with one of the shop cloths from the skipper. He cleaned the creature's blood off my armor, and then the camera lurched as he pulled off my helmet and set it aside.

On a cheap suit, removing the helmet would have killed the camera feed, but my Lady is well made, and her camera kept running. As a result, I found myself looking at my own body as Rupert wiped down my face with a gauze pad from the same damn first aid box he'd used on me when we'd flown back.

His movements were quick and efficient as he wiped the blood, mine and the creature's, from my skin. His face was blank as he worked, but there was something gentle in the way his hands brushed my forehead or cupped my cheek to push my head aside so he could clean my neck. He paused when he reached my wounded eye, and then, very, very carefully, he started cleaning the cut.

Behind him, I caught glimpses of Caldswell walking around the clearing, stopping occasionally to reach down and grab something. Ren followed him like a puppy, eyes wide and vacant as she strolled through the grass in his wake. When they passed out of the shot, I returned to watching the only thing left, Rupert.

He was worth watching. When I'd first seen him on the camera, he'd looked cold and collected, the man from the bridge. But while he'd been cleaning my cut, his expression had changed. His brows had dropped into a scowl, his mouth pressed into a thin line that was at odds with the gentleness of his hands as he worked. If I hadn't known better, I'd have said he looked almost possessive as he hunched over my prone body, his long fingers lingering on my face even after he'd wiped the last of the blood away.

Finally, he let me go and leaned back on his heels, looking me over like he was checking to make sure he'd gotten everything, and then his cold detachment was back as he balled up the bloody gauze and shoved it in his pocket. He'd just put my helmet back on my head when Caldswell came up and dropped my guns and thermite blade on the ground beside the skipper.

I winced when they hit. Didn't that idiot captain know how expensive my babies were? Caldswell stepped over my weapons as Rupert stood up, and they talked for a while. Or I guessed that was what they did. I couldn't hear what they were saying, and from the way my head was lying I couldn't see anything but their feet.

Finally, they broke apart, and Caldswell came to stand over me. The camera spun as he turned my head so that I was facing him, and then he took something out of his pocket. It was a flat square of folded leather, almost like a wallet. When he flipped it open, I saw it was a scan code badge, a palm-sized metal plate carved with blocks and bars meant to convey information to computers through cameras. My officers had used them to identify themselves to other units in the army, flashing their code at any camera for instant access. But the crest above the metal etched code block wasn't the usual officer's mark, or even some Terran nonsense. It was the royal seal of Paradox, and the moment my camera recognized it, my feed cut out.

I stopped the footage and skipped back, pausing a second after Caldswell flicked open his code badge. I hadn't been seeing things. The royal seal stood in proud relief above the scan code. It was the same seal that appeared on Devastators' armor, the mark of the king's trust. I was so busy staring at it, I almost missed the other crest beside it.

Next to the king's seal was a mark I didn't recognize, a black four-pointed star with a large stylized white eye at the center. Other than those two marks and the etched blocks and bars of the metal scan code below, there was nothing. No text, no name, no identifying number, nothing.

I restarted the video with trembling fingers. The interruption lasted only a second, but there must have been some time lost, because when my camera came back on, Caldswell was fitting my helmet back onto my head. Off to the right, I could see my clock had been reset during the gap. My vitals and my ammo counters were back to baseline as well, just as they'd been when I'd woken.

Once my helmet was back in place, Caldswell looked at me a moment, tugging his shirt collar into place like he was using my raised visor as a mirror. When he finished, he took a deep breath and said something that looked like *Ready?* Rupert must have said yes, because a second later Caldswell's whole face changed, contorting into rage. On the side of my camera feed, I saw my vitals spike as I woke up in a panic.

Hands shaking, I paused the recording on the image of Caldswell's angry face. I placed the handset gently on my knee and put my head in my hands. Closing my eyes, I took five deep breaths, and then, when I was as calm as I could expect to be, I set myself to the seemingly impossible task of figuring out what the hell I was going to do.

Three hours later, I'd watched the Bargain's recording a dozen more times, and I'd boiled things down to six absolute certainties:

1. The unkillable invisible monster had not been a figment of my imagination (I'd never believed otherwise, but it was nice to have proof).
2. Ren and the unknown black alien had saved me from the unkillable invisible monster.
3. Ren had something that could actually kill the unkillable invisible monster, unlike my bullets, plasma, or thermite blade.
4. Caldswell had a badge with the king's royal seal that could shut down my suit on sight.
5. Ren, Caldswell, and Rupert were part of a larger operation that went all the way to the very top levels of the Paradoxian government.
6. I was not supposed to know any of this.

I pried my fingers off my handset and leaned back, closing my eyes to think this through. It was clear from the way I'd seen Caldswell putting my helmet back on me that he'd meddled with my suit during the blackout, just as it was clear he'd lied to me when I woke up. But though I'd seen the truth of what had really happened in that clearing with my own eyes, I still didn't understand a bit of it, and I sure as hell didn't know what to *do*.

I knew what I wanted to do, of course. Mercs, the ones who survive their first year anyway, are creatures of instinct. Mine have always been good, and right now they didn't care about understanding. Right now, my gut impulse was to run. I didn't know what that black alien with Ren was, or why it seemed to be working with Caldswell, or where it had gone after saving me. I didn't know what kind of powers Ren had or if she was really Caldswell's daughter either. The only thing I did know was that what had happened in that clearing was *big*. Really big, the tip of an iceberg that could grind a disposable hired gun like myself into pulp if I let it.

The instinct to escape was so strong I actually had to ball my fists to not start packing. Looking back, I should have rolled with it. Every time I've ignored my instincts, I've regretted it. But loud as my need to run was at that moment, my ambition was yelling even louder.

Despite my confusion on pretty much everything else, one fact from this whole shitstorm had come through perfectly clear: Caldswell wasn't a trader. He wasn't a smuggler, either. I didn't know what he was, but the king's seal he'd flashed proved for sure that he was big. I'd never seen one in action before, but after watching my footage a few more times, I was now sure that the badge he'd used to shut down my suit was a Royal Warrant.

Though usually only given out to the most loyal and worthy of the king's servants like royal knights and Devastators, Royal Warrants could technically be given to anyone, even a Terran like Caldswell if the king thought he should have one. A Warrant gave the bearer the power to act in the king's name. On Paradox, a Royal Warrant would get you anything you wanted without question, and even in Terran space it was pretty much a free pass. I knew from Anthony that Warrants were carefully monitored. They weren't the sort of thing you could steal or fake, not without having a crash team of Devastators coming after you, anyway.

I stretched out my legs on my bunk and stared into the dark, thinking about how Rupert had told me right here a few days ago that it was an honor to serve under the captain. Now that I knew that Caldswell had a Royal Warrant, I was starting to believe it. But even as I tried to guess how in the universe a Terran captain had come into possession of the highest sign of the king's trust, a new realization was elbowing its way past my misgivings.

If Caldswell had a Warrant, then he was big. *Really* big. Big enough that he hadn't been exaggerating back in the infirmary when he'd said he could get me into the Devastators. Hell, if he was big enough to have a Royal Warrant, he could probably get me an audience with the king himself.

My whole body began to tingle with anticipation. My gut impulse to run was still strong, but ignoring it was getting easier and easier. After all, the whole reason I'd taken this job was to kick my career into high gear. Was I really going to chicken out and let a chance like this slip by?

With that thought, my disordered brain fell into place. A few moments ago, the question of what I was going to do with all these mysteries had felt overwhelming. Now, I realized the whole mess came down to a simple choice: did I listen to my instincts and run, or did I take a chance, see it through, and maybe end up a Devastator even sooner than I'd hoped? Did I pick safety or ambition? The slow and steady or the gamble?

I smiled. Put like that, it wasn't even a question. It was the same choice I'd made when I'd decided to take Anthony's tip and apply to Caldswell in the first place. Now as then, there was no doubt what path I'd pick. No one got to be a Devastator by taking the safe road.

My decision settled like a joint popping back into place, and I immediately felt better. I was back on target, back in the fight, and while curiosity over what I'd seen was still gnawing at my insides, I was more determined than ever that I would not screw this up. The blessed king had dropped a priceless opportunity in my lap, and I absolutely was not going to let it go to waste.

Riding my new burst of determination, I removed the Bargain chip from my handset and slipped it back into its dock in my armor's spine. I would have made a backup, but I didn't want to risk Caldswell discovering I knew more than I should. My Bargain would keep the truth in case I needed it, just like it was made to. Meanwhile, I would act like nothing had changed. I'd keep everything to myself and proceed exactly as I had before with no one the wiser.

Stupid as it was considering the risk I was throwing myself into, I was actually kind of excited. Working for a mysterious and powerful man under the auspices of the king sounded a lot more promising than being a ship guard for a cursed trader captain. And who knew? Maybe if I served Caldswell well enough, he'd bring me into whatever he was doing, and that would look *really* good on my Devastator recommendation.

No matter what, though, I could never let Caldswell or Rupert discover I'd found out their secret before they were ready to share it. Stepping lightly wasn't usually my strong suit, but I was pretty sure I could manage it this time. After all, they had no clue I knew what I knew. All I had to do was keep my curiosity from getting the better of me and it was going to be smooth sailing. Well, I thought, gingerly pressing my darkening black eye, as smooth as my sailing ever got.

Of course, just because I was going to be playing dumb didn't mean I actually had to *be* dumb. I wasn't about to do anything really obvious like question Caldswell, but I could do a little poking around using the resources available. Fortunately, I had a pretty good idea where to start, and since it was almost time for my shift anyway, I put on my suit and headed down the hall in search of Hyrek.

The xith'cal was where he always seemed to be, in his room. He screeched softly when I knocked, but the door unlocked a few seconds later without fuss, so it must have been the good kind of screech. I'd never actually been in his room before. Considering what he was, I'd half expected it to be the blood-splattered mess the xith'cal I'd fought had seemed to thrive in. Instead, Hyrek's cabin was almost homey.

It was a double bunk like the one Nova and I shared, but Hyrek had it to himself. He'd removed the beds and replaced them with an armchair large enough for a xith'cal. There was a large potted plant in the corner behind him, a lamp and a small chest with a thin rack for data sticks set on top, but that was it for furniture. Not that he could have fit anything else with the enormous chair taking up most of the room. I didn't even know how he'd gotten it through the door, but he was lounging quite comfortably when I came in, reading on his ledger. He put it down when he saw me and pulled his handset out of the front pocket of the large, formless scrubs he always wore, tapping the screen rapidly before holding it out to me.

Come to gawk at the civilized lizard?

"Might as well, so long as I'm here," I said, not bothering to lie since he was right, I had been gawking. "Where do you sleep, anyway? Do you just live in that chair?"

I sleep standing up, he typed. *That way I can get the drop on anyone who tries to come in without my knowledge. The chair is just a luxury for when I'm awake.*

He flashed a toothy grin at my shocked expression and nodded to my left. I looked over. Sure enough, there was a blanket bolted to the wall just beside the door. "Are you afraid someone's going to come for you while you sleep?"

Hyrek shrugged. *Old habits die hard.*

I nodded and made a note to ask Hyrek about his life before the ship someday when I was feeling brave enough to push a carnivorous lizard. "Listen," I said. "I need to look up some information about wildlife on Mycant. Do you have anything like that in your fantastically impressive collection?"

Hyrek arched an eye ridge at my comment, but then he leaned over, examining the data sticks on his rack with care. He grabbed one a few seconds later and held it out to me. I took it, turning it over to look for a label, but there was nothing except for a few marks in the xith'cal's chicken scratch across its front.

"Can I even read this?" I said.

I have every reason to believe you are literate, Hyrek typed back. *That's a collection of the official Republic Fauna Surveys from the last ten years as well as the Republic Exploratory Council's Census of Known Nonhuman Life.*

"And you think Mycant will be in here?" I asked, holding the delicate stick gently between my fingers.

If it's anywhere, Hyrek typed. *Unlike the Paradoxians, who never met a planet they couldn't terraform with bots before they'd even looked at it, the Terran Republic is usually very good about cataloging the native life on their colonies before they stamp it all out and repopulate with more human-friendly species.*

That insult wasn't even worth a comeback, so I just smiled. "Thanks, Hyrek. I'll get this back to you soon."

Take your time, he typed with a grin. *I completely understand if it takes you a little while to read something that doesn't have to do with killing or armor.*

I rolled my eyes as the xith'cal's unnerving teeth-on-metal laughter filled the room, but as I turned to leave, Hyrek made a trilling sound, and I glanced over my shoulder to see him holding his handset high.

You should put some ice on that eye.

"Thanks for the timely advice, Doc," I said, letting Hyrek's door slide closed behind me just in time to cut off another metallic snicker.

CHAPTER
9

Thanks to the planet layover, my shift switch was later than usual. We were already an hour into the *Fool*'s night cycle by the time I took over from Cotter, and most everyone was either already in bed or headed there. I lifted my visor to say good night to Nova when I saw her coming from the bridge, but rather than her usual cheerful reply, she stopped cold, hands going to her mouth.

"Deviana!" she cried. "Your eye!"

I winced, and then I had to stop myself from wincing again at the pain from the first one. I'd forgotten Nova had been on the bridge when we'd gotten back, which meant this was her first glimpse of my face. Must have been quite the sight, judging from her reaction.

"What happened?" she said, running up to me.

For a second I debated telling her. Not about Caldswell, of course, but about the invisible whatever. But even that suddenly felt like too much, especially since I liked Nova. She was one of the rarest things in the universe, a genuinely nice person, and I didn't want to tell her anything that could be dangerous for her to know.

"My own recklessness," I answered at last, which wasn't exactly a lie. "Took a spill when I was looking for the captain. But don't worry, it's nothing."

"It looks awful," Nova said, her pale face stricken. "Have you seen the doctor?"

"Yes." Again, not a lie. "But I'm fine, really."

Nova's worried look didn't ease up, but she eventually relented, though not before promising that she'd do some meditation therapy with me tomorrow to awaken my universal connection and speed my body toward wholeness. I had no idea what that meant, but I could listen to some weird space music with her for a while if it made her happy. Truth be told, my eye did hurt. I'd had far worse, of course, but unlike the leg I'd whacked on Rupert, I couldn't use my suit to take the strain off my face.

I put up with the ache for two hours before I decided I was being stupid and went to the kitchen for some ice. It was well into night cycle and the lounge was dark, but the runner lights on the walls were bright enough that I didn't need to switch on my suit's night vision. I took off my helmet and set it on the counter before going over to the freezer. I propped the door with my foot, using the extra light from inside to search the drawers for something to put the ice in so I wouldn't drip everywhere. I was still searching when I felt someone standing behind me.

My gun was in my hand before I could think. I whirled around, Sasha raised and ready, and found myself facing Rupert. He held his hands up, and I blew out a frustrated breath.

"Don't *do* that," I snapped, holstering my gun. "I'm going to shoot you one of these days."

"I thought you already did," Rupert said, lips quirking.

"*Without* a shield," I growled. I hate people sneaking up on me, especially in an utterly silent room where I really should have heard them coming. Rupert always seemed to move like a ghost, though, so I shouldn't have been surprised.

"What are you doing?" Rupert asked, putting his arms down.

"Getting some ice for my lovely new eye patch," I replied, pointing at my shiner. "What are you doing?"

"We have an alarm on both freezers and the fridge," Rupert said. "I was up anyway, so I decided to come check."

Elegant lady that I am, I snorted. "You wired your fridge?"

Rupert shrugged. "Can't have food going missing in deep space. And now that Cotter knows where I keep the beer, I've had to chase him out a few times."

The idea of Rupert running big, mean Cotter out of the kitchen was just too much. I burst out laughing, which was a really stupid thing to do with an injured face.

"Ow ow ow ow," I groaned, pressing my fingers into my cheek.

Rupert took my shoulders and gently pushed me out of the way. He grabbed a plastic bag from a cabinet I'd never have thought to check, filled it halfway with ice, and wrapped it in a clean towel. I put out my hand, expecting him to give it to me, but he didn't. Instead, he stepped closer and gently touched my chin, turning my head so he could see my injured eye in the dim light.

For a split second, his smile faded, and I caught a glimpse of the anger I'd seen on the video when he'd cleaned my cut. But even as I saw it, the look vanished as Rupert pressed the ice pack gently against my eye. The cold was an enormous relief, and I leaned back, letting my armor hold me up as the pain slowly drained away.

"How do we keep ending up like this?" I sighed.

"You keep getting hurt," Rupert said.

"I'm surprised you haven't started carrying an ice pack in your pocket by this point."

Rupert smiled, but he didn't answer. He didn't say anything for a while, and eventually I let my eyes flutter closed, giving myself over to the lovely feeling of being taken care of.

"I'm sorry you got hit."

I opened my uninjured eye. Rupert's voice was as soft as the pressure he put on my face, but his eyes were lowered, and I couldn't catch their expression.

"Not your fault," I said. "I decided to go out."

"You wouldn't have had to if we'd gotten back to the ship when we were supposed to," Rupert said, the words surprisingly harsh. "You wouldn't have been there at all."

If I was actually ignorant of what had happened in the clearing, I would have laughed. I'm a merc. A black eye is the sign of a good night, not an injury to be guilty over. Besides, how could he blame himself for my stumbling into wildlife? But I wasn't ignorant, and I knew what he was really apologizing for. He was sorry I'd gotten involved.

If I'd had any doubt before that the knowledge of what had really happened in that clearing was dangerous, Rupert's tight, worried expression would have stomped it out right there. But fool that I am, I wasn't afraid. I was touched by his concern. So much so that my chest hurt a little.

The way he was looking at me didn't help, either. Even in my suit, Rupert loomed over me, his eyes dark and tender in the low light when he finally raised them to mine. His fingers were still on my chin. They were warm, surprisingly so considering he'd just used them to shovel ice into a bag. They caressed my skin very slightly, and I shivered at the feeling, my gaze going involuntarily to his lips. They were close. All I had to do was push up on my toes to reach them. They would be warm, I bet, like his fingers.

I'd actually started to move before I realized what I was about to do. I froze, dropping my eyes from Rupert's lips to his chest. That wasn't much better. His chest looked solid and lovely, perfect to wrap myself around, but at least the reality of his dark suit brought me down a little.

What the hell did I think I was doing? There was a fine line between acting like I didn't know what had happened and willfully throwing myself into the fire. Rupert might be sorry I got hurt, but he was... I didn't even have a word for what he was, other than "involved." Very involved in things that could wreck me hard if I wasn't careful. But even if there was no danger or secrets, even if we'd been just a cook and a merc, getting tangled in the kitchen while I was on duty was simply too unprofessional for me to bear, and it was that more than anything else that got me to step back.

"Thanks for ice pack number two," I said, putting my hand up to take the ice from him. "I'd better get back to patrol. Have a good night, Rupert."

Rupert blinked like he was waking up, and then he stepped back to let me pass. "Good night, Devi."

Hearing him say my name like that, softly in the dark, did nothing for the lust I was trying to quash, but I forced myself to wave and smile as my feet got moving, taking me toward the cargo bay. When I heard the hallway door close behind him, I stopped and removed the ice pack, placing my fingers against my bruised skin. I brushed the cut on my cheekbone oh so gently, just as Rupert had done in the clearing, and took a deep, steadying breath to gather my wits.

I was on deep breath number three before I remembered I'd left my helmet sitting on the kitchen counter. I whirled around, silently cursing stupid merc girls who let handsome men walk off with their brains. I stomped back into the empty lounge, grabbed my helmet off the counter, and shoved it on my head. I dumped the ice pack in the sink for good measure before setting myself firmly back to work.

My eye ached for the rest of my shift.

True to her word, Nova was waiting with two meditation cushions when I got back to our room the next morning. My eye was throbbing and I wanted nothing more than to take a painkiller and fall into bed, but she was so excited about "realigning my core to the living energy of the cosmos" that I couldn't say no.

I let her sit me down on the pillow in something she called four corners position. It looked like normal old cross-legged to me, but I tried my best to keep my body just as she'd arranged it while Nova turned on her weird static music again. She sat down on the pillow across from mine and closed her eyes, instructing me in a dreamy voice to breathe deeply and imagine the endless void of empty space slowly filling with stars.

I'd filled my void with stars five times over and was starting to fall asleep by the time Nova announced the session was over.

"Do you feel better?" she asked, switching off the music.

"A little," I lied. I felt exactly the same, only now my legs ached from sitting still for so long. "Can't expect too much from my first session, though."

"It gets easier with practice," Nova assured me, getting up to collect the pillows. The session must have been much better for her than for me. Nova was practically glowing as I helped her toss the cushions back onto her bunk.

"Well, I don't have any plasmex," I said. "So I don't know if it'll ever really work for me."

"Everyone has plasmex, Deviana," Nova said, beaming. "It's a fundamental force of the universe, like gravity or the strong force inside atoms. Some humans are more sensitive to it than others, especially with daily practice, but everyone has at least a little." Her beaming smile faded a few watts. "Well, biologically speaking, humans and aeons have the least plasmex sensitivity of the known races. Xith'cal have significantly more, and the lelgis are said to hold it as the core of their senses, but please don't let that disturb your harmony. The only thing that truly matters is that we are all connected through plasmex in a great oneness that spans the whole of space-time. On a universal scale like that, minor biological differences become insignificant."

"Thanks," I said, eying my bed longingly. "I'll keep that in mind."

Nova caught my look and blushed, her paper-white cheeks turning bright red. "I'm sorry. I didn't mean to keep you up."

"No, no, no," I said hurriedly. I was almost frantic to reassure her. The thought that I'd hurt Nova's feelings made me feel like I'd just kicked a puppy. "It was really nice and it helped a lot. I'd love to do it again."

Nova peeked at me. "Only if you're sure. I don't want to bother you. I know how busy you and Mr. Cotter are."

I couldn't help it—I reached out with a grin to squeeze her bony shoulder. "Nova, you are a piece of good work, you really are. You are way too nice for this ship."

Nova's cheeks went scarlet again. "Oh, no," she said quickly. "It's the captain who was nice to take me in. I wasn't actually fully qualified to be a systems engineer when I started. Captain Caldswell did it as a kindness to my father."

I didn't stop smiling, but suddenly I was paying serious attention. "Really? How does your father know Caldswell?"

"I don't know, exactly," Nova said, suddenly looking sheepish. "Father always says that remembering the past is impossible when you are at one with a universe where time only moves forward, which makes it kind of hard to ask him questions like that. But I do know that my father put me here because he meant me to help with the captain's good work."

I had to fight not to look too interested. "Good work? What kind of good work? You mean charity?"

Nova shrugged, her brilliant smile returning. "I have no idea, but Captain Caldswell has always been good to me. We harmonize so well, I'm happy to help him any way I can." She glanced at her

handset, and her pale eyebrows shot up. "Oh dear, I have to relo-
cate! Basil's balance will be upset if I'm late."

"Basil's balance is eternally upset," I said, but Nova was already
out the door, waving at me as she went.

When she was gone, I hit the lights and fell into bed, but tired as
I was, I didn't pass out immediately. First, my eye was throbbing,
and second, I couldn't stop thinking about what Nova would think
if she saw the footage hidden on my Bargain. What part of that, I
wondered, would her father call "good work"? But, of course, fretting gave me no more answers, and eventually sleep took me.

Even with the knowledge of what had actually happened in the
clearing rattling around my head like an armed grenade, over the
next week I did an excellent job pretending nothing had changed.
As much as I'd love to attribute this to my fantastic acting abilities,
the real reason was that I was too busy spending every moment
of my free time cleaning in accordance with my punishment deal
with Caldswell.

I scrubbed every shower, toilet, floor, and sink on the whole
damn ship, and every time I thought I was finished, the captain
somehow found more. But if Caldswell thought to break me with all
this drudge work, he'd picked a sorry target. Like all Paradoxians,
I'd spent my first two years out of school at the bottom of the Royal
Army, and I'd scrubbed far worse than this.

When I wasn't cleaning, I was working. Cotter and I had
adjusted our patrol schedule so I got more time on the day cycle.
Even so, I was often bored, and while I would never slack on my
duty, I wasn't above doing a little reading while I was walking in
circles. I'd loaded Hyrek's compiled survey into my suit's memory,
and I read it whenever I had the spare time.

It was slow going. Not that I would ever admit it to the lizard, but the book he'd lent me *was* hard to read. This was partially because it was in Universal, not my first language, but mostly because it was exactly the kind of dry, overly specific scientific writing you'd expect from an official Terran survey. Also, it was huge. Unlike Paradox, which kept its colonies to a reasonable number, the Terrans had claimed so many planets I don't think even they could name them all.

Fortunately, the listings themselves were well organized and fascinating enough to keep me going. The survey was full of strange and sometimes wonderful creatures I'd never heard of. I found a whole list of critters I'd love to see in the wild, but there was nothing remotely like the thing I'd fought in the clearing. There was also no mention of anything like the black alien I'd seen standing behind Ren, among the xith'cal tribes or anywhere else.

By the time I finished the survey's last entry, I had a much better understanding of alien ecosystems but none of the answers I'd picked up the survey to find. I hadn't actually expected to find anything, of course, but I was still disappointed. Hyrek's survey had been a long shot, but reading it was safe and made me feel like I was doing something. Once I had no more reading to keep me occupied, patrol duty left me with way too much time to think, and my damned curiosity had started pushing my mind toward the more dangerous mysteries. Specifically, I started watching Ren.

Before Mycant, I'd paid the captain's daughter only cursory attention. I'd actually kind of liked her since she didn't bother me when I was working like most kids did. Now, I watched her whenever I got a chance, and what I saw only creeped me out more.

Even if I hadn't seen her drag me around with her mind or burn an invisible monster with her hand, one day of watching Ren for real would have been enough to tell me that Caldswell's daughter had something very weird going on in her head. First, while she clearly understood what people told her, she never spoke out loud. I'd seen her whispering to the captain and Rupert, but I'd never heard her voice or seen her talk to anyone besides those two. Second, she didn't make eye contact, didn't move unless someone guided her, and never showed an emotion except her usual blank stare. She was like a doll, or one of those creepy androids they used on the Terran core planets. If it wasn't for the fact that I'd seen her eat, I would have wondered if she was human at all.

The only thing that seemed to wake Ren up was her chessboard, but even there she was abnormal. I actually looked up the rules of chess in an effort to understand what she was doing, but while everything I read insisted chess was a two player game, Ren always played alone, moving both sides so quickly I could barely keep up until she reached checkmate. When that happened, she'd reset the pieces and start the whole process over without pause. She never even seemed to enjoy her games. It was more like playing was a compulsion, something she had to do rather than something she wanted.

I learned all of this from stolen glances, because another thing I'd discovered while I'd been watching her was that Caldswell and Rupert didn't just keep an eye on the girl, they controlled her like she was a prisoner in danger of bolting. They were never cruel or violent, but Ren never went anywhere or did anything without one of them beside her. Considering what I'd seen her do in the clearing, that wasn't actually so surprising. Couldn't let a girl with that sort of power and a seemingly empty brain run around loose. But their close watch made it impossible for me to get a chance to really look at Ren, and while I was dying to learn more about what she was, I wasn't about to take such a huge risk.

Or, at least, I wasn't until I ran headfirst into an opportunity that was simply too perfect to pass up.

It was early morning five days after Mycant. Cotter was still sleeping, so the lounge was empty except for the usual suspects. But while Ren was on the couch like always, Rupert was crouched on the floor behind the kitchen counter. He had the contents of the pantry spread out around him and was tapping on his ledger, muttering softly to himself in a language I didn't understand. It was so charmingly domestic, I couldn't help smiling.

"Counting the potatoes?" I asked, leaning on the door.

"Someone has to," Rupert answered, looking up briefly to flash a smile at me.

I smiled back and pushed off to continue my patrol, but my mind was racing. As soon as I'd seen Rupert's position, inspiration had struck. Down on the floor like that, he couldn't actually see Ren directly. For the first time since I'd started watching her, Ren was unguarded. This was my opportunity, I realized. But I had to act now, before Rupert moved.

The second I made my decision, I veered off my patrol path and cut across the cargo bay to the engine room. I climbed the spiral stairs on the other side and reentered the lounge from the hallway. Since it was day cycle, the lounge door was open, and I was able to step inside without a sound.

Like every public space on the ship, the lounge had cameras, but no one watched them actively, and anyway, I'd never been told specifically to stay away from Ren. I might be poking things that should not be poked, but according to ship rules and my own supposed ignorance, I was doing nothing wrong. With this in mind, I made a big show of being casual as I walked over and took up a position directly across the low table from where Ren sat.

I'd never been this close to her before, and I was a little disappointed to see that Ren looked anticlimactically normal. Just a scrawny teenage girl with olive skin and a cap of straight dark hair. She wore the kind of practical, boring shirt, loose pants, and plain slip-on shoes that clearly showed that her clothes were being picked for her, and I vaguely wondered if Rupert dressed her as well as everything else. Like always, she was staring at her game, her dark brown eyes large and unfocused even while her fingers moved the plastic chess pieces with machinelike precision.

Though I was now standing directly in front of her, the captain's daughter didn't look up at me. Using my rear cam to keep an eye on the kitchen, I bent over and waved my hand in front of her face. Ren didn't even blink. She kept playing her game without missing a beat, even when my hand had cut off her view of the board. Frowning, I tried again, this time skimming close enough to make her dark hair dance. Ren didn't so much as flinch, even when I almost clipped her nose.

I straightened up with a sigh. So much for learning something useful. The girl was about as responsive as a piece of machinery. I briefly considered touching her, but that felt like a step too far. I'd messed with her long enough, anyway. Rupert would be done counting soon, and I wanted to make a clean escape. Waving at Ren one last time, I started to walk away, but as I turned, something made me stop.

Ren had just reset the chessboard in the pattern I recognized as the start of the game, both colors lined up identically on opposite sides, but one piece was missing. One of the black pieces, the one called the queen, was tipped over on the far side of the table. Without thinking, I reached down and snatched up the little game piece. I was about to set it neatly in line with the rest of the black side when I realized that Ren had gone still.

No, not just still. She was absolutely frozen, like someone had paused her in the middle of an action. Queen still in hand, I leaned down to peer at her face. Her gaze was still focused on the chessboard, but her eyes were now as wide as they could go. I was just about to back away when I became aware of a pressure in my head. It was tiny at first, like sinus pressure, but it grew rapidly, and as it got stronger, a series of white static lines began to drop down my cameras with a soft, ominous crackle.

A hand grabbed my wrist, making me jump. I looked up to see Rupert standing right beside me. His face was almost too calm as he pulled my arm, my *armored* arm, aside and plucked the game piece from my gloved fingers. He replaced it at once, tipped on its side on the table just as it had been before. The moment it was back in place, the static lines vanished from my camera and the pressure lifted from my head, and Ren resumed playing like nothing had happened.

"Ren does not like her game disturbed," Rupert said, his voice low and controlled. "Please do not touch her things again."

Under normal circumstances, I would have asked him what the hell had just happened, but right then I was way too freaked out to push. I backed up with a murmured apology, though whether I was apologizing to Ren or Rupert, I didn't know. Rupert put his hand on Ren's shoulder as I walked away, almost like he was comforting the girl, but the way his fingers bit into Ren's skin reminded me more of a master holding back a rabid dog as I took off down the cargo stairs at slightly less than a panicked run.

I spent the rest of my shift playing the scene with Ren over and over on my camera. I'd caught everything—her crazed expression, the static lines, Rupert's incredible feat of strength—but I didn't know what any of it *meant*. I knew Ren was important, though not how or why. I also knew she was dangerous in a way I could not understand, and that frightened me more than I liked to admit.

I continued to patrol, but I didn't look at Ren again unless I had to. This was made much easier by the fact that she never looked at me either, or moved at all. As for Rupert, he acted like the whole thing had never happened, and I was happy to act right along with him. But the incident had put a sourness in me. I don't do well with puzzles in general, and this one seemed to be missing half its pieces.

The whole mess was driving me up the wall, and my body itched for some good, old-fashioned, completely nonmysterious action.

Luckily, I was about to get my wish. Our next jump was to the Recant, an asteroid field that was well inside the hunting grounds for Reaper's Fleet. I had no idea what kind of death wish drove Caldswell so near the xith'cal tribe who'd proclaimed him their sworn prey, but I wasn't about to complain. This far into xith'cal space, there was no way we could avoid a raid, and I was more than ready to take out my frustrations with some nice, visceral xith'cal slaughter.

My longing for battle must have scared them away, though, because the next few days were depressingly calm. The mining station we were headed toward was deep inside the Recant, where the asteroids were thick. Good for mining, bad for coming out of hyperspace. Because of the rocks, the gate had dumped us four days away from our actual destination, and after three days of getting dinged by space rocks without so much as sighting another ship, I was starting to feel like a caged animal.

"Relax, Morris," Cotter said, glancing up from the pistol he was cleaning as I entered the lounge on patrol. "You keep making that face it'll stick that way."

"Shut up," I growled, stalking past him to glare out the window at the rocks I was starting to hate.

We were speaking King's Tongue, but I guess the tone was clear enough, because Rupert chuckled. I turned my glare to him. He was sitting on the couch beside Ren with his long legs resting on the low table in front of him, reading something on his ledger and looking far, far too relaxed to suit my mood.

"I'm sure the xith'cal will be here to eat us soon enough," he said without looking up.

I was thinking up a good comeback to that when Caldswell's voice crackled over the com. "Security, get to the bridge."

"Come on, Cotter," I said, hurrying out the door, my anger forgotten in the thrill of potential action.

Caldswell, Basil, and Nova were all watching the screen when we came in. When I got through the door, I saw why. The bridge's enormous main screen was filled with the same space rocks we'd been flying through for days, but the thing taking up most of the screen's center was at least fifty times bigger than the largest asteroid. It was truly enormous—a dark, round shape blotting out the stars behind it, but more than that I couldn't see. The *Fool*'s lights were far too small to illuminate something this huge.

"What's that?" I said, lifting my visor. "A runaway moon?"

"No," Caldswell said without looking away from the screen. "That's a tribe ship."

I stared at the screen with new horror. I'd never seen a xith'cal tribe ship, but I'd heard stories. The xith'cal had no home planet we knew of, nor did they have colonies. Instead, they roamed the galaxy in gigantic colony ships. It wasn't unusual for a tribe ship to hold several million xith'cal, and I'd heard Reaper's Fleet had tribe ships large enough to hold tens of millions, which was why no one messed with Reaper.

Now that I knew what it was, I could see the thing in front of us wasn't actually round. We were looking at the ship nose on. As we slowly came around, I saw the vessel was long and cylindrical with a body that stretched back for miles, its impossibly huge sides riddled with bays and hangars for the fleets of slaver ships, battleships, and everything else the xith'cal sent out to prey on the lesser races.

"How did we get so close?" I whispered. Xith'cal didn't leave their tribe ships unguarded. You were usually attacked before you got within sensor range of one, which was why few people except the rare freed slave ever lived to tell about them.

"Because it's a ghost ship," Caldswell answered, leaning back in his chair. "Those things are usually lit up like Christmas, but look."

He pointed at the absolute black of the ship's outline on the screen. "Not a light to be seen."

I didn't know what Christmas was, but I had to grant the point that the tribe ship probably wasn't inhabited. If something lived there, we'd be under attack, not sitting here staring.

"I'm not picking up any heat signatures, either," Nova said, poking the impossibly complex screen in front of her. "The ship's been cold for a while."

"Do you think they abandoned it?" I couldn't think of a reason you'd just abandon a huge ship like that, but who knew why xith'cal did anything. Maybe it had dishonored them.

"I don't know," Caldswell said. "That's why I'm sending you two in to find out."

"Oh hell no," Cotter said behind me. "There is no way I'm going into a tribe ship, empty or not."

Caldswell looked at me, and I pursed my lips like I was thinking it over. It was an act, of course. I was itching for action, and this was exactly the sort of opportunity I'd been waiting for to show the captain my skills as something other than a ship guard.

"I'll go," I said. "I'm not afraid of an empty hull, and I've always wanted to see a tribe ship." I looked down at Cotter, who, without his armor, was an inch shorter than I was in mine. "If you're too scared, I can bring back some pictures for you."

Cotter shot me a nasty look. "There's a difference between brave and suicidal," he snapped. "And I don't see how going in there has anything to do with ship security."

"I'll throw in an explorer's bonus," Caldswell offered. "One thousand to each of you for every hour you're inside."

I whistled. Caldswell must really want something, because that was no small amount of cash. The same thought must have gone through Cotter's mind, because his shoulders slumped in resignation. "Fine," he said. "But first sign of trouble and I'm out."

"Fair enough," Caldswell said.

Cotter left to get his armor, but I stayed on the bridge, watching the tribe ship fill up the screen as we got closer. When Caldswell looked at me again, I smiled. It was time to do a little pushing.

"If I may ask, sir, why are you so keen on this?"

The captain folded his hands in his lap. "Just wondering what a dead tribe ship is doing this far out of its territory," he said. "These are Reaper's hunting grounds, but that's one of Stoneclaw's ships. Stoneclaw's hunting grounds are three days' jump from here, so you can see my interest." He shrugged. "It pays to be curious on occasion, and this is odd enough that I'm willing to take the gamble."

"How do you know so much about xith'cal?" I asked. "Did Hyrek tell you?"

"God, no," the captain said. "Hyrek keeps his secrets tight. No, I used to fight xith'cal when I was in the Republic Starfleet. Did raids to free slaves on occasion."

So Caldswell had been in the Terran Republic Starfleet. I filed that away for later use. "Slave raids, huh? Is that why Reaper's so angry at you?"

"One of the many reasons," Caldswell said, turning back to the rapidly approaching tribe ship. "Enough nosing, Morris. Get down to the cargo bay. We'll be close enough for you to hop over in a few minutes."

"Yes sir," I said, flipping my visor down so he wouldn't see my grin.

I jogged down the hall toward the cargo bay to start getting ready for a spacewalk, but as I turned into the lounge, Rupert's look stopped me cold. He glanced pointedly at the kitchen and stood up, leaving his ledger on the couch beside Ren. I followed a second later, confused. Rupert walked behind the bar and leaned on the counter. I followed suit, taking off my helmet so I could hear him without the com chatter in my ear.

"What is it?" I whispered, leaning in close so he could hear my lowered voice.

Rupert's face was perfectly neutral. To anyone else, he probably looked bored, but after trying so hard to break his bluff during our poker games, I knew his expressions better than I knew my own, and I could see from the tight set of his jaw that he was not happy. Very not happy.

"I don't like this," he said. He was looking at Ren, but his voice was pitched for my ears. The tremble in it was angry, but since he wasn't meeting my eyes, I couldn't tell if that anger was at me or for me. "This isn't your job."

I shrugged. "It's my job to do what the captain orders."

"The captain," Rupert started, then stopped, his jaw clenching tighter as he tried to find the right words. "Caldswell values his crew," he said at last. "But sometimes he values other things more. He thinks in terms of end goals and acceptable losses."

Most soldiers did, but there was something in Rupert's words that warned me that Caldswell's idea of an acceptable loss went a bit beyond what I was used to. I started to tell him I could take care of myself, but then Rupert actually looked at me, and the intensity of his expression stole the words off my tongue.

"You leave at the first sign of trouble," he said, his whole body taut as he leaned toward me. "Promise me, Devi. The first sign."

"First sign," I repeated, bumping his arm gently with my own. "I'll come back just fine. Promise."

He nodded and stood up. "Be careful," he murmured as I put my helmet back on.

"Always am," I said, lifting my visor to flash him a smile before I started down the cargo bay steps.

CHAPTER
10

Cotter was suited up by the time I made it down to the bay, and he didn't look happy about it. Despite Rupert's warning, though, I was getting sort of excited. I've always liked exploring, and after being cooped up for days with mysteries I couldn't solve, a chance to prove myself to Caldswell combined with poking around a ghost ship sounded pretty good to me.

While Basil was getting us closer, Mabel came out to help Cotter and me patch our video feeds through to the bridge so the others could watch the exploration.

"How do you stand seeing all the way around your head all the time?" Basil cried once my feed was running. "It's making me dizzy just looking."

"Guess my eyes are more advanced than yours," I said, glancing down at the text that had started scrolling across the bottom of my vision. "You see that, Cotter?"

"I see it," he grumbled.

The text was courtesy of Hyrek, who had agreed to watch and translate the xith'cal writing for us since no one else on the ship could read it.

"I hope you're charging a fat translation fee," I said.

You are the mercenary, Hyrek wrote. *I am the loyal crew member who does as his captain orders. Now, remember, stay away from anything that looks like this.*

The bottom of my screen filled with squiggles.

"What does that mean?" I asked.

"Slaughter Room" would be the closest translation, Hyrek replied. *Wouldn't want to offend your delicate sensibilities.*

Cotter made a strangled sound, and I rolled my eyes. "Let's get moving."

"Ready for pressure release." Nova's dreamy voice floated over my speakers. "Locking down."

There was a loud boom as the blast doors closed over the engine room and the door to the lounge. I stood impatiently, tapping my foot as I waited for the *Fool*'s vents to rescue what air they could. At last, when the atmosphere had dropped to nearly nothing, the new cargo doors rolled open, and Cotter and I stood facing the freezing blackness of space.

Basil had managed to get us right up beside one of the tribe ship's flight bays. The gravity had vanished with the air, and since I was the only one with thrusters, it was my job to pull Cotter out of the cargo bay and across the ten-foot gap between the *Glorious Fool* and the xith'cal ship. Fortunately, the floors were metal, and Cotter's suit wasn't so cheap that the boots lacked magnets, so once we were down we could both walk more or less as normal.

Going into the bay was like floating into an enormous cave in the side of an even more enormous cliff. It was pitch-black inside and so large that our suit lights barely made a dent in the darkness. The bay Hyrek had chosen for our entry was the biggest of all the ones we'd seen on this side of the tribe ship. From the shape, I'd guessed it was meant for supply freighters, a theory that was supported by the bank of shipping containers strapped to the back wall.

Cannon ammunition, Hyrek typed before I could ask.

"Guess they didn't get a chance to pack," I said, turning my light over the hundreds of containers.

"I don't think they had much of a chance to do anything." Caldswell's voice was deep in my ear. "Their ships are still in the bays."

The bay looked empty to me, but then Cotter whistled and pointed up. I raised my head and gasped. A half-dozen ships hung suspended from the ceiling above us. They were long-haul fighters, twice the size of the *Fool*, and though, as Nova always pointed out, there was no up or down in space and thus no way one could fall on me unless something pushed it, I moved to the wall anyway.

Cotter followed suit, and we hugged the line of crates until we reached a set of doors big enough to drive a tank through. There was a little red light glowing on the panel beside them, the first light I'd seen other than our own since we'd arrived.

That's the lock, Hyrek said. *Press the red button.*

I obeyed, hitting the glowing square hard with my finger. Something below us rumbled, and the door began to grind open.

"Some lock," I said, grinning.

Airlock, not door lock. The words looked just like all the others, but I could almost feel Hyrek's testiness running through the letters. *Tribe ships have no need for locks. Xith'cal who poke their snouts where they shouldn't don't last long.*

"Good to know," I said, stepping inside the airlock and waving for Cotter to follow. He came grudgingly, but he came. I hit the button on the other side as soon as we were both in, and the door to the hanger rumbled back into place. Though it didn't seem possible, it was even darker inside the airlock than it had been in the bay, but I could hear vents hissing overhead, filling the vacuum with atmosphere.

"There's some power, at least," I said, turning my headlamp toward the sound of blowing air.

"Gravity, too," Cotter said, settling more comfortably into his suit.

He was right. I turned off my magnets as I settled onto the floor under my own weight. The gravity was light, but it was definitely there, and in a few seconds, the air was as well.

My suit told me when the oxygen levels outside were acceptable, but I kept it sealed anyway. Humans and xith'cal can breathe the same air, but xith'cal prefer a good deal more arsenic in theirs. It wouldn't kill me immediately, but I had no interest in breathing poison, and since my suit could last sixteen hours before I needed to worry about my air supply, I saw no reason to.

Eventually the vents finished, and the door behind us, the one leading farther into the ship, opened with a creak, only to stick almost immediately. The crack was still enough for us to squeeze through, though Cotter was a tight fit. He cursed all the way, but even though he stuck to King's Tongue, Caldswell still snapped at him for it. Some things don't need translation.

The door let out into a large open space. Like the airlock, it was solid dark, but this room was so huge neither our lights nor my suit's night vision could penetrate to the end of it. We could see the floor, though, and what we saw there didn't make any sense.

"What the hell is that?" Cotter said, adding his light to mine.

I had no idea. It *looked* like a popped balloon. The thing shone iridescent purple in our floodlights, its edges reflecting rainbow pearlescence. It lay flat as a tarp on the ground, its surface wrinkled, like it was deflated. Beneath it, flat streamers peeled off in all directions like jellyfish tentacles. It was ripped in places, and there was something dark and sticky on the ground around it. Blood, I was willing to bet. Whatever this thing was, it had been alive once, and it had died a violent death.

"It's a lelgis," Caldswell said calmly.

I wasn't nearly as collected. I leaned down with a startled gasp, staring at the dead thing in horrified fascination. I'd never seen a lelgis, living or dead. Most people hadn't. The Terrans had discovered them seventy years ago when they'd just appeared out of nowhere with an enormous fleet and demanded tribute. There'd been a brief war, and then some agreement had been struck and the lelgis had pretty much kept to themselves ever since. They were supposed to be enormous and look like whale squids, but the thing on the ground couldn't have been much larger than me, even with the tentacles, and it was definitely closer to a jellyfish than a squid. Briefly, I wondered how it had moved around in life. Those flimsy tentacles didn't look anywhere near strong enough to hold that large, bulbous body.

"Are there more?"

Caldswell's question snapped me out of my fixation, and I straightened up, swinging my light across the floor. We found five more dead lelgis in the area directly around the airlock and then a sixth farther in, hanging from what looked like a tree.

It is a tree, Hyrek typed. *You're in an arbor. Look up.*

I obeyed, gasping in amazement. The room we were in was even larger than I'd initially thought, and it was filled with a canopy like nothing I'd ever seen. Enormous trees rose from several patches of dirt along the edges of the room, their wide, flat leaves forming an overlapping cover high above our heads. The canopy looked blue green in our floodlights, but most of the leaves' edges were rimmed with black.

They're dying, Hyrek wrote.

"What did you expect?" Cotter said. "No heat, no light, no water—assuming your plants drink water and not blood."

A tribe ship's heart is its trees. Hyrek's message came so quickly I could almost hear him slamming his claws against the panel. *They grow all through our ships, and their death is the tribe's death.*

"I'd say they outlived their tribe this time," I muttered, flicking my light toward a shape on the ground.

Dead xith'cal lay scattered all across the far side of the large room. They must have died a while ago, because the bodies were pretty well decayed, yet another reason I was happy I hadn't unsealed my suit. "That's strange," I said, turning over the closest body with my foot. "No bullet wounds. They weren't shot."

"They wouldn't be," Caldswell said. "Lelgis don't shoot."

There was something in the way he said that that killed my questions before they could form.

This makes no sense. Lelgis and xith'cal do not fight.

Hyrek had typed that to Caldswell, but I answered anyway. "I thought xith'cal fought everyone."

We fight to eat and for challenge, Hyrek wrote. *Lelgis are poison, and they do not fight as we do.*

"Well, something fought them," I said, sliding my light over the dead bodies, xith'cal and lelgis.

"Morris," Caldswell said. "See if you can get to a command room. Maybe there's some kind of record, a security camera, something that can tell us what happened."

"We need lights first," I said, looking around.

There's a door to your left, Hyrek typed.

It was as good a place to start as any, so Cotter and I dodged the bodies and made our way over. The doorway was rounded almost like a cave entrance and set into a metal wall that had been cast to resemble stone. Inside was a narrow stairway leading up.

Our people lived underground before we were forced into space, Hyrek wrote before I could ask. *Stoneclaw is an old tribe and keeps the old ways.*

"I wish they'd kept bigger doors," I said, sticking my head up the dark stairwell. "I don't think you'll fit, Cotter."

Cotter snorted. "Leave it to lizards to live in holes. Why even make something this small? Xith'cal are ten feet tall if they're an inch."

The males are ten feet tall, Hyrek wrote. *Females are significantly smaller.*

I frowned. "I don't think I've ever seen a female xith'cal."

Of course you haven't. Fighting and dying is for males. The smart xith'cal choose to be female—you live much longer. Hyrek paused. *Females are also in charge of all science and technical aspects of xith'cal society. That's how I knew the door in front of you went somewhere useful. It's a female door.*

As I read Hyrek's words, I suddenly thought about how small our xith'cal was compared to others I'd seen. Small and differently colored. Now was hardly the time to be pushy, but I made a mental note to ask him, or her, about it later. For now, we had more pressing business.

"Guess I'm the lucky girl," I said, stepping inside. "Cotter, keep watch. I'll see if I can't get us some light."

Cotter didn't even grumble at the order. Bad as standing around on an alien ghost ship was, at least this area was open and seemed relatively safe. Much safer than going up a small, dark tunnel into the unknown.

The stairs went up nearly thirty feet by my estimation, curving in a slow spiral so that I couldn't see the top until I reached it. The small room I came out in could have been a control room on any space station. There was a large exterior window looking down on the bay where we'd come in and the *Glorious Fool* beside it and a smaller interior window looking out into the canopy of dying trees. I couldn't see Cotter through the leaves, but one of the consoles had a blinking red light, and I decided to have a look.

I pushed the padded stool aside and stood in front of the console, shining my light on the various controls. "What now?"

Let's start on the upper left, second row, third from the top.

I found the switch easily, a fist-sized clunker covered in xith'cal scribble. It was heavy. If I hadn't had my suit, I probably couldn't have thrown it, but the Lady Gray had no problem. The switch flipped with a satisfying metal crunch. I was immediately rewarded by the whir of machinery.

Now go to the panel on the wall behind you.

I had to hunt a bit before I found what he was talking about, mostly because it wasn't a panel at all but a large box covered in ominous black markings. It was locked, so I ripped the cover off. Inside was a field of red toggles, each one carefully marked.

"Which should I hit first?" I asked.

I'm not sure. They're numbered, not labeled, Hyrek wrote. The words paused, and then I saw *Just hit all of them and we'll see what happens.*

"My kind of plan," I said, sweeping my arm across the lot.

Light flickered around me, and suddenly I could see, but only dimly. Soft red-orange light shone beneath the consoles and along the walls. The light through the window looking down on Cotter and the trees was a little stronger, but not much.

"Guess there wasn't enough power for the main lights," I said, flipping a few switches at random. "All I can seem to get are the emergency ones."

No, the lights are on, Hyrek replied. *Xith'cal eyes don't need the glaring light you humans seem to enjoy.*

The thought that this low, red glow was all the light I was going to get didn't thrill me, and I kept my suit's floodlight on as I walked over to the console in the corner below a bank of what looked to me like monitors.

"Okay, Hyrek," I said, leaning over the controls. "Let's see if we can't find out what happened between the squids and the lizards, besides the obvi—"

I froze. At first, even I didn't know why. All I knew was that my gut had clenched in the way that meant something was wrong. I stayed perfectly still, one finger poised over a switch at the base of the console like I was contemplating pressing it, and waited. A second later, I saw it again, a flash of movement in my rear cam.

I spun and fired before I could think twice. Sasha sang in my hands, firing a three-shot burst into the dark stair behind me. One of them must have struck true, because I heard a grunt, but before I could see what it was, something hard and heavy smashed me upside the head.

Had my stabilizers not been as good as they were, I would have gone over. Instead, I staggered, blinking against the spots dancing behind my eyes just in time to see a xith'cal step into the room.

It took me a few seconds to realize that, even though I was looking straight at it, I couldn't see the xith'cal clearly. Then I remembered that my floodlight was attached to my helm. That had been what the xith'cal had hit. Now that my thoughts were clearing, I could feel it, a pressure on the left side of my skull, and I swore loudly. The damn lizard had dented my helmet.

But my light wasn't the only casualty. In the distance, I could hear the thunder of Cotter's shotgun, but I didn't hear Cotter himself, even though I knew he had to be screaming into his com. I didn't hear anyone, nor did I see more of Hyrek's text scrolling across the bottom of my vision. The blow to my head had cut me off.

I swore a second time now that there was no one to hear and pointed my gun at the xith'cal. I couldn't get a head shot because of the angle, so I shot it in the upper chest. The xith'cal staggered into the wall as Sasha's armor-piercing round struck it, but it didn't scream. Instead, it dropped a little lower and started forward again.

Now that it was closer, even the terrible light couldn't hide that something was wrong with it. For one, there was a nice three-shot spread in its abdomen from my first attack. My second shot had hit just below the throat. None of those shots would kill a xith'cal, but together they should have been enough to make it retreat, or at least treat me with a little respect.

This xith'cal didn't even seem to notice. It kept coming, hissing at me as it did. But though it was stalking toward me, it wasn't stalking fast. It seemed to be having trouble standing. Actually, its movements were so jerky I began to wonder how it had clocked me so fast earlier.

And that was when I realized there were two xith'cal in the room.

I spun and shot the other one just as it jumped out from beneath the console I'd been crouching against. I hit it square in the head, but not, I realized too late, between the eyes. My shot grazed harmlessly off its skull ridge, not even slowing it down as it lunged. This one wasn't slow like the one in the tunnel. It was on me before I could dodge, shattering my shield in one hit as its enormous weight took me off my feet.

I didn't realize until the second xith'cal was on top of me just how much larger it was than the first. That one had been closer to my size. This one was eleven feet easy, an enormous warrior with more muscle than I'd known they could fit under those scales. He took me down like I was nothing and pinned me to the floor, locking my arms when I tried to roll into a defensive ball. I struggled madly, but even my Lady can't lift a ton of xith'cal with both arms flung sideways and no leverage. I kicked instead, pounding the xith'cal with my boots as hard as I could.

I might as well have been kicking a bulkhead for all the good it did. The xith'cal didn't seem to feel pain. It loomed over me, enormous and black, and then, slowly, it lowered its head until its breath was fogging my visor.

I'm not usually prone to panic, but I was panicking now. With my hands pinned, I couldn't even get Sasha up for a shot. All I could do was lie there as the xith'cal sniffed me, and I realized with dead certainty that this was it. After all those jokes about being a xith'cal's meal, it was actually about to happen. The xith'cal was so close now I could almost imagine I smelled its rancid breath even though my suit was still sealed. For a long second, it just sat there, staring at me through my visor, and that was when I saw it.

The xith'cal wasn't looking at me. It couldn't. Its eyes were covered by a white film, like a dead fish's.

I'd thought there was something wrong with the first xith'cal, but I *knew* there was something horribly, unspeakably wrong with the one on top of me. His scales, normally glossy black and razor sharp, were thin and chipped. Some were even torn at the edges, like something had been chewing on them. Beneath the ragged scales, his body was covered in what looked like furry black mold. His clouded eyes were deep sunken as those of the rotting xith'cal in the tree filled gallery below, and I could see that the skin around his snout was tearing, as though the stress of moving was too much for it. A wave of disgust washed over me at the sight, but it was quickly overwhelmed by a much larger wave of terror as the rotting xith'cal reared back and bit me across my left shoulder.

A xith'cal's jaws are its most powerful weapon, made to crunch through their own steel-hard scales. Xith'cal bites are the reason the Lady Gray's mesh plating is two inches thick instead of one, but pinned as I was with a warrior xith'cal's mouth completely around my shoulder, even the Lady's armor wasn't enough to save me.

I screamed in pain as the yellow teeth went through my suit and dug deep into the flesh of my shoulder. The bite crunched my collarbone like chalk, and for a moment I swore I could feel its teeth clicking together inside me. It was that feeling, that knowledge that I was completely and utterly screwed, that enabled me to do what I did next.

With a mad thought it took my suit two tries to confirm, I dropped my entire grenade payload from the chamber on my back, arming them automatically as they fell. All my grenades was probably a bit much, but if I was going to die, I was going to take this bastard out with me. The grenades hit the floor behind me with a soft ping, and then they exploded in a flash so bright my cameras went snowy.

The explosion blew us both up, and we crashed into the ceiling with enough force to distract me from the pain as the xith'cal's teeth ripped free. He might not have felt my kicks, but even xith'cal can't fight physics. The blast tore us apart. I landed on the floor, he landed on top of a console, crashing through it in a shower of sparks.

It must have been instinct, because the second I hit the ground, I rolled away. The fact that I should have been dead twice over felt like the only real thing in the world, but my suit had always been better at taking blasts than stabbings. Even better, now that the xith'cal's teeth were out of me, the Lady Gray's emergency measures were kicking in.

Pressure bloomed along my body as my suit filled with breach foam, an antiseptic white goo that filled the holes in me as well as the holes in my suit, stopping both my bleeding and the air leaks. It was too late, though. My suit was full of the smell of the xith'cal ship. It stank of decay, not the usual carnivore rotting meat smell of the xith'cal, but a necrotic, deathly rot like nothing I'd smelled before. For three seconds the urge to throw up was almost overwhelming, and then I felt the sweet prick of the cocktail needle hitting the back of my neck.

The cocktail is a Paradoxian military standard. When your suit senses you've taken a life-threatening amount of damage, it injects you with a powerful mix of painkillers, stabilizers, and adrenaline. My version also had some of the better black market battle drugs mixed in, because if I was going to go down, I was going to go down fighting.

The second the needle hit, the pain in my shoulder began to drain away. I could still smell the xith'cal's rot, but I didn't care anymore. There was no pain, no tiredness, no body at all, just me and my suit and the sweet, sweet song of the battle fury thrumming through us both.

I maintained just enough presence of mind to holster Sasha before I ripped Phoebe from her clamps. My suit adjusted immediately to support my useless shoulder, and I stabbed my blade through the xith'cal almost before the thermite could fire. His rotted scales and brittle bones melted under Phoebe's blazing heat, giving me no trouble at all as I yanked her blade up through his chest to take off his head.

I was moving for the second xith'cal before the first fell. The smaller one, the female I realized in my haze, was still crouched and hissing by the door. She lunged at me when I turned, and I sliced her almost casually, taking off her arm at the shoulder. The force of my blow flung her into the far console, but I didn't stop to see if she'd get up. Instead, I ran down the stairs so fast I felt like I was flying, Phoebe clutched against my side.

For the five minutes they're effective, battle drugs give you amazing clarity. Even though I felt like an invincible god as I tore down the dark tunnel, a calm, detached corner of my mind was watching the enormous red timers that had appeared on the edge of my vision. I had sixty-eight seconds before my thermite died, after which I would have to use Mia. It was much harder to shoot on battle drugs than it was to swing a blade, but I had no choice. If I didn't get medical help in the next four minutes and forty-two seconds, I wouldn't have to worry about my wounds or the xith'cal. The crash from the drugs would send me into an epileptic fit that would do the deed for them. But I'd pay the price later, if there was a later. For now, I had my five minutes, dearly bought, and I meant to use them.

My thermal scan didn't pick up any xith'cal in the gallery below, but when I exploded out of the tunnel, there they were, waiting for me like wolves around a rabbit hole. With the drugs pounding through my body, I moved faster than I've ever moved in my life. My thermite blade sang as it burned the air, slicing through the first xith'cal like he was made of paper.

These xith'cal looked the same as the ones upstairs, their scales rotted and black with mold, their eyes covered in white film. The females hung back, shambling and slow. The males were fast, strong, and aggressive as ever, but with room to fight, my drug-driven focus, and Phoebe burning like the sun, they never got close.

As I cut the second one down with a slice to the head, the calm, detached part of my brain stopped watching timers just long enough to look around for Cotter, but I couldn't see him anywhere. I couldn't see anything but xith'cal.

I don't know how many I killed. There seemed to be no end. I couldn't even make out what I was fighting half the time. It was all a dark blur of claws and teeth and rotting flesh. I moved in circles, cutting whatever I could, screaming battle prayers to the king at the top of my lungs as my white blade burned through the enemy like a falling star.

I was halfway through a xith'cal when Phoebe's light burned out. The timer had warned me it was coming, but the battle-mad part of my brain had been sure I could get at least one more. As usual, that part of me was wrong.

Eleven inches from freedom, Phoebe went dark, and her blade caught in the xith'cal's ribs. My swing ground to a halt, and I ground with it, stumbling into the lizard I'd been killing half a second earlier. The xith'cal screamed in my ear, the ragged metal sound cutting through the haze of the drugs just long enough to snap me out of my killing frenzy.

Quick as a thought, I dropped Phoebe's blade and danced back, grabbing Mia as I went. My plasma shotgun blazed to life, and I pumped a wide spread shot into the mass of xith'cal, blowing a hole I could run through. And run I did. Mia was powerful, but her power was limited. She had four big shots like that left in her if I was lucky, and even in my euphoric, godlike rush, I knew it was time to go.

The detached, rational part of me pulled up the map of the

ship my suit had been drawing in the background while we'd been exploring. But when the marker appeared to show my location, I felt a flash of terror strong enough to break through the drugs. The marker was in the wrong place. This whole time, I'd been cutting in the wrong direction. I was actually several dozen feet farther into the ship from the tunnel, and not, as I'd thought, toward the airlock.

If I'd been myself, I probably would have panicked then, but battle drugs make panic impossible. Instead, I turned around and started running in the right direction, which meant going back through the xith'cal I'd just broken free of. I shot again to clear another path, but right as the white wave of plasma left Mia's barrel, a big warrior jumped on me from behind.

I went down hard, skidding across the blood-slicked metal floor. The xith'cal on my back threw his head down to bite me, but to do it, he'd had to shift his weight, and that gave me my opening. I wrenched my arm back and shoved Mia's barrel right in his face, firing a tight blast that took his head off.

His weight wobbled, and I pushed myself up, shedding his body as I started forward again. The xith'cal were swarming now. I fired another wide shot and bought myself a few more feet, but when I went to fire again, all I got was a quiet click.

I pulled the trigger three more times before my drug-jacked brain caught up with what that clicking meant. Mia was dry.

It's a testament to how much I love my guns that I didn't toss her away. Instead, I swung her over my shoulder one-handed and clicked her back in place while my other hand grabbed Sasha. The second my glove touched my pistol's grip, her ammo counter popped up on my screen.

Twenty-five shots.

I had spare clips on me, but somehow I didn't think the xith'cal were going to give me the five seconds it took to reload. Not when they had me surrounded and all I had was a pistol. Twenty-five shots, then. I would make them count.

Still running, I brought up Sasha and pegged the xith'cal in front of me before my targeting system could catch up. Even with the drugs, it was a damn near perfect shot. I kicked its body out of the way and jumped, grabbing onto a tree branch fifteen feet above me.

The dying tree groaned under my weight, but it held long enough for me to swing forward and land on a xith'cal ten feet ahead of where I'd shot the last one, right on the edge of the circle that had formed around me. My suit doesn't weigh enough that I can kill a xith'cal by landing on it, so I shot the one under my feet as well. It was a hard shot, but my targeting system lined it up perfectly. The bullet landed right between the eyes, and the xith'cal went down without a sound as I landed on its crumpled back and kept running.

One by one, I shot the xith'cal. I didn't hit the head every time, but I didn't get caught either. And then, halfway to the airlock, everything went wrong.

I was down to five bullets, but as I barreled over the xith'cal I'd just shot, his death throes caught me on my injured shoulder. The blow hit me with a spike of pain even the drugs couldn't bury completely, and I stumbled.

It was barely a second, but it was enough. The moment I slowed, another xith'cal hit me from behind, crushing me under his weight. I flung Sasha over my shoulder and shot him using my rear cam, but his efforts to bite my head off knocked the barrel sideways and the shot went crooked, ripping through the scales on the side of his face but missing his brain.

I shot again, hitting him right this time, but the miss had cost me. Even as his grip weakened in death and I tore myself free, another xith'cal grabbed me around the waist. I shot him easily, but his weight slowed me further, and I looked up to see I was sur-rounded.

I shot the first xith'cal that came at me before my brain caught up with what had happened. I stopped, my lungs thundering, my ammo alarm screaming in my ear. One shot left. One shot.

I looked at Sasha as the xith'cal began to close in. An armor-piercing bullet could rip through my helmet with no effort at all. A quick death, painless and honorable, and with the drugs, I wouldn't even be afraid.

One shot left.

I raised Sasha to my temple with a silent apology to my beautiful suit for ruining it like this. Strangely enough, my last thought was shame that I'd failed in my promise to Rupert. But then, just as I was overriding the final safety that kept me from firing my gun at myself, I heard something that made me pause. The xith'cal were still packed around me so close that all I could see was their rotting flesh, but they were no longer looking at me. Instead, their heads were turned toward the sound I'd just heard. The sound of combat.

If I'd been myself, I would have taken this opportunity to run. But I was fearless and drugged, so I stood up to see what was happening. What I saw made even my drug-jacked heart skip a beat. There were even more xith'cal in the huge gallery than I'd thought, and wading through them, cutting them down like a thresher through grain, was the black alien from Mycant.

Though I'd only seen it through the grainy video, there was no mistaking that tall black figure. When I'd first seen it looming behind Ren, I'd thought it was strange and frightening. Now, watching it slice through the xith'cal like a hot knife through black snow, the only thing I could think was that it was beautiful.

Looking through proper cameras and not a compressed feed, I could see that its body was indeed armored like a xith'cal's. A healthy xith'cal with glossy, ink-black scales. Its claws were even longer than I remembered, and they shredded everything it touched. Its tall, armored body sang of speed and power as it sliced through the horde. No movement was wasted, no opening given. The black figure was so glorious, I didn't realize it was coming for me until it smashed into the line of xith'cal that penned me in.

It cut them down like all the others, and then it was standing over me. The black armor that covered its chest was rising and falling, like it was panting. Before my brain could finish that thought, the black figure crouched down and scooped me into its arms so quickly I didn't realize what had happened until it started running forward, carrying my armored body like I weighed nothing.

Pressed against the alien's chest, I was close enough to study its face. This was also as I remembered it, the sleek, black scales broken only by two narrow, glossy black eyes. There was the sharp mark of a nose and no mouth at all, just like before, and I knew it had to be the same one I'd seen with Ren.

As the alien carried me, it briefly occurred to me that I should be afraid, but my drugs made that impossible. Mostly, I was worried that my weight would hamper the alien's fighting, but I should have known better. The black figure moved like death itself, kicking the xith'cal away with enough force to send them flying into the distant walls. Its arms held me like a steel trap, squeezing so tight I couldn't even wiggle, and I felt a trickle of terror at the idea of being trapped. That trickle started a flood of panic of a different kind, and I snapped out of my focus on the alien to see my countdown timer blaring red at the center of my vision.

"Out of time," I muttered.

My rescuer looked down at the sound of my voice, and I tried to give it a reassuring smile. "Listen," I said calmly, hoping to the king that it spoke Universal. "In fifteen seconds, I'm going to look kind of scary." That was an understatement, but I didn't have time to explain. I could already feel the drugs fading, taking the last of my supernatural clarity with them. I started talking faster. "I'm locking my suit so I don't hurt you when I start to seize, but you need to get me to a doctor as soon as possible. My unlock code is five five six eight two."

The alien nodded and started running faster.

But drugs aren't a certain thing. Though my timer said I still had ten seconds, I could already feel the pain and panic coming back. But even as I clamped my teeth to keep from biting off my own tongue and prayed to my king to guide me to the gate of heaven, the honorable part of me demanded I take one last risk, just in case I didn't get a chance to say it later.

"Thank you," I said as my body began to shut down.

"No!" cried a deep, almost frantic voice. "Stay with me, Devi!"

The words sounded very far away, but I'd know that accent anywhere. That was Rupert's voice.

And with that realization, the first seizure hit, and my brain went black.

CHAPTER
11

I woke up in terrible pain. I was lying on something freezing cold and metal and my body was arching off it like I was trying to touch my stomach to the ceiling. I hadn't even known I could move like that, and I would have been impressed if my shoulder hadn't felt like it was being cut off. I heard an annoyed hiss, and then someone's arms pushed me down.

New pain rocked through me as I hit, and I might have started to cry. I certainly screamed, but whoever was holding me down with that impossibly strong grip didn't listen. I felt straps slide over me and cinch down as they tied me to the table. But even when I was lashed so tight my suit couldn't have gotten me out, the person holding me didn't let go.

I heard a voice begging, but it took me several seconds to realize it was mine. I should have been ashamed of myself, pleading like a dog on that table, my babbling voice switching from King's Tongue to Universal with no rhyme or reason, but all I could think about was the pain in my shoulder as another pair of hands, these gentle and cold where the others were hard and warm, tore out my collarbone. Or, that's what it felt like. They might have just been setting it, but they could have been beating me to death with it for all I knew. The world had shrunk to me, the table, the hands, and the pain, and when the cool hands stabbed something into my arm that made me sleep, I leaped gladly into unconsciousness, completely determined never to wake up again.

I did wake up again, but it wasn't nearly as bad as I'd feared. My shoulder still hurt, but the pain was distant, someone else's problem. I was still strapped down, but the straps made me feel safe instead of trapped. The cool hands that had torn out my bone were gone and the lights were dimmed, though I couldn't tell if that was because it was night cycle or out of courtesy to my eyes, which felt strangely raw.

I went to raise my hand to rub them and realized I couldn't. My arm was trapped by the hard, warm hands from before. The ones that had held me down.

The hands vanished the second I started to panic, and Rupert's face appeared above mine. He was saying something I couldn't understand, but the calm reassurance in his voice was clear even if the words weren't. He stroked the hair out of my eyes and then gently folded my hand in both of his. They were warm and strong, and I realized with a start that his arms had been the ones holding me down.

Somehow, knowing they were Rupert's took the panic away, and I collapsed back onto the table, tumbling into sleep as I hit.

The third time I woke up, it was for good.

I was lying on a gurney in the infirmary dressed in a white medical gown. The straps were gone, but I could feel where they'd been. If I could have gathered the strength to lift my head, I'm sure I would have seen bruises wherever they'd touched, but since I was sure of what I'd see, I didn't bother. Instead, I lay still and focused on getting myself together.

Battle drugs normally left me feeling like my head was going to explode for three days after, but this time, while I didn't feel great, I didn't feel like I was going to pop either. Mostly, I felt like my brain was full of cotton, which was much better, but I was having trouble focusing. Before I could get really worried about it, however, a handset appeared in the air in front of my face, its screen covered in angry, bold type.

Are you aware enough yet to be lectured?

"Not if you put it like that," I said. My throat was so dry, the words came out as a croak.

Hyrek's scaly face appeared above mine, and for a frantic moment, I thought I was going to have a panic attack. Just seeing him sent the memory of that horrible rot flooding back up my nose. I could almost feel the enormous weight of the xith'cal on my stomach, his milky eyes staring blindly at me as he bit down. But as my breath started to grow short, I forced myself to look at Hyrek's scales, to see how green they were, how clear his angry eyes were, and the fear gradually subsided.

"Okay," I whispered, flattening myself against the gurney. "What lecture did you have in mind?"

Hyrek snatched back his handset and clicked it furiously. *You nearly died three times in the last six hours, and do you know why?*

"Because my shoulder was nearly bitten off?" I guessed.

Your shoulder was the least of your problems, Hyrek clicked furiously. *Your* shoulder—he highlighted the word twice—*was set within five minutes of you coming in. It was the drug-induced convulsions strong enough to nearly break your spine that caused our difficulties. Do you have any idea how dangerous that sludge you pumped into your system was? I'm not even sure those drugs are regulated for human consumption.*

"Why Hyrek," I muttered. "I didn't know you cared."

I don't, Hyrek wrote, claws slamming down. *But if you die, Caldswell yells at* me, *and I'm not about to take the heat for your completely idiotic* and irresponsible use of illegal drugs in battle situations. *Honestly, you're lucky you have a nervous system left, or a brain for that matter. I thought for sure you'd fried both.*

"Nah," I said. "This isn't nearly as bad as last time."

Hyrek's scales stood up, and he gave an enraged snarl. *You've done this before?*

"Only twice," I lied. I'd done it four times, but this didn't seem like a good time to admit that. "Look, if it comes to dying or getting five more minutes on my feet, I'll take my chances with the seizures. We all do. That cocktail is standard Paradoxian issue." Well, mostly.

Hyrek threw back his head with a hiss. *And you call my people animals.*

That sounded like the perfect place to change the subject. "What happened to the ship?" I said, trying to sit up, only to lie back down immediately. Sitting was a very bad idea.

Hyrek glared at me again for good measure and then sighed, a low, whistling sound. *That's a complicated question. Your camera went out early, but Cotter's caught several shots of the xith'cal before he got away. I've never seen xith'cal like that. Those were not Stoneclaw's flesh.*

I wasn't quite sure what that meant from a xith'cal point of view, but I agreed. Those things may have been xith'cal once, but not now. "I don't know what they were," I said. "Xith'cal usually run cold, but I couldn't see these on my thermal scan at all." They'd been cold as the metal they lay on, I realized with a shudder of my own. Cold as death.

I stopped, suddenly terrified. One of those things had *bitten* me. "Oh, god," I moaned, staring up at Hyrek. "Please tell me I didn't get some kind of xith'cal rabies."

Hyrek snorted. *There are so many things wrong with that statement I don't even know where to begin. First, xith'cal and humans are completely biologically incompatible, which renders interspecies transmission of any sort impossible. Secondly, even if our races could infect each other, xith'cal are cold-blooded. Rabies only affects warm-blooded carbon-based Earth-descended life-forms.*

"So, that's a no?"

Definitively, Hyrek typed.

That made me feel a little better. Still. "Those lizards were sick with something," I said. "Did you send Cotter back in to get a sample? They were fast, but not smart. I bet we could lure one into the airlock and trap it long enough to get something."

Hyrek gave me a look that, on a human, would have been horror. *No, and we're not going to.*

"Why not?" I demanded. "I thought the captain was doing this because he was curious, and I want to know what the hell attacked me."

See for yourself. Hyrek set his handset down and walked over to the battered monitor on the wall, which was currently displaying my heartbeat and vital signs. He touched something on its side, and the screen flickered, changing to an exterior view.

The camera was on the tribe ship, which looked exactly as it had before, huge and dark, but no longer alone. It was now surrounded, as were we, by enormous ships like nothing I'd ever seen. They looked almost like deep sea creatures, thin and long with beautiful muted patterns in blues and greens. The things glowed with their own phosphorescent light, throwing lovely pale colors across the tribe ship's drab hull as they slid gracefully through the space around it like fish through calm water. So gracefully, in fact, that I didn't realize how big they were until one passed right over us.

"God and king," I hissed, cringing against the bed. The ship gliding over us was large as a Royal Cruiser, easily ten times the size of the *Fool.* "What the hell is that?"

Hyrek walked back to me and picked up his handset. *A lelgis battle fleet.*

"Oh," I breathed. I guess they weren't happy about the dead lelgis we'd found inside the tribe ship. But while I didn't know anything about the lelgis, I did know a thing or two about battle fleets, and this seemed like a pretty huge show of force for a relatively small number of dead squid. Of course, I'd only seen one room. Maybe it would have gotten worse if Cotter and I had been able to get farther in. "What do they want?"

The captain is talking with them now to try and figure that out, Hyrek typed. *If you could even call communicating with a lelgis talking, that is. They appeared five hours ago, and they've been circling like carrion eaters ever since.*

"Are they carrion eaters?" I whispered, my nose suddenly full again of the terrifying rotten smell of the xith'cal ship.

Of course not, Hyrek clicked. *They don't even honor their dead unless it's a central mind. They're all hooked up, you know. They have one mind that does all the thinking for a colony and controls the rest.*

"What, like a queen?" I said.

Hyrek shrugged. *You could call it that, though I don't think it's an accurate designation, as queen implies female. So far as anyone's been able to tell, lelgis don't have genders.*

I opened my mouth to ask another question but snapped it shut again when the *Fool* began to move. Basil must have had a heavy foot on the thrusters, because we jerked away from the tribe ship like we'd been burned, racing full speed in the other direction. As we fled, the beautiful shapes of the lelgis ships darted behind us with amazing speed, surrounding the tribe ship in seconds. And then, in a blaze that whited out the screen, they began to fire.

The tribe ship lit up as the lelgis' cannons crumpled its hull, tearing through the inner levels in waves of pale blue fire. They kept up the barrage the entire time we were flying out, and by the time I lost sight of the attack behind the asteroids that floated across our camera, the enormous tribe ship was all but destroyed.

"What was that about?" I cried.

I don't know, Hyrek typed. *And considering how fast we left, I don't think I want to. It's very probable that, were our captain not who he is, that fire would have consumed us as well.*

I went very, very still. "And who is our captain?" I asked, eying the xith'cal.

Hyrek glared down at me. *The kind of man the lelgis do not want to make an enemy,* he wrote. *I suggest you leave it at that, mercenary.*

I didn't need the growl Hyrek added. I let the subject drop instantly, but I didn't forget a word.

"Well, at least the lelgis had the right idea," I said. "Purging it with fire is the only good solution to a nightmare like that. Tell me how we made it out. I don't remember anything after the drugs crashed."

Hyrek leaned on the edge of my bed. *Cotter came out first, raving about monsters. We couldn't see your cameras, but we could still pick up your vital signs. We knew you were alive. The captain was trying to bribe Cotter to go back in for an extraction when you floated out on your own. We roped you in and sealed up. Once the air was back, Rupert unlocked your suit and carried you here. You've been my burden ever since.*

I closed my eyes so Hyrek wouldn't see the doubt in them. That wasn't what had happened at all. In addition to the extreme focus, or maybe because of it, battle drugs make sure you remember every detail of what happens while you're on them. I could see my rescuer clearly, the black scales, the blindingly fast movements. I'd thought it couldn't speak when it would only nod to me, but I knew I'd heard its voice at the end. Rupert's deep, accented voice, lovely even when it was frantic, telling me to hold on.

Hyrek's claw tapped me on the shoulder, and I opened my eyes to see his handset hovering above my face.

Get some rest, it read. *I'm going to get something to eat and then I'll be back. Punch the button if you need me.* He tapped the handset against the large red button on the gurney's arm.

"Gotcha," I muttered, turning over as much as the pain would allow.

The xith'cal's claws clicked on the metal floor, and then the door whooshed and I was alone. I lay there for a long time, trying to get my brain together enough to solve the puzzle I found myself in.

The biggest piece was Caldswell. Not only did he have a Royal Warrant, but the lelgis had listened to him. Before today, lelgis had been little more than spacer's tales to me. I'd been amazed to see dead ones, let alone a battle fleet. Now that I thought about it, though, I was having a hard time believing our captain had just stumbled upon a derelict tribe ship thousands of light years outside its normal range filled with sick xith'cal and dead lelgis right before a lelgis battle fleet showed up to destroy it. I mean, it *could* have happened—and I *could* wake up tomorrow and be the princess of Paradox.

Given how important Caldswell and whatever he was doing were to my future, I should have spent the next several hours obsessing over what he'd been after on that ship, why the lelgis cared, what the rotting xith'cal were, and why he'd sent Rupert to save me, but my brain kept sticking on that last one. When I'd first seen the black thing standing behind Ren in the video, I'd assumed it was an alien of some kind. Now, though, I knew, *knew* it was Rupert. Even if I'd imagined his voice at the end (and to be fair, the drugs had been fading at that point, so it wasn't impossible I'd hallucinated the words), Hyrek had said Rupert had been the one who'd gotten me out of my armor. The black scaly figure was the only one I'd given my emergency code to, and the Lady Gray doesn't give me up easily. Without the code or Caldswell's Warrant, I don't think anyone on the ship besides Cotter would have had the strength to rip me out. But Hyrek had said nothing about the captain or ripping, just Rupert pulling me out and carrying me to the infirmary.

I closed my eyes. If I'd come floating out like Hyrek claimed, that meant Rupert must have let me go before we got to the *Fool*, pushing me toward the cargo bay. I was a little insulted at the idea of being shoved off like so much unwanted baggage, but the more I thought about it, the more things started to click into place.

I'd known something was going on with Rupert, and the idea that he'd been the thing standing behind Ren in my video made way more sense than an unknown alien. I had no idea what the scales were or how they worked, but he'd crossed the vacuum in them and somehow gotten back onto the *Fool* without being seen, probably through the emergency hatch on the roof. I didn't know of anything that would let you do that other than a suit, but those scales didn't look like any suit I'd ever seen.

Breathing deeply, I thought back to my first glimpse of Rupert tearing his way through the xith'cal to get to me. The drugs brought the picture back crystal clear, and again, I was struck by how beautiful he'd been. How deadly. In hindsight, I should have guessed his identity earlier. The black scales were heavy, but the shape of Rupert's tall body was lovely enough to recognize beneath them now that I knew what I was looking at.

That thought made me smile. I might not know what to make of it, but it seemed I'd found out Rupert's secret at last, and I hadn't even had to break my promise not to question him about it. But my smile faded as quickly as it had come. Why had he risked that secret to save me?

After the drugs, my memories were less reliable, but I remembered Rupert's hands—how they'd held me down so I wouldn't hurt myself on the table, how gently they'd stroked my fingers and brushed my hair out of my face. I remembered the relieved look in his eyes as he'd talked to me, and that made me think back to last time we'd been in the infirmary together, when he'd treated the ankle I'd almost broken on his side. He'd been so worried that I'd be afraid of him, and I'd told him I never would be, right before I told him I wouldn't ask what he was.

A lot of things had happened since then, but had anything really changed? Then, as now, he'd taken care of me. He'd rescued me twice, I realized with a start, here and back on Mycant. Ren certainly wouldn't have yanked me out on her own. He'd made her save me, just as he'd come himself to save me this time. Now that I knew for certain, I couldn't sleep any longer.

Modern medicine is a wonderful thing. Back home broken bones had taken months to heal, but once I'd gotten into the military I'd never had to wait more than an hour or so. Bone knitting was expensive, but downed soldiers were even pricier. Apparently Caldswell agreed, because my broken collarbone had been knitted beautifully. Hyrek must have used a skin grafter and synthetic blood as well, because I didn't feel weak like I usually did after a big wound, and the skin of my shoulder was healed smooth with only a circle of faint red marks left to show where the xith'cal's teeth had dug in.

Sitting took me a long time, but that was mostly due to the painkillers Hyrek had pumped into me. Once I was up, I shook off the haze quickly, breathing long, deep breaths until the cotton-headed feeling went away. When I was thinking clearly again, I slid off the table and rolled my shoulder in a slow circle.

It was sore, but no more so than after a good workout. I tested my other limbs one at a time without incident, and my face broke into a grin. It looked like I'd danced out of death's jaws yet again.

I found my clothes in a bin by the door. My underarmor was a shredded, bloody mess, but someone had dug a fresh set of clothes out of my duffel, a red and gold T-shirt from the Kingston Armor

Rally, my purple capri running pants, and a fresh bra and underwear, both sky blue. Considering the color combination, I figured it had to be Nova, and I made a mental note to thank her as I shed the medical gown. Someone had washed the blood out of my hair as well, but drying spread out over my pillow had left it in huge, unmanageable waves. I combed it down as best I could with my fingers, and then, dressed and presentable as I could make myself, I slipped out the door.

It was night cycle, and all the corridors were dark. Even so, I moved like I was on a stealth stakeout, sliding along the walls to dodge the cameras, my bare feet silent on the padded rubber floor. I wasn't breaking any rules that I knew of, but I wasn't dumb enough to believe Hyrek or Caldswell would think very highly of what I was doing. If either of them caught me, I'd have to stop, and stopping was the last thing on my mind. So I kept quiet and low, sneaking down the spiral stairs to the *Fool*'s lower level.

By the time I got to the bottom, my heart was pounding so loud I thought I'd wake the ship. Part of it was anticipation, but mostly it was the need that always came over me whenever I'd narrowly escaped death. Much as we try to dress it up, fighting is an animal business. Even though I'd become a merc for the money and the glory and the chance to make a better future for myself, at times like this, when I'd cut it so close I could still feel death's breath on my back, all I wanted to do was throw myself into someone's arms and celebrate the fact that I was still alive. And here, now, after all that had happened, there was only one pair of arms I wanted.

The *Fool* had two levels of cabins. Nova and I were upstairs, along with Basil, the doctor, and Cotter. The lower level was the family floor where the captain and his daughter lived, along with Mabel. Rupert's room was down here as well, a small cabin tucked up against the back of the engine right next to Caldswell's suite. The drone of the long-haulers covered my footsteps, but even so, I crept like a thief until I was standing right in front of Rupert's door.

I felt strangely nervous as I reached up and knocked softly. Usually, this situation happened the other way around, with me being inside and the boy in the hall. But I was the one dangling this time, and I held my breath for several seconds until the door opened and Rupert stood before me.

I took a moment to drink him in. He'd always been lovely to look at, tall and handsome with his long black hair and bright blue eyes, but somehow he looked even better now. I must have woken him, because he was dressed in a soft white undershirt and navy sweatpants, the only thing other than a suit I'd ever seen him wear. His hair was free and hanging down around his shoulders except for the little bits that were sticking up from where he'd been lying on the pillow. His eyes widened when he saw who was at his door, and then he gave me an exasperated look. "You should be in the infirmary."

"I'm fine," I said, stepping a little closer.

His face grew wary, and when he spoke again, his voice was unusually low. "Do you need something?"

"Yes," I said, proud that my words weren't as breathy as I felt. "I need to thank you."

He pulled back, crossing his arms over his chest. "No need," he said, trying for casual and failing. "All I did was pull you out of your armor and get you to the infirmary. Anyone else would have done the same."

That wasn't all he'd done. I wanted desperately to tell him so, but I couldn't take that risk yet, so I settled for a half-truth. "No one else did," I whispered, stepping closer still. "Just you."

"I was doing my job," he said, his voice as quiet as mine as he looked down at me.

I smiled. "Last I checked, you were a cook, not security rescue."

I was so close now I could feel the heat of his body bleeding through his shirt. Slowly, hesitantly, I reached up to press my palms against his chest. His breathing hitched as I made contact, and his hands shot up to grab my arms like he was going to push me away.

But he didn't. He just stood there, looming over me, his eyes so dark I couldn't make out their color anymore. With my hands on his body and his palms wrapped around my wrists, I could feel the too-fast rhythm of his heart hammering against my skin.

"What are you doing?" he whispered. The question was little more than air.

"Thanking you," I breathed back, standing on tiptoe to press my lips to his.

He froze completely, his mouth like a wall against mine. I licked his lips with the tip of my tongue, waiting for him to respond, but Rupert was a rock beneath me, completely still. He didn't even seem to be breathing.

As the seconds ticked by, my stomach began to sink. When I'd decided to do this, the idea that he wouldn't want it too hadn't even occurred to me. I'd never had a problem like this before, but then I'd never gone after a man like Rupert before. Whatever he was, he wasn't a merc. He didn't live our rough-and-tumble, take-what-you-can-get life.

Oh god, I realized as my sinking stomach hit bottom, I'd just made a fool of myself, hadn't I? Maybe Caldswell *had* ordered him to save me. Maybe I was throwing myself at a man who was just trying to find a polite way to get me to leave, and this time I couldn't even blame it on the whiskey.

Crushed and embarrassed, I broke away, sliding my hands off his chest and out of his grasp. Knowing it was stupid, I glanced up at him through my lashes, but what I saw only drove the rejection deeper. His face was closed and cold, his eyes dark. The earlier warmth had vanished completely, and I knew, just *knew* I'd ruined everything.

"Listen," I started, looking anywhere except at his eyes. "I—"

Rupert grabbed me before I could finish, swooping down so fast it was like he teleported. One second we were standing apart, the next I was in his arms, crushed against his chest with my feet dangling off the floor and his lips on mine. He kissed me so hard I couldn't breathe, but I didn't need air. I didn't need anything except him. As soon as my initial shock faded, I flung my arms around his neck and pulled myself tight against the hard wall of his body, kissing him like I never wanted to stop.

And then it did.

Fast as he had scooped me up, Rupert broke the kiss and set me down, untangling my arms from his neck. We were both breathing hard as he stepped back, putting some distance between us. "I'm sorry," he said, running his hands through his hair and over his shoulders like he was trying to find something to touch that wasn't me.

"Why?" I panted. "I'm not."

Rupert shook his head. "It's not—" He stopped to steady his breathing. "It's not that simple, Devi."

"I don't care about simple!" I snapped, clenching my fists.

At this point, the need to confess was almost overwhelming. I desperately wanted to tell him what I'd seen, to tell him I knew everything, and none of it mattered so long as he'd just kiss me like that again, but I didn't dare. Not yet, not when he was pulling away.

"I know there are things you can't tell me," I said, breathing deep to keep my words from going choppy. "But I told you before, your secrets are yours. They don't have anything to do with us or what's happening right now." That wasn't entirely accurate, but, to my own surprise, what I said next was. "Between you and the truth, I'd rather have you."

Rupert closed his eyes. "It's not that simple," he said again. "Trust me, Devi, you don't want this."

I stiffened. "Don't think for one second you can tell me what I want," I said, my voice shaking with anger and frustrated passion. "Don't you *dare* assume you can tell me what I think. I'm my own person, I make my decisions. *I'm* the only one who knows what I want." My eyes narrowed. "And I fight to get it."

Tense as he was, Rupert's lips curled into a small smile. "I know that very well," he said, looking at me again. "But we can't. We have to stop, Devi. Now, while we still can."

He wanted me. The moment he told me we had to stop, I saw the hunger in his eyes, the wild longing I knew was mirrored in my own. My chest expanded with a deep, relieved breath. I hadn't been wrong before. Rupert did want me, then and now, and that was all I needed.

My arms shot out faster than he could dodge, wrapping around his chest until I was pressed flush up against him again. "You assume stopping is still an option," I said, rising up to kiss him on the cheek as I slid my way toward his ear. "But it's too late for that," I whispered when I got there, letting my lips feather against his hair. "Far, far too late."

Rupert made a sound deep in his chest. We stood there pressed together for a breathless moment, and then, like a dam breaking, he burst into motion. His arms slid down and scooped me up like before, like I weighed nothing. Cradling me against him, he stepped back into his room as the door slid closed behind us, locking with a soft click.

CHAPTER
12

For better or for worse, I've slept with a lot of men in my life. Some were better than others, but no one, *no one* has ever made love to me with the intensity that Rupert did.

After what had happened in the hallway, I'd thought it would be fast and wild, but Rupert took his time. He sat me down on the bed and peeled my clothes off, kissing me all the while until I could barely think. It wasn't just that he was a good kisser (he was), it was everything. The way his fingers clung to mine like I was the only thing holding him down, the way his mouth slid over my body like every inch of me was the most important inch in the universe, the way he whispered my name against my skin like a prayer, his lovely accent rolling the word into something so beautiful I barely recognized it.

I was less graceful as I yanked his shirt over his head, breaking the kissing only when I had to as I tore his clothes off until he was gloriously naked. His body was as beautiful as I'd imagined—long, hard, and lean as a fighter's, and he curled it around me like a cage as though he was afraid I'd disappear. He kissed me hard then, and I matched his ferocity with my own, tangling my fingers in his long, silky hair as I locked his mouth to mine.

After wanting him for so long, actually getting to touch him was its own kind of heaven. Even pressed naked against the wall of his chest, I couldn't touch enough. His fingers had always been warm when he'd touched me before, but he was on fire now. Heat poured off him like a radiator, warming me to the tips of my toes. His skin was surprisingly soft, a thin layer of silk over the steel of his body. His muscles clenched and rippled under my roving fingers, and his breathing grew ragged.

I grinned against him and kept going, running my hands over his shoulders, up his arms, down his back, over his chest, everywhere I could reach. The more I touched him, the wilder he became, pulling me against him with delicious ferocity. When he finally entered me, I couldn't help a moan of sweet satisfaction, but when he started to move, all I could do was hold on, my face buried in the crook of his neck as I let the desperate pleasure wash through me until all that remained was the intense feeling of being alive, of being cherished, of being the beautiful, precious thing he whispered I was.

I came once, hard and early, and then again, long, lovely, and slow. The second time I pulled him over with me, and we collapsed together onto the narrow single bunk. Boneless and deeply content, I rolled onto my side while he curled around me with his arm under my head and my back pressed against his chest. We were both sweaty, and my hair was clinging to everything, but I couldn't have cared less. I snuggled closer, stretching my whole body against his as he pushed back some of my wild hair to kiss the delicate skin under my ear.

Happy as I was, the heat of him was roasting me, so I pushed myself up and rolled over until I was lying on my stomach beside him. He kept his arms around me the whole time, watching me with a smiling, serene expression that was the most open look I'd ever seen on his face. His eyes were bright and blue as they studied me, taking in my hair, my face, the curve of my shoulders, the line of my back, everything he could see, like he was trying to memorize it. His hand slid up to stroke my cheek, and I leaned into the touch.

But as I turned to kiss his fingers, I caught sight of the thin black tattoo across his wrist I'd first noticed when he was chopping turnips what felt like forever ago.

I took his hand and held it in front of me, pulling his wrist right up to my face so I could examine the mark. I'd thought it was just a design, but up close, I realized it was writing. Like he'd taken a black pen and written a note across the inner skin of his wrist in a language I'd never seen.

"What does it say?" I asked, running my thumb across it.

He said something that sounded like water running down a mountain, all long vowels and fast slippery S's broken up by harder consonants.

"What?"

"This life for Tanya," he translated.

I bristled, instantly and irrationally jealous. He must have felt me stiffen, because he chuckled. "Tanya is my sister," he said, kissing my shoulder. "She died a long time ago."

There was an old sadness in his words that killed my jealousy faster than hearing she was his sister. "I'm sorry," I whispered, releasing his hand.

"I am too," he said, and I felt the bed shift as he lay back. "She would have liked you a great deal, I think."

"Really?" I turned to wrap my arms around him, sliding neatly against his side like I was made to fit there. "Anyone else I should worry about impressing?"

"No," Rupert said. "Just me, and I'm already very impressed."

I bit him, and he laughed, hugging me closer as he bent to plant a kiss on the top of my head.

Happy and more relaxed than I'd been in months, I lay against him, staring up at the ceiling in the half dark of the night cycle. I must have gotten used to Nova's taste in decor, because Rupert's room felt almost stark. It was shaped like an L with his bed taking up most of the long end and a rack of his ubiquitous suits along the short end, shoes lined up neatly below. Other than that, the room was bare as a monk's chamber. The only thing on the walls was the big energy pistol he'd used to fake holding Caldswell hostage on the bridge.

The gun hung in a dark leather holster on the wall above my head, its heavy inlaid pearl handle in easy reach from both the bed and the door. That made me smile. I also slept with a gun in easy reach. Only sensible thing to do. That thought pushed my smile even wider as I snuggled down against Rupert. Nice to see I'd picked a man with some sense for once.

"Devi?"

"Hmm?" I said sleepily. Rupert's voice was so quiet in the dark I could barely make it out. I was starting to doubt I'd heard it at all when he didn't speak again immediately.

"How much do you remember from the xith'cal ship?" he said at last, his arms tightening around me.

I hid my surprise at his question behind a long, languid stretch. This was probably as good an opportunity as I'd ever get to come clean, but the thought of saying something that could wreck the beautiful, contented peacefulness between us made my whole body twitch.

"Nothing much," I lied. "The drugs take as much as they give. Considering how I woke up, I don't think I want to know. Why do you ask?"

I knew I'd made the right choice when Rupert's body relaxed against mine. "Just wondering," he said, pressing me close with one arm while the other reached up to stroke my hair.

I buried my face against his smooth chest, breathing in his warmth. I hated lying to him so blatantly, but the more I thought about it, the more I convinced myself it was for the best. If Rupert thought I didn't know what he was, then he wouldn't worry about exposing his secret. So long as my ignorance kept us both safe, I would happily play dumb. Right then I'd have played anything if it meant he would keep holding me like this, petting my hair so gently, like it was the most wonderful thing he'd ever felt. With every stroke of his hand, the contentment sank deeper into my bones until, at last, I drifted off.

I don't normally sleep with my lovers. It goes against too many years of ingrained paranoia for me to let myself be that vulnerable, and then there's the part where I've never been quite sure I wouldn't attack them when I woke up to something moving beside me. I don't know if it was the lingering effect of the drugs, exhaustion from my injuries, or just something about Rupert himself, but I slept the whole night pressed right up against him. I woke when the lights came on for the day cycle to find Rupert up and already dressed, sitting on the bed beside me.

"Hey," I said, rolling over.

He grinned and leaned down, kissing me long and languid until I was very happy to be awake. But when I tried to put my arms around his neck and pull him down to join me, he gently caught them and pulled me up instead. "Time for you to get back to the infirmary," he said, handing me my clothes, neatly folded.

"You still have doubts about my health after last night?" I said as I stepped into my underwear.

Rupert just stood and walked to the door, watching me dress with a smile on his face. When I was decent, he caught my hand and pulled me into him. He'd kissed me when I'd woken up, but that kiss was nothing like this. That kiss had been slow and sweet, this one started hot and quickly grew to the intensity he'd had last night. He kissed me desperately, like he'd never kiss me again, his arms clenched so tight around my waist I couldn't do anything except lean into him.

Like I needed encouragement. I kissed him back with everything I had, matching passion for passion until we were both panting. When he finally pulled away, I thought it was to pull me back to bed, but he didn't. Instead, he straightened his jacket and stepped aside, opening the door to let me out.

I shook my head and stepped into the hall. "Get a girl all worked up..."

He chuckled, but he didn't touch me again. I pursed my lips at him in an invisible kiss and started for the stairs. He watched me the whole way, a strange, almost sad expression on his face. As I hit the second spiral, I saw him turn and walk the other way, down toward the end of the hall where the captain kept his quarters.

Hyrek was waiting for me when I walked back into the infirmary. He did not look happy, though I couldn't actually be sure of that. I've never seen a happy xith'cal to compare.

I won't ask where you were, he typed, claws moving over the handset with accusatory clicks. *But I would remind you that ignoring your doctor's orders and gallivanting around with a very recently healed compound fracture and the remnants of mind-altering battle drugs still in your system is only slightly less stupid than taking the drugs in the first place.*

"Sorry, Mother," I said, hopping up on the table. "For what it's worth, I feel fantastic. If you're half as good at carving up humans as you are at putting them back together, I'm almost sad you're not a butcher anymore. A great loss for the xith'cal race."

Hyrek didn't seem impressed by the compliment. *Butchering is male work.*

"Ah ha!" I cried, stabbing my finger straight at Hyrek's snout. "You *are* a female. I knew you were too small."

I'm not a female.

My face must have been a sight, because Hyrek laughed with a sound like a knife across glass. *Xith'cal are born genderless. We live in the hatchery until we come of age, doing both male and female work, and then we pick the gender that suits us best. I didn't like either, so I didn't choose.*

"You mean you're neither?" I said. "What, are you still a child then?"

Hyrek snorted. *Hardly. By human reckoning, I'm almost sixty. Neutrals live as long as females, who live twice as long as males.*

"So you just decided to be genderless?" I said. "You can do that?"

Obviously, Hyrek typed with a droll look.

I rolled my eyes and Hyrek sighed. *It's not a common thing. Tribe structure is rigid. Everyone has a place. Females are our thinkers, males are our warriors, females run the ships, males hunt. A genderless adult doesn't fit into the established order, so you can see how life could be difficult for those who don't choose.*

I remembered his sleeping arrangements with new appreciation. "That's why you're here, then? Because things got 'difficult'?"

Among other reasons, Hyrek typed. *I find living outside the tribe ship to be my safest option. Humans aren't exactly welcoming, but Caldswell has been my captain for many years now. He gave me a job and a haven when no one else would have me. I take my duties on this ship very seriously, which is why, the next time you come into my infirmary, I'm going to tie you to the table so you don't embarrass me again by wandering off in the middle of the night.*

"Sorry." And I meant it, sort of. "But I really am fine."

Hyrek's yellow eyes widened. *Are you a doctor?*

"No," I said. "But neither are you."

On this ship, I'm whatever Caldswell says I am, Hyrek typed. *Right now, I am your doctor, and when it comes to your level of "fine," my opinion is the only one that matters.*

I tried a few more arguments but eventually gave up. Arguing with Hyrek was like arguing with a dead apple tree—fruitless. Still,

I wasn't above giving him a smug grin when he was forced to admit after thirty minutes of tests that I was, in fact, fine.

"So what do I call you now?" I asked as I hopped off the table. "He? She? It?"

"He" is fine, Hyrek typed. *Humans are a backward sort of species that puts one gender before the other. Seeing this, I've found it's much easier to be thought of as male rather than female, especially looking as I do. And since the designation is meaningless to me, I don't see why I shouldn't take the easier choice.*

"Sounds sensible to me," I said, walking toward the door. "I'm going to check my gear and report in. Last chance to poke something."

Hyrek made a face. *I've had more than enough of that for the moment, thank you. I know staying out of trouble isn't exactly your forte, Devi Morris, but do try not to mortally wound yourself again anytime soon. You might not feel it at the moment, but the bone knitter and skin grafts did hurt you, and there's the trauma from the initial injury plus whatever you did to yourself with that poison you injected. The drugs seem to inhibit your response to normal pain-killers and sedatives. I had to give you enough to knock out a warrior xith'cal this time. It might get better, but I can't say for sure. Next time they might not work at all. So, please, save us all some trouble and try not to get anything else stabbed through you.*

"I'll do my best," I said, trotting into the hall.

I had absolutely no intention of getting my shoulder bitten off again anytime soon. Of course, I hadn't intended to get bitten this time either, but there wasn't anything to be done about that. Some mercs throw themselves into danger, but I've always tried to be practical. Still, taking shots was part of the job, and there was no way in hell I was going to start pulling my punches now.

For some reason, I'd thought my armor would be in its case. It wasn't, of course, because I was the only person who could open my case. But if it wasn't there, then I didn't know where it would be.

This kicked off a small panic as I went through the ship looking for it. Finally, I asked Cotter, and he led me down to the far corner of the cargo bay.

At first, I almost didn't believe the torn pile of silver metal on the ground was my suit. I fell to my knees, frantically gathering the Lady Gray into my lap. The ripped shoulder I'd expected, same for the large dent in my helmet, but the rest was a complete shock. Every single piece was damaged. My boots had huge claw gouges. So did my gloves. My four leg pieces were so mangled I was amazed I could still fit them together, and my chest piece was practically crumpled from the bite that had taken out my shoulder, plus three other bites that hadn't made it through.

It was astonishing to see. I hadn't even realized I'd been hit that much, but that was part of what battle drugs did—no pain and no fear meant you didn't notice when you'd been wounded. Still, the scariest thing by far was the condition of the suit's interior.

"God and king," I muttered, turning my chest piece over so I could get a better look. "I'm amazed I had any blood left in me."

"You started bleeding like a hose once the foam came out," Cotter said. "Charkov was the one who got you out and carried you to the doctor. He was scary intense. I didn't know a cook could move that fast."

I ran a finger over the suit's torn shoulder, and my chest tightened. My beautiful baby. My lovely suit. I forced myself to put the chest piece down before I cried in front of Cotter and set about looking for my guns.

I found them beside my suit and, praise the king, they were both fine. Out of ammo, but neither Mia nor Sasha had more than a few scratches. Phoebe wasn't there, of course. I'd lost her forever, broken and abandoned in some xith'cal's chest cavity. Fortunately, aside from the custom jointing to make her fit in my armor, my blade had been fairly unmodded. Replacing her would be nowhere near as impossible as replacing my other girls.

Cotter watched as I set my guns carefully aside, his suit creaking as he shifted his weight. "Listen, Morris," he said at last. "About what happened inside, how I left—"

"Forget it," I said, grabbing my left glove, the least damaged piece. "Getting out was the smart thing to do. If you'd stayed, we might both have gotten chomped. All I care about now is getting my suit fixed."

"It's a Verdemont suit," Cotter said. "Those come with a self-cleaner and auto-repairer in the case, don't they?"

"There's no *way* all of this is coming out with the self-cleaner," I said. "And this damage is far beyond what the repair system can handle. Not if I want my suit back this year, anyway."

Cotter shot me the most earnestly sympathetic look I'd ever seen on him. It was so sudden it made me tip back in surprise, though it really shouldn't have. He was an armored merc, after all. He felt the pain of a damaged suit just as much as I did. "What are you going to do?"

"Find a repair shop," I said, gently laying my glove on top of the rest of my suit before standing up. "A good Paradoxian one. There is no way in hell I'm handing my baby over to a bunch of pig-handed Terrans."

"Where are you going to find a Paradoxian shop out here?" he said, following me up the stairs.

I didn't answer because I didn't know, but I knew how to find out. Leaving Cotter to patrol duty, I jogged down the hall and burst onto the bridge. "Basil!" I called. "I need your help."

Basil and Nova were both standing at the top of the bridge by the sensor console, and they turned in unison to stare at me. "Well," Basil said. "Hello and good morning to you, too."

I was in no mood for his snark. My baby was hurt and I had to fix her. "I need to get to an armor repair bay," I said, hopping down the stairs to his pilot's nest. "A good one, by which I mean Paradoxian."

"Oh, I'm doing fine, thank you for asking," Basil said, slowly walking down the steps behind me. "So glad you're feeling better. Where did you learn to be so polite?"

"Basil!" I cried. "This is an *emergency*."

Basil flapped once, landing in his nest with a fluff of ruffled feathers. "That's funny, I didn't know powered armor died from lack of attention. Maybe we should get it a bed in the infirmary, too?"

"I'll put you in the infirmary if you don't get on this," I snapped. My suit was not a joking matter.

"Temper, temper," Basil said, but he brought up the star map.

The projected stars swung around him in a dizzying blur as Basil tapped the console in front of him with his long feet. After a few seconds, the rush of stars stilled on a gaseous planet with a large green moon.

"You're in luck," Basil said. "After that last fiasco, the captain decided to change course for the Republic. We're headed for the Jero System, but this is more or less on our way."

"What is it?" I couldn't read most planet codes without a dictionary on my best days. Reading them backward through the back of Basil's display was absolutely impossible.

"Seni Major," Basil answered, like this was too obvious for words. "According to the index there are a couple of armor repair places here, one of which lists itself as Paradoxian."

I leaned through his projected display to get a better look at the console screen. Sure enough, the repair shop he'd brought up bore the king's commerce crest. Even in the Republic, you didn't show that lightly.

"That'll do," I said, leaning back before Basil could bat me away. "How soon can we be there?"

"Four days," Basil said. "Assuming, of course, the captain approves the change in course."

"Where's Caldswell?" I said. "I'll convince him."

Basil frowned and punched another screen to his left. "He should be here by, ah..." He lifted his head high into the air with a smug toss of his crest feathers. "Right on time."

"Morris!" I heard my name before I heard the door open, and I looked over my shoulder to see Caldswell standing in the hall. He caught my eye and beckoned. "This way."

I stood up and marched after him. As I passed Nova, she gave me a relieved smile. "I'm so glad you're all right," she whispered.

"That remains to be seen," I whispered back with a pointed look at Caldswell.

The captain didn't say anything as he led me down the hall to the stairs. I swallowed as we started going down toward the lower level. The captain usually had no problem yelling at me in public. If we were going to his cabin, this was going to be bad. I scrambled to think of what I'd done that could have made him this mad, but the list was pretty long. It could be any number of things: the drugs, blowing off Hyrek's orders, the expense of the bone knitting I'd needed, forcing Rupert to come save me.

By the time we reached his door, I had no better idea what this was about than when he'd first called me down. His face was set in a calm frown, but I could feel the anger radiating off him like heat. He opened his door and waved me through. I went, putting on my best brave soldier face.

As expected for the captain, Caldswell's rooms were much larger than anyone else's. He had a sitting area with two small couches and a table, plus two bedrooms and a private bath. Best of all, he had a large window looking out the ship's prow into the endless space beyond. The metal floor was covered in a worn but nice carpet, and there was a small console in the corner with screens showing feeds from the various cameras all over the ship.

Through the door, I could see his daughter's room. It was small and plain, but that was to be expected. I'd never heard Ren express an opinion, much less actively buy something. The real surprise was that Caldswell's bedroom was equally bare, just a tiny room with a neatly made single bed, a nightstand with a lamp, a large blaster similar to Rupert's hanging on the wall. The only personal touch was a small picture in a glass frame, but from this angle, I couldn't see who it was.

Mabel and Ren were sitting together at the small table by the window when we entered. Ren was playing chess as always, only this time she was playing on a nice wooden board instead of the plastic set she used in the lounge. She didn't look up when we came in, but Ren never looked up at anything. Mabel, however, stood the second the door opened, taking Pickers, who'd been in her lap, with her.

The fat old cat jumped down with an accusatory hiss and ran for the hall. Mabel followed, giving me a sympathetic look as she slipped past us. I waited for Caldswell to shuffle Ren out as well, or at least send her to her room, but the captain said nothing, and I got a horrible sinking feeling in my stomach. Getting chewed out was bad enough; getting chewed out in front of a civilian, even one as weirdly vacant as Ren, was ten times worse.

Caldswell cleared his throat behind me, and I turned to face my fate. He'd closed the door and planted himself in front of it, arms crossed over his broad chest. The captain was not a tall man, but he was built like a brick, and now, trapped in the room with his fury, I suddenly felt very small. Even so, I refused to cower. I stood straight, eyes ahead with my arms at my side, military style, and waited to hear which of my numerous infractions he'd chosen to start tearing into me for first.

"I understand you spent the night with Rupert."

Despite years of training, I blinked. That was not on the list of things I'd expected him to be mad about.

"Did you?" Caldswell said.

"Yes sir," I said, a little late. "How did you—" I snapped my mouth shut before I could shove my foot any farther in. You didn't question your superior officer when you were getting chewed out. Fortunately, my insubordination didn't seem to make Caldswell's anger any worse, but the next words out of his mouth certainly took mine up a notch.

"Rupert told me."

My hands squeezed into fists before I could stop them. I might have marched out right then if the captain hadn't held up his hand.

"Before you take it out on him, you should know he didn't come bragging to me or anything like that," Caldswell said. "He only told me because he knew I'd find out, and he was trying to do damage control." The captain glared at me. "You're a terrible sneak, Morris. If Hyrek's report that you'd vanished from the medbay and couldn't be found wasn't a big enough tip-off, I keep motion sensor cameras on my door. Rupert's cabin is right next to mine. Your secret was out the moment the two of you decided to start necking in my hallway like a couple of teenagers."

I took a deep breath. Caught like an amateur. But though my fury was tingeing the room red, I forced myself to be still. I could be angry later. Right now I had to deal with Caldswell, who was glaring at me like he was trying to decide which piece to chop off first.

"This is my ship," he said, his voice low and deadly. "There are rules that must be maintained, and one of those is no fraternization. I'm not running a love shack here, Morris."

"I understand, sir," I said.

"I don't think you do," Caldswell said. "This isn't a big outfit like the Blackbirds. I can't just swap you around if things get uncomfortable. I fly a small ship through dangerous territory, and I will not have anyone's job compromised by personal feelings. I don't care how this infatuation started, but it stops right now. So long as you are on my payroll, you will not go near Rupert. You will not touch him, talk to him, or look at him unless it is directly related to your job. Do I make myself clear?"

"Very clear, sir," I said. "But, with all due respect, I don't see how my relationship with Rupert is harming the ship." I was treading on dangerous ground, but after last night, the idea of not being able to kiss Rupert again was making me feel pretty dangerous. "I've been a good soldier for you since I came onto this ship, and I mean to continue to do so. Rupert is not a distraction."

"Not for you, maybe," Caldswell said. "But you're not the only one who broke the rules, are you?"

His words were sharp and angry, and suddenly I realized that this was bigger than just me.

In hindsight, this was the place where I should have remembered that I was supposed to know nothing. This was the moment where a smart soldier would have lowered her head and kept her mouth shut. But I've never been good at playing docile, and my anger had me tight by the throat.

"This isn't about me sleeping with someone on the ship," I growled. "You're mad because I slept with Rupert."

"You're damn right I am," Caldswell said, his voice as angry as mine. "Your involvement didn't surprise me at all, but Charkov damn well knew better!"

"That's not fair!" I cried. "You can't just put all the blame on him like that!"

"I'm happy to blame you both!" the captain shouted back. "I

blame you for thinking with your hormones instead of your head, though with your record I should have known not to expect anything else. But Rupert knew *better.* He knew exactly how bad getting tangled with you was, but he did it anyway, and now he has to pay for it. How's that for fair?"

"Very well, sir," I said, looking him straight in the eye. "What's our punishment?"

"Charkov's punishment is none of your business," Caldswell said. "You I'm letting off with a warning."

"A warning?" He had to be jerking me around. After all that bluster, there was no way this was ending with a warning.

"Yes," Caldswell said. "Oh, I had something good, but Rupert volunteered to take the heat for you, so you get off easy today."

His words hit me like a punch in the gut. "He can't do that!"

"He damn well can if I say so!" Caldswell shouted. "Whose ship do you think you're on?"

I almost sealed my fate right then. I *almost* opened my mouth to ask him whose ship *was* I on, with a trader captain who did no trading, fought invisible monsters, kept his terrifying psychic daughter under guard like a prisoner, and flashed a Royal Warrant as though it were nothing. But I didn't. My ambition was finally beating its way through the burning fog of my anger, and I was at last starting to remember that this was the man who held my future in his hands. If I blew things now, all my work over the last decade was for *nothing.* It wasn't enough to douse my rage completely, but it let me get the control I needed to step back from the abyss.

"Whose ship, Morris?" The captain growled at me.

I clenched my teeth. "Yours, sir."

Caldswell nodded, a sharp jerk of his head. "Don't you forget it. Now, while I'm sorely tempted to come down on you anyway given how you've acted, I'm a man of my word. You're getting off today, but it's never happening again. I catch you doing anything on my ship you wouldn't do in front of your grandmother, I'm tossing you out at the next port. We understand each other?"

It was physically painful, but I ground the words out somehow. "Yes sir."

"Good," Caldswell said. "Now, I'd punish you for disobeying your physician's orders, but I'm pretty sure Hyrek's going to do that himself the next time you're under the knife, so for now you're back on duty. Any questions?"

"Yes sir."

His eyebrows shot up. I don't think he expected me to talk back after that display, but I had business to settle. "Do Cotter and I get our hazard pay for exploring that ship?"

"Yes," he said, eying me cautiously. "It should already be in your ship account."

I nodded. "Then, if you want me to keep doing my job, I need your approval to take the ship on a detour to a repair shop on Seni Major so I can get my suit fixed."

Caldswell frowned. "That's pretty far out of our way. Jero's a big colony—isn't there someplace there you can use?"

"I would shoot a Terran mechanic before I let him touch my Lady Gray, sir," I said. "Seni Major has a Paradoxian shop. If we can't go there, then I'll be doing my job in my skin until we can find a Paradoxian operation that's closer to your route."

Caldswell heaved an enormous sigh. "Fine," he said. "Tell Basil to set the course."

"Yes sir," I said, waiting.

He glared at me. "Dismissed."

I bowed and marched past him, desperate to get out while I was still in control. But I must have used up all my luck, because when I got to the door, Caldswell caught my arm.

"Remember what I said, Morris," he said, his eyes boring into mine as he held me with surprising strength. "Don't go near Rupert again. You disobey me on this, I'll kick you off so fast your head will spin, and you can kiss any hope of being a Devastator good-bye. Understood?"

My breath caught, and I actually had to fist my hands in my clothes to keep from punching him. "Understood, sir," I said, proud that I kept most of the murder out of my voice.

He let me go, and I stomped out into the hall. I heard his door close behind me, but I didn't look back. I didn't even look where I was going, which was how I almost ran into Rupert, who was waiting at the top of the stairs.

"*You*," I snapped, putting a good foot of distance between us. "You knew this would happen."

"I did," Rupert said quietly.

I lowered my voice to a whisper as well, which meant my next words came out as a hiss. "Why didn't you tell me?"

He looked at me skeptically. "I did try to warn you."

"Well, you could have been more specific with your doom and gloom," I said. "Or at least warned me you'd have to tell the captain." Not that it would have stopped me, but at least Caldswell wouldn't have caught me flat-footed.

Rupert had the good grace to look abashed, and I heaved a long sigh. "You shouldn't have taken the punishment yourself, either. What's he making you do?"

"Nothing too bad," Rupert said, pushing a stray lock of hair out of his face. I watched, envious. I'd liked his hair before, but after last night, running my fingers through it was one of my new favorite things. "I think the captain's more disappointed than angry. I let him down."

"Why, because you had a good time?" I scoffed. "Just because he's a sad sack doesn't mean everyone around him has to be."

That made Rupert smile, and the expression made my heart

clench. Suddenly, the idea that I couldn't kiss him right then was unbearable, and I closed my eyes in disgust. When had I turned into an infatuated teenager?

"Well," I said, getting hold of myself. "I guess that's that." I held out my hand. "Thanks for a good night, then. Sorry we won't be doing it again."

"Me too," Rupert said, taking my hand gently and then letting go at once, like touching me was painful.

"Come on," I said, forcing a smile. "We're still friends, right? I mean, he can order us not to talk all he wants, but I still need drinks."

Rupert nodded seriously. "Can't cut Devi off from her drinks. It would mean her death."

"I'm not that bad," I said, glancing at the hall camera. Caldswell hadn't come out of his room yet, so I would have bet my suit that he was watching us right now. Mature woman that I am, I gave the camera a nasty look and turned back to Rupert. "I'm off to go yell at a bird. See you around, okay?"

"Take care," Rupert said.

I waved at him and jogged away. I still wasn't quite in control of myself, so I didn't look back. If I did, there was no guarantee I wouldn't start crying out of pure frustration, and I would never live that down. Instead, I set my jaw and pulled myself together. I was Devi Morris, decorated war hero, former squad leader of the Blackbirds, and future Devastator. I was *not* going to get all mopey over a man, no matter how funny or handsome or good in bed he was. I was going to get my armor fixed, and then I was going to do my damn job, just like I always did. Rupert and I had both agreed it was over, so that was that. All we had to do was let last night go and everything could return to how it was before. Shouldn't be hard. We were both adults, after all. Rational people with careers and things in our lives we cared about more than each other, things we could easily lose by being stupid. With that in mind I was sure, absolutely positive, that we would have no trouble obeying the captain's orders and keeping our hands off each other. True, it might be hard at first after our intense connection last night, but given a few days I was sure life would go back to normal. No doubt. One hundred percent positive.

And that's what I told myself all the way back to the bridge.

CHAPTER
13

Of course, it wasn't that easy.

We were on our way to Seni Major with only a minimum of complaining on Basil's part. I'd packed my suit into its case as best I could, but though the cleaner had gotten most of the blood out, the automated nano-repair had barely made a start on the damage. Finally I just turned it off altogether and resigned myself to waiting.

That in itself was bad enough. Without my armor, I was useless. Unlike Rupert, I couldn't fire Sasha barehanded without risking a broken arm or worse. I could have fired Mia, but while a sixty-pound plasma shotgun is nothing in armor, it's pretty impractical in any other situation. I had my concealable pistol, but it was a weak, unmodified little peashooter I'd only bought because I couldn't stand going unarmed. It wouldn't even tickle a xith'cal, but I wore it anyway, mostly so I wouldn't feel so naked. Having it on my hip didn't help my mood at all, though, and that was a real pity, because something needed to.

With no armor, I couldn't do my job, which meant I spent most of the four-day trip to Seni with nothing to distract me from Rupert. Oh, I tried to ignore him, but as Caldswell said, the *Fool* is a very small ship. I'd never thought so before, but when you're trying to avoid someone, it's like the whole place shrinks. Suddenly, I seemed to be running into Rupert everywhere, and while he just smiled politely and went about his business, usually escorting Ren around or bringing food to whatever crew members couldn't be bothered to drag themselves to the mess, I stood there watching him like an idiot.

I couldn't help it. I'd been attracted to Rupert from the moment we'd met, but after our night together, it was like my body had become hyperaware of him. Sometimes I caught myself staring and looked away before it got too obvious, but mostly Rupert caught me, and then I felt nothing but fury at myself for turning into one of those pining, hopeless girls I used to make fun of. Truly, it was a pathetic display.

Strangely enough, it was Caldswell who came to my rescue. Unable to stand the idea of idle hands on his ship, he started finding work for me. I still had plenty of hours left from my punishment for Mycant to make up, so I spent most of my time cleaning. I scrubbed the cargo bay and mopped the hallways, cleaned the kitchen (while Rupert wasn't in it, thank the king) and the bridge, anything I could get to, really. It was stupid, brainless work, but I threw myself into it because it gave me something to do other than mope. I even put on one of the shapeless metal boxes Terrans have the gall to call armor and went outside to sand down the hull.

I actually liked hull duty. True, doing it in one of the *Fool*'s spare suits was nothing like doing it in my own armor, but it was still nice to be out. There's something about the cold silence of space that helps put your life in perspective. There was no rush, so I took my time with the work, picking the bits of shrapnel out of the hull in all the spots Mabel had marked and then sanding the rough parts down again with careful attention. Sometimes I just blatantly stopped working and stared at the stars as they slowly flowed past.

It was during one of these peaceful moments that I first saw them.

I'd just finished sanding down a particularly bad spot on the ship's belly and I was taking a break, hanging from my magnets as the universe flowed by when I caught a flash of movement by my foot. I looked down, worried that my sander had somehow broken its anchor and was now lost to the void, but what I saw put all other thoughts out of my head. A creature was sitting on the ship not three feet from me. It was small, about the size of a large cricket. I wouldn't have noticed it at all against the dark hull if not for the fact that the creature glowed with a soft blue-white light.

Entranced, I took a step forward, but the creature moved away before I could get close, dancing across the ship's hull like a crab scuttling across the sea floor. I tried again, but it was soon clear I couldn't get more than a few feet from the thing. Even worse, the shoddy Terran suit I was wearing didn't have a camera, just a large plastic face shield, so I couldn't even zoom in. I had to settle for watching from afar.

I sat down, staying very still in the hope that the thing would come closer. But while it did skitter around me, it never came any nearer. Seeing it from many different angles gave me a pretty good idea of its shape, though.

It looked sort of like a spider, but with more legs. It was mostly legs, actually. The long appendages made up the vast majority of its size, sprouting off a tiny abdomen no longer than the first joint of my pinky. The legs were curled rather than jointed, almost like the thing was walking on bending wires, and they gave it a sort of soft, bouncing motion, like it was moving underwater.

In addition to the blue-white glow, the creature was semitransparent, like its body was made of frosted glass. It had three large, bobbing antennae sticking up from its head, or what I assumed was its head. It had no eyes that I could see, so I couldn't be sure.

After I'd watched it bounce around for almost five minutes, the tiny creature vanished right in front of me. Not like I lost sight of it or it jumped or anything like that—I mean it *vanished*. Poof. It happened so suddenly I actually lunged forward, like I could catch it. I couldn't, of course, not in Caldswell's slow brick of a spare suit. I looked anyway, just in case, but I didn't see it again before it was time to go in.

I thought about telling someone what I'd seen, but as soon as I was back inside, the wreck my life had turned into came crashing back down. It was dinnertime, and most of the crew was in the lounge to eat. Rupert was serving, and, since this was a perfectly normal crew function, I sat down to enjoy some completely irreproachable time in his company.

During the two days since Caldswell had ordered us apart, I'd almost convinced myself that Rupert really had let it go. While I was watching and moping, he seemed completely himself. He was polite, if distant, though that was probably my fault, since I kept staring at him. Still, he never showed any sign that he regretted how things had ended, or that he thought of me at all.

Tonight was no different. He handed me my plate with the same half smile he gave everyone and kept his eyes on his work. I ate in sullen silence until Nova showed up and started into some enormous story about a problem with the scanner array they'd been having all day.

I threw myself into conversation, glad to have something, *anything* to pull me out of my self-pity. Plus, it made Nova so happy to talk about her job, and her joy was infectious. By the time we were done eating, I was actually relaxed enough to laugh at her terrible Basil impressions, which was why I didn't notice Rupert behind me until he reached over my shoulder to take my empty plate.

He must not have expected me to lean back, because when I did, my back bumped into his chest. We both froze. Pressed against him, I could feel his heart thudding and the tension in his muscles as he held his breath. And then he was gone, clearing my plate away with a soft apology for bumping me.

Nova noticed none of it. She just kept telling her story, hands waving excitedly, but I couldn't make sense of her words anymore. My brain was caught in a loop, replaying the last few seconds over and over. I hadn't seen Rupert's face during the exchange, but somehow I was sure he'd been looking at me. In the split second we'd been pressed together, I'd felt him stop just as I had.

It might have made me a terrible person, but the knowledge that he wasn't actually as calm as he put on, even just for a second, was a huge relief. But even as the discovery comforted me, it started my thoughts down all kinds of dangerous paths. Paths that led to me doing something dumb, like cornering him and kissing him until we both couldn't breathe. I was actually planning how I could do it when my good sense slammed back in like a kick in the teeth, and I knew I had to get out. So, with a hasty apology to Nova, I excused myself and headed for the cargo bay.

There is no better cure for a traitorous brain than exercise. I ran twenty laps around the empty cargo bay and then did push-ups until my arms gave out. I was about to start on my sit-ups when I heard someone open the door from the lounge. For one stupid moment, I hoped it was Rupert, but when I looked up it was Hyrek who was standing on the stairs above me.

He held out his handset. *I need to run a few more tests. Are you free now?*

"Free as I'll ever be," I panted, standing up. "Do you want me to shower first, or can I be sweaty?"

Hyrek wrinkled his snout. *You stink either way, so let's just go now.*

I shook my head and followed him up the stairs.

The tests he wanted were blood tests, so I sat on the table while he drew three vials and took them off to the machine in the corner.

I'd pushed my muscles too hard in my little hissy fit exercise session, and now that I was still, my body was knotting up. I stretched my shoulders and arms while he worked, trying to ease the burn that ran through my upper body. I was flexing my calves in a futile attempt to head off the cramps when a light moved across the top of my vision. I looked up more out of habit than anything else and froze in place, legs still extended.

The glowing bug from outside was crawling on the ceiling.

The first thing my brain did was list all the sensible reasons why I couldn't be seeing what I was seeing. First, the thing from earlier had been outside the ship. We were sealed against the vacuum, so unless it had come in with me, there was no way it could be inside. Second, the ship had air, pressure, and gravity. A deep-space creature should have been smashed flat by any one of those, but the little glowing bug was skittering along just like before, hopping delicately on its long, bouncy legs. The lights didn't seem to dim its glow at all, either, though its frosted glass body was harder to make out against the white ceiling than the dark hull.

I slid off the table very slowly, trying for a better look, but as before, the thing shied away from me. I couldn't even get close enough to be sure it was the same one from outside, though considering I'd never seen anything like this up till now, I was skeptical that there would be two different glowing space bugs on the ship today. I was trying to think of how I could get around behind it when I heard Hyrek's claws clicking.

I looked up. He was standing over the analysis machine, staring at me strangely as he held up his handset. *What are you doing?*

"I'm trying to catch that bug thing," I said, pointing at the glowing creature on the ceiling.

Hyrek followed my finger, and his expression grew bewildered. *Bug thing?*

"Yes, look." I pointed again. "It's hard to see against the white, but it's there, left of the light about three feet and moving toward the wall."

Hyrek gave me one more skeptical look and walked across the room until he was standing right under the place where I was pointing. I started to yell at him not to get so close or he'd scare it away, but the bug didn't seem to notice him. It just kept gliding silently along the ceiling, its antennae waving right above Hyrek's head.

"Hold still," I said, creeping forward. "I don't think it sees you."

The second I moved, the bug bolted, running toward the corner. I froze, but it was spooked now. It turned its antennae toward me one last time and then ran straight through the wall like a ghost.

"Did you see that?" I cried, running over to the wall. I jumped up, slapping my hand against the place where the bug had passed through, but I felt nothing at all, not even a change in temperature. I looked over my shoulder at Hyrek, but the xith'cal was standing very still. I was about to ask what his problem was when I met his eyes, and then I knew.

He hadn't seen it at all.

After that, I had to sit through a lot more tests.

"I'm fine, Hyrek," I groaned, trying to pull the IV out of my arm. "I'll swear it by the Sainted King if you want. Will you please let me go?"

Hyrek swatted my hand away. *I don't believe in the Sainted King,* he typed furiously. *You should just be grateful I didn't strap you down.*

I flopped my head back on the bed with a frustrated growl. "I've been under a lot of stress. People see things when they're under stress, right?"

I'm more inclined to believe it's a lingering reaction from the drugs, Hyrek typed before setting down his handset to poke another needle into my poor, bruised arm. *I've never heard of any of those particular compounds causing hallucinations,* he wrote when he was done. *But then, I've never heard of anyone taking all of them at once either, so I wouldn't be surprised by anything at this point.*

"What are you even looking for?" I asked as he carried another vial of my blood to the analyzer. "It's not like you're going to see hallucinations in my blood."

Hyrek typed something and held the handset up over his shoulder. *You never know. And for your information there are certain chemical markers that can indicate the presence of hallucinogenic conditions in humans. Just because I haven't found any yet doesn't mean I won't.*

"It doesn't even matter," I said. "I know they're hallucinations now, so I'll just ignore them. No problem."

What fantastic logic. A gun-happy merc who sees things—I'm feeling safer already.

"It's not like I'm seeing hordes of xith'cal," I said. "They're just bugs, and not even real-looking bugs. I'm pretty sure I can handle it."

He turned around. *Have you seen any more?*

There was actually one walking across the table right behind him, but I sure as hell wasn't going to tell him that. "Of course not. All I've seen is a lizard wasting both of our time."

Hyrek made a sound like tearing sheet metal which I'd heard often enough by this point to guess was some kind of xith'cal curse. *I can't find anything wrong with you physically,* he typed at last. *But that doesn't mean you're healthy.*

"What else could it mean?" I said, exasperated.

The xith'cal tilted his head and clicked his handset several times, like he was writing and erasing something over and over. *You smell odd,* it read when he finally held it up.

I rolled my eyes. "I thought I smelled terrible."

You do, he typed back. *But it's a different kind of terrible than usual. At first I thought it was something lingering from the tribe ship, but that would have faded days ago. This smell is only getting stronger.*

"Great," I sighed. "I stink and I'm seeing things."

I don't think the two are related, Hyrek typed. *But I don't know anything at this point. I'd like to keep you here overnight for observation.*

"All you're going to observe is me sleeping," I said. But Hyrek was immune to reason, so I spent the night tossing and turning on a gurney with four machines hooked up to me. By the time the lights came on for day cycle, even Hyrek had to admit I was fine, and I was given the go-ahead to get back to work.

As I walked toward the door, the xith'cal stepped in to block my way. *You will tell me immediately if you see anything else,* he typed, sticking the handset right in my face. *That is a direct order given on the captain's authority.*

"Yes sir," I said, doing my best to look docile and contrite. Hyrek didn't buy it for a second, but he stepped aside, and I stepped into glorious freedom.

Thankfully, I didn't see the glowing bugs again before we reached Seni Major.

Unlike most places named Major I've been to, Seni Major was actually pretty big for a moon. The colony it supported was large as well, mostly logging companies lured by the shallow-sea rain forests that covered the entirety of the planet's equator. We landed at Station One, the largest city and capital, which looked like a village compared to Kingston but was a thriving metropolis so far as colonies went.

Because Seni Major was covered by one enormous shallow sea that never went more than a hundred feet deep, Station One was built on pilings, the buildings standing on stilts above the turquoise water. Even though the whole place had been logged thirty years ago to make way for development, the enormous trees were already back, shooting up from their root knots deep in the water below wherever there was room between the houses.

This overgrowth shaded the city beneath a huge green canopy. Several of the trees were blooming, and the boardwalks were littered with deep pink flowers as large as I was. If I hadn't been in such a terrible mood, I would have thought it was lovely.

But I wasn't here to gawk. The moment the ramp came down, I'd marched off the ship with my armor case bumping behind me and caught the first water taxi I saw to Kingston Armor Repair. It turned out to be a short trip. The shop was less than five minutes by boat from the spaceport. I felt better the moment I saw the king's flag above the door, but what really brought a smile to my face was the professional-grade refactory attached to the shop's rear.

When employing mechanics to work on something as complicated and expensive as custom armor, dress is very important. Fortunately, I was an old hand at these things, and I'd come prepared. I was dressed today in my favorite dress, a long, thin, clingy sheath in a rich dark purple that made my skin glow. I'd even dug out my makeup and done up my hair in a twist, and though I refuse to wear any shoes I can't run in, I did have on my nice sandals. All the pieces were pretty standard, but put them together with the right attitude and I looked like an incognito noblewoman, which was exactly the point.

I had the armor mechanic's full attention the second I stepped into his shop.

"My lady," he said in King's Tongue, bowing low. "How may I help you?"

Paradoxian law requires that you correct anyone who mistakes you for a noble the second it happens, but while I am the king's servant unto my death, this wasn't Paradoxian space and I was no longer in a Paradoxian company.

"I need this repaired immediately," I said in the airy, haughty voice I'd heard nobles use as I slid my armor case onto his counter. His eyes widened at the Verdemont crest, and I knew that if he hadn't believed I was a noble before, he certainly did now. Verdemont is quality.

"I don't know if I have the expertise to repair a suit like that, lady," he said apologetically. "With that sort of custom work, I—"

"I know," I said, cracking the case open. "That's why I asked the Master Armorsmith to load my schematics in the repair system's memory."

His face brightened considerably when I mentioned schematics. All armor aficionados love getting their hands on custom design sheets. But his smile fell to horror when he saw my suit's condition.

"God and king, Lady," he whispered, pulling out my dented helmet. "What happened to this poor suit?"

"Xith'cal," I answered, which was close enough to the truth.

The mechanic stared at me, jaw slack. From the look on his face, he was clearly trying to envision what kind of horrible circumstances would allow a noble lady to be chewed on by lizards, but peasants did not question nobility, and I certainly wasn't going to volunteer any information. "How soon can you have it done?"

"I'll have to refactor everything," the mechanic said, looking down in dismay at the Lady's piled pieces. "With the schematics, though, I should be able to get it done by next week."

I froze. "Next week?"

The cold threat in my voice had the desired effect. The words were barely out of my mouth when the mechanic began to sweat like a fever victim. "I can move some other clients, my lady," he said, keeping his eyes down. "Would tomorrow please?"

"It would indeed," I said. "The name is Morris."

His face went white as paper. I just smiled. After all, it's not my fault I share a surname with the infamous Baron Morris of Summerland.

While the mechanic closed the Lady's case and lugged her into the back, I plopped myself down on one of the three battered plastic seats by the open door overlooking the canal and the market on the other side. He put my suit down nervously on his work table. "I will not be done until tomorrow, lady. Surely, you would rather—"

"I'll wait," I said. I knew more about the Lady Gray than anyone except the Master Armorsmith of Verdemont himself. I might not be a mechanic, but I knew more than enough to recognize when something was being done incorrectly. Paradoxian or not, there was no way in hell I was going to let some colony tinkerer be alone with my armor.

Peasants do not talk back to nobles, and since I had obviously made up my mind, the man had no choice but to let me stay. I sat on the edge of the chair in the doorway, alternating between watching him like a hawk (and offering my pointed opinion whenever he did something I didn't understand or approve of) and catching up with the rest of the universe via my handset, since Seni Major actually got timely news updates, unlike the other backwater planets we'd been to. Even when I was reading, though, I had one eye on my suit.

Watching my suit get repaired is always a harrowing experience. My Lady is as near and dear to me as my own flesh, and seeing her crushed pieces being fed into the refactory put me in a vicious, protective mood that Seni's suffocating humidity wasn't doing anything to help. By the time he was ready to start work on my chest piece, the mechanic and I were both shaking, him from nerves and me from the pressure of not vaulting over the counter, snatching my beautiful Lady out of his hands, and fixing her myself. Still, other than the flashes of murderous rage, I'd thought I was keeping a pretty good hold on things until I heard a deep, familiar laugh from the street outside.

I whirled away from the mechanic to see Rupert standing on the boardwalk, his hands filled with bags from the market across the canal. "You know," he said, making no attempt to hide his amusement, "he'd probably work faster if you weren't hovering like you were about to eat him."

Considering the fool I'd been making of myself for the past several days, you would have expected the smile on Rupert's face to send me fluttering into the air. You'd be wrong. No amount of smiles could distract me when my precious armor was in someone else's hands.

"I'm just sitting here," I said, crossing my arms so he wouldn't see the white-knuckled grip I had on my handset. "It's not like I have anything else to do."

"In that case, let me put you to work," Rupert said, holding out a hand laden with bags. "Help me carry these to the ship."

My eyes widened, but Rupert just stuck his head in the shop door. "You won't mind if I take her away, will you?"

The mechanic gave Rupert the kind of reverent, thankful look usually reserved for the veneration of saints. "No, my lord. I will continue my work at full haste."

Rupert glanced down at me and gallantly held out his elbow. I didn't want to take it, but after that display I had little choice. Snarling at him and demanding to stay didn't fit the noble lady I was half pretending to be.

Besides, even with my armor in such dire straits, I wasn't completely immune to Rupert. Not when he drew me up and linked my arm through his, guiding me down the flower-strewn boardwalk. Of course, there was no way I was going to let him pull a stunt like that without repercussions, either.

"Why did you do that?" I hissed, twisting my head to keep the armor shop in sight as we walked away. "Who knows what that idiot will do if I'm not there?"

"Nothing half as terrible as he'll do by accident while shaking in fear of your wrath." Rupert's voice was measured and calm, but his eyes were twinkling with suppressed laughter. "Trust me, I'm saving your Lady Gray."

He might have had a point there. I was still stewing, of course, but as we walked down the crowded boardwalk, I realized this might not be so bad. Because of the oppressive heat, Rupert had shed his jacket and rolled up his shirtsleeves. My dress was sleeveless, and the touch of his skin on mine went a long way toward helping me get over my fury. It must have affected Rupert as well, because we got almost a full block before he remembered the excuse he'd used to drag me out.

"Here," he said, handing me two bags full of vegetables I didn't recognize. "Earn your keep."

I sighed dramatically as I threaded the handles through my fingers. "Fighting xith'cal isn't enough? I have to be a mule, too?"

"It happens to the best of us," Rupert said, rearranging his remaining bags to balance the weight. "Though with your natural stubbornness, I'm sure you'll do fine."

"And here I used to think you were so charming," I said with mock despair, swinging the bags as I walked.

Rupert chuckled but didn't reply. We walked another block in silence, and then he asked, "Why did Hyrek put you back in the infirmary?" His voice was light, like he was just making conversation, but I could see the tension in his shoulders.

"Nothing serious," I said. "Just more tests. He found nothing, just like I'd told him, but the old lizard doesn't like being wrong."

The tension eased out of him, and I tilted my head back to peer at his face. "What, concerned?"

His eyes stayed locked straight ahead. "You of all people shouldn't question my concern for your well-being."

There was no anger in the words, but I still felt like I'd been punched. I dropped my head, staring at my feet while I silently chewed myself out both for being a jerk and for the surge of giddy joy that came from knowing he'd worried about me.

"Rupert," I said at last. "I—"

"We should pick up the pace," he said, stepping out ahead of me. "Rain's coming."

I had no idea how he knew that. The sky, what bits of it I could see through the canopy, was clear blue. But the locals were clearing the boardwalk, and as we reached the spaceport, the rain started to fall.

We broke into a run, but by the time we'd made it to the elevated deck where the freighters were docked, it was pouring buckets of warm, tropical rain. My long dress was soaked through in seconds, and with the wet skirt tangling my legs, I started to fall behind. The downpour was so heavy I was having trouble seeing Rupert even though he was only a few steps ahead, so I was caught by surprise when his hand grabbed my arm and pulled me sideways.

I stumbled out of the rain into the shelter provided by the wing of an old planet hopper that, judging from the empty engine casing and the rust on its hull, wasn't leaving anytime soon. There was room to stand beneath the wing, though not to do much else, and I found myself panting inches away from a soaked Rupert surrounded by a thick curtain of rain.

I shoved my bags into the dry space under the planet hopper and braced my hands on its rusted hull as I caught my breath. Rupert hadn't appeared to mind the run at all, but by the time I straightened up, his breathing was quicker than usual, his chest rising and falling clearly beneath his drenched shirt. For a moment I just stood there, tracing the beautiful, lean lines of his body with my eyes, and then I forced myself to turn away before I did something stupid, like touch him. Instead, I focused on pulling the now-useless clips out of my soaked hair, but I couldn't see what I was doing, and the hair kept getting caught. I was about to give up when I felt warm hands push mine aside.

Rupert turned me around and began gently pulling the clips out until my hair was hanging free. I expected him to let go then, but he didn't. Instead, he stood just behind me, his warm fingers brushing my wet hair down my back.

"Here," he said at last, his hand darting over my shoulder to give me the clips.

"They're yours anyway," I joked as I took them. "You won them."

"They look better on you," he said softly, his fingers brushing my neck one last time.

The intimate contact left me shaking, and I cast about desperately for something to ground myself until I could get back under control. I settled on assessing the damage from the rain. My makeup was washed clean away, which I counted as better than being half washed and streaky, but my clothes were ruined. In addition to being soaked, my pale sandals were now black from splashing through puddles of tarmac grime. The run had also left long splashes of black sludge on the side and back of my dress where my feet had slung it up. I growled in frustration, partially because I'd ruined my favorite dress, but mostly because I looked disgusting in front of Rupert.

That thought made me even angrier. What the hell was I doing, worrying over my appearance in front of a man I was supposedly done with? I clenched my teeth. What was I doing fretting about how I looked to *any* man? Had I left *all* my dignity behind in Rupert's room?

"What?"

I jumped. Rupert's voice was closer than I'd expected. His hand touched my shoulder, steadying me.

"You're angry," he said quietly. "What's wrong?"

"Nothing," I snapped. "I'm just pissed because my dress is ruined." I looked down again at the long black splashes, and I nearly had to laugh—it was that bad. "God and king, I look terrible."

"No you don't," Rupert said.

"I look like a drowned rat," I protested.

His next words were so soft I nearly lost them in the rain. "You're beautiful, Devi."

I looked over my shoulder to see him staring down at me. He was so close, the rain dripping out of his hair landed on mine. The tropical water was warm, but it was nothing compared to the heat in Rupert's eyes as he looked at me. I think I stopped breathing then, my fists clenched so tight the hair clips dug into my palm.

A mercenary knows how to make fast decisions in the field. Even if he hadn't just said I was beautiful, the look in his eyes told me everything I needed to know. Rupert wanted to kiss me, badly.

Actually, I was pretty sure he wanted to do a lot more than kiss me, and he was fighting himself over it. I wanted to kiss him just as much, if not more, but unlike him, my mental battle was quickly settled. After all, Caldswell had told us to keep away from each other on his ship, and we weren't on his ship. We were standing in a tiny shelter surrounded on all sides by a rain that hid the rest of the world, and that little bit of logic was all I needed.

I moved so fast even Rupert couldn't dodge. One moment I was looking over my shoulder at him, the next I was pressed against his chest with my arms around his shoulders and my mouth on his, the hair clips clattering to the ground at my feet. I must have surprised him, because he stumbled back into the planet jumper's hull. I took advantage of the position at once, pinning him against the metal wall with my weight as I kissed him like I'd been dying to since the morning I'd left his room. For a second he just stood there, stunned, and then he was kissing me back, his warm hands sliding over my wet dress to lock me against him.

I moaned at the touch, and his breathing hitched as his fingers dug into me. Before I could adjust, he flipped our positions, lifting me up and turning so that I was now the one pinned against the ship with Rupert all around me. He kissed me hard, his grip so tight it was almost painful, and then he pulled away so fast I nearly fell.

I stumbled, grabbing the planet jumper's hull for balance as I tried to figure out what the hell had just happened. Rupert was now standing at the other end of the rain shadow, as far from me as possible. His back was turned, so I couldn't see his face, but I could see his muscles clenching under the clinging fabric of his wet shirt, his shoulders pulled up tight as a fighter's just before he delivers a deathblow.

"I'm sorry."

His voice was so resolute I wanted to cry. But I didn't cry. I got mad.

"Why are you always apologizing?" I yelled. "Caldswell may own us when we're on his ship, but we're not on his ship now. I wanted that just as much as you did, so don't you dare apologize to me!"

Rupert dragged his hands through his dripping hair. "I shouldn't have allowed this to happen," he said. "Any of it. It's my fault."

He turned then, and his face was the cold mask I'd seen on the bridge when he'd held a gun to Caldswell's throat. "This can't go on, Devi. It ends now."

"Why?" I shouted. "Because of Caldswell? Because you're all part of some huge secret and can't get Devi involved? Bullshit, Rupert!"

I was saying too much, but I didn't care. I was so sick of lies, mine and his. So sick of secrets. I'd told him before that I wanted him more than I wanted the truth, and I'd meant it, but this was different. If he was going to deny something we both clearly desired so badly, then by the king I was going to know *why*.

I lunged forward, slamming my fists against his chest as hard as I could. I've knocked over bigger men with that move, but, as always, Rupert didn't even wobble.

"Tell me," I said, staring up at him. "If something's wrong, tell me. If it's dangerous for us to be together, then tell me why. If it's because being with me will wreck your career with whatever Caldswell's into, then tell me that. Just *tell* me why you're pushing me away. Whatever it is, I can take it. I'm the merc, remember? There's nothing I can't handle. But don't you dare act like you were the only one who made these decisions. The idea that you 'allowed this to happen' is crap and you know it. Everything between us was a two-person gig, and I won't let you take it all on your shoulders. But don't you think for a damn second you can just push me away and not tell me why like I'm some weak little girl who can't take the truth."

"I don't think you're weak, Devi," Rupert said. He wasn't shouting. I'd never heard him raise his voice, actually, but there was an edge to his tone that made me cringe. "But it changes nothing. What happened between us was a mistake."

"It was *not* a mistake," I hissed.

"It was," he said. "*My* mistake. I was wrong, I put you in danger, but now I mean to make it right."

"There's nothing to make right!" I cried. "What danger am I in from you?"

Rupert looked away, and I felt his chest rise under my fists as he took a deep breath. Even with his head turned, I could see him icing over, shutting me out. Panic gripped me, and I leaned closer like I could somehow pull him back.

"There's nothing more to discuss," he said with cold finality, hands coming up to push my fists away. "This is ov—"

"I know what you are!"

Like a switch cutting off, Rupert's body went still, but I refused to be distracted. I'd just played my final card. It was now or never.

"I lied about what I remembered from the tribe ship," I said, staring up at the profile of his closed-off face. "I remember everything. I saw you there. I heard your voice, that's how I know you saved m—"

Rupert moved so fast I didn't even see it. One moment he was turned away, the next he was facing me with one hand gripping the back of my skull and the other over my mouth, cutting off my voice. His grip was painful, his hand burning hot against my lips, but it was the look in his blue eyes that got me most. They were wilder than I'd ever seen them, and I realized with a cold clench that Rupert was terrified.

"Not another word," he whispered, his fingers shaking. "Don't say another word. Whatever you think you remember, whatever you think you saw, it was nothing."

I made an angry sound of protest against his palm, and Rupert's fingers tightened until my jaw ached. "*Nothing*," he hissed. "You will never speak of this again. Not to me, not to the captain, not to *anyone*. Do you understand?"

"No!" I shouted, finally getting my hands up to rip his away. "You think I can't see what you're doing? You're trying to save me again, but I don't *need* saving." I clutched his hand in mine. "You don't have to lie or hide from me. Please." I could hear the desperation in my voice, and it's a testament to how afraid I was of losing him that I didn't even care. "*Please*, Rupert, tell me what's going on."

Rupert stared at me for a second, and then, like a falling tower, he slumped forward. His hands slid down to encircle my waist, and he pulled me close, his face landing in the spill of my wet hair where my neck met my shoulder. "I want to," he whispered against my hair. "I want to talk to you, Devi. So, so badly. But I can't. Once you know, there's no going back. It's no world for you."

"Shouldn't I be the one to decide that?" I said. My voice was low and angry, but I couldn't help leaning my forehead into the warm comfort of his shoulder.

Rupert raised his head with a jerk, and for the first time since the night we'd slept together, his calm mask vanished completely. "Why is everything a fight with you?" he said, eyes flashing as he grabbed my arms. "This isn't a contest, Devi. You can't just throw yourself at it until you win. I'm not keeping things from you because I enjoy it. It's *dangerous. I'm* dangerous!"

"So what?" I shouted. "My whole life is dangerous!"

"Not like this!" Rupert shouted back.

We stared at each other for a moment, our bodies tense like we were about to start fighting for real. But then Rupert closed his eyes. Feature by feature, his face relaxed, the cold calm falling back over him like a winter fog.

"This is over," he said softly, dropping his hands and stepping back so that we were no longer touching. "All of it. You will never speak of what you saw again, and in return, I won't tell the captain you kissed me."

My mouth fell open. "Are you threatening me?"

"Yes," Rupert said, looking at me through narrowed eyes. "Because you won't listen to anything else. In any case, this is never happening again. Everything between us is finished."

"The hell it is!" I shouted, lunging forward to grab him. But as my hands shot out, Rupert vanished into the rain like a ghost.

I stumbled as my fingers caught nothing, blinking at the blank wall of water where Rupert had been a second before, and then I turned and slammed my fists into the planet jumper's hull with a furious scream. The old ship rang under the blow like a gong. I hit it again for good measure before sinking to the ground and wrapping my aching hands around my knees.

I don't know how long I stayed like that, sitting on the dirty cement with the rain all around me, but by the time I stood up, the downpour had slowed to a drizzle. I brushed the grit from the pavement off my ruined skirt as best I could, and then I grabbed all the bags, the ones I'd been carrying as well as the ones Rupert had left, and carried them to the ship.

Mabel must have been busy while I was gone, because the cargo bay was nearly full. Caldswell and Basil were sitting in front of the piled boxes on a pair of battered folding chairs, watching the last of the rain.

"What happened to you?" Caldswell said, eying my wet clothes as I climbed the ramp. "I thought you were getting your suit repaired."

In an incredibly unprofessional move, I threw the shopping bags straight at his chest. To my disappointment, his chair didn't even tip as he caught them. "Is there something you'd like to discuss, Morris?"

"No sir," I said. "Just returning your property, sir."

He frowned, but I didn't wait around to answer more questions. I stomped up the stairs, through the mercifully empty lounge, and into my room. Nova was sitting on her bunk, but before she could ask what was wrong, I grabbed my towel and headed for the showers. I didn't even bother to strip out of my wet clothes, just shut the door and turned the water on hot as it would go. As the scalding stream rolled over me, I peeled off my wet dress, balled it in my fists, put it to my mouth, and screamed into it until I was reasonably sure I wouldn't shoot something.

Needless to say, I screamed for a long time.

CHAPTER
14

When I finally dragged myself out of the shower, the first thing I did was grab my handset and send a message to Anthony.

Considering how we'd parted when I'd left Paradox, running to Anthony now was pretty low, but he was the only person I knew who was high ranking enough to get me the information I needed. Rupert could threaten me all damn day, but if he thought I was going to bow my head meekly and slink off, he had another thing coming. If he wouldn't tell me what was going on, I would find the truth myself.

Righteous anger sent my fingers flying over the projected keyboard as I typed a long, detailed letter describing everything I remembered about Rupert's other form. I stuck to the basics, describing the black scales, incredible strength, and impossible speed but leaving out all the damning details like where I'd seen him and why I wanted to know. I also left out Caldswell and his Warrant. Even in my rage, that was a hornet's nest I did not want to kick, especially not with Anthony involved. But I was going to find out what Rupert was if it killed me. I was done being coddled, done being patronized. Rupert was wrong, this *was* a fight, me versus him, and from here on out, I was going on the attack.

I sent the message using the planet's network rather than the ship's. Seni Major sent communication drones into hyperspace every five minutes, so it would get there faster, and there was no chance of Basil seeing the letter and busting me. As an extra precaution, I used my old address from the Blackbirds. Not only would this make sure Anthony knew the message was really from me, it would keep Caldswell out unless he was ready to hack the Blackbirds' private mail.

Message sent, I closed my handset with a triumphant click and threw myself back on my bunk. But the satisfaction of sticking it to Rupert was short-lived. Bit by bit, my righteous fury was dying down, and as it went, the enormous wave of misery it had been holding back started to break through.

As much as I tried not to think about it, my brain kept flashing back to Rupert burying his face in my hair. Rupert kissing me. Rupert, vanishing into the rain.

Wetness began to pool behind my eyelids, and I put my pillow over my head, shutting out the world as shame overtook me. I was *not* crying. I hadn't cried since I was fifteen. I *didn't* cry... and yet all I wanted to do was break down sobbing.

I tried in vain to summon up my old standbys. Couldn't cry now, had to focus on my job. After Rupert's threat, I was pretty sure he wouldn't tell the captain about our conversation, but I was beginning to regret sending that message to Anthony. The size of the risk I'd just taken was only now starting to hit, and I suddenly realized that I might have just blown the career I'd worked my entire life for out of anger over a *man*.

That thought was the straw that broke the Devi's back. The wetness behind my eyelids began to spill over and seep into the pillow I was pressing against my face. A sob jerked in my chest as I curled over in self-loathing. God and king, how much lower could I sink? What had I *become*? This had to stop. Right now. I had to get myself togeth—

"Deviana?"

I jumped and then nearly died of shame. I'd been so wrapped up in my misery, I'd totally forgotten Nova was in the room. Pulling myself together with a harsh breath, I pushed the pillow down slowly, so the case would wipe the wetness from my face, to see Nova peeking at me from the top bunk.

"Do you want to talk about it?" she said softly.

I sighed. "Not particularly."

Nova bit her pale lip. "Do you want to play cards, then?"

The question was so sweet and unexpected, I actually smiled. Cards seemed an odd way to end what was shaping up to be the worst day of my life, but hanging out with Nova suddenly sounded a lot better than crying in my bed like an idiot over things I couldn't change. "Sure," I said, pushing myself up. "I'd like that."

We spent the rest of the afternoon and evening sitting on Nova's bright purple meditation pillows playing poker. We didn't talk much. I didn't trust myself not to explode, and Nova was far too nice to pry, but it was soothing just to sit and play.

We called it quits at dinnertime. Not willing to face the lounge for obvious reasons, I skipped on food and went to bed early. I didn't cry again, thank the king, but I spent the night tossing and turning and thinking way too much. By the time I left to pick up my suit early the next morning, I had a new perspective on things.

Oh, I was still furious with myself. I'd lost my cool and acted like an idiot over a guy in a way that endangered my career, something I'd sworn I would never do. But as I'd fought tears and pitched a fit, I'd slowly come to a new understanding of *why*. The reason getting dumped by Rupert had affected me so much more than ending things with any of my other lovers was because Rupert wasn't like my other lovers, and I didn't know how to deal with that.

I hadn't exactly been a normal girl growing up. I'd always been the most aggressive person around, and for some reason boys liked that. And I liked boys. I was also an idiot teenager with a body that was way more grown-up than her decision-making skills, which meant I made a lot of stupid messes before I shipped off for my mandatory two-year service to the crown.

The army grew me up a lot, and the boys slowed down, though they never stopped completely. I was still human, after all, and soldiers aren't known for their celibacy. I did stop making messes, though, both with my heart and theirs. The situation with Anthony before I'd joined Caldswell's crew was my first slipup in years, and that wasn't even my fault. He was the one who'd changed.

But the mess I'd made with Rupert dwarfed everything that had come before it, only this time, it looked like the one left in the mud was me. After years of perfect performance, I'd slipped up big-time. I've never exactly been great at being honest with myself, but I could no longer deny that I was falling in love, and I was doing it with the worst man possible.

It was enough to make me spit. Love was the last thing I wanted. I had ambitions, I had a career ahead of me. Love ruined careers. It certainly seemed to be ruining mine, but I didn't know what to do about it. I felt helpless, like I'd just taken a sucker punch for a fight I hadn't even known I was in, and that made me feel more murderous than anything else. Nothing pisses me off like being weak.

These thoughts were still boiling in my head as I let myself into the repair shop and found the Lady Gray waiting for me in her case with the mechanic standing proudly beside her. I inspected my baby millimeter by millimeter. When I was satisfied that everything looked correct, I put her on and jumped back and forth over the canal until I was sure.

For all my hovering, the mechanic had done a good job, and I tipped him well out of the fund Caldswell had set up to help pay for my repairs. The rest of the fund, plus a good chunk of my own earnings, went to pay for the actual work and the materials. Verdemont suits were as expensive to repair as they were to buy, but being back in my armor made me feel better than I had in days.

Because of the Republic's ridiculous public armor laws, I couldn't wear my suit back to the ship. With deep regret, I packed the Lady back into her case and left the shop in my civilian clothes. After paying for the repairs, I didn't have the money to catch a taxi, so I started walking, my armor case bumping along behind me.

It was still early, but the boardwalk was already packed with people going about their business, mostly loggers rushing to catch the high-speed trains out to the work camps. I kept my suit close and my head down, threading my way through the crowd as I tried to work out a plan to repair the mess I'd made of my life.

My relationship with Rupert was clearly over. Even if he hadn't said so yesterday, I would have ended it now that I'd realized I was falling for him. But much as I wanted to, I couldn't just make myself stop caring, so as I walked, I set down firm guidelines. No more drinking with Rupert and no more moping over what I couldn't have. My only love would be my armor and my ambition, just as it always had. I'd been slacking on my training sessions anyway, so I'd go back to those. I'd have to find a thermite blade to replace Phoebe, but until then I could work on my hand-to-hand with Cotter. I needed more practice against Count-class armor anyway.

I'd almost managed to get myself excited about this new life of work and discipline when a shadow fell over me. I jerked to a stop and looked up to see a man I didn't recognize blocking my way. I placed him in his early forties, not tall, but broad shouldered and imposing. His hair was sandy brown and military short. He wore no uniform or identifying mark, but he carried himself like a soldier even as he leaned against one of the boardwalk's quaint, old-fashioned lampposts.

We were on a pedestrian bridge that spanned the wide stretch of shops leading up to the starport. The way was narrow, and this man was taking up most of it. Normally, I wouldn't have hesitated to walk over him, but I didn't want to lug my case over him as well, so I stopped and gave him a glare that should have been enough for anyone with an ounce of sense to get the idea and move along. Unfortunately, this man seemed to have no sense at all, because he smiled wide at me and started talking.

"Good morning, pretty lady. Where are you off to?"

I blinked. He was speaking King's Tongue. Paradoxians and Terrans both came from Old Earth, but we hadn't been separated long enough that you could tell us apart by sight.

My first thought was that the mechanic had blabbed about me, but then I remembered I was hauling a Verdemont armor case. That was as sure a giveaway as my accent to anyone who knew enough about Paradox to speak the king's language. But though I had no reason to think the man was anything other than what he appeared, a lonely Paradoxian expat flirting with a fellow peasant girl on a sunny morning, I didn't let my guard down.

"Shove off," I told him with a look that said I meant it. "I've had a bad last few days. You don't want any of this."

The man pushed off the lamppost to block the way completely. "Thought you'd be used to bad days," he said casually. "Aren't you one of Caldswell's security dogs?"

My hand went immediately to the gun on my hip. My concealable pistol might be accurate as a blind man on a dark night compared to Sasha, but it would still take an unarmored man down, and I didn't have to be accurate when we were this close. The man lifted his brows when the gun came out, but he didn't panic or raise his hands. He just looked at me with a sort of lazy half smile, thumbs tucked in the pockets of his worn pilot's jacket.

"No need to be uncivil," he said. "My friend works at the traffic control tower and saw you leaving Caldswell's ship yesterday. I've heard a lot about the *Glorious Fool*, and I thought this would be a good chance to satisfy my curiosity."

"About what?" I said, lowering the pistol but keeping my finger firmly on the trigger.

He shrugged. "I've heard that ship is cursed. Is it true?"

"I can't speak for curses," I replied. "Caldswell attracts trouble, sure, but that's to be expected when you go around sticking your nose in hornets' nests."

The man laughed much harder at that than I'd expected. "That bad, eh?"

"Some trouble is worse than others," I said, eying the railing that walled us in. He'd shifted back toward the lamppost. I could get by him if I squeezed.

"Like that xith'cal tribe ship?"

I dropped the handle to my armor case and stepped in, bringing my pistol right up against his stomach. I hadn't actually thought much about the tribe ship since I'd survived it. It was burned and I'd had bigger things on my mind. But the only people who knew we'd been there were the crew and the lelgis. There was no reason this man should know anything, and the fact that he did was proof enough for me that he was up to no good.

But if the man was bothered by the idea of a bullet taking up residence in his small intestine, he didn't show it. The cocky smile never left his face as he leaned down, dropping his voice to whisper in my ear. "Now, now, hear me out. I'm not after your ship or Caldswell, all I want is the truth. Tell me what happened out in the asteroids and I'll make it well worth your while. Won't take half an hour, and then you can scurry back to your tyrant with no one the wiser."

"Or I could shoot you here," I growled.

He straightened with a shrug. "Or that, but this isn't the king's land, girl. The Republic doesn't respect duels, and even in the colonies, the police tend to react badly when people start shooting on a nice street like this."

His eyes flicked to the people on the bridge across from us, the happy morning shoppers talking and strolling with no clue about what was going on a few dozen feet away. I glared at him one last time before holstering my gun. "Let me pass."

The man didn't move a muscle. "Last chance to make some money, little mercenary," he said sweetly. "If we have to do this the hard way, you won't like it."

I laced my fingers together and cracked my knuckles. "For your information, the hard way is usually my favorite. I told you I was in a bad mood, and nothing cheers me up like a good fight."

We stared at each other for five long seconds, and then the man stepped aside, holding out his arms in a grand gesture. I grabbed my case and marched past him, hand on my pistol the whole time, but he made no move to follow. He just stood there watching me with that cocky smile until the doors hid him from view.

The moment I was inside the terminal, I ducked into the ladies' room and put on my armor. Suited up, I hoisted my now-empty armor case onto my shoulder and ran back to the *Fool*. My newly refactored legs cleared the quarter-mile stretch to the freighter landings in forty seconds. Cotter was on duty when I came in. I grabbed him and called the captain to come down to the cargo bay.

"This had better be good," Caldswell said when he stomped down the stairs a minute later.

"Someone just cornered me on my way back."

That got his attention, and he listened gravely as I described the man who'd stopped me and recited our conversation. "Do you know him?" I asked when I'd finished.

"I might," Caldswell replied. "Thank you, Morris. I want you both on guard until we take off. If you see anyone lurking around, get a picture and let me know."

"Sir," Cotter said, saluting.

I saluted as well, but the captain was already on his way back upstairs.

"What do you think that was about?" Cotter said.

"No clue," I answered. "But burned or not, nothing good comes out of that tribe ship. Let's just keep an eye out."

Cotter looked nonplussed. "You really think he's that dangerous?"

"Let me put it to you like this," I said. "Whoever that man was, he didn't flinch when I dug a gun into his stomach. That means he's either very well trained, very crazy, or he knew my shot wouldn't hurt him. Whichever of those is the truth, I don't want to mess with it."

Cotter shook his head. "You're bad as the captain about attracting trouble, you know that?"

I shrugged. "It's always been a talent."

Cotter snorted, and then he gave me a once-over. "Kind of sad to see you back in your suit. I was enjoying watching you scrub the floors."

"I'll scrub them with your face if you like," I said.

Cotter laughed long and loud. "Good to have you back. Honestly, I'm really sick of working double shifts."

I nodded sympathetically. "I'll put in some extra once we're back in flight."

"You sure?" he said. "Caldswell ain't paying you overtime."

"Caldswell doesn't pay me if he can help it," I replied. "But it's no problem. I owe you for covering, and anyway, I'd like the extra work."

"Needed it" was closer to the truth. Work was my way out of the hole Rupert had put me in. Fortunately, Cotter didn't argue too hard.

We spent the next three hours in surprisingly companionable company staking out the ship. It was good to be back on my game, and by the time we lifted off, I was almost feeling back in control.

The next day I threw myself at my work with a vigor that surprised even Caldswell. I double-checked all our security records and then spent three hours in the cargo bay recalibrating my suit, since the repairs had undone all my custom settings. I changed my emergency lock code, not because I thought Rupert would use the old one against me, but because I didn't want to be beholden to him for anything ever again. This time, though, I made sure the number was encrypted into my ship record. No point in having my lovely Lady ripped to shreds again just because no one knew how to get me out.

When I was on duty, I patrolled like we were in a war zone. When I was off duty, I exercised and did target practice. I also went through my catalogs and researched new thermite blades that would fit Phoebe's empty niche in my suit.

I couldn't afford anything right now, but I was pretty sure I could guilt Caldswell into fronting me the money. After all, it was his fault I'd lost Phoebe in the first place, and it was in his interest to make sure his mercs were well equipped. In the meanwhile, Cotter let me practice with his ax. The huge blade was too heavy for my suit and utterly ridiculous, but I enjoyed it all the same. I enjoyed anything that kept me busy and safely away from the things that weren't a part of my life anymore.

I must have done too good a job distracting myself, though, because I'd completely forgotten about the glowing bugs until I almost walked into one.

I was going through the lounge on patrol. It was very late, well into night cycle. Other than Caldswell, who was watching the bridge, I was the only person awake, so I was being a little more casual than usual, walking around with my helmet and gloves off. I stopped the moment I saw it, and then, since no one was around to report my weird behavior to Hyrek, I took a chance and leaned forward for a better look.

This glowing bug was different from the one I'd seen before. It was about the same size, but where that one had long antennae and scuttling legs, this one was perfectly circular with a hole in the middle, like a tire. It glowed with the same beautiful blue-white light though, shining like a star in the darkened lounge. A long tail covered in short, glowing fuzz extended from one side and moved with tiny flicks, propelling the creature through the air away from me.

Just like before, the thing wouldn't let me get close to it, so I stopped trying before I drove it off. Instead, I put my helmet back on to get a look at it through my cameras. But when my cameras came on, the glowing bug had vanished.

It reappeared when I lifted my visor but vanished again when I put the visor back down. For whatever reason, it seemed to be invisible to my cameras. I took my helmet off again and leaned back against the lounge windows to consider what that meant.

It was very possible the thing was, in fact, a hallucination, but I just couldn't believe that my brain would make up something as pointless and random as a tiny glowing bug to express its displeasure. But if it wasn't a hallucination, I had no idea how to explain something only I could see that didn't appear on cameras, could live on ship and out in space, and didn't want me getting close to it. Hallucination or not, though, the creature was pretty as it floated through the air.

I was watching it turn in little circles when the sound of a door opening made me jump. My hand went to Sasha at once, and I looked up to see Rupert and Ren come into the lounge. They were both dressed and awake like it wasn't four hours before the morning alarm. Rupert looked as surprised to see me as I was to see them. The captain's daughter, as usual, didn't seem to notice me at all.

I let go of my gun and straightened up, putting on my gloves quickly before Rupert noticed I'd been slacking. "What are you doing up?"

"Ren was hungry," Rupert said, helping the girl to the couch before heading for the kitchen.

I started to make a joke that this was an intergalactic crisis when I remembered I wasn't joking with Rupert anymore, so I said nothing. But I didn't want him to think he was driving me out either, so I leaned back on the window and watched Ren instead.

I hadn't actually looked at her much since my unnerving disaster the last time, but there wasn't much to see. She looked exactly the same as she always did. Rupert hadn't set her chessboard out, so she just sat on the couch staring blankly with her hands crossed in her lap. Even knowing how crazy she was, watching someone sit and stare wasn't exactly riveting. I was about to drop my visor and get moving when Ren lifted her head.

Such a tiny movement shouldn't have put me on guard, but it was so quick, and this was *Ren*. She never moved unless someone made her. Without thinking, I lifted my head as well, following her eyes to see what had caught her attention.

My stomach turned to ice. The glowing creature was hanging above the main mess table like a snowflake, and Ren was staring straight at it. I looked at it, then at her, then back at the creature as it floated off toward the kitchen where Rupert was pulling things out of the fridge. Ren's eyes followed it the whole time, and then, just as quickly as she'd looked up, her head snapped toward me.

For the first time ever, Ren's dark brown eyes met mine full-on. It was more like being looked through than looked at, but as much as I wanted to, I couldn't turn away. Just when I was sure I couldn't take any more, Ren's face lit up in an enormous smile.

The expression was all encompassing, the kind of smile you'd see on the face of a true believer witnessing a miracle. The smile changed her, made her beautiful, a dangerous, doomed sort of beauty that was painful to look at. And then, as quickly as it had come, the smile was gone. Ren looked away, and I collapsed against the window.

"Devi?"

I raised my head. Rupert was leaning over the counter. "Are you all right?"

"Fine," I said, straightening up. "Just fine. Go back to your cooking."

I could see he didn't believe me, but I didn't give him a chance to push the issue. I nodded to him and Ren and then turned back toward the cargo bay. I caught one last glimpse of the glowing creature sliding through the wall before the door shut behind me.

The incident with Ren shook me so badly I almost told Hyrek about it the next morning. After all, if two of us were seeing the things, they couldn't be all in my head. But even if Caldswell let her talk to the xith'cal, relying on the testimony of an insane girl who didn't speak to prove my own sanity wasn't an appealing prospect. In the end, I decided to get a neutral third-party opinion, and when Nova took her morning break, I caught her in the hall and pulled her into our room.

"What's wrong, Deviana?" Nova said, sounding truly concerned.

"Nova," I said. "What do you see when you see an aura?"

Nova paused, thinking this over like I'd asked her some sort of great universal question, which, to be fair, maybe I had.

"It's usually a glow around the person's head," she said at last. "Most people's are too faint to see much, but some are brighter.

They change all the time, though, growing and shifting color as the person changes." She looked at me with a frown. "Yours was strong when I first met you, but it's been dim now for a while. That usually happens because of stress or grief." Her frown became gentle, and she laid her hand on mine. "Is there anything I can help you talk through?"

"No, but thank you," I said. I was actually very touched by the offer. Of course, I still wasn't quite sure I actually believed in auras. Nova had been in the room when I'd had my little breakdown, and anyone who'd been paying any sort of attention would have noticed how snippy I'd been since the tribe ship. But I could see from Nova's face that she believed she saw something, and considering *I* was the one seeing glowing bugs, I didn't have much room to judge.

"Do you ever see other things?" I asked. "Besides auras, I mean."

Nova furrowed her brows. "Like what?"

"I don't know." I stalled. "Just anything odd that can't otherwise be explained."

"Oh, I see stuff like that all the time," Nova said, her face breaking into a serene smile. "The universe is filled with phenomena beyond our comprehension. It's part of what makes life so beautiful."

That sounded promising. "Have you ever seen anything on the ship?" I asked. "Anything glowing or floating?"

Nova thought for a moment, then shook her head. "I don't believe I've seen anything that matches that description. Have you?"

"Oh, no, of course not," I said, scrambling. "Just something I read about plasmex users being able to do."

"Don't believe everything you read," Nova said, her voice angrier than I'd ever heard it. "Some people seem to revel in ignorance and misinformation. One time, *News Net* called our entire colony a *cult*." She gave an insulted huff. "Can you imagine?"

"No," I said, shaking my head. "The press will say anything."

"I know," Nova said. "It's awful the way some people attack those who seek knowledge."

She would have said more, but something in her pocket started chiming. She dug out her handset, which was now bright purple and covered in little glittery stars. She flipped it open, and her face fell. "Would you be offended if I put off our talk until later? Basil needs me on the bridge. The captain changed our course last night while everyone was asleep and now things are sort of chaotic while Basil sorts out the star maps."

"We changed course?" I said. "Why? Where?"

"I'm not sure," Nova said. "Some kind of last-minute trade tip. But we're going to the terraforming base on Republic Colony Falcon Thirty-Four."

I stared at her, appalled. "What the hell are we trading on a terraforming base?"

Nova spread her hands in the helpless gesture she always used when discussing the captain's eccentricities. "I'm sorry I couldn't help you more, Deviana."

Her genuine niceness snapped me out of my frustration, and I gave her a wide smile. "You helped, Nova. Thank you."

She beamed at me and left, walking back into the hall in that floaty way of hers. I waited until the door closed before I let my face drop into a scowl. Technically, I was off duty and should have been sleeping, especially with a planet stay coming up, but I couldn't resist checking out Falcon 34.

My handset didn't have much. Falcon 34 appeared to be every bit the middle-of-nowhere speck it sounded like, another brand-new claim for the Terrans with a population of less than ten thousand, most of whom were laborers on the terraforming platforms that were still working to make the planet habitable. Certainly not the kind of place you took a private trade ship to, or anything else for that matter.

Lying back on my bunk, I wondered briefly if Rupert would be going with Caldswell on this "last-minute trade tip" before I remembered that I wasn't worrying about Rupert or secrets or anything other than my job anymore. With that thought firmly in mind, I pulled the sheet over my head and went to sleep.

I was glad I'd found out where we were going from Nova, because no one else seemed to know we'd changed course until we landed on Falcon 34 seven hours later. The planet proved worse than I'd feared. There wasn't even a proper spaceport, just a stretch of mountain that had been leveled to form a landing space for supply freighters.

The planet looked to be nothing but dry, flat, yellow desert broken up by long mountain ranges. With clear air and no vegetation, I couldn't tell if the mountains were ten or a hundred miles away. They were big, though, and if it wasn't for the fact that I was here under duress, I might have called them majestic in a desolate sort of way.

The terraforming was far enough along that the air was breathable, if thin, but not so far that there was a suitable atmosphere to bounce the fantastic heat from Falcon 34's sun. It was a hundred and forty degrees in the shade, and even though the ship's climate control was going full blast, we started feeling the heat immediately. I could even feel it through my suit, and Cotter was sweating openly, but it wasn't until Basil started proclaiming that he would die of heat exhaustion that the captain pulled some strings and got everyone rooms at the soon-to-be colony governor's mansion.

This cheered the crew up immensely, especially Basil. I suspected Caldswell must have flashed his Warrant, because the terraforming office, which couldn't be bothered to return our calls half an hour ago, sent a complimentary shuttle not ten minutes after the captain's announcement. The whole crew loaded in, even Hyrek, much to my amazement.

"I thought you never left the ship," I said as he climbed in.

He gave me a cutting look and held out his handset. *Xith'cal do best between seventy and ninety-five degrees. The ship's interior rooms were one hundred and ten when I left. Compared to that, a night listening to Basil complain about the accommodations in a mansion is nearly tolerable.*

"Don't eat the staff," I said.

Hyrek turned up his snout so fast I thought I'd actually insulted him, but then I saw his handset. *Spoilsport.*

I laughed and closed the shuttle doors, waving as the crew flew off toward the tiny smudge of the villa's climate-controlled dome on the horizon, the only spot of green in any direction.

Cotter and I weren't going, of course. Whatever Caldswell was here for, we still had a ship full of cargo to watch. Caldswell wasn't going to the mansion either. He, Ren, and Rupert had left right after Caldswell made his arrangements with the colony brass, flying their skipper off into the desert. It was the same little trio who'd gone out on Mycant, and, just because I could, I started watching my clock like a hawk. But it stayed perfectly on time, and I didn't feel so much as a tremble of a quake as the afternoon wore on and the temperature crept up.

We closed up the ship and shut down everything we could except the air, but it didn't make much difference. By the time it was my turn to eat dinner, I was sweating buckets even in my suit. Cotter wasn't much better, and we eventually gave up any pretense at decorum and sat sprawling on top of the cargo watching last year's gladiator world championship on the cargo bay vidscreen. I already knew who'd won, but watching two enormous suits of armor chop each other to pieces took my mind off the heat, and it wasn't like we were actually slacking on guard duty. After all, with us sitting on the cargo like we were, any would-be thief would have to steal us, too.

By the time the sun had set, taking the temperature down just a little, we'd reached the semifinals, and I was bored stiff. Even with heat parboiling my brain, there's only so much show fighting I can take. I didn't feel like patrolling, though, so I pulled out my handset to see if Anthony had written me back.

Checking while I was on the ship was risky, but with the crew gone and Cotter half asleep beside me, I felt I could chance a look. I wasn't actually expecting an answer yet anyway. We could terraform planets and jump ships through dimensions, but no one had ever mastered real-time communication across the universe. My message would have been relayed through hyperspace on the back of whatever drones were available, but even if it had made it to Paradox the night I'd sent it, Anthony would still have to actually read the thing and reply, something he'd never exactly excelled at. Add to that the part where I'd asked him a question that might take some research, and I didn't expect to hear anything for at least a month. So you can imagine my surprise when I found that a message bearing Anthony's ID had arrived the day we'd left Seni Major, a mere nineteen hours after I'd sent the first one.

And not just any message, either. The letter was encoded with top military security. I didn't even know Anthony had access to that sort of encryption, much less the freedom to use it writing notes to *me*. I glanced at Cotter, but he was completely absorbed by the carnage on the screen. That was about the best distraction I could ask for, and I casually turned over on my side, using my body to block my handset screen as I unlocked the message and began to read.

> *Devi, love, as you probably guessed from the encryption, what I'm about to tell you is top secret. I could lose my job five times over for this, so I hope you'll respect the risk I am taking for you and listen for once.*
>
> *I did some checking with a contact who knows about this sort of thing, and he believes the scaled figure you described is a Terran weapon called a symbiont. They were used against us in the Border Wars, but the Ter-*

rans supposedly destroyed them all decades ago because of their extreme instability. Thanks to that, our info is a bit out of date, but I can tell you that symbionts are alien parasites, created in the lab and put into a human host.

*Since we've never caught a symbiont alive to test, we don't know their exact abilities, but we do know they're incredibly strong, fast, and damn near unkillable. They can also switch back and forth between the thing you described and their old, human body. Don't let that fool you, though. Symbionts are **not** human. If you've really seen a symbiont, Devi, I need you to let me know right away. If the Terrans are breaking their treaties, I have to report it to the king's office immediately.*

In the meanwhile, I want you to forget Caldswell and get out of there. I know you're dead set on a quick promotion, but this is too much. Symbionts are a death sentence to everyone around them, and you can't be a Devastator if you're dead. Please, Devi, for once in your life use your damn sense and come home. Contact me the moment you're safe and I'll send someone to pick you up.

See you soon, A.

PS: For the love of the king, don't even think about fighting one. Even Devastators don't take symbionts solo. You see one, you run as fast as you can in the other direction. We'll talk more when you're home safe. I'll be waiting.

"Morris?"

I looked over to see Cotter staring at me. "You all right? Your suit's shaking."

"Heat's getting to me," I said, standing up. "Cover for me, would you? I'm going to take a quick shower."

Cotter shrugged, but I was already walking away. I made it all the way up the stairs, through the lounge, and into the hall before I whipped out my handset to read the message again.

It didn't get any better the second time, or the third. By the fourth reading I gave up on all pretense and sank to the floor so I wouldn't fall.

Anthony was wrong, of course. No matter how sure his contact was, there was no way Rupert could be one of those things. He was the picture of control and discipline, so much so that I wanted to strangle him sometimes. He certainly wasn't unstable, though he was surprisingly strong. And fast. And able to shoot Sasha without breaking his arms and get knocked across the bridge without taking a mark. And he was able to change shape into that alien... thing.

I looked back down at Anthony's message. My hand was shaking so badly I couldn't read the text, but I wasn't really trying to. My mind was back on Seni Major, looking up at Rupert's cold face against the rain as he'd said he'd put me in danger, that *he* was dangerous. At the time I'd thought he was full of it. Now, though, I wondered if he hadn't been speaking literally.

One of the things I loved about Rupert was how intense he was. I loved how tightly he held me, how hard he kissed me. I'd thought it was a sign of how much he wanted me, but now I wasn't so sure. What if he'd been like that because he was fighting for control? What if I really *had* been in danger when he'd taken me to his room?

Even as I thought it, I dismissed the idea as absurd. Angry as I was at Rupert, I couldn't believe he'd hurt me. Not physically, anyway. I scowled at that thought and looked down at Anthony's message one last time, and then I deleted it.

I deleted all the backups too, wiping my whole box. My gamble had paid off. Anthony had given me the truth, just like I'd wanted, but I didn't care anymore. I was tired of gambling, tired of worrying, tired of getting hurt. This shit was way too heavy for me.

Before I could chicken out, I deleted my Bargain footage too, all of it. I knew I'd probably regret it later, but right now, all I wanted was for this to be over. Rupert, Caldswell, Ren, mysteries—I wanted all of them out of my life. I was going to finish this damn tour, and when the Devastators asked me about my time on Caldswell's *Fool*, I'd tell them I fought a lot of xith'cal and put up with a lot of bullshit, but I'd never tell them a damn thing about alien monsters, not the invisible ones or the ones with kind smiles. Rupert could keep his damn secret; I was *done*.

When I'd cleaned everything off my Blackbird box, I sent another message to Anthony, a perfectly innocent one, through the ship system. I thanked him for being such a sweetheart, but I'd been overreacting. There was no need to report anything or send someone. I was fine, and I'd see him in a few months when my tour with Caldswell was up. I put the message on Falcon 34's queue to go out on their daily communication drone, and then I pushed myself off the floor to go take that shower. I was thinking about how lovely the water was going to feel when the first blast rocked the ship.

Even with my stabilizers, I was thrown against the wall. The explosion was powerful enough to tip the *Fool* up on its side, and I almost fell again as the ship slammed back down so hard the lights flickered. By that point I had an emergency signal out on all channels. I heard Cotter's alarm go out a half second later, and then everything in my helmet went silent as a jamming field landed on the ship like a hammer.

"*Shit*," I whispered, flicking through channels as fast as I could think. "Shit, shit, *shit*."

All outside channels were black, and there was no getting through. I could still get Cotter, though, and I patched him straight in, switching one of my camera feeds for his just in time to watch a second blast explode right in front of him.

"*Cargo door!*" he shouted in my ear.

"I see it!" I yelled back. "Hang on, I'll—"

I cut off as something hit the bridge door with an enormous clang. The bridge and engine room doors had locked automatically when I'd sent the emergency signal, and while the bridge door wasn't blast rated, it was still a good inch of solid steel. That didn't seem to matter to whatever was hitting it, though.

The first blow bowed the door out a foot, the next took it off its track altogether, crumpling it to the ground as a wall of smoke billowed into the hall. The explosion I'd felt must have been for the entry shutters on the bridge, I realized belatedly. They'd blown the windows off the ship's nose, and now there were three armored figures barreling at me through the destroyed bridge door.

I shot the first before he was more than a shadow in the smoke. Sasha stung him clean in the head, and I grinned at the sound of tearing metal as my anti-armor gun did her magic. The suit dropped with a clatter, blown clean open.

"Terran armor!" I shouted to Cotter. "Two up here, entry on the bridge."

"Four here!" Cotter shouted back. He was almost laughing, and I heard the crunch as his ax came down. "Three now! Terran tin cans, let's tear 'em up!"

"Copy," I said, ducking into a crouch as I fired my second shot at the next target.

Sasha may not be much against xith'cal, but when it comes to shredding armor, you have no better friend. Her armor-piercing rounds spin, going through the target like a cannon blast. The enemy had larger suits than mine, larger even than Cotter's, but the gulf between a custom Paradoxian suit and Terran assembly-line wear is too wide to be crossed by mere mass.

I dropped the next target with an arm shot while he was still trying to get his hulking shoulders through the shattered bridge door. I could have had the head, but I wanted someone alive when it came time to sort out who to blame for this mess. I'd aimed for the joint, but Sasha hit him so hard we took his arm clean off. The soldier went down with a scream I could hear through his helmet, and then the sound cut off as my third target dropped back to grab the injured man's boots and tug him back into the bridge, out of the breach path.

I paused. In my experience, a pirate would have just stomped over the downed man and kept coming. Pulling him back minimized losses and cleared the attack path. It was what I would have done, a merc maneuver. I glanced at the man I'd killed earlier. His armor was still Terran and terrible, but it wasn't bad for what you could get in this part of space, and it wasn't the sort of ragtag suit you saw on criminals.

"Cotter," I said, catching my partner's attention. "Don't get in too deep. We're dealing with a crash team."

"A piss-poor one!" Cotter crowed in my ear. I glanced up at his camera just in time to see the flash of his ax as he crunched through the man in front of him. "Two more came in while you were playing up there, but they're on the floor like the others. Five down now, and the rest are keeping their distance."

"How many is 'the rest'?" I asked, keeping Sasha trained on the bridge door.

The only answer I got was Cotter's laugh as his shield ate a hail of bullets. They stuck like caught flies in the wall of invisible plasma. Mine would have broken after half so many, but the big suits had their advantages, and strong shields was a large one. Even so.

"Get some cover, you skullhead!" I shouted, eying the red warning I could see flashing on his display through our shared camera. "You take another of those and you'll be sprouting leaks."

"The day some Republic hack armor team gets a shot on me is the day I die of shame," Cotter said. "Mind your six, Morris."

A bullet whizzed above my head, and I hit the deck just in time as three more followed. They were shooting at me from the smoke cover of the blown-out bridge. With a silent apology to Basil and Nova, I grabbed a grenade from my back and tossed it through the bridge door. The soft, too-innocent clink as it bounced down the bridge steps was lost in the hail of gunfire, but the explosion that followed lit up the bridge like the noon sun.

The blast wasn't enough to take down the shooters, but it flushed them out nicely. I caught the first man through with a clean shot to the throat. The next learned from the mistakes of others and came in low. My first shot whizzed over his head, but my second caught him in the shoulder with enough force to send him flying back into the ruined bridge.

"What the hell?"

Cotter's surprise cut through my focus, and I risked a glance at his camera feed.

What I saw put everything else out of my mind. Cotter was standing with his back to the wall of cargo. As he'd told me, five dead mercs lay on the ground in front of him, their shoddy armor no match for Cotter's ax. Five more mercs stood at the base of the blown-out cargo ramp with their heavy rifles trained on Cotter, whose shield was now dangerously low. But Cotter wasn't even looking at the firing squad. His eyes were on the two smaller figures standing silhouetted against the starport's floodlights.

Next to the assault team's hulking armor, they looked almost fragile, but I knew better. Their bodies were covered in overlapping black scales, and their faces were nothing but glittering eyes and terrible, alien features. It was the thing Rupert had been on the tribe ship, the shape he'd used to save me. *Symbionts*, my mind whispered, making my skin go clammy.

But even though Rupert was the only one of those things I'd ever seen, I never once thought he was one of the two in the cargo bay door. For one, Rupert's alien form was tall and lithe, just like him. These were both stocky and large, and undoubtedly our enemies. They were standing almost casually, their glossy black eyes looking at Cotter like he was the bug, not them, and I felt an icy stab of fear.

"Cotter," I whispered. "Cotter, get out of there."

Cotter didn't answer, or maybe he didn't hear me. By the time I'd spoken, he was charging forward, ax raised in a battle cry.

The two black figures didn't move until he was nearly on top of them, but when they did, it was like death himself had come down to show us how it was done.

CHAPTER
15

Cotter did a lot better than I thought he would.

The two black figures were just as fast as I remembered Rupert being, their long, curving claws tearing through Cotter's armor like he'd torn through the Terrans. His straining shield broke the second they hit it, the suspended bullets falling with a clatter. But even shredded and shieldless, Cotter was still nearly a thousand pounds in his armor, and he'd thrown every last ounce of it into the ax strike that caught the smaller of the two symbionts square in the side.

The blow sent the symbiont flying into the bulkhead, and I almost cheered at the crunch it made when it hit. Would have cheered, actually, if three bullets hadn't just stuck in my shield right in front of my face.

I snapped back into my own fight with a string of expletives that would have made my army sergeant proud. Two mercs had cleared the bridge door while I'd been distracted, and the rear soldier's arm was already moving in a throw. I spun on instinct, kicking the grenade with my boot even as I heard the whistle of the rising charge reach its final octave. Any other suit would have been too slow, but my Lady isn't any other suit, and she proved it yet again as my kick launched the grenade right back at my attackers. They didn't even have time to duck before it exploded in their faces.

Whoever these mercs were, they used a much heavier ordnance than I did. The grenade blast blew me down the hall and them back into the bridge. My suit shifted my shield to take most of the impact, and I was back on my feet in a second. I should have charged then, run in and finished off the two mercs with Sasha while they were still on their backs, but my mind was half on Cotter anyway, so when his scream tore through my com, my attention snapped right back to his camera.

My run-in with the grenade team couldn't have taken more than ten seconds, but that had been enough for Cotter's fight to turn. He was down, his garish yellow armor crumpled and ripped like foil around him. His faceguard had been ripped open as well, and his suit was full of blood.

But Cotter was a Paradoxian, a soldier to the end. Even bleeding and on his back, he had his gun in his hand and was firing over and over again into the chest of the black figure standing on top of him. If he'd been firing an anti-armor pistol like Sasha, one shot would have been enough to blow the thing back, but Cotter's sidearm was standard issue, and he might as well have been shooting pellets for all it seemed to bother the symbiont.

My targeting system beeped in my ear, and I glanced at my own cameras to see one of the men I'd blown into the bridge getting back on his feet, but by this point I didn't care. I was running full tilt down the hall toward the door to the lounge. I heard the man shoot me, felt the pressure as the last of my shield caught the shot before flickering out, but I couldn't tear my eyes away from the black figure as it slowly reached down past Cotter's camera to wrap its hand around my fellow merc's head. The last thing I heard was Cotter's scream and the roar of his gun as he fired one final time before his feed went dead.

I've been in armored combat for nine years. During that time, I've seen more men killed than I care to count. I'd watched men die through their own cameras like I'd just watched Cotter. Some mercs swear it gets easier, that you get used to it in time. I never have, and by this point, I'm pretty sure I never will.

Cotter's death hit me like a kick in the stomach, and I stumbled, though there was nothing in my way. For one second, I let the death wash over me, and then, as I'd been trained, I boxed it up and set it aside. Never shame your comrades by letting their death get you killed, my drill sergeant used to say. Never dishonor the dead by smearing your blood on their hands.

As though summoned by the memory of my old commander's voice, the sharp focus of the battle rage settled on me like a mantle as I dove out of the hallway and into the lounge. The second I was in, I whirled around and slammed my fist down on the blast-door switch. The heavy panel dropped like a hammer, walling me off from the men coming from the ship's shattered nose. This also meant I was now locked away from the rest of the ship, giving them free rein over the bridge and anything else they wanted from the cabins and infirmary, but that was a risk I had to take. I was alone now, and I couldn't afford attackers at my back.

There were two armored mercs coming up the cargo bay stairs when I'd hit the blast door. I took them both out the second they stepped into the lounge, Sasha ripping through their helmets like the steel plating was paper. I reloaded after that, tossing my half-spent clip into the kitchen just in case I survived this. I'd had twenty shots left, so I didn't really need to reload, but I'd realized by this point that I was likely going to die, too. With that in mind, conserving ammo, even expensive ammo like Sasha's, just seemed pointless.

Reloaded, I crouched low and checked my density sensor. I could see the armored mercs clearly. The ones from the bridge were spreading out down the hall I'd abandoned, but they were ignoring the dropped blast door, no doubt realizing, as I had, that I'd be dead soon enough from their companions downstairs. That suited me just fine; one less thing to worry about.

Putting them out of my mind, I shifted my attention to the cargo bay. Down there, the mercs were more gun-shy. They hovered at the edge of the blown-out cargo bay doors, scared off by Cotter's grand last stand and my own execution of the two mercs who'd gone up to corner me. Other than Cotter's fading signature, though, I couldn't see anything in the cargo bay itself. The symbionts weren't showing up at all.

I switched back to my normal cameras. The outlines of the armored mercs vanished from my screen, but they weren't the real threat. What I had to watch out for were the monsters my sensors couldn't see.

I swallowed, remembering Anthony's warning that even Devastators didn't take symbionts one-on-one. My equipment was good, but I wasn't a Devastator yet, and unlike Cotter I didn't have a thousand pounds or an ax. I didn't even have my thermite blade. If I was going to have any chance at all, I had to get the first shot.

Crouching low, I ran into the kitchen. My plan was to use the bar as cover for a better chance at getting the drop on whatever came in next. When I ducked below the counter, though, I found something I didn't expect.

The bar that separates the kitchen from the rest of the lounge is held up by two sturdy metal poles, but lying between them was a third pole. The spare was braced against the underside of the bar by a box of dried noodles and the soup pot that was too big to go in the cabinet. Like the others, the spare rod was steel, thick walled and heavy, about thirty pounds. Without my armor it would have been slightly too heavy to be a good weapon. In my armor, it gave me an idea.

Quietly as I could, I grabbed the metal pole and wrapped my hand around one end, squeezing until the metal collapsed into something resembling a sharp point. Satisfied, I hefted the pole in my left hand while keeping Sasha firmly in my right. Armed as best as I could manage, I settled down to wait.

I heard the symbiont the moment it entered the lounge. It moved quiet as a barefoot man. Quiet as Rupert, I realized with a pang. But I was listening hard and my speakers were very good, and I caught the soft click of its black claws on the lounge's metal floor. If the symbiont had had sensors like mine, it would have found me instantly, but it must not have, because it paused just inside the doorway, and that was when I attacked.

I shot up and jumped sideways over the counter, shooting the second I was clear. The move was too fast for my computer, but I didn't need my targeting system for a shot this close. Sasha's bullet hit the symbiont square in the head, right above where its ear should have been, slamming it into the wall.

The moment the shot left my gun, I charged, throwing my suit's strength behind the metal pole in my left hand as I stabbed for the symbiont's stomach. I'd expected piercing the black scales would be hard, but even though my suit would never throw around the sort of weight Cotter's did, I was sure I could punch the pole through. That is, I was sure until I actually tried to do it.

Stabbing the pole into the symbiont was like trying to drive a toothpick through a rock. The sharp point snapped the second it made contact, and then the pole snapped again just above my grip. The symbiont's stomach wasn't even dented, but I could see its layered black scales rattling, scraping together just like they did on an enraged xith'cal.

But though my assault had proven useless, I'd still surprised the thing, and I dropped the bent, useless pole to grab the symbiont's neck instead. Using all my suit's strength, I pinned it to the wall with one hand while I pressed Sasha against the side of its skull with the other. As soon as the barrel was firm, I fired three more shots in rapid succession.

I was about to land another when the symbiont's arm shot out and slammed me right in the chest. The blow knocked me back, and I hit the ground hard. I had one second of scrambling before the black figure was on top of me, the clawed hand wrapping around my throat as I'd just held its.

Even as the symbiont pushed me down, part of me couldn't believe this was happening. Counting my initial attack, I'd shot this bastard four times at point-blank range in the *head*. Even a Devastator would have gone down under fire like that, but while the symbiont was bleeding now, the blood red and human looking as it splattered across my visor, the head wound didn't seem to slow it down at all.

Its weight was like a boulder on my stomach as it pinned me to the floor, using its legs to hold mine flat. It held my right hand and gun down with its left while its right hand worked on prying my helmet off. My left hand was free, and I got several good punches on its shoulder, but the alien didn't even seem to feel it. Its entire focus was on my helmet, and its arm was so strong I could feel the pulling all the way down to my toes. But the Lady Gray doesn't give up easily. Despite the creaking, my locks held firm, though they wouldn't for much longer under that sort of pressure.

By this point, my mind was scrambling. I didn't know why the symbiont was so intent on getting my helmet off, but I knew the moment my locks popped, I was dead. But what could I do? I was on my back with my gun hand pinned and my punches useless against the symbiont's alien strength. I was outmatched in every way. I would have dropped my grenade string like I had back on the xith'cal ship if I'd thought it would have broken the thing's hold, but with my helmet lock about to go, a blast like that was more likely to rip my own head off than do any good.

I was fighting the urge to panic when a fresh drop of blood hit my visor, drawing my eyes up to the hole my shots had hammered into the thing's armored skull. The wound was on the side, so I couldn't get a good look at it from this angle. I could see something, but it took me several seconds to recognize that the dark, matted strand sticking out from the black armor's head was *hair.* Bloody, dark brown human hair. And that was when I knew what to do.

I flung out my left arm and felt along the floor until my fingers found the dented length of the broken pipe I'd dropped earlier. I wrapped my hand around it and, throwing every bit of power my suit had left into my arm, swung the pipe up like a spear. I hadn't even looked to see what end of the pipe I'd grabbed, but a little luck was still on my side, because it was the sharp, broken end that I slammed with all my force into the side of the symbiont's skull, right where the hair stuck out.

Since none of my other hits had meant a thing, the symbiont had stopped paying attention to my flailing. It had dismissed me, and because of that, it lost the precious second of reaction that could have saved its life. The dodge, when it came, was too little and far, far too late. My makeshift spear sunk through the hole my shots had made, and the black scaled body went stiff. The grip on my neck slacked, then fell away as the symbiont slumped forward on top of me.

I knew it was dead, but after watching the thing soak four head shots, I wasn't taking chances. I scrambled out from under it and locked my gun against its bloody temple. But as I squeezed the trigger to fire one last shot, just to be sure, my body froze.

My first thought was that all the pulling on my helmet had broken my suit, but the Lady was working fine. It was my own body that was frozen. My muscles simply refused to listen to anything my brain said. I was paralyzed, stuck like a bug in glue. I couldn't even move my eyes, so though I heard someone enter the lounge, I couldn't see who it was until he reached out and gently plucked Sasha from my now-limp hands.

"I told you you wouldn't like the hard way."

I would have jerked at the familiar voice if I'd been able to move, but even my paralysis couldn't stop the growl that rose in my throat as the man who'd blocked my way on the boardwalk at Seni Major ducked down to look at me through my visor. "Nic," he said calmly. "Would you ask Miss Morris for the emergency unlock code for her armor?"

There was some shuffling, and then a pale young man I'd never seen before knelt beside me and turned my head so I was looking him in the face. "Deviana," he said, his voice richer than anything I'd ever heard. "What is your emergency code?"

The stiffness in my throat and mouth vanished, and I took in a breath to tell them exactly where and how they could shove my emergency armor code. But the words that left my mouth were not the ones I'd meant to say.

"Eight six four five three."

As the code left my lips, my armor dutifully shut down. My cameras went dead, my locks popped, and the Lady Gray fell off me like a shed skin. When it was done, the man from Seni Major lifted my helmet off my head with a smile that I would have given every gun on Paradox to punch off his face.

"Get her up and make her comfortable," he said, tucking my helmet under his arm. "Miss Morris and I have a chat to finish."

I wanted to struggle. I wanted to scream. I wanted to shoot every single person in the room, even the dead ones, but all I did was stand when Nic bade me and walk over to the bar stool that the third person, a woman about Nova's age, pulled out.

She met my eyes, and I expected her to order me around like Nic had, but she didn't say anything. Instead, a wall of force landed on my shoulders, and I collapsed onto the stool. The wall wrapped around me like a blanket as soon as I was down, but I barely felt it. I'd finally put two and two together.

"You're plasmex users."

"They're much more than that," the man from Seni Major said, striding over to stand in front of me. He was speaking Universal with no accent at all, and I dismissed my earlier assumption that he was Paradoxian. No Paradoxian could be this much of a backstabbing coward.

He waved his hand, and Nic and the girl fell back, though the girl kept her hand on my shoulder. "I think we got started on the wrong foot," the man said, leaning down with the same winning smile he'd flashed back on the boardwalk. "My name is John Brenton, and believe it or not, I'm one of the good guys."

"I don't believe anyone who calls himself 'one of the good guys,'" I snapped, pushing as hard as I could against the invisible pressure. "And if you're trying to play the shining knight, you're doing a damn poor job." I glared pointedly at the dead symbiont by his feet.

Brenton suddenly looked sad. "He wasn't trying to kill you, you know. His name was Anton Mikel, and he was a good man. I would never have sent him to subdue you if I'd thought there was a chance of either of you getting seriously hurt."

"He killed Cotter!" I yelled, jerking halfway off the stool before the girl caught me.

"Your partner was a Paradoxian skullhead," Brenton said dismissively. "Not the sort who'd listen to reason even if we had offered him a surrender."

He was right, but I certainly wasn't going to tell him so. I think Brenton saw it on my face, though, because his smile turned into a smirk as he continued.

"If we're reckoning blood debts, Miss Morris, I believe I'm the one coming up short. The two of you killed a dozen of my mercs, though neither of us can beat your captain when it comes to blood spilled." He leaned back and tilted his head like he was trying to get a better look at me. "You know, none of this would have happened if you'd just told me what I wanted to know back on Seni."

I lifted my chin stubbornly and kept my mouth shut.

"You're awful loyal for a merc," Brenton went on when it was clear I wasn't going to rise to that one. "I can't believe Brian's changed so much in the last five years that he's become likable enough to inspire genuine loyalty in the people he hires to die for him. Tell me, mercenary, what did he pay you to buy such stubborn silence?"

I shrugged. "Nothing special. He gave me a job, and I honor my contracts."

"She's telling the truth," Nic said behind me.

Brenton heaved a long sigh. "You Paradoxians and your damn honor." He wiped a hand over his face and started again. "You know, you don't look like a dumb girl. Aggressive as a mad mountain cat certainly, but not dumb. You must have realized by now that your captain's not the trader he pretends to be."

I kept silent, which was answer enough.

"He's no smuggler, either," Brenton continued. "Or spy, or anything so nice."

He paused there, letting the words dangle. Rupert had warned me once that just because someone baits you doesn't mean you have to bite, but I guess I don't learn, because my curiosity snapped it up. "Okay." I sighed. "What is he?"

Brenton crossed his arms with a thoughtful look. "That's a complicated question. Back when I worked with him, I used to think of us as brave heroes giving our lives to defend the galaxy from what it cannot fight on its own."

I arched an eyebrow at the overblown rhetoric, but Brenton just kept going. "There are things in this universe we do not understand, Miss Morris," he said. "Things we cannot see, cannot detect, and yet they could wipe us out, all of us, without even noticing we were here."

As he spoke, my mind flashed back to the thing I'd fought in the woods on Mycant, the invisible monster that wouldn't die no matter how much I carved it up.

"Ah." Brenton's voice stopped my thoughts cold. He was closer than I'd realized, staring into my eyes like everything that had just flicked through my brain was written there for him to read. "You've seen a phantom."

I briefly considered lying, but I had a feeling the Nic kid would know. Anyway, there was still a good chance this Brenton was going to kill me. If I was going to die, I'd at least die with some answers.

"I fought something," I said. "It was huge and invisible. My cameras didn't work around it."

"I'm surprised your suit worked at all," Brenton said. "Phantoms and technology don't get along."

"What are they?" I asked, leaning forward as far as I could. "You said they could wipe us out—how? What do phantoms do?" Because other than messing up my suit and knocking me around and being unkillable, the big invisible monster hadn't seemed that much more dangerous than any other big animal. Certainly not the intergalactic menace Brenton was implying.

"No one knows for sure," Brenton said. "Suffice it to say, phantoms break what we know about the rules of normal space. They move through the universe seemingly without care for gravity or distance, and they're attracted to habitable planets. Leave one there long enough and the whole place starts to crumble."

I swallowed, remembering Mycant's quakes. "What about time?" I demanded. "What do they do to clocks?"

Brenton looked at me sharply. "You really did fight one, didn't you?"

"Don't act so surprised," I said, tossing my head as much as I could with the pressure. "I'm pretty tough."

"I know that," he said, glancing at the dead men on the floor. "I'm not surprised that you beat it, but that Caldswell let you live afterward."

My mouth went dry, but I couldn't let him see my reaction, so I set my jaw and stared him down. "Why would the captain kill me?" I said. "I saved him."

Brenton shrugged. "That's never stopped him before."

I gave Brenton a dangerous look. "Look, I'm not Caldswell's biggest fan, but he's my captain. So far as I'm concerned, you're no more than a pirate invading his ship, and the moment your little freak shows let me go, I'm going to make sure you join your fellow 'good man' down there. Now, are you going to tell me about the time thing or not?"

My threats rolled off Brenton like rain off a mountain. "I think I've given you quite enough information for free," he said, dragging one of the stools over so he could sit facing me. "Are you familiar with chess, Deviana?"

"No." His subject changes were giving me whiplash. I really hoped this all came together soon. I hate puzzles enough on a normal day, there was no way in hell I was going to spend my last minutes of life playing guessing games.

"Ancient game of strategy," Brenton continued, settling onto his stool. "Two equal armies fight until a king is captured. It's a game of risk and reward where it's not uncommon to sacrifice even your most powerful pieces to protect your objectives or corner the enemy."

He placed his hands on his knees, and his face grew wistful. "Brian, your dear captain, is an excellent chess player, and he takes great care to stock his ship with useful pawns. But though Caldswell is king on his little *Fool*, he always seems to forget that the king is a piece like all the others, and that he is being moved just as much as the rest of us."

I leaned back into the invisible wall. "Does this have a point?"

"My point, dear," Brenton said, "is that if you're going to play with Brian Caldswell, you need to understand that it doesn't matter how well you honor your contracts or how many times you save his life. The moment you become a liability to his game, he'll sacrifice you without pause, just like he does all his other pawns."

That was just going too far. I didn't need Brenton's cryptic bullshit to know I'd seen something I shouldn't have in that clearing. If Caldswell was really as ruthless as Brenton claimed, he would have eliminated the risk entirely and shot me while I was unconscious, but he hadn't. Instead, the captain had gone out of his way to cover things up so I could stay on as his merc. He *had* sent me onto the tribe ship, but it's a merc's job to do dangerous work, and when things had gone to hell, Caldswell had patched me up instead of letting me die. Sure he was a jerk and a killjoy, but while I hated him sometimes, the captain had never acted as less than what he was: an officer trying to keep a rowdy but useful subordinate in line, and that was something I could understand and appreciate far more than I did the man in front of me.

"You're very quiet all of a sudden, Miss Morris," Brenton said, leaning forward with a smile. "Did I upset your view of your captain?"

"Not at all," I said. "You actually helped me put things in perspective. I don't know what Caldswell's up to, but it's not my job to ask questions, is it? I'm a merc, I follow orders, and Captain Caldswell has been nothing but a captain to me. A captain, I might add, who has the respect and loyalty of his crew. In the months I've worked for him, I've never seen him needlessly waste the lives of those under his command. On the contrary, I've seen him go through great trouble to protect his people, which is more than I can say for you."

Brenton glowered at me. "You don't know what you're talking about, girl."

"Don't I?" I snapped, letting my eyes drop to the bodies of the two mercs I'd shot when I first entered the lounge. "You can tell a lot about a man by how he treats his hired guns, John Brenton. Even though you had two symbionts with you tonight, you sent that crash team in here to die."

Brenton went very still. "What do you know about symbionts?"

"I know they could easily have killed Cotter and gotten me down without the aid of your Terran tin cans," I said. "And you knew it, too, but you didn't want to risk your 'good men,' did you? No, you sent in the hired armor to soak up some bullets first."

I gave him a look of pure disgust. "I've worked for men like you," I continued. "Pricks who treat mercenaries as disposable shields to protect higher-value targets. Whatever you may think of Caldswell, he'd never have sent those poor Terran bastards up against two superiorly armored opponents in close quarters. The captain can be a right ass sometimes, but at least he gives a damn about whether people die, hired guns or not. And he certainly would have given Cotter a chance to surrender if all he meant to do was corner a merc with some plasmex and babble nonsense at her."

Brenton stared at me for a long time after I finished, and then that smug smile was back. "Believe me, Miss Morris, I could tell you stories about your captain that would make what I've done here seem like—"

"You just don't get it, do you?" I snapped, lurching forward against the barrier until I was nearly in his face. "You think that just because Caldswell did something worse, it makes your sins go away? Bullshit. Why should I even believe you, anyway? You come in here, lose a bunch of men, kill my partner, tie me up, and then you try to say you're better than Caldswell? *Please.*"

"I'm sure Brian would be touched by your loyalty," Brenton snapped. "But let me ask you a question. If Caldswell was really the hero in this, if he was *really* the good captain you claim he is, why does he kill everyone who gets close to the truth?"

I wanted to call bullshit on that, but I couldn't. Not after Rupert's behavior on Seni. I could still see him in the rain, staring at me with horror as he pressed his hand over my lips and told me I'd seen nothing on that tribe ship. I might be pissed at him at the moment, but I wasn't stupid enough to think that Rupert's fear was unfounded. Whatever secrets Caldswell was keeping, they were the killing kind, but that didn't mean I was about to give this man an inch.

My determination must have been clear, because Brenton's scowl fell into a tired frown. "Let me lay it out for you plainly, Miss Morris," he said. "You might not think much of me at the moment, but for all your misplaced faith in our dear Captain Caldswell, you have to know that you're dead if you stay on this ship. I don't know how you've avoided it so far, but now that you've talked to me, Brian doesn't have a choice. He'll kill you for sure. Or he would, if I hadn't gotten you first."

I looked at his face and saw what was unsaid. This man was going to kill me. The knowledge wasn't even frightening after everything that had happened. I was mostly just annoyed he was being so damned high-handed about it.

"Do it if you're going to, then," I said, staring him straight in the eye so he'd know I wasn't afraid. "At least I took one of your freaks down with me."

"Sorry," Brenton said. "But you'll have to wait a little longer. First, I need to know what happened on that xith'cal ship."

I couldn't help it. I started to laugh. "Then you should have asked me about it before you told me you were going to kill me. I'm not exactly inclined to talk now, am I?"

"But it doesn't have to be like that, Deviana," Brenton said, his voice going smooth. "As you're so keen on pointing out, I'm not Caldswell. All I want is the truth. Answer my questions about what really happened on that ship and I swear I'll answer yours in kind.

I'll tell you about the phantoms, about Caldswell, anything you want to know, and in the end, I'll let you go free."

"You're shitting me," I said. "You'd just let me walk?"

"Of course," Brenton said. "Caldswell's the one who kills to keep secrets. I kill to bring them out." He held out his hand to me. "This is your only chance, Deviana. Tell me what happened on that ship and I'll have Evelyn let you go right now."

I stared at him hard, but so far as I could tell, Brenton was in earnest. "Why is the xith'cal ship so damn important?" I asked. "It's gone. The lelgis burned it to a crisp. If you were after anything, it's space trash now."

"That's why we need you," Brenton said. His expression never changed, but I could hear frustration creeping into his voice. "Do you think Caldswell just stumbled into that tribe ship? The Recant asteroid belt is almost two light years from end to end. The odds of finding anything in that by chance, even something as huge as a tribe ship, are astronomical. The only way Caldswell found it was because someone tipped him off."

I'd already guessed as much, but Brenton wasn't finished. He pulled back his hand and leaned in, lowering his voice even though there was no one but his own people to hear. "The xith'cal were doing something on that ship," he whispered. "Something that terrified the lelgis. You were there when they burned it, how many ships did the lelgis send?"

I almost answered before I remembered I wasn't telling this man shit. When it was clear I wasn't going to say anything, Brenton answered for me.

"A dozen at least," he said. "That's a full battle fleet, and all to burn one ghost ship that couldn't fight back. I want to know *why*. The lelgis are creatures of nearly pure plasmex. Their drones are disposable, they don't fear guns or ships, and even the xith'cal don't raid them. They've had nothing to fear in the whole of their history, so why are they so afraid now? What were the xith'cal doing?"

"How the hell should I know?" I snapped.

"Because you were there," Brenton snapped back.

He stopped and took a deep breath. "They might not look it, but the xith'cal are brilliant bioengineers," he said, calmly now. "They've changed their own race countless times over the centuries, increasing their senses by a factor of ten, making themselves immune to nearly every disease, and specializing the genders so intensely that male and female xith'cal are almost separate species. Controlled evolution, their females call it, but Stoneclaw is a tricky old girl. Her tribe focuses on biological weapons. I think Stoneclaw was building something on that ship. Something that could threaten even a lelgis hive mind."

"So?" I said. "What do you care if the lizards and the squids fight?"

"I don't," Brenton said. "But to kill a lelgis, you'd have to make a weapon that destroys plasmex, not flesh. And *that*, little mercenary, is something I'm very interested in indeed."

He bent down again, planting his hands on my legs so that he was leaning completely into my personal space. "This could be the most important event of our lifetime, Deviana," he said, his dark eyes boring into mine. "I *have* to know what was on that ship. The proof might be long burned to ash, but anything could be a clue. I need you to tell me exactly what you saw in as much detail as you can remember, and we don't have time for that here."

He held out his hand again, his fingers hovering right under my chin. "The choice is very, very simple," he said quietly. "You can stay here and die, or you can come with us and live. I'll swear by anything you like that you will be unharmed, and for every answer you give me about that ship, I'll answer a question of yours in turn.

It'll be tit for tat all the way, and when it's done, we'll set you free. I'll even make it worth your while. We're not without resources, and Paradoxian mercs still like money, right?" He gave me an earnest smile. "What do you say, fair deal?"

He was so close now I couldn't have looked away from his eyes if I tried. But I didn't try. I stared him down, baring my teeth like the animal I was right then.

"Go," I said slowly, because whatever he thought, I was no snitch. "To." I'd die as a Paradoxian should, as Cotter had, with my honor intact and my enemy defeated, even if that defeat was nothing but denying him the information he'd killed us to get. "Hell."

Brenton closed his eyes and sat back. His offered hand dropped to his hip, and I knew this was it. But as I silently said my final prayers, Brenton pulled out not a gun, but a sleek handset.

"I didn't want to do this," he said softly, flipping open his handset and mashing a button. "But this is too important to sacrifice on the altar of Paradoxian honor."

I braced by instinct, ready for a bomb or something equally horrible. Instead, I felt Nic slip away behind me. Half a minute later, I heard soft footsteps on the stairs.

"Your refusal is noted," Brenton said, holding out his arm as the footsteps came closer. "But your cooperation is no longer required."

I was about to ask what the hell he meant by that when the girl stepped into view.

She was so emaciated, I almost wasn't sure she was a girl at first. Her body was little more than bones and sallow skin. Her long hair, dull and gray brown as heat-spoiled chocolate, hung limp and brittle from her scalp. Her head was down and her bony shoulders were shaking, but it wasn't until Brenton pulled her into his arms that I realized the girl was sobbing, crying in great heaves, though she made no noise at all.

"I'm sorry," Brenton whispered, hugging the girl close. "I'm so, so sorry. But I need you to do it one more time. Please, Enna, just one more time."

He stroked the girl's shoulders until they finally stopped shaking, and the girl pushed away from him enough to look at me. The moment her eyes met mine, I froze. The skeletal girl in Brenton's arms was Ren.

Even sunken with hunger and screwed up with more emotion than I'd ever seen Ren show, that face was definitely Caldswell's daughter, except that was impossible. I'd seen Ren leave with Caldswell myself not five hours ago. She'd been fine then, as fine as Ren ever was, anyway. She'd certainly looked nothing like the wasted waif cowering in Brenton's arms. I was wondering about the odds of Ren having a twin sister when a beeping interrupted our little tableau.

Brenton pulled out his handset. "What?" he barked, holding it in front of him so he wouldn't have to let go of the girl.

The man on the other end was a merc if I've ever heard one. "Sir, we found the records you wanted. You were right. Caldswell sent both hired security into the ship, but only the female was injured."

Brenton's eyes found mine. "Injured how?"

"Bite across the shoulder," the man said. "Nearly took her arm off."

"Thank you, commander," Brenton said slowly, closing the handset with a click before looking at me like he was seeing me for the first time. "You were bitten?"

I fixed him with my best not-giving-a-shit glare. "Have you ever fought a xith'cal? Bites are part of the package."

Brenton ignored me. He stood up, keeping a careful hand on Enna as he got in my face. "What game are you playing?"

I was so over this. "You tell me!" I shouted, kicking at him as much as the invisible wall would allow. "You're the one who's the truth crusader!"

Brenton ignored my outburst, straightening back up with a

confused frown. "I don't understand," he said. "If you survived being bitten, why the hell is Brian letting you run around loose?"

"Because that's what he pays me for!" I yelled. "I'm his god-damn security!"

Brenton clamped his jaw shut, obviously upset. He studied me for a few more seconds while I did my best to look as surly as possible. But just as Brenton's staring was getting unbearably obnoxious, his face changed.

He was still looking at me, but his expression was totally different. Wondrous, like he'd just seen a mystery of the universe unfold before his eyes. "My god," he whispered. "He doesn't know."

I threw back my head with a frustrated hiss. Brenton didn't even notice. "Brian didn't know what was on that ship!" His shout was almost gleeful. "He just followed the tip. He doesn't know why the lelgis were there, or what Stoneclaw was actually doing, or *you*. He doesn't know what you've—"

Brenton cut off at once, but he couldn't quite get his joy in check. He took a deep, satisfied breath and looked at me the same way I'd look at a shiny new gun. "Well, well," he said, his voice thick with smug happiness. "If you really were bitten, then there's a chance everything isn't lost. Someone up there must like us after all."

"No one likes you," I snapped. "And that bite healed a long time ago, sorry to disappoint. Now, would you please stop talking and just shoot me?" Because listening to him babble about shit I didn't understand was getting really, really tedious.

Brenton shook his head, grinning so wide I could see his back teeth. "No shooting today, darling. Hell, if this works out, I'll take a bullet for you. After all, you're the one who's going to help us save the universe."

He reached out and clapped me on the shoulder so hard I nearly fell off the stool. As I was recovering my balance, he glanced over my head. "Nic!"

The man behind me stepped forward, and Brenton gently pushed the emaciated girl toward him. "Change of plans. Get Enna out of here, and don't let her touch the merc."

Nic nodded and reached out to take the girl, who'd started her silent sobbing again. Just as his hand touched her arm, the unmistakable sound of gunfire rang out outside the ship.

Brenton went for his handset at once. "Report!"

No one answered. Outside, the gunfire cut off abruptly, and then two mercs in full armor came flying through the cargo bay door.

I couldn't see them land from where I was sitting, but the crash I heard was enough to tell me they'd hit the far side of the cargo bay. I stopped worrying about them a second later, though, because the next thing I saw come through the blown-off door was Rupert.

Funny enough, the very first thought that crossed my mind was how much he must have been holding back during our fight. He was still dressed in his suit, without a speck of sweat despite the heat, and he was holding a third merc in full armor above his head. It took a few moments for me to process that last part, actually. The merc had to weigh close to nine hundred pounds, but Rupert hefted him like he was made of air and plastic, hurling the man across the cargo bay to join his friends before turning toward us.

He spotted me at once, and his face fell into the most deadly snarl I've ever seen on a human. But then he saw Brenton, Enna, and Nic, and his expression changed from rage to horror. For a split second, everyone just stood there, and then Brenton shoved Nic and Enna down as Rupert charged.

Even though I knew what he was now, Rupert's speed still shocked me. He was faster than I was in armor and almost as good a jumper. He cleared the stairs up to the lounge in one leap, landing in the doorway. But his next move wasn't for me, it wasn't even for Brenton. When Rupert lunged, he lunged at Enna, his hands going out to snap the skeletal girl's neck.

He would have made it, too, had Brenton not gotten in the way. He caught Rupert's wrist when Rupert's fingers were an inch away from the sobbing girl's throat, and the two men stopped cold.

"Nic," Brenton said, his voice calm. "Evelyn, get the daughter and the merc out of here. Nothing else matters."

Nic nodded and scooped the thin girl into his arms before setting off down the stairs at a dead run. Rupert tried to follow, but Brenton threw him over his shoulder. Rupert hit the far wall of the lounge hard enough to dent the metal, but it barely seemed to faze him. He was up and about to go for the girl again when Brenton, moving with the same impossible speed Rupert had shown earlier, slammed into the wall on top of him, his hand on Rupert's throat.

"Hello, Charkov," he said. "Been a while."

"Not long enough," Rupert growled.

Brenton flashed Rupert a bloodthirsty grin, and then he began to change.

When I'd read Anthony's letter, I hadn't fully comprehended the reality of a symbiont. Even though I'd seen two today, and killed one, I still thought of them as things, alien enemies to be defeated. I had not yet stopped and worked through what it would mean to have an alien presence living inside you that came *out*. Now, I saw it all too well.

With a whisper like a slicing knife, black scales sprouted from Brenton's body. They pushed clean through his exposed skin and cut through his clothes like razors, shredding his shirt and pants, even his heavy boots, to tiny scraps. The scales grew like leaves, overlapping across his muscles and down his limbs, sliding over him like black water until every glimpse of flesh was hidden.

The entire process took less than a count of three, and when it was done, the thing holding Rupert was no longer human. It was the Terran weapon that even Devastators didn't fight alone, the symbiont, a huge, black-scaled alien creature with Brenton's cocky stance and glittering, alien eyes that made my skin crawl. That was the last impression I got before the symbiont lifted Rupert and threw him through the blast door.

Not into, *through*. Rupert's body tore through the three inches of reinforced steel like they were cardboard and crashed into the bulkhead across the hall. He hit with a clang that made me wince and dropped hard, landing facedown.

"You're not going to last long like that, Charkov," the black thing called in Brenton's voice.

I thought Brenton was being optimistic about Rupert lasting at all. That had looked like a finishing blow to me. But then, to my amazement, Rupert pushed himself up to his knees and looked at me.

There were so many emotions on his face right then, I couldn't place them all. Rage was there, certainly, but also fear and shame, guilt and something warm, an echo of the intensity that was always in his eyes when he looked at me. It lasted only a moment, and then Rupert dropped his head, and blackness bloomed across his body.

Like Brenton's, Rupert's change took only three heartbeats. Black scales sprouted from his skin, slicing through the dark suit I'd come to love so much, covering his face, his hair, all of him I could see. The scales rustled softly as they fell into place, glossy and hard under the ship lights as the remaining scraps of clothing slid away. When he stood at last, he wasn't Rupert at all. He was the black figure from the tribe ship, the one who had saved me.

"Get the merc out!"

Brenton's shout startled me, and for a moment I didn't know who he was yelling at. Then I felt a pressure on my chest, and I realized the girl behind me, Evelyn, was trying to yank me off the stool using the invisible pressure. Only it wasn't working.

"I'm trying!" she cried. "She's resisting!"

If I was, I didn't know it, which was a shame. If I'd known what I was doing, I'd have tried to do it harder. I wished she hadn't drawn my attention to whatever it was, because the moment she told me I was resisting, I apparently stopped, and the pressure slammed down so hard I fell off the stool. The fall dazed me, and Evelyn took her chance, dragging me like a hunting trophy toward the stairs.

Out in the hall, Rupert sprang forward. I was pretty sure he was going for me this time, but, as before, Brenton blocked him. My breath caught. If Brenton had been fast as a human, he was unstoppable now. He was in front of Rupert almost before Rupert was off the ground. But Rupert was fast, too, and the moment the situation changed, he changed with it, turning his lunge into a flying elbow that hit Brenton square in his scaled jaw. The men tumbled to the floor in a black tangle, but that was all I could see before Evelyn hauled me down the stairs.

CHAPTER
16

I don't like being dragged around, and I like being tied up even less, but the absolute last straw was being made helpless. My body was frozen under Evelyn's invisible pressure. I couldn't even kick as she bumped me down the stairs, tugging me behind her like a trussed-up hunting trophy. I could feel Rupert and Brenton's fight through the metal floor, but I couldn't *do* anything, and as I watched the lounge door grow smaller and smaller, something inside me snapped.

I'm no stranger to anger, especially the killing kind, but this? This was rage like I'd never felt. It was like a dam broke in my chest, and raw fury, white hot and sharp as a thermite blade, came thundering down through my body, filling me to bursting.

All at once, I stopped going down the stairs. The pressure holding me frozen was still there, but I could feel it getting thinner. Above me, Evelyn was staring down in horror. She was drenched in sweat and her whole body was shaking, though I couldn't tell if it was from effort or fear.

"Stop fighting!" she screamed, her voice shrill. "You'll kill us both!"

Effort and fear, then. Ignoring her warning, I bared my teeth and let my rage carry me. Her shaking grew worse as the pressure on me grew softer and softer until I could move my body again. It was just a little, but it was enough for me to flip myself over onto my stomach and push up to face her.

The moment I turned, I stopped so abruptly that even my rage flickered. With everything that had been happening, I hadn't noticed the creatures. Now that I was staring directly at Evelyn, I couldn't not see them. She was covered in glowing bugs. They were crawling through her hair, floating over her face, passing through her wide, terrified eyes like ghosts. Some were so tiny they looked like pinpricks; others were nearly the size of my thumb. Some had wings, but most were little more than bundles of spindly legs.

Their collected glow was bright as moonlight on her skin. It was so beautiful, so strange and terrifying that for several moments I could only lie there and stare. My hesitation almost let her regain control, but then the anger came pounding back, and my fist started moving toward her chest like a punch in extreme slow motion.

We fought for every inch, but whatever I was doing, I was winning. As my hand crept closer and closer to her chest, the bugs began to move away from where it would land, opening up a clear spot just above her stomach. On impulse, I opened my hand, no longer punching, but simply reaching toward her, my fingers straining.

This seemed to panic the glowing creatures. They fled from me, climbing up into Evelyn's hair and down her legs. As they ran, I had a fleeting moment of regret I wouldn't get to touch one, but I forgot all of that when I caught sight of my fingers.

Where my hand was closest to Evelyn, my fingertips were black. They looked almost sooty, like I'd brushed them against an exhaust pipe. The black was so out of place, I thought that it must be another hallucination, but Evelyn saw it, too. I knew, because she started to scream.

"No!" she wailed. "Don't touch me!"

But it was too late. My fingers brushed against her, and the blackness on the tips vanished like it had been rubbed off by her shirt. The pressure holding me lifted in the same instant, and Evelyn tumbled to the ground.

Suddenly free, I collapsed as well, falling down the stairs on top of her. This scattered the last of the bugs, but I could barely see them leaving through the fit Evelyn was throwing. She writhed on the floor, screaming and tearing at her chest like she was trying to rip something out. I scrambled, trying to get off her before her thrashing threw me farther down the stairs. I'd just gotten a knee on the ground when I saw the blackness creeping up the skin of her neck.

I jumped back like I'd been burned, catching the railing just before I tumbled head over heels into the cargo bay below. I kept myself from falling by sheer luck, but I couldn't manage to focus my body to do more than hold on. All my attention was on Evelyn as the blackness spread across her skin.

She thrashed wildly, screaming as black slid up her chin and down over her arms until she looked like she'd been rolling in soot. The more it spread, the wilder her struggles became until, just as it reached her hairline, she jerked to a sudden, unnatural stop. Her cries cut out like someone had sliced the feed to her throat, and she lay still, her face frozen in terror.

It was so horrible, so strange, that I actually stood there gaping like a fish for several moments before my battle sense kicked back in. Gritting my teeth, I crouched down, but I couldn't make myself touch her. There was just something too wrong about the black body to risk touching.

In the end, I settled for holding my fingers under her nose, but it didn't tell me anything I didn't already know. The girl was dead. Whatever I'd done had killed her.

I snatched my fingers back, staring at them like I'd never seen them before. They looked normal, no sign of black at all, but my skin tingled painfully where the sooty stuff had appeared. On a hunch, I moved my fingers under my own nose, breathing deep to try to catch a snatch of Hyrek's "odd smell," but I got nothing. Just the usual slightly sweet silicone smell of my armor lining and—

A crash from the lounge snapped me back into the present. In a flash, I forgot the dead woman, the creatures, and the strange black stuff on my fingers and her skin. I shoved the whole thing out of my mind, spinning on my toes as I ran up the stairs to help Rupert.

I stopped when I reached the lounge's landing and ducked low. I might have come to help, but I wasn't about to throw my currently unarmored self into a fight between two Terran super soldiers. Instead, I remembered my training and played it smart, dropping down to the ground with my back safely to the doorjamb before peeking my head around to look inside.

What I saw wasn't good. Blood was splashed on the floor, and though I couldn't see whose blood it was, Rupert was the one with his back to the wall while Brenton was on the attack. Rupert had height and reach, but Brenton was larger and, I was willing to bet, more experienced. He would dart in to strike at Rupert and then, when Rupert dodged or countered, dart out before Rupert could reach him.

Rupert was entirely on the defensive, and if he kept fighting like that he would lose. He must have known that as well, because his counters were getting more reckless, wilder. He was trying his best to break out, but Brenton was keeping him penned in like a pro. However, though Brenton currently had the edge, it was by a tiny, tiny margin, and neither man had the spare attention for me.

That was my saving grace. Quiet as I could, I slipped inside the lounge. My armor was piled in the corner, and the temptation to run over and put it on was almost unbearable. But even on my best days, I'd never been able to get into my armor in less than nineteen seconds, and nineteen seconds was eighteen too many with Brenton not ten feet away. So, rather than head for my armor, I snuck along the wall to the kitchen counter where Brenton had laid my gun after he'd taken her from me.

Before I could chicken out, I shot up, grabbing Sasha off the counter as I did. The noise caught Brenton and Rupert's attention, but even their ungodly speed wasn't enough to beat years of training. I lugged Sasha up, my arm straining against her weight now that I had no armor to help me, took aim at Brenton's head, and pulled the trigger.

I've fired Sasha outside of armor only once, just to see if I could do it, and nearly broke my arm. This time I wasn't sure if I'd been so lucky. Sasha's kick blasted through me like a rocket, slamming my back into the counter so hard I almost blacked out. But even as I hit, my mind was past the pain. All my attention was on Brenton.

The shot was so perfect even I couldn't believe I'd done it without armor. He'd been turning to look at me when I'd fired, and the bullet had caught him right between the eyes. If he'd been a xith'cal, he would have been dead. Considering I'd shot his goon four times in the head, though, I knew it wasn't enough to kill, or even really hurt him. Still, Sasha's punch knocked him flat on his back, and that was all Rupert needed.

He was off the wall and on Brenton before I could breathe. He attacked with all the pent-up fury of a cornered animal that's just broken free. Brenton defended well, but with Rupert holding him down, he couldn't get off his back.

Gasping from the intense pain of slamming my back into the kitchen counter and possibly breaking my arm at the same time, I pushed myself up and switched Sasha to my left hand, which was still working. My right felt like it had been run over by a truck. I couldn't even move my fingers.

Looking back, I should have taken this chance to run over and get my armor on, broken arm or no. Mia would also have been useful, but I couldn't get myself going, not even to grab my plasma shotgun. I was mesmerized by how amazingly fast Rupert and Brenton were moving.

Anthony had said symbionts gave their hosts increased speed and strength. Watching the real thing in action made his warning sound laughably understated. There was no word I knew in any language to accurately describe the speed and deadly power of the fight in front of me.

The symbionts were moving so fast their scales whistled through the air. Every time Rupert struck and Brenton dodged, the blow dented the floor. I could actually feel the fight echoing through the metal under my feet like a jackhammer, and the longer I watched, the more I realized that I might not be able to land a shot even with my suit's targeting system. The symbionts were simply too strong and too fast for my Lady. If the power didn't seem to come at such a high price, I might have been jealous.

I was about to go and get my armor on anyway when I heard something coming up the cargo bay stairs. The footsteps were so fast and heavy, I almost thought it was Cotter before I remembered Cotter was dead. When I turned, though, I realized I'd been half right. There *was* a dead man running up the stairs, just not the dead man I'd thought.

The symbiont Cotter had sliced just before he'd gone down lunged through the door from the cargo bay. His side and front were still gaping and bloody from the gyro ax, but the black scales had closed over the hole enough to let him stand. Still, the wound slowed him, and that was the only way I managed the miracle that happened next.

The injured symbiont never saw me. His attention was all on Rupert and Brenton. He charged forward, claws ready to rip into Rupert's exposed back, but before he'd taken more than one step, Sasha's bullet hit him solid in his injured side.

I've never been as good a shot with my left hand as I am with my right, but Cotter's ax had left me a pretty wide target. Even so, I almost didn't make the shot. As I raised my pistol, I hesitated. My left arm isn't as trained as my right, and even if I did manage to relax enough to spare my bones, shooting with my weaker hand would almost certainly dislocate my elbow. I had one arm out of commission already, the idea of losing the other scared me witless.

But as the injured man's claws reached out for Rupert, little things like broken arms and the almost certain grisly death that would come if I didn't kill the newcomer with this shot became trivial. I'd faced my death several times today already. I'd embraced it, even demanded it. I was not afraid of death, but the idea of living on knowing that I had let Rupert die, knowing that the man I loved was gone and it was my fault because I'd been too slow, because I'd been a coward, that was more than I could bear.

Sasha's shot exploded in my ears, and the force of her kick knocked me all the way to the busted blast door. I landed on my back, my head slamming into the floor so hard I saw stars. My left shoulder and arm felt like they were on fire, and I *knew* I'd broken something this time, but I couldn't work up the strength to care. It took everything I had just to stay conscious as I lay panting on my back, ears ringing, which was why I didn't see or hear the symbiont until he was on top of me.

The first thing I noticed was that he was bleeding freely from his side, and I felt a surge of triumph. I'd hit him. But the triumph burned out as he raised his black fist. Not hard enough. That was my last thought before the symbiont slammed his claws into my stomach.

"No!"

The word came from two throats, Rupert's and, to my surprise, Brenton's. Another time that would probably have struck me as significant, but at the moment I was too focused on the feeling of the hand in my guts to think much about it. I did feel when someone ripped the symbiont away, though, because his crushing weight on my hips vanished, and then a pair of steel-hard arms scooped me off the ground.

I don't think I could have fought those arms if I'd tried, but I didn't have to, because it was Rupert's voice that rumbled through the chest I was pressed against. "Hang on!" he shouted at me.

I obeyed as best I could, curling my body around his as he backed through the busted blast door into the hallway. In front of us, I could see all three of the symbionts who'd stormed our ship: the one I'd killed, still on the ground, the one Cotter had chopped and I'd shot lying on the floor, dying if not dead, and Brenton pushing himself up from where Rupert had left him. Brenton stared at Rupert a moment, and then he lunged forward, grabbing the bleeding symbiont and running down the cargo bay steps so fast he seemed to fly.

"Rupert," I whispered as he turned and started running down the hall in the opposite direction. "Rupert, they're getting away."

"Hush," he said. I felt his chest tense, and then the black scales covering his face slid back and Rupert, my Rupert was over me, his eyes set forward with absolute focus as he turned us into the medbay. "I'll take care of them later. All that matters right now is that you don't die."

He laid me down on the emergency gurney in the corner, the one with the trauma shell that's saved for really, really bad cases. I didn't want to go under the black shell. Rupert must have seen the fear on my face, because he leaned down and kissed me quickly.

"Everything will be all right," he said, his voice determined. "I won't let you die, Devi."

And then he closed the trauma shell over me, and the world vanished.

* * *

I don't know how long I was under the black healing shelter of the trauma shell, but I hated every second of it. Trauma shells surround you in a field that slows your body down to nothing. That might not sound so bad, but the reality is that you feel like you're constantly on the edge of suffocating. Plus, they're dark. Being in one always made me think of being buried alive, though usually I had drugs to get me through.

No such luck this time. Rupert must have pulled my hand out to put in the IV at some point, because I could feel the pressure of the needle in my skin just as I could feel the hazy weight of high-grade painkillers on my mind, but I couldn't seem to pass out. Hyrek had mentioned something about the battle drugs ruining all normal painkillers for me, but I hadn't realized just how bad that would be until now. Of course, I should have been ecstatic I was alive to be in this much discomfort, given everything that had happened, but feeling like you're about to run out of air at every moment makes it harder to appreciate the little things, so I just focused on trying to stay still and wait it out.

I must have drifted off at some point, though, because Caldswell's voice woke me up. He was whispering, but even when he pitches it low, Caldswell has a captain's voice, and it was enough to snap me out of the light sleep I'd managed.

"...better this way," he was saying. "Dammit, Rupert, you think I like this? She's the best merc I've had in a decade. That was Mikel's body in there. He was an Eye for ten years before he turned, and she took him out like so much trash. You don't let someone that good go without sound reason, but she knows too much. I've bent the rules for her twice already, I can't keep doing it. She's hovering on the edge of death as it is. Let her rest. She'd want it this way."

"Devi would never want this." The voice was so cold and angry that it took me several moments to recognize it as Rupert's. "Not like this, Brian." I'd never heard him use the captain's first name before, either. He said it like a curse.

Caldswell's sigh was more tired than anything else. "She knows what you are now for sure," he said, calm and reasonable. "The tribe ship I could excuse since she was half dead and high out of her mind, but this? This is unrecoverable. And since whatever idiot blew up my bridge completely destroyed the security feeds, we have no way of knowing what Brenton told her. Considering he was here waiting with his daughter while we were out chasing nothing, though, I'm betting this whole planet was a setup."

"Even more reason not to do this." Rupert's voice was desperate now, almost pleading. "If all Brenton wanted was information, he could easily have gone after the crew. They were the softer target and they've been with you longer. But he specifically came to the ship and interrogated Devi. He even tried to take her with him. She knows why, she could tell us—"

"Brenton wants to destroy everything we've suffered all these years to protect," Caldswell snapped. "I don't need a detailed description of his plans to know he was going to use Morris against us."

I felt the table creak beneath me, and I realized Rupert had grabbed it, denting the metal right by my arm. Caldswell took a deep breath at the sound, and I got the strangely distinct impression he was rubbing his eyes.

"If it was just that Brenton wanted her, I'd let things slide," he said. "But she's seen too much. Also, as you've just proven, she compromises *you*, and that's a risk I can't afford."

Rupert didn't answer, but I could almost feel the silence getting colder. Caldswell must have felt it, too, because the next words out of his mouth were the gentlest I've ever heard him speak.

"I tried to warn you," he said softly. "I *told* you not to get attached. No matter how you try to protect them, it always ends up like this. *Always*." His voice was so longing, I started to wonder who Caldswell had lost. "I wish we had the time to work through this more gently," he continued, his tone shifting back to his usual brisk command. "But we're up against the wall here. She has to go, now, before the crew comes back. The only question left is do you want me to do it, or do you want to do it yourself?"

The silence stretched on so long I was afraid I'd passed out again, but then Rupert answered, his voice so low I could barely hear. "I'll take care of it."

There was a creak as Caldswell left. I heard Rupert step away, and then the scrape of a chair as he dragged it across the room to sit beside me, his forehead resting on the table next to my shoulder. I held my already short breath, waiting for him to do something, but all I heard was his low, steady breathing until, at last, it lulled me back to sleep.

I woke next to bright light as the trauma shell was peeled back. I tried to cover my eyes, but I couldn't move. Neither of my arms would obey me. In the end it didn't matter, because something leaned over me, blocking the light. It was Rupert.

"Shh," he whispered when I flinched. "I have to be fast. Your body isn't stable enough to be out of the shell for long."

I hadn't realized I'd been trying to get away until his voice made me stop. My brain was fuzzy and disconnected, but the conversation I'd overheard before was still with me. I'd been sure Rupert was here to kill me, but the moment he spoke, I knew I was wrong. No one who came to kill you could talk like that, and they certainly wouldn't worry about you being out of the shell for too long.

He reached out and gently cupped my face. I relaxed into his touch, letting myself revel in a moment where I was alive, no one was trying to kill me, and Rupert was here, safe and whole beside me. He was so close I could feel his breath against my lips, but while his voice was soft, his tone was almost frustrated.

"Devi," he whispered, dragging my name out with a long sigh. "You make me lose all sense. All my life I've trusted my control even when I trusted nothing else, but when I'm with you, it all vanishes." He kissed me gently. "You make me crazy, do you know that?"

Inappropriate as it was, I couldn't help myself. "A lot of people tell me that," I croaked, smiling against his mouth.

He broke away from me, ducking his head. For a second, I thought he was laughing, but there was no laughter in his voice when he spoke again.

"When I saw you on the floor, saw him jump on you, I thought I was too late." His lips were pressed against the hollow at the base of my throat, and I felt the words more than I heard them. "I thought I'd lost you. I didn't know I could be that scared anymore."

He took a deep breath and raised his head to look me in the eyes again, tightening his grip on my face so that I couldn't look away. "I love you," he said, his voice hard and earnest. "And I won't let anyone take you away."

My poor heart, already abused by the trauma of the last few hours, skipped a beat at his words, and the only thing that kept me from throwing my arms around him was the fact that I was too weak to move. "I'm not going anywhere," I said, struggling to get enough breath behind the words. "I lo—"

He cut me off with a kiss. "No," he whispered, his voice rough. "I might not be strong enough if I hear that." He kissed me again and leaned forward, his hair falling over my face as he lowered his mouth to my ear.

"I don't deserve to hear that," he murmured against me. "I've done—" He stopped, and his fingers began to tremble. "I do terrible things, Devi. Terrible, necessary things that I cannot undo.

Would not undo. What you've seen is just the surface. What I am, what I've done..."

He pressed his cheek against mine with a deep breath, like he was trying to pull himself together. "You deserve better," he continued at last. "I put you in danger just by being near you. You've seen what I am, but what you don't know is that I chose this. I *chose* to become a monster. I thought I had nothing left to lose, nothing I could put in danger. The day I accepted the symbiont, I thought the only thing left for me in life was my duty, but I was wrong." He kissed my cheek. "I found you. You're the bravest, craziest, most extraordinary thing I've ever seen. When I look at you, I forget that my soul is sold already, that I have no right to feel the happiness I feel around you, to love you like I do."

I struggled against him as he spoke, trying to get my stupid body to cooperate long enough to tell him I didn't care about any of that. That I thought he was plenty deserving, and my opinion was the only one that mattered. But Rupert was already raising his head to look at me with blue eyes so frighteningly intense I lost the little bit of breath I'd managed.

"I will not let him kill you," Rupert said, each word sending tremors down the fingers that had never left my face. "If he wants you dead for knowing too much, I'll make you know nothing. If he would kill you because you make me weak, then I'll make sure you never look at me again. I'll do whatever I must to keep you safe, and if you hate me for it, all the better. I can bear that. I can bear anything if it means you stay alive."

I couldn't, and I started to tell him so, but Rupert was too fast. He leaned down and kissed me again, hard and desperate, and then pulled out of my sight. The bright light hit me as soon as he vanished, forcing me to close my eyes.

When I opened them again, there were two people standing over me. Rupert was there, and Ren stood at his side. The real Ren, not that skeletal shadow that had been with Brenton. This Ren was calm and still as a doll, her blank, dark eyes expressionless as ever.

Rupert reached out one last time, trailing his finger down my cheek. "Good-bye, Deviana," he whispered.

Rage surged strong enough to push me up. I wanted to yell at him, to ask what he thought he was doing and how the hell he thought he could just say good-bye after telling me all that. I'd barely gotten more than a half inch off the bed before Ren's hand covered my face. I jerked away in horror, but her fingers were gentle as they followed my movement, and then a soft, female voice whispered in my mind.

Sleep.

And I slept.

I woke to the feeling of something sharp poking my hand, but my eyes stuck shut when I tried to open them. I tried harder, but nothing I did could unglue them. I was starting to get a little panicky when someone wiped a wet cloth over my face, and the gunk vanished. I blinked at the sudden bright light, and as things slowly came into focus, I saw there were words floating in front of my face.

Welcome back to the land of the living.

The words vanished, and I turned my head slightly to see Hyrek standing beside my bed, clicking unhurriedly on his handset.

How do you feel?

I considered the question for a moment. "Not like much of anything, actually," I answered at last. "Tired, mostly."

Hyrek shook his head. *That's because you've been under the bone knitter twice in less than a month. Your nerves are fried. Didn't I tell you to stay out of trouble?*

"Are they coming back?" Because the idea of fried nerves definitely did not appeal to me.

They should, Hyrek typed. *Assuming I don't have to patch you back together again for at least another forty-eight hours.*

"No promises," I grumbled. "What happened?"

I was hoping you could tell me, Hyrek typed. *So far as we've been able to gather, pirates hit the ship while we were staying at the not-quite-as-finished-as-advertised governor's mansion. Caldswell came back when he got the alarm to find you down and Cotter dead.*

I sank into the bed. I didn't remember any of that. The last thing I remembered was lying on the cargo watching old gladiator matches with Cotter. I didn't remember a fight, and I certainly didn't remember Cotter dying.

That thought made my chest clamp up. I wasn't sure how, but I had the feeling his death had been glorious, worthy of memory, but I couldn't make my brain form any pictures. I was about to ask Hyrek another question when the door opened and Caldswell came in.

"How's our hero doing?"

The question was genial, but one look at Caldswell's face told me he was anything but happy. Of course, what captain whose ship had just been hit and crew killed would be?

"I can't remember anything," I said, staring up at him.

Caldswell shrugged. "To be expected. You took quite a blow to the head, though why you were out of your armor is anyone's guess."

My eyes widened. I could think of no reason why I would ever get out of my armor while on duty.

"You were roughed up pretty bad," he continued. "We had to keep you under the trauma shell until Hyrek could operate. You're lucky to be alive."

I rubbed my forehead, trying to make the memories surface.

Hyrek glanced at me and typed. *I'm sure it will come back. Your brain is still trying to heal. Even your hard head can't take everything.*

I shook myself and sat up a little. "Is there a video or something I could watch?"

"No." Caldswell sounded pretty bitter about that. "They blasted the bridge when they came in. You and Cotter took out plenty before you went down, though, so whatever you did, you did it well."

"Thank you, sir," I said, more out of habit than anything else. It didn't feel right accepting praise for something I had no memory of doing.

"Get some rest," Caldswell said, gently patting my shoulder. "We're stuck here until Mabel can patch the *Fool* up enough to make the flight to a real repair shop, so no rush. Just take it easy and try to get some sleep."

"Yes sir," I whispered, though I didn't feel like sleeping anymore. I felt restless and angry. Far more angry than I should be over lost memories that would probably be coming back. As I watched Caldswell leave, I noticed someone was waiting for him in the hall. It was that tall man, the cook. The moment I saw him, a wave of revulsion hit me in the chest.

I looked away in disgust. The feeling had come out of nowhere, washing through my body like a flood. It was so strange that I forced myself to push up a bit and look again.

The wave hit me just as hard the second time, but I was expecting it now and I was able to keep looking. Caldswell was standing in the door, talking softly to the cook. I couldn't hear what he was saying, but the raw anger was clear in every line of Caldswell's body. I had no idea what the cook could have done to make the captain so furious, but Caldswell looked ready to murder him on the spot.

That didn't seem to bother the cook, though. He just stood there and took it, his face neutral. Finally, Caldswell stomped off, waving for the cook to follow. He did, but as he passed the door, his eyes met mine.

The revulsion hit me so hard I nearly threw up, but the surge of anger that came right after was what knocked me back down on the bed. I sank into the pad, completely confused. What the hell was wrong with me? I didn't even know that much about the cook, not even his name, actually. I knew I didn't like him, but surely not liking someone wasn't enough for a reaction this strong.

Hyrek touched my shoulder, holding his handset out. *What's wrong? Your blood pressure just shot up.*

"I have no idea," I confessed, covering my face with my hands.

Hyrek grabbed my head and turned it, peeling back my hands to examine my eyes and mouth. His nostrils quivered as he did, and he jerked away.

"What?" I asked, tensing. "The smell again?"

Hyrek nodded. *Worse than before.*

I knew I'd regret asking, but I couldn't help it. "What do I smell like?"

Hyrek set his jaw stubbornly and didn't answer. I was beginning to worry he wouldn't when he reached down and clicked his handset, turning the screen toward me.

Rotted meat.

I looked away in revulsion. I could hear him typing something else, but I shook my head. "I asked," I muttered. "Thank you, Hyrek. I'd like to sleep now."

He tapped my arm gently and left me alone. I lay in the bed for a long time after that, hands pressed against my eyes as I tried to figure out what had happened, how Cotter had died, what Hyrek's smell meant, and why I was so angry. Mostly, though, my thoughts kept drifting back to the cook's eyes. I hadn't realized until now that they were blue, but it was the expression in them I couldn't shake. I'd never had anyone look at me with such a strange mix of loss and triumph, and it bothered me.

Finally, exhausted, I kicked everything out of my mind and focused on going to sleep. Tomorrow, I would remember. Tomorrow, I would know what the hell was going on with my life. Tomorrow, things would make more sense.

I held that hope like a prayer until sleep took me at last.

ACKNOWLEDGMENTS

I owe much thanks, admiration, and adoration to my editor, Devi Pillai, who stuck with me through countless edits to get this book right. If I hadn't already named a character after you by accident, Devi, I would have done it on purpose. Thank you for everything.

extras

www.orbitbooks.net

about the author

Rachel Bach grew up wanting to be an author and a super-villain. Unfortunately, supervillainy proved surprisingly difficult to break into, so she stuck to writing and everything worked out great. She currently lives in Athens, Georgia, with her perpetually energetic toddler, extremely understanding husband, overflowing library, and obese wiener dog. You can find out more about Rachel and all her books at rachelbach.net.

Rachel also writes fantasy under the name Rachel Aaron. Learn more about her first series, *The Legend of Eli Monpress*, and read sample chapters for yourself at rachelaaron.net!

Find out more about Rachel Bach and other Orbit authors by registering for the free monthly newsletter at www.orbitbooks.net.

interview

When did the idea for Fortune's Pawn *first come to you?*
One summer day in 2011, I decided I wanted to read an action-packed space romance. I looked and looked, but I just couldn't find one that scratched the right itch, so I wrote my own. This is why being a writer is awesome!

Okay, so that's not really how it happened. I've actually been playing around in the world of Paradox for years. Devi started as a side character in an entirely different novel about the Blackbird Mercenaries, but when she stole the show and refused to give it back, I had no choice but to give her her own series. Then I wrote about half the book before I realized it needed to be first person, not third, so I had to go back and redo everything. So yeah, she *really* muscled her way into the spotlight.

How was the transition from fantasy to science fiction?
Astonishingly easy. There's a reason the two genres are mentioned together so frequently (so much so that they've merged into the übergenre of SF/F). Both feature created universes, significant personal actions, epic landscapes, and high-stakes scenarios. Both can even have magic! The only real difference is flavor and, of course, just how bound you're willing to let yourself be by the realities of science.

But that goes for fantasy, too. Just as a hard-core military fantasy might get into the nitty-gritties of a prolonged siege that a lighter fantasy would gloss over, so lighter sci-fi can play a bit looser with the rules of the universe for the sake of the story. Because in the end, it's the fiction half of science fiction that matters most.

That said, I hope any physics majors reading this will forgive me if something I mention in the book turns out to be physically impossible.

What was the inspiration behind Devi Morris?

I am a huge, huge fan of in-your-face, make-no-apologies female badasses. As I said earlier, Devi has been in my head for years, so her inspirations are wide and varied. There's a lot of Toph Beifong from *Avatar: The Last Airbender*, some Paksenarrion from Elizabeth Moon's amazing *Deed of Paksenarrion*, a little Killashandra from Anne McCaffrey's Crystal Singer series, and a whole ton of Ellen Ripley from the *Alien* movies.

But all of these were just influences. Like all of my really good characters, Devi arrived fully formed in my head all on her own, guns loaded, ready to roll. Characters like this are both frustrating and amazing to write. Amazing because they write themselves, and frustrating because they occasionally write themselves in *completely the wrong direction*. This aside, I wouldn't trade Devi for the world. She's a force of nature, an unreliable narrator, and a complete joy to write, and I wouldn't have her any other way.

Fortune's Pawn *takes place in such a unique world. What was it like, creating such an intricate world with so many different species interacting and conflicting with one another?*

This was where having the universe percolating in my head for years really helped out. By the time I started *Fortune's*

Pawn, I knew my world on the sort of deep, familiar level that normally requires several books to achieve. There's actually a ton of stuff about Paradox I had to cut out because there was just no way to fit it into Devi's story.

My number-one rule for any world is that everything has to be understandable and connected. Things can't just exist only because I think they're cool or they help the plot along, there has to be a reason. Technology is a tool that changes the world for people who use it. Whenever I make a new place or add a new bit of tech, I'm always asking myself "How would people live here?" or "How would this change people's lives?" and then I try to show how these changes and adaptations influence the society. This is the fun part of world building for me, trying to imagine how people would use things like jump gates and powered armor to change the way they live. I do this for every world I create, but you just can't beat sci-fi for truly epic scale.

Along with the different species come different names. Was there a specific inspiration for names such as Lady Gray, Paradoxian, xith'cal, Hyrek...?
Fun fact: the actual name the original Earth colonists gave planet Paradox was "Paradise," because it *was* a paradise, a beautiful, Earthlike planet just waiting to be colonized. But then horrible things happened, a lot of time passed, the language changed, and the name got transposed to "Paradox." That's the setting explanation, but the reason *I* named it Paradox is because the planet itself is a paradox: a hyper-advanced spacefaring society that still uses a feudal system, scorns democracy as heretical, and worships a divine god-king (and yes, I did take liberal influence from *Warhammer 40k*'s Divine Emperor).

Unfortunately, Paradox is the only name with a good story behind it. Everything else was named according to what I thought would be appropriate and/or cool at the time.

Speaking of, how do you actually say "xith'cal"?
I say it ZITH-cal, but you can say it however you want! I am not proprietary about my names. For example, I pronounce Devi's name "Dev-ee," but my editor at Orbit, whose name ALSO happens to be Devi out of SHEER AMAZING COINCIDENCE (my Devi was Devi years before I got Devi as my editor, but how's that for amazing?), pronounces it "Dave-ee," just like her own name. Am I going to tell my editor she's mispronouncing her own name? Hell no! So go ahead, pronounce everything however you like. So long as you enjoy the book, that's all I care about.

What is next for Devi and the Glorious Fool?
Well, as you can probably tell from the end of *Fortune's Pawn*, things are about to go from bad to worse. Everyone's going to have to pay for their actions in this book, especially Rupert, and the heat will be turning way up. Fortunately, Devi's got it covered. Mostly. Sort of. In a "down to my last bullet and there are two enemies left, but if I shoot them both through the head in the same shot, I've got this covered" kind of way. Ah, Devi, you just don't know when to quit!

if you enjoyed
FORTUNE'S PAWN

look out for

TRADING IN DANGER

by

Elizabeth Moon

ONE

Kylara Vatta came to attention in front of the Commandant's desk. One sheet of flatcopy lay in front of him, the print too small for her to read upside down. She had a bad feeling about this. On previous trips to the Commandant's office, she had been summoned by an icon popping up on her deskcomp. Those had all been benign visits, the result of exams passed in the top 5 percent, or prizes won, and the Commandant had greeted her with the most thawed of his several frosty expressions.

Today it had been 'Cadet Vatta to the Commandant's office, on the double,' blaring out over the speaker right in the middle of her first class period, Veshpasir's lecture on the history of the first century PD. Veshpasir, no friend to shipping dynasties, had given her a nasty smirk before saying, 'Dismissed, Cadet Vatta.'

She had no idea what this was about. Or rather, she hoped she didn't. Surely she had been careful enough . . .

'Cadet Vatta,' the Commandant said. No thawing at all, and his left eyelid drooped ominously.

'Sir,' she said.

'I won't even ask what you thought you were doing,' he said. 'I don't want to know. I don't care.'

'Sir?' She hated the squeak in her voice.

'Don't play the innocent with me, Cadet.' Rumor had it that if his left eyelid actually closed, cadets died. She wasn't sure she believed that, but she hoped she wasn't about to find out. 'You are a disgrace to the Service.'

Ky almost shook her head in confusion. What could he be talking about?

'Going outside the chain of command like this' – he thumped the sheet of paper – 'embarrassing the Service.'

'Sir—' She gulped, caught between the etiquette that required silence until she was given leave to speak, and a desperate need to find out what had the Commandant's eyelid hovering ever nearer to its mate.

'You have something to say, Cadet?' the Commandant asked. His voice, like his face, might have been carved out of a glacier. 'Do go ahead . . .' It was not a generous offer.

'Sir, with the greatest respect, this cadet does not know to what the Commandant is referring . . .'

His lips disappeared altogether. 'Oh, you can play the innocent all you want, Cadet, and maintain that formal folderol, but you don't fool me.' He paused. Ky searched her memory, and came up empty. 'Well, since you insist, let's try this: do you recall the name *Mandy Rocher*?'

'Yes, sir,' Ky said promptly. 'Second year, third squad.'

'And you can think of no reason why I might connect that name and yours?'

'Sir, I helped Cadet Rocher locate a Miznarii chaplain last weekend, when Chaplain Oser was away . . .' A dim glimmer of what might be the problem came to her but she couldn't believe there would be that much fuss about a simple little . . .

'And just how did you locate a Miznarii chaplain, Cadet?'

'I . . . er . . . called my mother, sir.'

'You called your mother.' He made it sound obscene, as if only the lowest criminal would call a mother. 'And told your mother to do what, Cadet?'

'I asked her if her friend Jucha could refer me to a Miznarii chaplain near the Academy.'

'For what reason?'

'I told her that one of the underclassmen was overdue for confession and the Academy chaplain was out of town.'

'You didn't tell her what he wanted to confess?'

Ky felt her own eyebrows going up. 'Sir, I don't know what he had to confess. I only know that he was in distress, and needed a chaplain, and I thought . . . I thought it would save trouble if I just got him one.'

'You're not Miznarii yourself . . . ?'

'No, sir. We're Modulans.' Actually, they were Saphiric Cyclans, but that was such a small sect that nobody recognized it, and Modulans were respectable and undemanding. You could be a Modulan without doing anything much at all, a source of some humor to more energetic sects. Ky found Modulan chapel restful and had gone often enough to acquire a reputation for moderate piety – the level most approved by Modulans.

'Hmmph.' The Commandant's eyelid twitched upward a millimeter; Ky hoped this was a good sign. 'You had no idea that what he wanted to confess concerned the honor of the Service?'

Her jaw dropped; she forced it back up. 'No, sir!'

'That he made a formal complaint to this Miznarii, in addition to his confession, which the chaplain took immediately to the Bureau of War, where it fell into the hands of a particularly noxious bureaucrat whose *sister* just happens to be on the staff of *Wide Exposure*, so that I found myself on the horn very early this morning with Grand-Admiral Tasliki, who is not amused at all . . . ?' It was not really a question; it was rant and explanation and condemnation all in one. 'The bureaucrat spoke on *Wide Exposure*'s "Night Affairs' program at 0115 – clever timing, that – and this morning all the media channels had something on it. That's only the beginning.'

Ky felt hot, then cold, then hot again. 'S-sir . . . ,' she managed.

'So even if you did not know, Cadet Vatta, what Cadet Rocher wanted to confess, you may be able to grasp that by going outside the chain of command you have created a very *very* large public relations problem, embarrassing the entire general staff, the Bureau of War, and – last but not least – me personally.'

'Yes, sir.' She could understand that. She could not, she thought, have anticipated it, and now she was consumed by curiosity: what, exactly, *had* Mandy Rocher said? They weren't allowed access to things like *Wide Exposure* except on weekends.

'You are an embarrassment, Cadet Vatta,' the Commandant said. 'Many, many people want your hide tacked on the wall and your head on a pike. The only reason I don't—' His eyelid was up another millimeter. 'The *only* reason I don't, is that I have observed your progress through the Academy and you have so far been, within the limits of your ability, an exemplary cadet. When I thought you'd done it on purpose I was going to throw you to the wolves. Now – since I suspect that you simply fell for a sob story and your entire barracks knows you have a soft spot for underdogs and lost lambs – I'm simply going to take the hide off your back in strips and see your resignation on my desk by 1500 hours this afternoon.'

'S-sir?' Resignation . . . did that mean what it sounded like? Was he kicking her out? Just because she'd tried to help Mandy?

Now the eyelid came all the way back up. 'Cadet Vatta, you have – unwittingly, perhaps – created a major mess with implications that could damage the Service for years. Your ass is grass, one way or the other. You could be charged, for instance, with that string of articles beginning with 312.5 – I see by your expression that you have, belatedly, remembered them . . .'

She did indeed. Article 312.5 of the Military Legal Code: failure to inform superior officer in a timely manner of potentially harmful personnel situations. Article 312.6: failure to inform superior officer in a timely manner of breaches of security involving sensitive personnel. Article 312.7: failure to inform superior officer in a timely manner of . . . rats, rats, and flying rats. She was majorly doomed.

'I . . . wasn't thinking, sir.' That was not an attempt at apology, merely a statement of fact.

'Fairly obvious. What did you think might happen?'

'I thought . . . Mandy – Cadet Rocher – was so upset that day – I thought if he could see a chaplain and confess or whatever, he'd settle down until the regular chaplain got back. He had those exams coming up, and they were group-graded; if he didn't do well, his squad would suffer for it . . .'

'What you don't know, Cadet, is that Rocher had been avoiding the regular chaplain's cycle; his so-called emergency was of his own making. He wanted to talk to someone outside the Academy, and you made that possible.'

'Yes, sir.'

'And you didn't tell anyone at all about this, did you?'

'No, sir.'

'Easier to get forgiveness than permission, is that what you were thinking?'

'No, sir . . . not really.' One of the places where Modulans and Saphiric Cyclans disagreed was about the giving of aid. Modulans felt that moderate assistance should be moderately public – one did not make a huge display of charity, but one allowed others to know charity was going on, to set a good example. Saphiric Cyclans, on the other hand, believed that all help should be given as anonymously as possible. Now was probably not the time to talk about that difference.

'I am so reassured.' The Commandant's eyelid quivered. 'Cadet Vatta, it is unfortunate that you have to suffer for a generous impulse, but we need naval officers with brains as well as kind hearts. You will not return to class. You will, as I said, present a letter of resignation which does not mention any of this, and cites personal reasons as the cause, by 1500 hours. Sooner, Cadet, is better than later, but first you will go to Signals, and make contact with your family, so that you will be able to leave quietly and quickly when that resignation is approved.' The look he gave her now was warmer by a few degrees, but still not cordial. 'Staff will pack up your things; they will be at the gate when you depart.'

'I . . . yes, sir.'

'And yes, you infer correctly that you are not to speak to any of your former associates. Your departure will be explained as seems most expedient for the Service.'

'Sir.' Not speak to anyone. Not to Mira or Lisette . . . not to Hal. *Only another few months, and we can –* but not now, not ever. Please, please, let no one figure out . . .

'You are dismissed.'

'Sir.' Ky saluted, rotated correctly on her right heel, and left his office, her mind a blur. Signals. She knew where Signals was. She passed without really seeing an enlisted man in the passage, and another at the head of the stairs down to the classroom level. Halfway to Signals, her mind clicked on long enough to panic . . . She had to call her family, tell her father and, oh heavens, her *mother* that she was disgraced, dismissed . . . Her brothers would all . . . her cousins . . . Uncle Tomas . . . Aunt Grace, worse than Uncle Tomas, who would say again all she had said when Ky first went to the Academy, laced with *I told you so* . . .

She felt the tremor in her hands, and fought to still it. Now, for this short period of time, she was still a cadet, and now, for this short period of time, she would act like one. Even as the dream went down in smoke and ashes, even then . . . her stomach looped wildly once and settled.

At the door of Signals, a uniformed guard stared past her.

'Cadet Vatta, on order of the Commandant,' she said.

He stepped aside, and she heard him murmur into his comunit 'Cadet Vatta at Signals, sir.'

Commander Terry had the watch in Signals; his expression suggested that her family were loathsome toads, and she was toad spawn. 'Vatta,' he said, minus the honorific.

'Sir.'

'Which contact number?' As if having more than one number were also a crime.

'Vatta Enterprises,' Ky said. 'They have a relay—' Wherever her father was, they could reach him, or give her a link to the senior Vatta onplanet.

'We would prefer that you make a direct call.'

She knew her father's mobile number, of course, but he'd often said he hated the damned thing, and would leave it on the bedside table as often as not. That meant her mother might pick it up, the last person she wanted to talk to. Vatta Enterprises would ring his skullphone, which he couldn't take off. She didn't have that number; no one did but the communications computer at VE.

She rattled off the string for the mobile, and mentally visualized the arc of blue, best fortune, of the Saphiran Cyclan wheel, as Commander Terry nodded to the rating who entered the string.

'Name?' Terry asked abruptly. Ky startled. 'The name of the person you are calling,' he said.

'Sir, my father, sir. Gerard Avondettin Vatta. But if my mother—'

'You are permitted one call, to one recipient, Cadet Vatta.' Commander Terry picked up the headset and held the receiver to his ear. Ky waited, the blue arc fading in her mental eye. Then his hand twitched. 'This is Commander Terry at the Naval Academy; I need to speak to Gerard Avondettin Vatta.' A pause, then: 'Kylara Vatta will speak with you.' He held the headset out to Ky.

She was not even allowed to speak from a privacy booth. She had known the call would be recorded, but at least a semblance of normal courtesy would have helped. She could feel tears swelling now, stuffing her nose. She fought for calmness as she took the headset and put it on. Enough of this; she turned her back on Commander Terry without permission.

'Dad, listen—'

'Ky, what's wrong? Are you hurt?'

'Dad, no, I'm fine, please listen. I have to leave, I have to leave today. Can you send somebody to the gates?'

'Ky, what is it?'

'Dad, please. I have to resign. I have to leave. I don't have any money for transport; I need a way to get home—'

'What—!' She could hear the explosion building up, the familiar prelude to the famous roar. Then it ended, surprising her into silence. His voice gentled to a soft growl. 'Ky, listen, whatever it is, we can help. Let me call the Commandant—'

'No, Dad. Don't do that. I'll explain when I get there, only help me get there, please?'

'When do you need transport?'

She looked at the chronometer. Only 0935. Surely she could write a resignation that would satisfy the Commandant by noon.

'By noon, if that's possible.'

'For you, Kylara-mish, five minutes would be possible. Only tell me, has someone hurt you?'

Later, she would consider whether Mandy Rocher had hurt her; now she wanted only to get away. And even if Mandy had, she had made it possible; it was her own fault. 'It's not that, Dad.'

'Good. Because if any one of those fisheaters had laid a finger on you—'

'Dad, please. Noon?'

'At the gates. On Vatta honor.'

'Vatta honor.' The signal died, and she handed the headset back to Commander Terry. He took it without comment, and gave a curt nod.

'Get on your way, Vatta.'

'Yes, sir.' She needed a place to write the resignation; if she was forbidden to return to her quarters, where could she go? Outside, she found the answer, of sorts: the wiry gray-haired senior NCO who had been her year's nemesis in the first four quarters, and an increasingly valuable resource ever since. She had not, she remembered, taken MacRobert's advice on the matter of Mandy Rocher.

'Commandant's library is empty, Cadet Vatta,' he said now. 'Fully equipped.'

'Right,' she said. She would not cry. She would certainly not cry in front of this man. He turned to lead the way and she followed.

'Right mess you made of things,' he said, when they were around a corner from Signals.

'Yes,' Ky said.

'I won't say I told you so,' he said. He just had, of course, but she didn't answer. 'I daresay you feel bad enough already.'

A shadow of a question in that. Anger stirred suddenly, beneath the anguish. 'Yes, I do,' she said, hearing the sharp edge to her own voice.

'Thought so,' he said. 'Here you are.' He opened the door for her. She had never been in the Commandant's private library before; the long narrow room held not only racks of ordinary books and journals, but shelves of ancient books like those in her family's oldest house. A long table ran down the middle of the room, and at one end someone had set out a stack of white paper and a selection of pens. 'It's appropriate that a resignation of this type be handwritten,' MacRobert told her. 'You can use the voice recorder or the keyboard to rough it out, but it's better to stick to the simplest format . . .' Someone had also laid out a copy of *Naval Etiquette: Essentials for Officers*, and the hand reader.

'Thank you,' Ky said. It was still not 1000 hours. Her world had ended less than an hour ago. She had another couple of hours . . .

'What time did you arrange transport for?' MacRobert asked.

'Noon,' Ky said.

'I'll see that your gear is at the gate by 1130,' MacRobert said.

'Thank you,' Ky said again. She felt unreal, still, as if this were a dream, as if she were floating a few centimeters off the floor.

'I'll leave you alone,' MacRobert said. 'When you're finished, you can leave the resignation here—'

'The Commandant said on his desk,' Ky said.

'That's right. And so it will be; just tell me when you're finished.' He nodded and went out, shutting the door silently behind him.

She put *Naval Etiquette: Essentials for Officers* into the reader and found that someone had already bookmarked the section on resignations. Voluntary and involuntary, sections of the legal code relating to, forms of appropriate and inappropriate . . . She paused there and looked at the appropriate wording for resigning one's commission while in command of a ship, while in command of a flotilla, while between commands, while on leave, while suffering an incurable mental or physical condition precluding further duty ... That's me, Ky thought. Suffering from an incurable tendency to trust people in trouble and help lame dogs.

She turned to the keyboard – she didn't trust her voice to use the speech-activated system – and copied in the phrasing. 'I, [name], hereby resign my [cadetship/commission] for reasons of [reason.]' 'I, Kylara Evangeline Dominique Vatta, hereby resign my cadetship for reasons of overwhelming stupidity and weak sentimentality.' No, that wouldn't do. 'For reasons of totally unfair blame for something I didn't do.' That wouldn't do either. 'For reasons of a mental illness called gullibility?' 'Softheartedness?' No.

Tears blurred her vision suddenly; she blinked them back. Memory stirred, bringing her Mandy Rocher's image as he sat, shoulders hunched, hands trembling a little, telling her that he had to find a chaplain, he really did. Had his hands trembled with secret laughter that she was so easy to fool? Had he looked down to hide the scorn in his eyes? He was such a little . . . little . . . she searched her vocabulary for a sufficiently descriptive phrase. Insignificant. Forgettable. Boring. Pitiful. Nonentity. And to lose her cadetship because of *him*!

She would get him someday. Vengeance, said her grandmother, was an unworthy goal, but this was a special case. Surely this was a special case.

'I, Kylara Evangeline Dominique Vatta, hereby resign from the Academy for reasons that reflect on my ability to carry out the duties of a naval officer.'

Close. Not quite yet.

She looked around the room, squinting to bring the titles of the old books into focus. Herren and Herren's *Chronicles of the Dispersion*, all ten volumes. Her family owned III through X, but I and II were very rare indeed in paper form. Cantabria's *Principles of Space Warfare*, evidently a first edition. She longed to pull it down and check, but was afraid to. A row bound identically in blue-gray cloth . . . logbooks, the old-fashioned kind. Those would be centuries and centuries old; she got up and looked at the names on the spines. *Darius II*, *Paleologus*, *Sargon*, *Ataturk* . . . she felt the gooseflesh come up on her arms, and looked quickly at the last, least-faded volume. *Centaurus*. Not in fact centuries old, not even one century: these were logs that the Commandant had kept, his personal logs from every ship on which he'd served. She'd once memorized the sequence on a dare. Her fingers twitched. What had he thought, felt, done as a young man on his first ship?

She would never know. She had no right to know. The adventures she had hoped to write into such logs herself would never come her way now. She made herself step away from that shelf and look at another. History here, biography there, reference works on all the neighboring states, on the biota of First Colony, on the ecology of water gardens . . . Water gardens? The Commandant studied water gardens?

A sound outside in the passage startled her and sent her back to the table, but the footsteps passed by. She stared at the screen again. 'For reasons of . . .' Back to the hand reader. Alternate phrasing: 'due to.' Clumsy.

Never say more than you need, her father had said; her mother had muttered that Kylara always said more than she needed.

She'd stop that right now.

'I, Kylara Evangeline Dominique Vatta, hereby resign from the Academy for personal reasons.' Short and . . . not sweet. Nothing about this was sweet.

She stared at the screen a long time, glaring at the tiny blue words on the gray screen. Then she moved the paper over and copied the words very carefully, in her best script, the handwriting of a properly-brought-up child and good student.

Panic gripped her when she had signed it. She did not want to do this. She could not do this. She must do this. She looked at the time, 10:22:38. Had destroying her life really taken so little time?

A tap on the door, then it opened. MacRobert again, this time with a large silver tray. A teapot, incongruously splotched with big pink roses. A pair of matching cups, gold-rimmed, on saucers. A small plate of lemon cookies, and another of tiny, precisely cut sandwiches.

'The Commandant will be joining you,' MacRobert said. He set the tray on the end of the library table, picked up her resignation, and walked out with it. Ky sat immobile, staring at the steam rising from the teapot's spout, trying not to smell the fragrance of cookies obviously fresh from the oven, trying not to think or feel anything at all.

The Commandant's entrance brought her upright, to attention; he waved her back down. 'You've resigned, sit down.' He sighed. His left eyelid was back up where it should be, but his whole face sagged. 'Pour out, will you?'

Ky carried out the familiar ritual, something she didn't have to think about, and handed him his cup of tea. He waited, and nodded at her. She poured one for herself. It was good tea; it would be, she thought. He took a sandwich and gave her a look; she took one, too.

He ate his sandwich in one bite, and sipped his tea. 'It's a shame, really,' he said. 'Here I had a perfectly good excuse to remove your internal organs and hang them from the towers, make an example of you . . . It's my job, and I'm supposed to relish it, or why did I ask for it? But you were a good cadet, Mistress Vatta, and I know you intended to be a good officer.'

Then why did you make me resign? That was a question she must never ask; she knew that much.

'In consideration of your past performance, and on my own responsibility, I've chosen to let you keep your insignia and wear it as you depart; I trust your sense of honor not to wear it again.'

'No, sir,' she said. The bite of sandwich she had taken stuck in her throat. She had not even considered that he might demand their removal. The class ring on her finger – Hal's ring, as he wore hers – suddenly weighed twice as much.

'It's hard for you to believe now, I'm sure, but you will survive this. You have many talents, and you will find a use for them . . .' He took a long swallow of his tea, and actually smiled at her. 'Thank you for not making this harder than it had to be. Your resignation was . . . masterful.'

The sandwich bite went down, a miserable lump. She wasn't hungry; she couldn't be hungry. She ate the rest of the sandwich out of pure social duty.

'I understand you've arranged transport for noon?' he asked.

'Yes, sir.'

'You don't have to say *sir*, Ca – Mistress Vatta.'

'I can't help it,' Ky said. Tears stung her eyes; she looked away.

'Well, then. I would advise that you go out at 1130, while classes are in session. MacRobert will remain with you until your transport arrives, to deal with any . . . mmm . . . problems that may come up. Since the story broke on the early news, the media have been camped at our gates; it'll be days before that dies down.'

For a moment she had been furious – had he thought she'd do something wrong? – but the mention of media steadied her. Of course they would be trying to get in, trying to interview cadets. Of course the daughter of the Vatta family would interest them, even if Mandy hadn't mentioned her, and someone would be bound to have a face-recognition subroutine that would pop out her name.

'And there's another thing.' She had to look at him again, had to see the expression of mingled annoyance and pity that was worse than anything he might have said directly. 'The Bureau demands – I realize this isn't necessary – a statement that you will consider all this confidential and not communicate with the media.'

As if she would. As if – but she took the paper he handed her and scrawled her name on it in a rough parody of her usual careful handwriting.

'You have almost an hour,' the Commandant said. 'MacRobert will fetch you when it's time.' He drained his cup and picked up one of the lemon cookies. 'And – if you'll take advice – drink the rest of that tea, and eat those sandwiches. Shock uses up energy.' He rose, nodded to her, and went out, shutting the door softly behind him.

To her shame, Ky burst into tears. She snatched the tea towel off the tray and buried her face in it. She could always claim she'd spilled the tea; she wasn't a cadet; she didn't have to tell the strict truth. Five hard sobs, and it was over, for now. She wiped her face, spread the tea towel out again, and set everything back on the tray in perfect order. No – her cup was almost full. She drank the tea. She ate another sandwich. Disgusting body, to want tea and food at such a time.

The silent room eased her, made calm possible. She got up and paced the circuit, looking at the titles again. Then she took down the logbook labeled *Darius II* on the back. Just this once – and what could they do to her if they disapproved?

When MacRobert came for her at 1127, she was deep into the logbook, and calm again.

* * *

Outside, the weather had changed, as if her fortune changed it, from early morning's sunshine and puffy clouds to a dank, miserable cold rain with a gusty wind. Her luggage made a pile in the relative safety of the gateway arch; she stood in the shelter of the sentry's alcove, where she could just see the street beyond, and the gaggle of reporters on the far side. She was still in cadet blue; the sentry ignored her, and MacRobert checked off her bags on a list before turning to her.

'They'll be near on time?' he asked.

'I expect so,' Ky said. The lump in her throat was growing now; she had to swallow before she could speak.

'Good. We'll have to frustrate the mob over there . . .' He cocked his head. 'You're not half-bad, Vatta. Sorry you stepped in it. Don't forget us.' His voice seemed to carry some message she couldn't quite understand.

'I won't,' she said. How could he even suggest she might forget this? Her skin felt scorched with shame.

'Don't be angrier than you have to be.'

'I'm not.' She might be later, but now . . . anger was only beginning to seep toward the surface, through the shock and pain.

'Good. You still have friends here, though at the moment there's a necessary distance—' He looked at the clock. 1154. 'Excuse me for a few moments. I'll be back at 1200 sharp.'

Ky wondered what he was up to, but not for long. The chill dank air, the gusts of wind, all brought back to her the enormity of her fall from grace. She was going to have to go out there, in the cold rain, and pick up those bags and put them in the vehicle in front of everyone in the universe, obviously disgraced and sent away, and be driven home to her parents like any stupid brat who's messed up. Like, for instance, her cousin Stella, who had fallen in love with a musha dealer and given him the family codes. She remembered overhearing some of that, when she was thirteen, and telling herself *she* would never be so stupid, *she* would never disgrace the family the way Stella had.

And now it was on all the news, whatever had actually been said, and it was all her fault.

A huge black car whizzed past the entrance, flags flapping from its front and rear staffs, and she saw the reporters across the way turn, and then rush after it. 'The back entrance!' she heard one of them yell. Their support vans squealed into motion, turned quickly across the street, and sped after the black car. She glanced at the clock. 1159. She stepped out of the alcove into the archway and saw a decent middle-aged dark blue car swerving over to stop at the archway. Twelve hundred on the dot. Two men – the driver and escort – got out of the car.

'I'll help with these.' MacRobert was back, and already had two of her bags in hand. 'Vatta, you get in the car. Jim, get her trunk,' he said to the sentry. In moments, Ky was in the backseat, her luggage stowed in the trunk or beside her, and the two men were back in the car.

'Take care, Vatta,' MacRobert said. 'And remember what I said; you have friends here . . .'

At the last moment, she stripped off the class ring and handed it to him. 'You'll know where this should go,' she said. She couldn't keep it; she could only hope that MacRobert would get it back to him discreetly, that Hal would understand.

The car moved off, sedately, rejoining the traffic stream, and turning at the first corner; Ky glanced to the right and saw a crowd of news vans partway down that block. What, she wondered, did MacRobert want her to remember? That he was kind as well as brusque? Or how stupid she'd been?

The Vatta employees in the front seat didn't talk on the way to their first stop, the warehouse office at 56 Missalonghi. There, the escort got out and her uncle Stavros climbed into the backseat with her.

'Kylara, my dear . . . are you all right?'

'I'm . . .' She did not want to come apart in front of Uncle Stavros, father of the notorious Stella. 'I'm fine.' A lie, and they both knew it, but the right thing to say.

'We're going over to the airfield—' That would be the private airfield, of course. 'You'll be on a flight to Corleigh; your parents had to run over there to take care of some business a week ago.'

Ky put her mind back to work: Corleigh. Tik plantations. Source of both wealth and problems, because the labor force knew all too well what tik extract brought on the interstellar market, and felt they weren't getting enough of the profits. 'Pickers or packers?' she asked.

Her uncle nodded approvingly. 'Packers. The pickers

got a new contract last year, and the packers insist they add more value and need another two percent on top of the five percent increase year before last.'

She hadn't seen the sales figures for tik extract since the holiday before last. 'So . . . what's the quote running?'

'Thirty-eight two seven – down a hundredth from last year; Devann's come into production, though we judge their product only third-rate. I think the market'll be back up, but we'll see.'

Ky knew her uncle had brought this up mostly to distract her, but it did make the journey easier. 'What's their production base?'

'Twenty thousand hectares, five thousand in eight-year-olds, five each in seven, six, and four. Rumor has it they lost their entire planting five years ago, and all the surviving trees lost a year's maturity. Soil's good, climate's marginal.'

'Labor force?'

'Well, now, that's more of a problem for them than they want to admit, and that's where their quality falls off. They recruited from the immigrant lists, and none of 'em are experienced. Most of the ag-credentialed immigrants are row croppers who know nothing about trees. What I hear from the market is that their pickers are damaging the fruit, and the packers aren't tossing the damaged stuff. It's been a year longer than they planned, after all, getting any income off the place at all, so they're trying to make it up.'

Ky glanced out the window as the car swerved; they were nearing the private airfield now, and a truck with the blue and red Vatta Transport insignia had slowed for the turn into the cargo bays. Their car sped on to the passenger entrance, paused at the check station for their driver to flash the scans, then followed the service road past the elegant little charter terminal with its tropical garden and colonnade, for those departing or arriving on chartered flights, and on around past the private terminals to the Vatta Transport complex, all in blue with red trim. Sitting out on the apron was the sleek little twin-engine craft in which Kylara had flown from island to island most of her life.

'You can't pilot yourself today, Ky,' her uncle said, as the car slowed. 'Under the circumstances—'

Her vision blurred. She knew she wasn't safe to pilot anything, not like this, but –

'It's Gaspard; you remember him.' She did; Gaspard Ritnour had been her first flying instructor, though the family wasn't supposed to know that. 'Let's get you aboard.' Kylara moved quickly from the car to the aircraft. Automatically she put her feet in the right places on the step and wing, and started to slide into the copilot's seat.

'You'd better ride in the passenger compartment,' her uncle said.

Ky felt herself flushing. 'I won't try to grab the controls,' she said.

'It's not that, Ky,' her uncle said. 'Gaspard – explain it to her; if she's going to ride up front you'll have to take steps. I need to get back—'

Ky buckled in and one of the ground crew slammed the door.

TWO

Ky said nothing as Gaspard finished preflight; he didn't explain what her uncle had meant. She sat quietly, waiting. One thing she'd learned at the Academy was how to wait without fidgeting. She did not even put on the copilot's headset.

Gaspard murmured into his own voice pickup – contacting traffic control, she assumed. Then he turned to her.

'Put your headset on,' he said.

'Why?' Ky asked.

'You're visible up here.' It took her a moment to figure out what he meant. Anyone looking in – with a long lens for instance – could see her, whereas back in the passenger compartment the smaller windows had little shades.

'Damn,' Ky said, snatching the headset. It wouldn't be enough, she knew. She shrugged out of her uniform jacket and tossed it onto the seat behind; Gaspard pointed behind her. A Vatta crew flight jacket, matching Gaspard's, hung there. She pulled it on quickly, then twisted to see if she could shut the window shades back in the passenger compartment . . . but someone had already done that.

'They'll assume a regular flight crew,' Gaspard said. 'Unless you're sitting there in cadet blue . . . with insignia . . .' Ky fumbled at her blouse collar; she'd forgotten the collar insignia, which a long lens might be able to catch. They were embroidered; she would have to turn the collar under. She did that while he signaled the ground crew, and let the plane roll forward slowly.

'Better,' Gaspard said.

Would the headset obscure enough of her face, though? She swung the voicelink up as far as possible. They were out from between the Vatta hangars, onto the taxiway. A single-engine yellow plane swung onto the taxiway in front of them. Ky looked down at the familiar checklist. If she was to be the copilot . . . this is what she would be doing.

They moved on. As they passed the little terminal parking lot, Gaspard said, 'Do something that looks good.'

Immediately, Ky pulled up the manual checklist and reached overhead as if going through a final preflight.

'What I love about flying with you, Ky, is that you always react the right way,' Gaspard said. Ky looked at him, surprised; the grin he was aiming down the centerline of the taxiway looked genuine. 'That couldn't have looked more natural if you'd rehearsed it for days. I spotted a fire truck in the wrong place. Now . . . we're going to be really exposed during takeoff and for the first hour. Since you're already up here, and I entered for two crew just in case, you'll have to stay here.' He paused. 'I know your uncle said no flying, but someone's got to be traffic watch, and if you can help . . .'

'I can help,' Ky said.

'Good. I'll take 'er up, but you stay on the controls with me.'

Ky turned up the volume in her headset and heard traffic control give them clearance for takeoff after the little yellow plane. They paused as the yellow plane swung into position; she could see it shudder and then begin its takeoff roll. She checked the boards. This plane had every avionics gadget, and an AI autopilot perfectly capable of handling almost every contingency, but Gaspard preferred to take off and land on manual, to keep his skills current. 'And because it's just plain fun,' he said now, as he usually did. 'There's something atavistic about shoving the throttles forward myself.'

She felt the same way, as they turned into position and the power of the engines fought the brakes for a moment before Gaspard released them. She loved it all, from the acceleration down the runway to the moment when they left the ground to the steep climb out over the factory district.

Once they were a half hour offshore, at cruising altitude, Gaspard relaxed and pulled out his hotpak of coffee. 'Well, girl, I'm not sure what anthill you kicked – or kicked you – but your father and uncle were certainly upset. Want to tell me about it?'

'I . . . can't. Can't fly and talk about it, anyway.'

'Fine. Let me finish this and I'll take it back.' He

swallowed quickly and relieved Ky at the controls. 'Not that I'm pushing you, you understand, but.' But he wanted to know. Of course.

'I had to resign from the Academy,' Ky said.

He whistled. 'Didn't you keep your antifertility implant up to date?'

'Not that! I wouldn't . . . !' She stole a glance at him.

'Sorry,' he said. 'It's just – what else could make you do it? Your family's not yanking you out for some business reason . . . ?'

'No,' Ky said. 'I . . . did something stupid. It caused a stink. Such a big stink they wanted me gone.'

'You? I can't imagine what big stink you could cause. Now if you were a bonehead like that kid who told a Miznarii priest that he was being treated unfairly and prevented from practicing his religion, and that the service was hostile to Miznarii and had a policy of putting them – how did he say it? first in danger, last in promotion – that is what I'd call a big stink.'

Ky's heart sank. 'That . . . was my fault.'

'Your fault? How? You aren't even . . . oh shit, Ky, you were just helping someone again, weren't you? What'd you do, get him in contact with this Miznarii?'

'Yes.' She could hear that her voice was choked with tears.

'Um. I can understand they might be peeved with you – it's headlined in the news – but it's not bad enough to make you resign.'

'They think it is.'

'They'll wish they hadn't,' Gaspard said. 'Though it

may take them a while. So . . . you're in disgrace, is that it?'

All the misery broke through, and she felt tears burning in her eyes. She couldn't speak.

'Thing is, Ky, disgrace doesn't last forever.' She caught the quick movement of his head as he turned to look at her and looked away, out the window, where a blanket of cloud lay between them and the East Shallows.

'It can,' Ky said.

'Usually doesn't,' Gaspard said. 'Whatever stupid things you do, you can do smart ones later.'

'Somehow I don't think so,' Ky said. 'When I try my hardest, that's when I do stupid things.'

He looked at her. 'It's not my place . . . ,' he began.

'Oh, go on, everyone else will lecture me, too.'

'I'm not going to lecture you.' He looked out the side window, sighed, and engaged the autopilot. 'Logged: all boards clear, no traffic reported or scanned. Estimated flight time three hours fifteen minutes.'

'We'll be home in time for supper,' Ky said. Her throat closed again. It had all happened too fast. She'd awakened as a senior cadet, in the honor squad; she'd eaten breakfast at the head of a table of cadets, in charge of that table, reminding the lowly cads to sit straight on the edge of their chairs and take no sugar in their drinks. She'd eaten that scrap of lunch in the Commandant's library as a disgraced ex-cadet, and tonight she would eat supper in the family dining room, the family disgrace come home to roost.

'You want to talk about it?' Gaspard asked. He was

only ten years or so older than she was, she thought. Younger than the Commandant or her father, older than all but one of her brothers.

'You know.' Her hands moved as if of themselves. 'I tried to help, and it blew up in my face.'

'You know this kid well?'

'Mandy? He's – he was – in my diviso. Last year the cad intake officer asked me to take him under my wing. Third-years get handed a cad to baby-sit. Mandy was mine. He had a rough time, being Miznarii, but he did fairly well.' The Miznarii considered even implants immoral modifications of the basic human, so those of their children seeking higher education were always at a disadvantage. They attended only those institutions where students had to study without implant assistance, but, as with the Academy, the other students had used them before.

'As well as you did?'

'No, but—' Her voice trailed away. Who would expect a Miznarii from Cobalt Hole to do as well as she had? 'Better than expected,' she finished.

'So . . . you give the kid a model he can't reach, and he asks you to do him a favor, and then he backstabs you. Think he did this just to cross you?'

She hadn't considered one way or the other. What did Mandy's intention matter? It was betrayal even if not intended.

'I think . . . I think he meant to get the Academy in trouble.'